BUILT ON SAND

SAND

SR KAY

Built on Sand

S R Kay

www.1889books.co.uk

ISBN: 978-1-915045-22-5

CHAPTER ONE

It mustn't tip. It must stay upright. Elsie headed up towards the Town Hall, holding the envelope as steady as her nerves would allow. She concealed the inscription against her coat. "For Mr Asquith," it read.

The wind tugged at the hem of her coat; she had to hold on to her hat, well pinned though it was. She tucked her muffler a bit tighter around her neck, breathed out long and slow to steady her nerves and continued down past the shops illuminated by their Christmas lights. This was justified. Everything else had been tried. This was about the right to live.

Fargate was busy with people on their way home. Shop windows competed to draw in passers-by with electric fairy lights and gifts for "Your darling wife" – beautiful necklaces she could only dream about, boxes of chocolates or crackers from sixpence a box. Smith would not get her any such thing. He regarded himself as a practical man and he provided gifts to match. A new teapot, or a toasting fork. On their first wedding anniversary he had announced excitedly that he had a surprise for her.

'What is it?'

'I'll show thi, come on.'

He had led her by the hand to the scullery, opened the door and said: 'There: what's tha reckon to that, then?'

She'd stood looking at her scullery, looking for something that she should be grateful for.

'Well?'

'What am I looking at, Smith? All I can see is the scullery – same as it was last night.'

'No, look closer.'

'What at?'

'The clothes wringer.'

Then she noticed. 'Oh. It's got new rollers.'

'Thought tha'd like that! They're beech wood, good quality. Fitted 'em myself. Tha was allus complaining about the old ones being worn out.'

1

What could she do but say thank you, and give him a kiss on the cheek?

She slowed past Coles' bright and colourful window displays, enticing you, like she was simply an ordinary shopper, like this was just an ordinary day. She crossed Church Street finding gaps between the motorcars and horse-drawn carriages. The post box was over by the corner outside Pawson and Brailsfords.

She stopped by the parish church gates and looked around her, convinced she was being watched. She sought out eyes upon her, but everyone was going about their business. She should act normally, like she was just posting a letter.

The pillar-box stood before her. She held the envelope upright, rested it on the lip of the opening and sent it tumbling into the box before crossing quickly over to Cole's corner. When she reached the entrance she heard a shriek. She turned to see smoke rising from the pillar-box. The crystals and acid were doing their job. Someone shouted: 'A bomb! A bomb!' A police whistle sounded. She froze in panic. People were running away from the scene. Then a man appeared from somewhere with a bucket of water and poured it through the slot of the pillar-box. The smoke stopped, and Elsie walked away.

How far she had come. Prim and proper little Miss Elsie Green: scholarships, maiden to a May Queen, Lincoln Cathedral chorister, role model to pupils. There was no going back.

*

'They've been bloody at it in Sheffield now.'
Elsie pulled the pan out of the soapy water and inspected it.
'I said they've been at it again.'
'Who have?'
'Thy lot.'
'My lot? What have those Quinn boys been up to now?'
'Not thi cousins – thy suffragette lot. They've done it now. Blowing up post boxes in Sheffield.'
'Oh? Where was that?'
'In town, right by the gates of the parish church. And one in Brightside.'
That must have been Mary, she thought. She had met her at the kitchen of one of the organisers where they put the vitriol into little cork vials and divided the Berthollet salt that Miss Schuster had

brought up from London into little packets. 'It seems somehow fitting that they should call it oil of vitriol doesn't it?' 'No. It should be called "oil of patient determination." All the vitriol comes from the government.'

Smith tapped the newspaper for emphasis. 'They've gone and done it now – totally alienated anyone who had any sympathy for them. Them post-boxes could have contained dying wishes, or money to stop orphaned children from starving.'

'Oh, don't be so melodramatic. They'll only have been bills and invoices, letters from banks and solicitors.'

'I think tha'll find it not me that's being melodramatic. What a way to go about business. Trying to get people on side by threatening public safety and the Royal Mail.'

She dried her hands on her apron. 'But where has asking nicely got them? For over sixty years women have been asking nicely.'

'This isn't the way to persuade anyone.'

'But no one listens. They attack property because it's all they're bothered about. They despise *people*. When property is attacked they take note. Your miner and docker friends don't ask nicely – they go on strike, they blockade, they burn mine owners' property, and they get concessions.'

'It's not the same. There is a much bigger struggle going on than the pathetic little obsession of your Mrs Pankhurst, but she's too narrow-minded to see it. She cares nowt for the real struggle for power based on wealth.'

'I know all that. But this is half the population who have no say – until we resolve that...'

'But there you are, it's not *either or*, is it?' He reached for his boots from the hearth. 'Your lot campaign against a good Liberal and would rather end up with a Tory. They try to persuade people to vote against everything the government do. It's women's suffrage or nothing – never mind universal suffrage. There's plenty of working men what's got no vote neither.'

He was now up on his feet, gesticulating. Elsie stood there with her tea towel in her hand as he directed all his anger at her – as if it were her fault.

'Sorry: no pensions, shite working conditions, but don't worry: at least we've got a handful of propertied women the vote! I'm off down the Arms.'

3

The back door closed and the house shook. She sat down at the table and her tears welled up. He could be so cruel. She knew all that, understood all that. Of course she did. Surely he could see that if mothers and daughters and sisters had a vote they would change everything for the better? They did not run off down the pub to escape – they were the ones who were left to feed their children, or worry about their husbands down the mines and in the forges, and whether they would return home in one piece.

Why was he so quick to condemn? At times when his eyes flashed like that, she felt he hated her. Blamed her for the loss of his son. He hadn't suffer like she had done: having had a bond with him growing inside her, talking and singing to him every day. To then know he had departed, and still to go through the pain of his birth. To gaze upon his perfect yet lifeless little body. To not be allowed to bury him properly. No, he had just ranted and raved and left her to it, taking his comfort from a steady flow of Gilmours.

If only she could conceive again and fill their home with a family. Perhaps it would not be all so intense, so much depending on her, on her ability to provide him comfort. It would give her a focus. She'd be able to cluck round like all the other mothers on the street had done the week before, when heavy snow fell. She could have warmed mittens on the range so that they could join all the other children on the street sledging down the hill on contraptions made by skilled fathers, or, less than skilled, older siblings – brought up from cellar and wiped clean of cobwebs and coal dust, or hastily knocked together from bits of tin and wood.

***

Smith kicked a stone in the street and sent it smacking into a wall and out into the darkness. It wasn't supposed to be like this. He wasn't brutish, but he couldn't stop himself. It was like scratching an itch. Why did she challenge him all the time? She just wouldn't be beat. He found his old friend Charlie sitting at the bar of the Danville Arms.

'What kept thi?'

'Nowt. Just arguing with the missus.'

'What now – the usual Saturday night sport?'

'Nah. Bloody suffragettes.'

'No, not that again. What's she been saying about that Pankhurst lot now?'

4

'She's one of 'em. Sticking up for them bombing stuff. All her spare time's taken up wi' it now. House is neglected. Some evenings I've got home to find no more than a jug of beer on the table and a note saying my dinner's in the oven.'

Charlie shook his head slowly. They both drew on their glasses of beer and lit a cigarette. He watched Charlie through the cloud of smoke narrowing his eyes as he took another drag.

They went way back – he'd known him for as long as he could remember. Mucked about together as kids as part of the Notty Cliff gang, got into scrapes, got out of scrapes, played on the rec until all hours. Then Charlie, pushed by his dad to do something useful with his life, had gone off to join the army at the first opportunity, following in his uncle's footsteps and into the Sherwood Foresters. Smith was a couple of years younger and took up an apprenticeship at a saw blade makers when he left school. They'd lost touch until they met up a few years later when Charlie was on compassionate leave for his father's funeral – killed when some water got into his furnace, showering him in molten metal. It was in the pub afterwards that Smith saw him – majestic in his uniform, holding forth on tales of life in Aden and Malta – with a group of apostles sat around him, open-mouthed. As soon as Smith moved into his circle, the parable stopped abruptly and he had jumped up: 'Bloody hell, is that Smith?' He had shaken his hand enthusiastically. 'Tell me everything you've been up to. How's your old ma? Best gingerbread I've ever tasted. Are you still in touch with the others?'

They had reminisced, and shared stories of various conquests. Charlie didn't take much priming before all his yarns of army life started. He had left Smith torn between thinking what a marvellous thing army life was and wondering whether his old friend was a fantasist – over-embellishing stories to make the dull monotony of drill and night-watch seem something that it was not. Smith was plied with beer until he felt quite unsteady on his feet.

It was after Smith fell out with the chargehand at the works that he wrote to Charlie asking his advice on joining up. A few months later he was a raw recruit in Aldershot in the same regiment as Corporal Charles Jepson.

When Charlie's service ended he had got a job with the Midland Railway at their locomotive department. Then when Smith was faced with having to do the right thing by Elsie he confided in Charlie. He'd already completed his seven years short service so didn't have to apply for compassionate grounds. Charlie put in a good word for him and he got a job as a fitter's mate at the depot.

' 'ere, tha going to t' meeting tomorrow?'

'Yeah. Shall I pop round for thi on my way up? We could go over the back way to Grimesthorpe across the fields.'

'Sounds good to me. I'll perhaps slip a couple of bottles into my pockets for refreshments.'

'You heard owt else about what went on?'

'Well, the word is he might have given the scabbing bastard a little push on the shoulder for being a mouthy get, but it were no more than that.' He demonstrated with a light shove on Smith's shoulder.

'And he's done for assault for that?'

'It's all trumped up. They've been out to get them that were solid in 1911 ever since – make an example of 'em.'

'Are they really that daft? They must know we won't stand for it.'

'It's all over the country too. They're heading for a national strike if they keep it up.'

They were joined by a couple of mates from the depot, so got the dominoes out and played for penny stakes. By the time the bell rang at the bar, *All right, gentlemen. Can we have your beer off now, please*, Smith had a little pile half an inch high.

'Right then, Charlie. I'd best be getting back. I'll see thi.'

'Aye. Ta-ta.'

CHAPTER TWO

Mary was already waiting for Elsie in the Chapel Walk shop and had a big girlish grin on her face – bursting to say something. She was only a couple of years younger than Elsie but her mannerisms and her round, freckled face and big eyes made her look younger.

Elsie took her through to the back room. Mary took both her hands and jigged about.

'We did it!'

'I know. What was it like?'

'I didn't see anything. I simply posted the letter and kept walking – not daring to look back – there were quite a lot of people out and about – I had my hat pulled down as far over my face as I could.'

'You made it into the newspaper, though.'

'Not like yours. What happened? Did it explode?'

'Of course not – when I looked back it was smoking a bit, then someone put it out with water. No worse than you get from a bit of fat spilling over into the fire really. They make it sound so dramatic, talking about bombs, when it was no more than setting a few letters smouldering.'

They took a bundle of newspapers out and headed up towards the Victoria monument. Most people chose to hurry past, avoiding eye contact as if they were unclean beggars. Others uttered words of contempt: haughty women carrying packages to awaiting carriages, feeling the tremors at the foundations of the baroque edifices of their femininity. Or stuffed shirts and starched collars flashing looks of hatred. How dangerous their ideas!

Others still would find sport in goading them or "learnin' 'em a thing or two."

'Look 'ere, love, it's not that Asquith. You know what he's up against in the Lords. The real power's still wi' the King and the barons. They'll never let the likes of me get a say, never mind ordinary women. That's where your fight is, not with Asquith.'

'But aren't the Liberals just as much a part of the problem?'

'Happen as not. You've got to bring the lot down.'

'Exactly. But giving women votes will be a step towards that, surely?'

'Goo on then. Gi' us one of them papers, love.'

'Thank you, sir.'

They went to a cafe for lunch afterwards and ordered a pot of tea and sandwiches.

'Are you scared, Elsie?'

'What of?'

'That they might find out it was you,' she whispered.

'No. No one saw me. And how could they prove it was me anyway? Besides they'd have come knocking by now if they had. Don't worry, Mary.'

'No. You're right. You always have the right answer. Always explain things - got the knack. I would have liked to have had a teacher like you. It's not fair.'

'No – and it's a waste. Not just me, but all the others. All that training, and not put to a proper use.'

'Marrying shouldn't make a difference.'

'Once we have the vote, such nonsense will soon end, don't you think?'

'Oh yes. We will change so much. That's what scares them.' Mary wiped a crumb from her lips with the napkin. 'Would you not rather have carried on teaching than get married?'

'It's easy to say yes, looking back. But I didn't have a choice at the time.'

'What do you mean?'

'Me and Smith... I got into trouble.'

'Oh... but – '

'I miscarried.'

'Oh, I'm sorry Elsie. I shouldn't have asked.'

'Don't be a silly. It is better to be able to talk about these things. I was whisked off my feet I suppose.'

'He is rather charming though, isn't he?'

'Yes, he can be very charming, especially when he chooses to be. And back then, when he was in his dress uniform, he looked very fine. He was attentive and flattering, and I fell hopelessly in love with him.'

'Where did you meet him?'

'In Lincoln. That's where I did my teacher training at the Church college there. We used to go up to the cathedral every Sunday morning to the service. And one day Smith was there with his regiment – they were out in Lincolnshire on manoeuvres or shooting practice or whatever it is they do. He took a shine to me. Love on first sight he said.

'I didn't see him at first – but he said he never took his eyes off me all the way through the service.

'Afterwards he contrived to be waiting around outside as we filed out: he touched his cap and smiled at me. I must have blushed terribly, I know.

'He was a sly one. He still is. He tracked me down with all the skill of a Mohican scout. Imagine my surprise when I was walking through the castle grounds with my best pal, Irene, and him and Charlie, his partner in crime, were sat on a form as we went by. They jumped up and doffed their caps and introduced themselves, and asked if they might stroll with us.

"Thank you, but we really couldn't," we said.

"What rot! Why ever not?"

"Well, the college doesn't like us to associate with gentlemen."

"What nonsense. This is not the nineteenth century. What harm can there be in a little polite company?" Smith said.

'His mate, Charlie, looked all sad like a small boy who'd lost his best marble, and he made Irene laugh.

"Oh, come on, Else," she said. "I do get somewhat bored listening to just your opinions all the time."

'I gave her a withering look. It was a beautiful spring afternoon, with the leaves on the trees still looking perfect, and sunlight dappling the paths. Try as I might to stick with Irene, I failed. I think they had planned to split us up all along. I ended up by myself with Smith.

'He charmed me – talking of the cathedral and the service that morning. He seemed to have a fine ear for music. He was so polite, and the most pleasant company. And it felt a thrill to be away from the college and its rules and constant female companionship. It was quite daring. He was interested in everything I said about college life – about the hockey team and our trips to play matches. They had only recently got back from having been stationed in Ireland at the time and he told me all about army life and the things they got up to relieve the boredom. Somehow we got onto politics – I probably asked him about the Irish Question and set him off. Universal adult suffrage, seizing power in Parliament through the Labour Party and Trades Unions – all that.

'You know, it was very exciting for me to hear – I'd been quite sheltered, I suppose. That conventional view that women's roles and strengths are different – definitely the college ethos. I never really challenged it and certainly was appalled by the tactics and the shrill voices of the suffragettes.'

'Shrill voices, Elsie?'

'I don't think that now of course, but back then I was quite the prim, little schoolmistress. I'd read about Adela's antics with a good deal of disdain – climbing up drainpipes to address the mob, and all that.'

'Who are you calling a mob?' Mary laughed. 'I was in the town that evening – me and my big sister were staying with my aunt and uncle. We'd gone in with our uncle to see a torch-lit procession of the unemployed. I remember Adela speaking to the crowd – the police did everything to try to shut her up. They roughed her up a bit too, the brutes!'

'I'd have disapproved highly of her antics. Very unladylike and lacking in manners.'

'And now look at you!'

'I know. After, I started to show an interest in the debating society at college – we even had a debate on women's suffrage.'

'So, did you see Smith again soon after?'

'Yes. I'd given so much information away about myself, not knowing. I played in a hockey match against Sheffield Training College up at High Storrs one day, and Smith was in the crowd watching – he was on leave. I was very flattered and we exchanged a few words and he asked if he could write to me.'

'Then what?'

'So, I said yes, of course. I was completely besotted by then. I would have married him then and there if he'd asked. I didn't get to see him much because he was on a posting to Plymouth, and in September I took up a teaching post at a school in Tinsley. We wrote to each other and when he was given leave he'd come up to Sheffield. He'd meet me at the school gates and take me for tea and out to the pictures or the varieties. I could see no wrong in him. He was intelligent, polite, very considerate and had a head full of exciting ideas about how our generation were going to change the world for the better.'

'I sometimes wish my Robert were a bit more lively like that – doesn't have strong opinions on anything. When I ask him something it's always: "I don't rightly know, Mary." Or: "I 'spect so." "I reckon you must be right." '

'Oh, but he dotes on you, that's why. If you were to marry him, he would devote himself to you entirely. He's as steady as they come.'

'I know but he's never going to whisk *me* off *my* feet. And Smith is such a dish.'

'Well, I can't say I wasn't physically attracted to him, but I admired and loved him so much more than that. But that was part of the trouble. I think I loved him much more than he loved me. Once we were married, he had got what he wanted and stopped trying. I gave up everything for him – I gave up the profession I had worked hard for – really hard. Two years of college, two years at the Pupil Teacher Centre, and at school, earning my scholarships.

'I used to wait all day for him to come home so that I could tell him how much I loved him, and look after him. But he wasn't the same – he didn't rush home to me to hold me in his arms. He'd often be late back, having been to the pub after work, and would sit down in his chair without even taking his mucky jacket or boots off – after I'd spent all day cleaning and making the house nice. I'd give him his tea and he'd often go out again, or just sit in front of the fire reading his newspaper, not wanting to be interrupted.

'But every now and then he'd do something – put his arms around me – or rest his hand on my ever-rounding belly and that would be enough. He was never unkind to me back then, when I was expecting, but there was no passion. He has a coldness; for him, marriage, love even, is a necessary inconvenience.

'I had mood swings, accused him of not caring. "Sometimes I think you no longer love me." I'd throw at him. Seeking reassurance. "Oh come off it, Else," he'd say. "Of course I do. What rot! There's no point getting upset. Be reasonable." Reasonable! What has reason got to do with it? Did I apply reason when I fell in love with him? Then he'd sulk, or storm out, and I'd feel guilty, cry and beg for his forgiveness. "It is just your condition making you say these things. You should rest," he'd say.

'He's basically selfish, despite all his talk about the common good. He only does things if they make him happy, if they satisfy his own pursuit of pleasure or an easy life. He wooed me not for my sake but for his own gain – I sacrificed everything to him, set it all out in front of him to take as his, but he never sacrifices the slightest whim for anything that is just for me. There is always a calculation going on – if he gives something, does he get even more back. You're better off with a man like Robert, who would rather live with you in poverty than without you in wealth. You shouldn't keep him waiting for too long, Mary. If you wait for the perfect time it may never come.'

'Are you still trying for children?'

'No. Not really. Not now. We did, but I've rather given up hope. It's been over a year since I lost the baby.'

'That's not so long.'

'No, perhaps. But I wonder if something is wrong.'

Mary took her hand across the table and gave it a squeeze.

'I was happy, Mary. I felt the child would make up for so much – make my sacrifice worthwhile. As it became more real, as the baby kicked inside me, it became for me a kind of freedom – I no longer waited eagerly for the sounds of his boots down the passage. I was less dependent on the little signs I looked for that he might still love me. I had another focus – someone who needed my love so much more. But then afterwards it was even worse – like he blamed me for what had happened.

'Can we really find happiness, Mary? Isn't there something always denying us? Look – I'm sorry. I have rather gone on a bit. We'd best get back to the shop and give them our takings.'

*

'How was your meeting last night?' Elsie was putting tea on the table. Smith had been to bed for the afternoon to get some rest before his night shift.

'Good, yeah. The stewards are going to go back to the managers with an ultimatum. There's another meeting Thursday evening. The pressure's building for another strike.'

'Can we manage if that happens?'

'Why ever not? Thousands do. Somehow or other. Why don't tha bloody well support me for once?'

'I'm not saying I don't. It was just a question about practicalities.'

'Tha could always go cap in hand to thi folks.'

'That's not fair. All I was doing was asking. It's got nothing to do with my parents. I'm not saying I'm for or against a strike.'

'That middle-class, do-gooder Pankhurst woman of yourn. She's agin us. Only bothered about women's votes. Men who have the vote shouldn't strike and damage wealth, but should queue up with their votes: "Please sir, can I have some more." It doesn't work like that.'

'Did I ever say it did? Just eat your tea, Smith. I'll go and fetch your work clothes.'

'No. Sit. Sit with me and eat. I didn't mean to go on, lass.'

She pulled up a chair and took some bread for herself.

'It just makes me mad. People can't see what's right in front of them. Just giving people votes won't solve anything. Most people are too stupid to know how to vote. They'll not think for themselves. They'll simply do as they're told.'

'That's why better schools are needed, and properly trained teachers.'

'Like you, you mean?'

'Yes, like me.'

'I'm not talking about bookish learning, about Shakespeare and the Romans, but proper political education through trade unions.'

'The two aren't mutually exclusive. Just because you never got on at school doesn't make it wrong. It can be as much about learning to think as about learning facts.'

Smith either held his tongue or knew he had nothing more he could say. Elsie glanced at him but his head was down, eyes on his plate. Little more was said. She fetched his boots, loosened the laces and placed them on the hearth, aired a clean shirt and neck cloth over the back of the chair and put a flask and his snap into his bag.

As soon as he had closed the door behind him she packed her own bag – another flask of tea and a box of children's chalks.

She headed for the tram stop on Burngreave Road, leaving enough of a gap between Smith's departure and her own.

Should she have played the good little wife and not argued back? He hated being reminded of her education. He always said he had learnt more in the army than eight years in school. That's as maybe, but he still had a chip on his shoulder. He always used to say it was her intelligence as well as her looks that first attracted him, but now when she used that intelligence it annoyed him – like it was a thing to be tamed and put in a cage, dangerous if it was let out. When he was the lion tamer controlling her mind and her body he was happy. All she had asked was a question about practicalities in the case of a strike but he took it as a challenge. Not that she was worried about the money – from her short spell teaching she had saved several pounds from her twenty-eight shillings a week. Hidden away for a rainy day, unknown to Smith.

Trams packed with weary men, women and children headed up Spital Hill in the opposite direction, their headlights piercing the gloom.

She had arranged to meet Molly, the new organiser, at Lady's Bridge. She'd only been with them a few weeks and brought back that spark that had gone out when Adela had left, leaving only Miss Schuster in charge. Efficient, controlled Miss Schuster. She was a brick, of course, but spinsterish, and her slight German accent gave her a coldness, put her at a distance, always making Elsie feel she was being assessed. On the other hand, Molly was a force of nature, fizzing with passion for the cause. She was a similar age to Elsie, someone you felt you'd always known – had grown up with, even. She had brought new ideas with her from across the Pennines and a certain aura from her association with the Pankhursts.

'Glad you made it. Are you all right for time?'

'Yes. He's on nights, so he'll suspect nothing as long as I'm back before him. Where are we going?'

'I thought we could brighten Rotherham up tonight. It's much better when you come along: all those artistic flourishes you add. People actually stop to admire the craft that has gone into the designs – it's not just my bold statements.'

'I'm excited about this. I've got some ideas based on some jewellery I was looking at. I've got plenty of green and white but the purple was a bit harder to find.'

They waited for a through-tram to Rotherham and had to stand downstairs – it was packed with men and boys on their way through the Don Valley. A distinctive metallic smell clung to the coarse fabrics of their clothes, mixed with aromas of tobacco and sweat.

'Where did you learn to draw?'

'I was quite good at school. Then at the Central School we had art lessons – there wasn't an art room at the school so we had to walk across to the School of Art – Miss Nott used to do life studies with us – drawing hens and the like. Only one boy rather spoilt it by throwing bread crumbs he had saved in his pocket.'

'Typical boy.'

'Yes. Making up for his inadequacies – drawing attention to himself.'

'Rather than *actually* drawing.'

'What? Oh yes. Exactly.'

They got a seat after Savile Street where many got off to go to work at Cammells.

'What is Mrs Pankhurst really like? I mean, is she nice? You hear stories.'

'I'm not sure nice is a word that jumps to mind exactly. She'd be the least favourite of your two grannies. Not the one you'd run to if you fell over. But does it really matter what a leader is like if they inspire people?'

'I suppose not. I wouldn't have got involved had I not seen her speak. It was at the Montgomery Hall. Cissie, a friend from college, who I met up with by chance, suggested we go along to see for ourselves. It was about the Conciliation Bill or something like that. I'm not good at understanding all those bills and amendments. It was something about her I fell in love with, I suppose.'

'Me too. She holds you in the palm of her hand, doesn't she?'

'She spoke with such passion about how they would take on the Government. March up to Parliament and refuse to move if the Bill didn't get through.'

'Black Friday?'

'Yes. You know Miss Schuster was there? She told us how they were groped and assaulted by the police. Up until then I'd believed what I'd read in the newspapers.'

'That's what they do: close ranks, twist the story.'

'Anyway, after, me and Cissie started going to all manner of meetings. The police stole our placards from us when we tried to protest at Churchill's visit to Sheffield. We were held back outside the Albert Hall by dozens of them.'

'It's to Churchill that I owe my job here.'

'How's that?'

'That famous meeting at the Free Trade Hall when he was there with Grey – '

'You were there! When Annie Kenney and Christabel – '

'No. I wish. But it was all over the local papers about this shocking, unladylike behaviour.'

'What? Having opinions?'

'Yes, shocking. You know that stuff about Christabel spitting at the police – all made up. Anyway, I was at my evening class – we'd been discussing what had happened at home as well as before class. The headmaster used to prowl around supervising the classes, and he stopped and made some quip about the Free Trade Hall meeting. Then proceeded to read the report to us out loud from the newspaper he had tucked under his arm. I must have raised my eyebrows or rolled my eyes or something because he jumped at me: "What are you smiling for, young lady? Do you uphold the conduct of this lady in spitting in the face of a policeman?" I said something like: "No, it is a waste of good spit, if you ask me" or some such – it made everyone laugh, anyway. Not a very ladylike reply.'

Elsie laughed out loud and several passengers turned to look.

'That was it for me, after that. My mother and all her girls got involved with the WSPU.'

When they reached Rotherham they alighted.

'Come on, let's go and find a dreary spot to decorate.'

'Are we writing anything in particular?'

'No, not tonight. It's more about being seen: to have a presence. Then when we've meetings to advertise we can come back.'

'They sat on the pavement underneath a gaslight near to the parish church and got out the chalks. Passers-by stopped to see what they were doing. Elsie was working around her initial, white chalk lettering – a simple: GIVE WOMEN VOTES – in a floral design of twisting willow-like green leaves and purple flowers.

' 'ere are you them women what wants to wear trousers?'

'Could you imagine me in trousers, sir?' said Molly, looking up and fixing the man's gaze.

'No, miss. Not trousers. But you lot are wanting to be the bosses.'

'No. We only want what men have got.'

'Well, I ain't got nowt – you're welcome to haife on it.'

'Very kind, I'm sure.'

'Well, if I ain't got a vote I don't see why you should.'

'Nor do we. Men and women of all classes should have a vote.'

'Aye. Right enough. Night, miss.'

Others were less amenable to a discussion and told them to: 'gerroff out on it,' 'get yerselves home, and see to yer husbands, or they'll be getting their seeing to elsewhere.' Which caused hilarity amongst their pub-bound mates.

Elsie and Molly had long since ceased to be shocked by some of the vile comments they got.

Some people, though, were appreciative of Elsie's creativity – some shop girls stopped to talk.

'That's right pretty, that, miss. I wish I was that clever.'

'Thank you, that's kind.'

'Will they ever give us a vote then, miss?'

'Not unless they have to – that's why we have to keep the pressure up.'

'You should get involved,' said Molly. 'We need strong young women like you. Take one of our handbills to read about it.'

'Oh, I don't think so, miss. I don't think my Harry would like it, miss. But good luck to you.' And they wandered off.

Elsie was finishing off another design, and Molly had moved on to a nearby wall, when Elsie sensed someone standing next to her. She looked up and there was the tall figure of a constable looming over her. He shone his lantern onto the pavement, illuminating the violet, green and white artwork.

'What's all this then?'

Elsie froze. She felt her insides twist and seize up, a panic rise in her throat.

Molly came over. 'Good evening, sir. I've got a handbill you can take if you are interested in our cause.'

'I'm obliged, miss, but I'm going to have to arrest you.'

Molly smiled at him; a sweet smile, like he had offered her a rose. 'Whatever for?' – looking at the silverware on his tunic – 'P.C. 127?'

'For wilful damage.'

'We've not damaged anything. One sharp shower of rain and it will all be gone.'

'Then for causing a nuisance on the highway.'

'Under which category would that be? We have not thrown or permitted to be thrown any filth or matter onto the carriageway or footway.'

'It is drawing on a pavement.'

'Oh no. I think you're getting muddled with drawing a wagon or cart on a footway – not drawing in chalk.'

'But what you have written on the wall: "Liberals break promises, suffragettes break windows." That is condoning a crime.'

'It's a simple statement of fact.'

'And you are causing an obstruction.'

'We're not. Look, we'll move on if you would like us to.'

'Yes please, miss.'

'Right. We'll go then.'

'Goodnight to you.'

'Goodnight, P.C.127. And thank you for everything you do to keep us all safe.' Molly's teeth flashed white in the darkness.

'It's very pretty, miss.' The policeman nodded towards Elsie's design. She felt a glow of pride.

They gathered up their chalks and left.

'You really are very good, Molly. I do believe you could charm the birds out of the trees.'

'Oh, I just find being nice works better than being nasty.'

'And you seemed to know the law better than he did.'

'It helps to know where you stand. We've had talks from lawyers – we're getting some real expertise built up. Come on let's go and get a drink from somewhere before the last tram back. We've earned it.'

CHAPTER THREE

Winter snows cast a temporary veil of purity over blackened buildings and muddy roads and causeways, until it too turned as grey as a starched collar on the neck of a foundry clerk or the net curtains of a woman full of the best intentions.

The Board of Trade enquiry into the Midland Railway dispute was slapped over with crude brush strokes after a good old dipping in a bucket of slaked lime. Railway workers held meetings, passed resolutions, recruited and organised and threatened. But the managers were so inept that they rubbed further salt in the wounds by sacking a guard called Richardson for refusing to follow an instruction to take more than the regulation number of trucks for a ten-ton brake van – and on the not insignificant gradients between Chesterfield and Sheffield, to boot.

The government ditched its Franchise Bill, which resulted in more disgraceful scenes at Westminster, more arrests of unladylike ladies, more windows hammered, more pavements chalked, more newspapers sold, more meetings attended – and disrupted, more accusations hurled. On golf courses frequented by virtuous gentleman, carefully manicured greens were dug up by women of no virtue, determined to prove that they deserved never to be allowed a say in the rule of law.

The tragedy of Antarctic explorers appeared to bring the nation together in a moment of reflection on the importance of life, of sacrifice and of national consciousness, but nothing had really changed. While Oxford and Cambridge gentlemen were unwavering in their belief that their values and methods were those of the Almighty, that the study of ancient languages and dead civilisations was what was required to reverse the decline in modern western civilisation and far superior and more useful than the tawdry pursuit of science or the seedy business of engineering, the lower classes simply followed the waving flag.

Molly was a rising star in the suffragette movement and was attracting attention for all sorts of reasons. Earnest young men started coming into the shop on Chapel Walk offering to help out – to carry newspapers or run errands. Elsie bathed in a little of that starlight. These young socialists were full of ideas of how they were going to change society: a state medical service and preventive medicine, raising the school leaving age to fifteen, a minimum wage, boards of control for key industries, and retirement pensions. They were unstoppable; they had the rising tide behind them, irresistible logic and irrefutable evidence of decay of the old order. They brought not only fresh ideas to the shop, but also bon-bons, and little bunches of violets and wood anemones to set on the counter. Elsie looked forward to these visits and the exchange of ideas, not to mention the occasional sugared almond. She was flattered to have attention paid to her and her opinions sought. It was also nice to have help in distributing newspapers at the monument.

Not everyone approved in equal measure. The ladies of Fulwood and Ecclesall disapproved of men hanging around the shop. They were scornful of Molly – probably jealous thought Elsie. They were the ones who Molly called the "fish course martyrs." She told a story of once visiting the home of a rich sympathiser in Manchester who sat in her lavish parlour surrounded by silverware, extolling the virtues of sacrifice. She did the voice so well that her listeners always exploded with laughter: "Of course, all of us have many demands made upon us, and yet we must get more people to support us. It is no use people saying they cannot afford any more. There are always ways and means, if it is only cutting out the fish course at breakfast and giving that…"

One of Elsie's favourite young socialists was called Henry. He was so young he still had no beard worth lifting a razor to, intense blue eyes and blond hair neatly parted down the centre. He worked at the Kelham Island electric power station for the trams and threw himself into everything he did – his work, his trade union, the Labour Party, and the Ethical Society. He'd regularly call at the shop after his shift to see if there was any news or any interesting speakers coming up at the monument.

It was also occasionally helpful to have someone in the background in case things got awkward, or spirits rose too high. When, for example, an ardent member of the publican-supporting arm of the Tory Party had tried to snatch the bundle of papers that Elsie had over her arm and Henry had moved him on. He did it very tactfully, not in a way as to place himself in control. He was not aggressive. He quietly stepped up and spoke to the man: 'I can see you are a keen supporter, sir, but if you want that many newspapers you'll have to pay for them first.'

The friends of the man laughed at him, and they went swaying on their way. Henry nodded to Elsie and left her to get on with her work.

Afterwards Molly and Elsie were heading back down Fargate accompanied by Henry and Jack, a young man who appeared to have taken a shine to Molly.

'There's a bunch of us going up Hillsborough on Sunday night to go to Joe Pointer's meeting. We might have a bit of fun. Are you two coming?' Henry asked.

'We'll spread out around the hall in twos so that they don't suspect anything.' It was Alf Barton who spoke – one of the best speakers the Socialists had. 'We'd perhaps be best splitting up once we get off the tram as well, in case they try and turn any of us away.'

'I don't suppose there'll be much of a police presence though, will there, Alf?'

'No – they save that for the Liberals. A Labour man like Joe Pointer will just have to fend for himself, with perhaps one bobby posted outside.'

Elsie got off the tram with Mary.

'I'm not sure I could ever speak with the confidence that these men do,' Elsie said.

'It's all the same, whether they're right or wrong, isn't it? They still make out they know what they're on about.' Mary put on a deep voice: 'Let me make myself absolutely clear. I stand before you in complete control of my bladder... er, brief, and can assure you that I have all the facts up my er... ar... sleeve.'

Elsie giggled. 'Stop it, Mary. Someone will hear you. Come on, let's go in.'

Inside the auditorium of the Phoenix they found a seat right in the middle of the stalls. It was a full house by the time the ILP Member of Parliament for Attercliffe took to the stage.

Before he even opened his mouth to speak, a voice shouted out: 'Are you going to withdraw that contemptuous article in the Guardian?' It was Alf Barton.

'Sit down, will you,' responded one of the stewards.

Pointer raised his hand for quiet. 'As regards the article, everyone who knows me knows that the next time I run away from anything will be the first.' Elsie felt quite sorry for him already. He did not have an unkind face – he had nice eyes, a smooth, high brow and a rather smart moustache: long and twisted to a point at the ends.

'What are they talking about?' Mary asked Elsie.

'I don't know. It's perhaps his attack on socialists not in the Labour Party – what they were talking about on the way here.'

'You cannot represent the people until the women have votes!' They recognised Molly's voice across the auditorium.

'Please. I know many of you have grievances – if you let me speak I will pick up on many of them as I go, but we will not make progress this way, if you continue to upset the whole meeting.'

'But Westminster has no legitimacy when it denies more than half of the population a say!'

'It is not as straightforward as you might like to think.'

'It never is for you!'

'We Labour Party MPs are betwixt two fires.'

'Three!' There was laughter around the hall. The honourable member's face was flushed – it was getting warm in the auditorium and he was wearing his jacket and waistcoat.

'Yes, if you like: three. First of all, the Conservatives and Liberals say the Labour Party is going too fast. Some of our friends in the Social Democratic Foundation say we are not going fast enough. Then the ladies say we are not going at all. I have got to this point, that I am conscious to avoid displeasing. In future I am going to look a little after myself.'

'Look after your pocket!'

The meeting settled down somewhat and he got onto his views on the Minimum Wage Act and explaining the Parliamentary process.

Mary shuffled in her seat next to Elsie. 'Women's suffrage! No taxation without representation!'

Elsie started – she hadn't been expecting Mary to get involved. Mary was beaming – clearly very pleased with herself for doing her bit. A few men in tweed turned to see who the harridan was. Some tutted and twitched their whiskers.

'Look, no matter how much you interrupt I will not be made to alter my course. I will deal with the Suffrage Bill in due course.'

'Take it first!'

'No, I shall not. And if I don't reach the bill tonight that will be because of your interruptions and you will say I am the worst of the five Sheffield members.'

Another shout from Mary: 'So you are!' Where had she got all this courage from? She was becoming a proper militant. Elsie felt under pressure. She didn't want to appear timid. Didn't want to let her friends down.

Joseph Pointer spoke again: 'You say that, and yet I have always voted for the women. But what I want to see is a franchise for everyone: men and women alike, not just a few well-to-do women.'

There were more interruptions, and patience started to wear out. There were cries of 'Chuck 'em out.'

'No. I do not want any of that. These women are presuming on their sex. Men would not be allowed to do as they are doing. If you really want to be trusted on equality with men then you should observe the decencies of public meetings. Don't you think it peculiar that the other members for Sheffield who have not voted for the women always get off scot-free, whilst the one who has always voted for them gets treated like this.'

'That's because as a member of the Labour Party you can do more to help our cause than all the other four, and yet you do not. That's why our grievance is against you.' It was Molly speaking again.

'Look, when I became a socialist – '

'A what?'

'When was that?' There were guffaws of laughter.

'I have found that since, since I have been in the ILP, that all the time among socialists is taken up in fighting each other, instead of the enemy.'

He dragged it back to the minimum wage and was challenged over the lack of Labour Party support for the minimum wage for the miners.'

'When are we going to have a decent minimum wage for women?'

Elsie wished she thought of that.

'When some of you get a bit more sense.'

'Of all the –' Elsie muttered to Mary. She wanted to shout out something witty and incisive. She was letting them down.

'That's an outrageous thing to say.' Elsie recognised Jack's voice from the balcony. She should have said that herself.

The MP got onto the question of the franchise. He was accused of not keeping his promises. He shook his head. 'But I have.'

'Then why don't you do something?' Another female voice from across the auditorium.

'I suppose what you ladies want us to do in the House of Commons is what you are doing now. All I can say is that they would not treat us as tenderly as we treat you. The ladies want us to make government impossible until they get the vote, but that is not what I am going to do.'

There was applause around the theatre from his supporters. She had to say something. The thought of getting to the end of the meeting and not having done her bit! How would that look?

Pointer picked up again: 'Unless I can take women's suffrage as part and parcel of the Labour programme I am not going to have it at all.'

Her heart was racing, she was perspiring and her mouth was dry.

'The view from where I sit in Westminster is clear: the women must get the public behind them, and then they will get what they want, but public opinion is not behind them.'

'It is!' There, she had done it.

'If only you would go about things more reasonably with your propaganda, then you would have the country behind you. You have lost support, and handed the argument to those who say women are too emotional, too hysterical to exercise the vote responsibly. Every man who has supported them they have gone against. The militancy now going on is the greatest obstacle to women's suffrage. How is breaking the law going to help your cause for a say in forming it?'

'That's nonsense, and you know it!' She had broken the spell over her now. 'If the miners, or other strikers, break the law you listen and act. We have tried for sixty years being good little ladies. It would still get us nowhere in another sixty.'

'I think my point is proven,' the M.P. replied superciliously.

'You're a disgrace,' shouted Henry from the balcony. 'A traitor. No wonder the party is deserting you.'

There was a commotion as shouting started up above, with others taking up positions on one side or the other.

Pointer sat down and lit a cigarette as the pandemonium continued. Mary patted Elsie on the hand. 'Well said.' She swelled with pride at having found her voice.

The chairman of the meeting came down off the stage and tried to calm everyone down. Elsie looked at Pointer. Was he at all upset that he was not trusted, or was he so thick-skinned he didn't care either way. Perhaps he was not as nice as she first thought. Looking after himself.

At the end of a meeting Elsie heard Molly and some of the others singing as they left: 'The People's flag is deepest red, It shrouded oft our martyred dead.' She and Mary followed the singing band out of the hall and joined in the chorus, the only bit Elsie knew.

She felt elated coming out into the cool evening air amongst her friends. She had stood up to a Member of Parliament and put him in his place.

A bit of a scuffle started, followed by a stand off with insults being hurled.

Elsie and Mary scurried off down towards Hillsborough Corner to catch the tram. The others caught up with them shortly after, Henry appearing from out of a nearby pub, smiling.

'Did I miss owt?' said Henry.

'Pointer started defending what he said about Tom Mann – that he deserved six months in gaol, if not more.'

'Yeah, of course. Six months for pleading with soldiers not to shoot strikers?'

'You'd've thought our *Independent Labour* Member of Parliament would have understood that.' The words Independent and Labour were spat out with a sneer.

'You wonder whether they get taken over by the establishment as soon as they get to Westminster. Feed 'em a few nice dinners in the Palace, port and cigars, and even a patternmaker from Attercliffe starts acting like Lord Pointer from the Manor of H'attercliffe.'

'It's always the same – mad-eyed soldiers just firing into the crowd: Featherstone, Llanelli.'

'And don't forget that bastard Churchill sending the troops against the miners in Tonypandy.'

'How come you missed some of the meeting?' said Elsie.

'He got thrown out by a couple of heavies.'

'Did they rough you up?' said Jack.

Henry was all smiles. 'Nah, not much, but it was worth it. And I'd do it again – the hypocrite.'

'He only does it to make a show.' Jack put his arm round Henry and gave him a shake. 'Not a proper meeting unless you get chucked out, is it Henry, old lad?'

Henry grinned at Elsie and shrugged.

When she got home, Smith was sitting at the table, still in his jacket turning his cap round in his hands.

'Tha were a bloody disgrace.'

'What do you mean?'

'Tha knows.'

'I have no idea.'

'At the meeting.'

'You were there?'

'I bloody were. Like Saint fuckin' Peter – denying thi bloody existence. Where's your respect?'

'Respect? Surely that's something that has to be earned.'

***

Smith joined the steady stream heading out at the end of the shift.

'See thi tomorrow then, Arthur.'

'Aye, that tha will, Smith, lad. More unbounded joy with them there boiler tubes.'

'Can't wait.'

It was now light at home time, lifting his spirits; gone were the depressing winter evenings when he trooped to work and home again in the dark. He looked for Charlie near the main gate, and hung back to wait for him.

'How's thi day been?'

'Not bad, thine?'

'Same as yesterday. Same as tomorrow.'

They got into their stride as the first pint beckoned.

'Strike's off then,' said Smith. 'At least until the next time they get their arses and elbows mixed up.'

'I reckon they backed down when they saw what they were up against: now we're a two hundred thousand strong *National* Union of Railwaymen.'

'And thousands still joining. Is he back in work again, yet?'

'Richardson? Yeah, I believe so. 'ere, did tha read what Keir Hardie said about 1911?'

'Nah, what was that?'

'It were in yesterday's paper: that the main reason it were called off was pressure from the army. Because of Agadir and a plan to send troops quickly to Antwerp to defend France, they needed the railways running to mobilise men quickly. Paid 'em off apparently. It's all coming out now because of this new talk of military build up.'

'But that's all blather, ain't it?'

'Of course, yeah. Asquith reckoned there's nowt to say we've got to send troops to France, that we've good relations with Germany. Let 'em squabble over Strasbourg – it's nowt to do wi' us.'

They stopped off at the Carwood Hotel. A little oasis amongst blackened brickwork, chimneys, overhead pipelines, the thumping of tilt hammers and deep rumble of rolling mills. It was packed out inside.

'Ey up, Bob?' said Charlie, seeing one of their workmates at the bar. 'Tha buying?'

'No. Sod off. I only won forty shillin'. If I started buying rounds, I'd soon have nowt left.'

'Tight bugger,' said Charlie laughing.

'What's that about?'

'Oh, just he was bragging about having made forty bob up at the Sky Edge tossing ring, so everyone's been begging all day, winding him up. I bet he wishes he'd never said owt. All sorts of daft stuff – dying relatives, sick children needing cures at the seaside, that sort of thing.'

'We should perhaps take a wander up there for a little flutter one pay day.'

'Let's grab that seat – them two are getting up.'

Charlie got out a blackened clay pipe that had survived many an outing against the odds and spent a minute or two filling the bowl with precision before handing the leather pouch to Smith.

'What is it? Looked like tha were about to say summat.'

'Nah. I were just thinking.'

'What, Charlie? I know thi well enough.'

'It were just… Tha getting on all right with thy lass?'

'Apart from the usual, yeah. Why?'

'No, it's probably nowt.'

'Come on. If tha's got summat to say, best get it said.'

'It were just… I heard someone talking.'

'What about?'

'About them suffragettes at the monument handing out papers.'

'She were up there, I suppose. Showing hersen up?'

'Yeah. But it weren't that. It were at snap time, and I overheard one of the lads having a go at 'em and saying summat like "Smith's lass…" and then going on about these young fellas they had in tow – like some sort of entourage. It were nowt more than that, but perhaps tha ought to have a word.'

'Who were it gossiping like a fishwife? Tha'd best tell whoever it were that I'm coming to shut his slack jaw up for him good and proper.'

'No need – I put him straight already – told him there was no better woman and that he should put his own house in order and keep his nose out of other people's business if he didn't want it breaking. There's nowt in it, I'm sure.'

'No. Course not.'

The cool evening air made him feel a bit light-headed as they clapped each other on the back and headed home. Something was nagging at him. He didn't believe it for a minute. Elsie wasn't like that – whatever her views on votes, she wasn't disloyal. She had made her vows and believed in them – she might be strong willed, but she never put her opinions before their marriage. They'd argue, but if push came to shove she'd always look him in the eye and tell him that he came first. And yet lately she had been a bit different – dressing different somehow – she said she had to be smart in the shop or when talking to people to persuade them. He'd caught sight of her adjusting her hat in the mirror and smiling to herself. He would be cautious – not say anything to make himself look stupid. Just keep an eye open, play it long; that was the best strategy.

CHAPTER FOUR

The first blossom appeared in the hedgerows in the country lanes around the city, furniture was heaved out into backyards for a good airing, leaving patches of floor that hadn't had a proper scrub since last year, and whitewash was daubed on pantry walls and slopped on floors. In town, pavements looked a little cleaner and shop awnings a little brighter; heads lifted a little more skywards, and yearnings for the countryside of forefathers re-awakened.

'Elsie, Molly, what are you doing next Sunday?' said Jack, from where he was leaning against the counter of the shop next to Henry, cluttering the place up and getting tutted at by fish-course martyrs.

'Cooking the Sunday dinner, going to church – the usual,' said Elsie.

'Not much,' said Molly. 'Why?'

'Me and Jack are off walking with the Clarion Ramblers into Derbyshire,' said Henry. 'And we're going to call in on Edward Carpenter. I'm a huge fan of *Towards Democracy*. It will be like meeting one of my heroes – and we always have a good old debate on our walks. Say you'll come, won't you?'

'No. I'd probably best not,' said Elsie. 'But thank you.'

'Are you sure, Elsie? I think I should like to go,' Molly said.

'No. It would be too much trouble.'

Henry looked deflated.

Miss Schuster clapped her hands. 'Come along now. These boxes of ribbons won't unpack themselves, ladies. Gentlemen, if you don't mind...'

***

'I'm meeting up with Charlie after tea.' Elsie looked up from her plate but didn't say anything. 'What's tha going to do tonight?'

'Oh, I have some mending to do, and I'll read a book that someone lent to me.'

'What's that then?'

'It's on the mantelpiece.'

Smith mopped up his plate with a bit of bread then stretched and went and stood by the fire.

He picked the book up off the mantelpiece.

'*Towards Democracy* – bloody hell, lass. Tha's getting some ideas. I thought it were the latest tuppenny novelette tha'd borrowed.

'What is this? Chuffing heck. "The sun, the moon and the stars, the grass, the water that flows around the earth, and the light air of Heaven: To you greeting. I too stand behind these and send you word across them." What the bloody hell is this?' He looked at her. She was still sitting at the table; her cheeks were flushed with embarrassment. She looked beautiful and vulnerable.

'It's poetry.'

'Poetry! Not the word I'd use for it – bollocks: pretentious bollocks. I thought from the title tha'd seen some sense. Reading summat decent, summat about the Labour Party.' He flicked through the book. 'Does tha understand all this?'

She got up to take the book off him, like she was trying to protect it.

'Not all of it. I don't think you always have to understand poetry – the words themselves make you feel something whether you fully understand the poet's intention or not.'

'What a load of crap.'

'I wish you'd mind your tongue.' Her dark eyes flashed at him. God she was beautiful.

'I just say things how they are – plain speaking.' He grabbed hold of her and pulled her towards him, held her face in his hands and kissed her mouth, smothering her with passionate kisses. She fought against him to start with. Then she relented as he overpowered her. Let him kiss her till he'd taken his fill.

*

Getting off the tram on Duke Street, Smith and Charlie headed up towards Sky Edge with Tom and Morris: two shunters from the depot.

'I tell you what, though, it's good to get out of the house and spend a bit of time with the lads,' said Smith.

The pikers were out – at least that's what they assumed they were: men standing at the side of the road and on the track up to where the tossing ring was located. These pikers were rough-looking men you wouldn't want to mess with – employed by the boss who ran the ring to maintain discipline, to keep rivals away and to look out for any police wanting to stop the fun. In addition, some young lads acted as scouts to outrun anyone approaching, particularly the police – so that the ring could be quickly dissolved if there was a raid planned.

There was a small crowd of maybe twenty or thirty gathered around the pitch – a flattened piece of ground – lit by lanterns on poles. Keeping order were a couple of men, the ponters, armed with walking canes – maintaining the edge of the ring, supervising the betting and collecting and the distributing the money. Smith's sense of excitement built as they approached. Some of the men were smartly dressed, wearing overcoats with astrakhan collars, and round felt hats – not quite respectable in looks – not like those you might see at the Lyceum Theatre or attending a function at the Cutlers' Hall. These men had not inherited their money, nor earned it through stocks and shares, nor even through running successful manufactories. One had a flattened nose – evidence of a career in the boxing ring, or of having upset too many people, another a thick brow ridge and dark, heavy eyebrows that were not the features of a finally bred descendant of one of the Conqueror's barons, but of an altogether more deeply rooted bloodline.

'Heads, twelve shillings.'

The call was made by the man in the middle of the pitch – the toller. A young man with ginger hair and a neat beard stepped forward with a pile of coins.

Smith and the others just watched, acclimatising to their environment and getting the measure of the play and the players. The toller was a jovial man: clean-shaven, quick eyes, quick fingers and quick-wits. He wore a green silk scarf tucked under his chin and a matching handkerchief flopping out of the pocket of his Norfolk jacket. Always jollying people along, teasing their money out of them, taking two shillings from the stake as his toll and piling up the remainder and the counter-bet in the centre of the ring with a flourish.

'All right then, gentleman. A lovely little pile of shiny silver portraits of Queen Vic, King Eddie, and there's even a spanking new Georgie Porgie half-crown in there, worth at least two and six!'

There was the sound of beer bottles clinking together around the ring as he placed the three halfpennies on his fingers, gave a little twirl and flicked the coins spinning into the air. There was a pause and a hush. 'Heads it is: pay the gentleman. No? Leaving it in? We have twenty-four shillings on tails. Who's going to heads it?'

31

This time the pile of silver was a couple of weeks' wages. The ginger-haired man raised his arm in the air when the call of tails was made and his friends all cheered and slapped him on the back as they anticipated a few drinks coming their way.

'Right then, gentleman. Let's start again. Shall we try twenty-four shillings for tails, anyone? Anyone out there got the guts, or the style?'

And so it went on. The crowd ebbed and flowed but still grew as more joined than left. Charlie gambled twelve shillings and lost it to a huge man in both height and girth, someone Smith thought he recognised, but couldn't quite place. Morris won over a pound on his stake.

'Right then, lads. I can see one or two of you are a bit shy. Shall we start at six shillings on heads.'

Smith handed over his money to the ponter closest to him. A shilling of this went into the toller's pocket.

His stake was matched by the man who looked like an ex-boxer. The crowd of eager faces murmured in anticipation; some putting on side bets between themselves. Then the chatter quietened out of respect for the game. Smith couldn't see beyond the ring; beyond the faces illuminated by lamplight under a cloud of tobacco smoke. A bulldog strained at his lead and was jerked back.

'That's two heads.'

He felt good. Luck was flowing around him, he knew.

'I'll stay in on heads, please.'

'So who'll put me ten bob on tails?'

The same man fumbled in his trouser pocket for a half sovereign and threw it onto the ground.

Smith watched the coins rise into the night: spinning well – no trickery going on. The first coin he saw land on the compacted mud was a tail. For a fraction of a second he was sickened, followed by joy on finding the other two had landed heads. He knew he should take the money. He had taken most of it from the housekeeping tin, after all: he needed to put ten shillings back in.

'Tails this time.' If Lady Luck stayed with him he'd walk away with two pounds, slip the ten shillings back, and still end up with nigh on thirty shillings profit.

The same man tossed in a sovereign.

'A chance to win back your gold, sir, on heads? Right you are.'

This time as the half pennies rose Smith lost them in flight – catching only a few flickers as one briefly caught the lamplight.

'That's two tails and a head. Feeling lucky again?'

'No. Not this time.' Smith was handed the coins and slipped them into his pocket.

They hung around a bit longer to get their breath back then decided to head for a drink. Charlie patted Smith on the shoulder, 'Right, you jammy bastard, tha's buying.'

Smith laughed. 'Not a problem – what's it to be? Whiskies all-round boys?'

'You recognised the big fella didn't you?' said Morris.

'I thought I did. Who was it?'

'Foulkes.'

'Of course: legend of a keeper! Thought I recognised him,' said Charlie. 'Bloody hell. He looks even bigger up close. If he'd been wearing a striped jersey I would've known him for sure. Well, I must say, that eases the pain of losing twelve bob.'

They got talking about the prospects of the Sheffield teams for the following season as they headed down the hill: whether United could turn things round on the Wednesday.

They went in the first pub they found, then went for a few more when they reached the pubs in town.

He woke up in his chair with one boot off. Where had he been? Oh yeah – he wasn't quite sure how he'd got home. Charlie had been there. What an evening! Was it morning? No, still dark. No fire – no wonder it was so bloody cold. He fumbled on the mantelpiece for the matches and knocked something off with a crash.

'Bloody, bollocking bollocks!'

He struck a match and looked at the clock – gone half two. Time for bed. There was a light.

***

Elsie had sat up in bed suddenly awake, with a sense of dread. Was it the sound of breaking glass that had woken her? A burglar?

'Smith,' she whispered, and reached over to wake him. He wasn't there. Then she realised it was probably just him getting back late. She lit a candle, put on her dressing gown, and went downstairs.

'Smith, is that you?'

'Yes. Good eve– Good… Hello.' He was on his hands and knees.

She saw her shepherdess and suitor smashed into pieces on the floor, Smith groping about trying to collect them together, blood

33

dripping from the palm of his hand onto the rug.

Tears welled up in her eyes — her mother and father had bought that as wedding present. It was not only the value — it was German porcelain — but she used to take it down off the mantelpiece and imagine their story, admire the detail on the little fruit basket and the dog at her feet.

'It'll glue back together, love.'

'Give it here: you've done enough damage. Get up to bed.'

She swept the pieces up with a dustpan and threw them in the bin, then went back upstairs with a strip of bandage. Smith was sat on the bed trying to get his socks off. She dressed the cut on his hand, got him into bed, and went round to her side where she blew out the candle. He came fumbling over in the dark and she tried to push him away, but he was too heavy and too strong. He stank of beer and tobacco.

She didn't have to put up with it for long before he rolled back over. She was wide-awake. She got up, used the chamber pot and then went downstairs to wash him off her. She sat at the table and wept.

CHAPTER FIVE

She woke when the light crept through the curtains. Smith was fast asleep and snoring gently. She slipped out of bed and gathered her clothes up off the chair where she had laid them out ready for church the night before and crept downstairs.

She boiled the kettle over the gas ring and made her breakfast. She cut up some bread for Smith and got his plate and cutlery out, some marmalade, and fetched two slices of bacon from the meat safe and put them into a cold frying pan with a scoop of lard. She left two eggs on the side. There: he'd have to manage. He was always going on about having had to cook breakfast while in the middle of nowhere in the army.

She wrote a note and left it on the sideboard: "Gone for a long walk with friends. Back teatime."

She had decided in the night that it was a case of self-preservation – to get out of the house and away from Smith. It was only after she had reached this resolution that she had felt settled enough to return to bed and get some sleep.

There was a small group of people at the foot of the Town Hall steps as she approached. They didn't notice her; they were all so engaged in some discussion or other, with Molly the centre of attention.

It was Henry who spotted her standing quietly at the edge of the group waiting for an opportunity to make herself known. He skipped round the group and held out his hand, smiling.

'You came! How awfully good of you.'

He then went spinning into the cluster of people stood around like a ball into skittles, ignoring any conversation going on. 'Look everyone, Elsie's here. She said she couldn't come. Bert, have you met Elsie? Molly, Elsie's made it after all. Did you bring some snap, Elsie? Just some cake: that's awfully good. We all muck in anyway – we end up with a right feast.'

Their route took them up through Heeley where a few more joined their band. Then, emerging from the city, they got into their stride and filled their lungs with clean air and their minds with clearer thoughts.

They talked with enthusiasm for the future.

'It is inevitable that we will win,' said Henry, waving his arms around like he was invoking the trees and the sky to support him. 'Even with a limited presence in Parliament we already have seen great reform – workers' compensation, pensions... That is down to pressure from the people.'

'But don't you see, those are no more than bones thrown from the rich man's table to keep the dogs happy. We're better off directing our efforts at organising within the trades unions and getting real power – economic power. That's more effective than a miserable vote every five years, where you get to choose between some drunken sot of a Tory or a Liberal who tries to tiptoe his way past raging fires without ever trying to extinguish them.'

'But we've got labour candidates too.'

'Yes, if you want to waste your vote voting for the man who comes third, go ahead, because that is the case too often and they laugh up their sleeves all the way to Westminster. It's exactly what they're banking on.'

'But surely neither route rules out the other?' Elsie said. 'Surely the struggle can go on both inside Parliament and within the trade unions.'

'Well-spoken,' said Molly. 'These men always see things in black or white.'

They passed Millhouses and went up through the woods where they started to sing. They started with a rousing old Montgomery favourite: *Burst every dungeon, every chain, Give injured slaves their rights again,'* followed by Mather's Repentance: *When the battle is won, And our race fully run, We to mansions of glory shall fly; There eternally praise, The blest Ancient of Days. For His love made us ready to die.'*

Then they struck up what had become their anthem:

'England Arise! The long, long night is over,
Faint in the east behold the dawn appear;
Out of your evil dream of toil and sorrow,
Arise, O England, for the day is here.'

Elsie couldn't join in to start with, not knowing the words, but managed to sing along with the choruses. Some lines of the song took her by surprise:

By your young children's eyes so red with weeping,
By their white faces aged with want and fear,

36

By the dark cities where your babes are creeping,
Naked of Joy and all that makes life dear,
From each wretched slum,
Let the loud cry come,
Arise oh England for the day is here.'

Tears came to her eyes and Henry produced an immaculate cotton handkerchief from his pocket. She handed it back to him.

'You can keep it. There'll be other songs too.'

'Thank you.'

They stopped for some lunch in a glade in Ecclesall Woods, carpeted by bluebells, sharing out bread and cheese and some pickles that someone pulled out of their knapsack.

'You've got a nice voice,' said Henry.

'Thank you. You have too.'

'It was written by Carpenter, that.'

'Was it? I've heard it before but never sung it.'

'I'll teach you the words.' He ran through it with her two or three times so that by the time they began again on their approach to Millthorpe she could sing all the words.

The house stood alone a short way from the village, nestled amongst trees like it had sought, and been granted, permission from them for its existence; they'd shuffled up a bit to make room, then draped an arm over it.

'The orchards and gardens over there used to belong to Millthorpe too,' said Henry. 'They used to grow all their own food.'

They went through a gate in a stone wall leading to a track that went down the side of the house. Ivy grew up its walls and birds were already rediscovering their ancestral homes in its eaves. Bert Ward, the leader of the party, went up to the door of the house and knocked to announce their presence.

'Was he expecting us?' asked Elsie.

'I shouldn't think so. It doesn't quite work like that. People often visit in the afternoons and Edward and George are accustomed to receiving them.'

'Who's George?'

'He's Edward's friend and housekeeper.'

Elsie had many follow-up questions that she didn't know how to frame.

They filed into the house one by one, shaking hands with the man who had let them in.

'I'm George, pleased to meet you.' And it was clear he genuinely was. His hand was dry and rough and his handshake was enthusiastic, though not as if he had a point to prove like many men. It was not the handshake of a man who wanted to ingratiate himself or the shake of a self-important man or one who wanted to assert himself, using his handshake as a statement of hierarchy or establishment of a natural order.

They gathered round a large, rustic looking table – the men all electing to stand. Elsie looked around her – the room was very plain and simple: whitewashed walls and a stone flag floor with rag rugs, a fireplace with an unlit fire and a large case clock ticking loudly in the corner. No gewgaws or trinkets anywhere to be seen.

'You're welcome,' said George. 'Let me go and fetch Edward, then I'll make some tea. He will be pleased to see you.' He skittered off with the eagerness of a border collie and returned soon after, heralding the arrival of Carpenter. Elsie was immediately struck by Carpenter's presence, as if royalty had entered the room. It was not his attire – a rather shapeless old suit, a badly tied necktie, and bizarre, oriental-looking sandals on his feet – no, it was something else: an aloofness perhaps, a separateness. His eyes moved about nervously, as if as he surveyed the party; did she detect an irritation in his demeanour, a resignation to an inconvenience? But he spoke kindly and said he was honoured that they had walked so far and how it was refreshing to be able to open his house to the outside world and find fellowship of ideas and spirit. He was very well spoken – like one of her old college masters, not at all like George whose speech showed little refinement.

'George, would you be kind enough as to fetch some glasses of milk and some cake or some tea for our friends.'

He sat at the head of the table while George went off to find refreshments.

'I'm so terribly bad with names, please forgive me if I don't remember your names, other than Mr Ward's, of course; though I am sure I have made the acquaintance of some of you before. Tell me what news there is. What is your take on the international situation?'

The leaders of the group engaged enthusiastically in discussions with Carpenter as Elsie tried to take it all in, and as George went back and forth with teacups and glasses of milk.

Henry was soon earnestly wading into the discussion. 'Isn't it like you describe in *England's Ideal* – that people desire to take more than they receive – to occupy a big house, with servants, living off dividends. That can only be maintained and expanded if more people are exploited, with an ever-increasing access to new markets to exploit and resources.'

'You may be right,' said Carpenter. 'But how do you get from there to militarism?'

Elsie thought Carpenter already knew the answers to the questions he put – like a schoolmaster pushing his pupils to think.

'Well, you said something like the "canker of effete gentility has eaten into the heart of this nation." The same could be said elsewhere in Europe. They want us to out-do Germany and France. I don't think I'm making sense...'

'I think you are. Please, do continue.'

'So maybe... what I'm saying is... if these classes of parasites living off the labour of others are expanding, then they need more to feed off. And that puts pressure on commerce to expand – our spheres of influence then start to collide. We maintain our Empire through our navy, but Germany is jealous of that. So they expand their influence through their Ottoman corridor to the Gulf by building a railway. They crave access to oil.'

'An interesting angle. You think the sabre rattling is an assertion of strength to enable them to continue to consume more than they create?'

'I hope it is only sabre rattling.' It was Connie who spoke, a women Elsie knew from the shop. 'But how many more clashes over things like Morocco can there be before Germany push the French and British into biting back?'

'Indeed. And our young friend, here, has hit a nail full square on the head. It is in the nature of capitalism to be voracious. To demand return on investment. And that is only achievable by exploiting others. By not being honest about the price paid for labour or resources. It is no different now to the seventeen nineties when the rich cried treason when people demanded a vote, or during the Corn Laws, when they preserved their wealth by taxing the poor.'

George had been busy the whole time taking cups away and bringing the same ones back, replenished for others, since there was clearly insufficient to provide them for everyone at the same time. His labour on behalf of the idlers was now at an end and he sat on the arm of Carpenter's chair, leant towards him and put his hand on his shoulder.

'My dear George. Have we gone on too long?' Carpenter patted him on the thigh.

'Not at all; you're talking about important things. I can see that. Only, I wondered whether our guests would prefer to leave the stuffiness of the room and enjoy the garden.'

'An excellent idea. We can continue to talk outside.'

They streamed out, shepherded by the great man. Elsie let them go; she felt overawed by the company, the conversation always one step in front of her. She kept up with it but not so fast as to be able to contribute without risk of feeling foolish.

She was about to follow when she noticed George also hanging back.

'Shall I help you clear the things away?'

'No, thank you. Leave 'em. I'll sort it later.'

He had blue eyes, deep set, and a drooping moustache over his rather long upper lip, the whole creating a rather quizzical but sad countenance.

'After you,' he said.

'Have you known Mr Carpenter long?'

'Over twenty years, now.'

'And you look after the house yourself?'

'I do.'

'It's nice.'

'Thank you. I'm really lucky – I can't imagine anywhere better to live. And the Royal Oak is right handy too, when I get fed up with his lordship.'

Elsie didn't know how to react. His face remained impassive. Then there was a spark in his eye and he laughed, so she was able to smile also.

'Would you like me to show you round the garden, or perhaps you'd rather be joining the discussion.'

'No, I'd love to have a look round, if I may. We seem to have been engaged in serious discussion all day.'

George walked slowly beside her indicating the best path to follow.

'It's not at its best at this time of year. You should come back when the flowers are all out. Perhaps you would like to see Ed's writing hut – most people usually do.'

'I would. Thank you.'

'It's where he wrote *Towards Democracy*.'

'I've been reading that.'

He stopped and looked at her. 'And what do you think of it?'

'It's very good. It's…' she hesitated a bit too long. The twinkle came back to his eye.

'And do you understand it?'

'Well, perhaps not all of it, but…'

He smiled, 'No, neither do I,' and laughed. 'But I'm just a simple man.'

'I don't believe that for one minute.'

The hut was nothing like she imagined. It was a rather crude affair, made with little skill: a few logs arranged vertically with a small thatched roof – barely big enough for a single chair.

'You see, he's not so grand after all, is he?'

'No, it's very plain. But a beautiful spot – it must be wonderful to sit and write to the sound of the stream.'

'And then to be able to bathe when you get hot and bothered.' Again that spark in his eye.

'Oh yes.'

As they walked back towards the city it was as if they were re-entering the real world after being somewhere that rules of society didn't apply. Elsie had so many questions, but how could she possibly ask them? It seemed to be only she that had any sense of puzzlement. She knew she should be shocked, but perhaps it was her own perception that was askew.

Gradually their band dwindled as they returned to town – some, still not having had their fill of talk of social change, had decided to go to the monument to see who was speaking.

'Would you like me to walk you home,' asked Henry.

'No. No, thank you,' she replied.

***

Smith had started the Sunday off with gold in his pocket: three half sovereigns, along with whatever housekeeping money he'd not spent on drinks. By the end of the day it had all gone – including the housekeeping.

It wasn't his fault. He'd woken late, wondering why Elsie hadn't got him up to go to church. When he'd opened his eyes, the house was quiet and the time for church had been and gone. Perhaps she'd gone on her own. He found her note when he got downstairs, scrunched it up and threw it into the cold fire. Sod her. She'd gone off and left him to fend for himself – and no fire in the hearth, no breakfast made. This was what it was coming to.

He cooked his bacon and eggs over the gas ring; a long afternoon on his own loomed ahead of him, waiting for her to return. Damn it – he wasn't going to do that. What sort of milksop would mope around waiting for his wife? Instead he went round to find Tommy. Tommy lived in a house in Newhall where he rented a room off a widow who let three of her rooms out. They went on to meet up with some of Tommy's friends and had spent the afternoon playing cards, drinking and smoking. His fortune had turned and he kindly redistributed his winnings of the night before, plus everything else in his trouser pocket, as he'd tried to claw it back. When they broke up he handed his pocket watch to Tommy in exchange for ten shillings to put back in the tin.

'Pawn it if you like and give me the ticket. Once I've got some cash I'll get it back.'

Elsie was back home before him. The fire was going and a smell of shepherd's pie was already filling the room. She was standing at the sink washing and picking over the greens. He dropped a half crown piece, a couple of shillings and a sixpence in the housekeeping tin on the sideboard.

Best to go on the offensive. 'Where the bloody hell's tha been?'

She looked at him coldly. Like she knew what he'd been doing – throwing it back at him when it was her in the wrong, not him.

'I've been out walking. I said in the note.'

'Who with?'

'With friends from the shop. Are you drunk again?'

'No, and don't start.'

He sat in his chair and took his boots off.

'You've no right to go off and leave your husband like that.'

'Oh, don't be ridiculous. The Victorian with his good little wife! I have every right. And the state you were in last night: you needed to sleep that off, so don't try to take the moral high ground, because from where I'm standing you're well down in a ditch.'

'Tha bloody...'

She carried on trimming stalks off the greens. He stared into the flickering, hissing flames of the fire.

CHAPTER SIX

One afternoon, as Elsie arrived at Chapel Walk prior to going out selling papers, an impromptu meeting was taking place.

'What do we know about this pilgrimage?' Mary asked.

Molly and Miss Schuster were dividing newspapers into bundles of a dozen.

'Not much – it's the polite, respectable ladies, who are gathering to ask awfully nicely to be allowed, if it isn't terribly inconvenient, that they may have a vote if they promise ever so much not to be hysterical,' said Molly.

'Are we going to do anything? Should we support them?' said Elsie.

'Let's see how much momentum builds – if nothing else it could be a good opportunity to sell some more newspapers. Perhaps we could open some eyes?'

Miss Schuster spoke: 'We should be careful, though. We are all on the same side after all; so we should wish them well.'

'What if we could make use of the opportunity to put on a meeting afterwards to highlight the need for deeds not words?'

'That's a very good idea. Perhaps we could show people what we are up against – we could discuss the "Cat and Mouse Act." '

'There have been some powerful first-hand testimonies,' said Elsie. 'There was, oh, what was her name: Lilian somebody, who is severely ill with septic pneumonia after repeated forcible feeding. Simply awful. Could we get an actual hunger striker to address a meeting?'

'I think we perhaps could. It's an excellent idea. We'll put it to the committee,' said Miss Schuster. 'I can write to the London Branch and ask for help.'

Elsie popped out to the post office with some letters to catch the afternoon post, leaving them to their discussion. She wasn't gone long, but when she came back there was a small package for her.

'It was delivered by an errand boy from Walsh's,' said Mary.

'I wasn't expecting anything.'

'Aren't you going to open it then?'

'Ladies? Newspapers?' said Miss Schuster, from behind the counter.

She popped the package into her bag, and they picked up a bundle of papers each and left the shop. It wasn't until later that she remembered it, when she reached into her bag for her purse for her tram fare home. She took her ticket off the conductor and unwrapped the brown paper. Inside was some tissue paper and inside that a necklace of gold-coloured metal with fake pearls and green, coloured glass in the string, and with pendant violet drops. At least she assumed it was pinchbeck and glass, what else could it be? It was pretty though: the colours of the movement: green white and violet – GWV – give women votes. Subversive jewellery.

There was no note to say who had sent it. But it was lovely. What did it matter? Not that she'd have many chances to wear it. Perhaps if she went to the college reunion in a few weeks' time? She'd never been before, and it would be such a nice break to get away for a day or two and meet up with some of her old college pals. She allowed herself a smile and hid the necklace at the bottom of her drawer when she got home.

***

The tea things had been cleared away. They were still sitting at the table under the light of the gas lamp. Smith was reading the *Sheffield Guardian*, Elsie the *Suffragette*.

There was a knock at the door and it opened before either of them got up. It was Charlie.

'Ey up! Look at you two boring so-and-sos. Get your boots on – Gracie's waiting outside – we're going for a nightcap or two.'

Elsie got to her feet and Charlie came over and gave her a kiss on the cheek.

'It's all right, Charlie. I'll give it a miss. I'm a bit tired.'

'No, you won't, come on. Grace is counting on you coming. She only said she'd come if you were.'

'Oh, all right then. I'll go and change – I can't go out like this. I'll not be a minute.'

'You're just fine as you are.'

'To you maybe.'

'What's that supposed to mean?'

'No, I didn't mean…'

Charlie laughed. 'Go on, hurry up.'

Smith got his boots from the side of the hearth.

'You two getting on a bit better then?'

'Oh? Yeah. You know… I broke one of her wedding presents the other night, so that didn't help. I'll replace it when I get a bit of cash together, but it's not easy.'

'Never is.'

'I don't know how we'll manage once kids come along.'

'But you do, somehow. I don't know. Grace seems to stretch it out. Oops – I'd better tell her we're on our way.'

Elsie came down; she was wearing a long navy skirt with matching jacket and white blouse – the one with the fancy embroidery and lace. She glanced at Smith to check it was having the desired effect. He offered his arm and they stepped out together.

Charlie and Grace were waiting at the end of the passage Grace immediately grabbed Elsie off Smith's arm.

'Look at you! You look lovely. Come on let's walk ahead of these two scruffs.'

Smith watched them heading down the street in front; Elsie taking her long lilting strides and Grace struggling to keep in step with her. If they were elemental, Elsie was water: cool and constant, with a strength beyond that which was apparent. Grace was fire: all sparks, flames and heat, immediate and quickly responsive – she was not Smith's type though: he tired of her quickly, but she was a laugh and she was good-looking: round face, big eyes and blonde curls, enjoying life and the people around her, no matter who they were. And a nice figure: probably using a corset – wasn't there something fine in the unlacing of a corset, releasing what was inside, not that Elsie believed in the virtues of figure – child-bearing hips and a cleavage any man would be happy to bury his face in. Charlie was a lucky man.

'She's got some class, has Elsie,' said Charlie. 'Look at her. It's her that has grace.'

Smith smiled to himself. It was if they were both breaking the Commandments given to Moses.

Charlie went on: 'If she were walking down Oxford Street or even t' Champs Elysee, tha wouldn't pick her out as a Sheffield lass. We should treat them to a night out sometime. Tha off on Easter Monday?'

'Yes. United at home to Sunderland.'

'They'd love that! No, how about that new picture house up Attercliffe – the Globe – they say it's quite the thing – like a palace inside with fancy tiling and plush seats.'

'I saw it the other day – that revolving globe is quite summat ain't it, all lit up at night-time?'

'There's a film I wanted to see about the railways as well, this weekend. An engineer trying to kill one of his rivals or something.'

'Probably a scab.'

They chuckled. The two women looked around to see what they were laughing at, then scornfully turned back again.

'Sounds a good idea.'

'I had another idea too. I've been thinking about thy lass and her suffragette ideas. My Grace knows some very influential people in the anti-women's suffrage thing. I reckon if Grace were to get Elsie to go along she might see things different.'

'I can't see it. She wouldn't go to such a meeting.'

'It's got to be worth a try though surely? She needn't know what she was in for – it could just be an invite to afternoon tea, or summat.'

***

Smith needed to make a bit of extra money. He needed to get his watch back before Elsie asked questions about it, and they couldn't be roughing it in the thre'penny seats. And they were in arrears on the rent and the coal bill. Whatever he made, he wouldn't chuck it away this time. All he needed was a little investment up front – the few coppers he had in his pocket weren't enough, and now the housekeeping tin was empty. She must have taken it and hidden it after his exploits at the weekend – she wasn't daft. If only he could find a couple of half crowns he could do what he did last time, easy – just a few shillings to prime the pump. He could hear her downstairs. He slid the top drawer of the chest very slowly so that it wouldn't squeak. This was where she kept her various undergarments. He checked his hands to make sure there was no oil still on them from work, and without taking anything out felt down to the layer of brown paper at the bottom and slid his hand under the pile of cotton and fine woollen garments. His hand contacted a packet of some sort. He pulled it out and with it came a handkerchief caught up in the fold of paper. The packet was just heavy enough to hold a few coins. He heard the sound of the oven door being shut and the coals being raked. He sat on the edge of the bed. He looked at the handkerchief: it was not obviously a woman's one – no lace on it or anything fancy. Why did she have one of his handkerchiefs in her drawer? He unfolded it – it wasn't his – it had initials stitched into a corner: HP.

Inside the folded brown-paper packet was some tissue paper, and inside that a necklace, one he'd never seen before: gold set with stones. Fancy-looking. He was in two minds as to whether to storm down and confront her, or to bide his time. Likely as not she'd have some plausible explanation and he'd just be made to look a fool, or he'd have to stick to his guns and not back down. God only knew where that would lead. No, he'd have to keep his powder dry. In the meantime he still needed to raise some cash.

Smith met up with his mate Tommy on the corner of the Corn Exchange. They went into the Market Hotel for refreshments to ease the walk up Duke Street, but then, on emerging a few minutes later into cool air, and as the Park Hill stretched before them, hopping on an approaching tram seemed a better idea.

'Managed to rustle a few bob together then?' said Tommy.

'Only just – a couple of items from the sideboard, and my best suit and boots are in the popshop. With a bit of luck she'll never notice. I'm going to need luck as well: I've only got seven and six. It'll be all or nothing for me.'

It was dark when they approached the Skyring. Smith's heart was thumping. The darkness was punctuated by the glow of cigarettes moving about outside the circle of men's backs forming the small lamp-lit arena, two or three deep.

Smith and Tommy had to bide their time before they reached the front row. Tommy was first in with a twelve-shilling stake which he lost straight off. Undeterred, he went right back in with a silver crown and a shilling which he flipped spinning through the air into the toller's palm.

'Thanks, but you can leave the showmanship to me.'

'Who will tails it for six bob? Very good. Best of luck, fellas.'

Tommy clawed himself back to breaking even and then went up in the next toss.

'I've got a good feeling about this,' he said, before blowing his winnings and being back where he started from.

'Can I put six bob on heads, please,' said Smith.

A middle-aged man, rather worse for wear – scruffy hair, unshaven, and somewhat dishevelled clothing – handed some money to match it.

'Oh dear, oh dear. There's coppers in here. Am I going to have to count it out? You know we much prefer silver and gold. Ain't that so gentleman? Silver and gold. That's what dreams are made of… That's five shillings and tenpence ha'penny. You're a bit short.'

'Tell me about it,' the man replied.

'That's fine,' said Smith. 'Let him play.'

'Very generous of you, sir.'

The man acknowledged Smith with his empty grey eyes.

'That's three heads.'

The other man's head dropped onto his chest and he melted away into the crowd.

'Keep it in,' said Smith. 'On heads again.'

'Right you are. That's just shy of eleven shillings on heads. Who'll tails it for an approximate quid?'

A young man stepped forward – athletic looking, dressed in a long, pale-coloured Mackintosh, smoking a cigar – and tossed in a half sovereign, flickering gold in the lamplight. It landed right next to the pile of coins.

'That's better – no need to count that. Good luck gen'lemen.'

The toller balanced the halfpennies on his three middle fingers then flipped them.

'Two heads.'

'I'll leave ten bob in, please. Tails this time.'

The same young man matched it and lost again. There was a murmur.

'Same again, please: ten bob on tails.'

Again it was matched by the same man. A heavy silence fell, Smith closed his eyes. The only sound was the slap of coins on the mud.

'Two tails. Same again?'

'No. I'm out, thanks.' He had gone from seven shillings in his pocket to a little over two pounds. He was euphoric. Everything was going to be all right now.

'Here, I can get my watch back now. Did you pawn it, Tom?'

'No, as it happens. I never did. I'll only charge thi a few pints of beer as interest too. How's about that?'

As they were leaving the ring, Smith felt a hand on his shoulder.

'Not so fast.'

He spun round – suddenly primed. It was the young man in the raincoat.

'You stung me for thirty shillings.'

Smith was now fully alert, ready to get in the first blow. He locked onto the man's gaze ready for what came next. He sensed Tommy at his shoulder ready to back him up. The man broke into laughter.

'Your face! I wasn't going to do anything. I'm just joking. It would be suicidal to take you and your mate on.'

'It would, yeah.'

'On my own, anyhow. Where are you boys heading?'

'Town.'

'Come on. I'll buy you a drink.'

'No, it's all right. I've got my winnings.'

'Oh yeah – *my* money.' He smiled. 'I won't take no for an answer. You'll offend me if you don't accept.'

'No, really. We'll just get off.'

Suddenly the man became very serious and spoke in a low voice: 'I don't think you heard me. I said you'd offend me if you don't accept my hospitality.'

Tommy stepped in. 'Shake the gentleman's hand, Smith. It's very kind of you, er…'

'John James Murphy. You might have heard of me going by the name of Spud.'

Smith shook the man's hand, but said nothing. It was like he thought of himself some kind of big-shot that everyone would know about, but Smith didn't want to say he'd never heard of him.

'No hard feelings, eh?'

'No. No, you're all right. You just caught me by surprise – you were lucky.'

'Yeah, yeah, could've had my block taken off, eh?'

'Well you know – it's sometimes best to get in first and ask questions later.'

'Quite so. You boys fighters then?'

'No. Ex-army.'

'Oh. I see. Disciplined fighters – lucky shave then?' Murphy laughed. 'Not seen you boys in the Park before?

'No, we're over from Burngreave?'

'They've a good little set up here, don't you think?'

'Yeah, yeah, it's not bad.'

'I thought you were decent in letting that old fella carry on the bet even though he was short.'

'Well, you know…'

'It was daft of me to bet against you after. That gesture must've

49

put the big fella on your side, to be sure.' Murphy laughed, as if at a joke he'd made.

Murphy lined up the drinks at a pub tucked down a side street amongst the densely packed houses of the Park. He was on nodding terms with one or two of the clientele and on first name terms with the landlord.

'So, where do you boys work at?'

'The railways.'

'Oh, that's good.'

'Is it?'

'Well, yeah. My associate – he's away on business right now – was only saying the other week how we needed to expand into the railways. I'm sure you boys would be up for a chance to top up your wages?'

'How's that?'

'My associate is always on the lookout for decent fellows like yourselves to help out with opportunities. One of the things is a weekly coupon on football results. Do you boys know a bit about the game?' They nodded. 'It would be a simple case of distributing coupons during the week, and collecting them back in with the shilling stakes, then handing out winnings on the Monday. You earn commission at two shillings in the pound. How does that sound?'

'But the football season's nearly over.'

'B' Jesus! What do you want? Look – see how it goes. When my associate gets back from his little… er, holiday, if he is happy, then there might be other opportunities.'

'So how does it work? What are these coupons?' said Tommy

'They've got the weekend fixtures on them – not the obvious ones of course.'

'So, not on Villa beating Woolwich you mean?'

'If you say so. I don't follow it that closely. I'm not the expert in that. I don't look after that side of the business. We'd end up broke within a fortnight if I did. So there's usually fifteen games on the coupon and you get odds of between eleven to one for predicting four home wins, twenty to one on four draws and a hundred and fifty to one on four draws and an away win – that kind of thing.'

'What if we get caught?'

'Best not to get caught.'

'But if we did?'

'We can't do business with people who are so stupid they get caught.' He smiled. 'But you boys ain't stupid, I can see that. You won't get caught. But if someone were to snitch on you there's nothing to worry about. The worst they can do is fine you a tenner.'

'Bloody hell – you reckon that's nowt to worry about?'

'Look, that's the worst. And we'd always pay the fine for you. We look after each other, see? What do you say?'

It certainly seemed a sure-fire thing to Smith.

Tommy nodded too. 'Go on, then. I'm in, Mr Murphy.'

'Spud: we're mates now, ain't we?'

'Yeah. Right-ho, Spud.'

Smith nodded. 'So what do we do, Spud?'

'Go to the Old Hussar on Scotland Street tomorrow night, if you reckon you can sell some before the weekend matches. Ask for Pete – tell him I sent yer – and he'll sort everything. You only need to take a few to start with – see if you like it – no pressure. Best starting small, so you are, and building a loyal customer base amongst trusted friends.'

He went up into town and found Pete, in the pub. He took two-dozen coupons, which he sold at the workshop. He didn't have to work too hard to sell them either: discussion on football results was a favourite topic at snap time, especially as the season was coming to a head. And how difficult could it be to pick out four wins or four draws? For just a shilling you could earn ten bob, easy. It spread by word of mouth and Smith had sold them all by Friday. The collected coupons were checked off in a little book and returned with the stakes. Smith picked up two shillings and ninepence ha'penny in return. He reckoned on doubling that the following week.

CHAPTER SEVEN

Grace called on Elsie, as arranged, on her way to afternoon tea at the house of Mrs Jeffrey Channing who lived in a large villa on Burngreave Road, the other side of the cemetery. Elsie had tried to turn down the invitation but was in danger of being considered rude, so relented. 'No, you must come,' Grace had said. 'Mrs Channing was so good to h'invite me the other day at church when we were arranging the flowers. She said I had a fine eye for it. She's a teacher, you know, like you – she's very involved with the Sunday school.'

'Do you know who else will be there?'

'Oh, yes. I know a couple of the ladies who are h'invited. I was h'onoured to have been round to the house of Mrs Potts, who is a good friend of Mrs Channing also. And Mrs Archibald Yelverton, she is the wife of the owner of Yelverton and Sons, you know: the saw manufacturer at Neepsend.'

'Does this fine lady not have a name of her own? I don't suppose her mother christened her Archibald.'

Grace ploughed on. 'There will also Miss Violet Lofthouse, I believe, who it is rumoured may be getting h'engaged to a cousin of the Duke of Norfolk.'

Poor Grace, she tried so hard to live up to her name, but it remained a shackle. One of those Sheffield women who strove to rise above backyards, washing lines and outdoor privies, who tried so hard not to drop 'h's that she peppered her speech with them when not necessary – putting on h'airs and graces. Elsie suppressed a giggle.

Grace strutted quickly through the cemetery. 'It always gives me the creeps in here.'

'I find it rather peaceful. Not a bad final resting place.'

'I'd rather not think about it.'

They walked up a curving gravel drive to the front door of the house, approached the porticoed entrance and rang the bell. Poor Grace took a couple of deep breaths. This was of some significance to her, but it was nothing compared to singing at the cathedral or going round to Canon Rowe's house for tea after you'd won a prize for an essay.

Their coats were taken and they were shown through to an overly furnished drawing room where several overly furnished ladies were already sitting in conversation.

Their hostess rose to greet them. She was a rather ugly woman in her fifties: a jowly, somewhat manly, face that would be better suited to a headscarf and being behind a butcher's stall at Norfolk Market than under a large hat with an ostrich feather in it, and a figure that would look comely in an apron, but rather ridiculous in folds of pearly grey satin.

'How do you do, Mrs Jepson. So good of you to come.'

'It's an honour, Mrs Channing. This is all so charming. Let me h'introduce you to my good friend, Mrs –'

'Oh, Grace! Everyone just calls me Elsie.'

'… my good friend, Elsie.'

'How very modern of you. You young ladies never cease to amaze me. In that case you should call me Winifred.'

'Elsie went to teaching college. She was a teacher before she got married. Her husband was in the same regiment as my Charles.'

'Which college were you at, Elsie?'

'Lincoln. The Diocesan College.'

'Oh, how splendid. My husband knows the music master there, Dr. Bennett. Do you know him?'

'Oh, yes, I was in the choir.'

'Then you must give us your opinion on Elgar. Let me introduce you to my guests.'

Elsie and Grace shook hands with the four ladies: the one called Archibald, Mrs Potts who went by the female name of Gladys, the demur Miss Violet, and a Mrs Mary Colquhoun, enveloped in pale blue chiffon.

'We were discussing The Music Makers. Mrs Potts heard it performed in London and thought it rather tawdry.'

'Oh, but you can't call Elgar tawdry,' said Elsie.

'But surely he is not in the same league as Mahler, Wagner, the great Russians, or even Brahms?' said Mrs Colquhoun, in her clipped, Edinburgh accent.

'I'm afraid I don't get to go to concerts these days, but at Lincoln we performed the Sea Pictures. They capture England perfectly. Mahler is all very good and jolly – but it cannot resonate an English soul, like Elgar, or Stanford, surely? The flamingo's call may stir the soul of a Hottentot, but it is the blackbird that can make an Englishman weep.'

'Oh, well said, Elsie,' said Winifred Channing. 'I do believe you hit on the truth there. No one does a melody like Elgar. Would anyone care for some gingerbread? It's something I pride myself on. I take a special care to oversee its preparation in the kitchen.'

A parlour maid stepped forward in her pristine lace apron and cap and offered the plate around to the ladies.

'So do you have equally modern views on the role of women, Elsie?' said Winifred.

'Oh no. Not really. There's nothing new about my views.'

Winfred Channing raised an eyebrow. Elsie looked round the room. Miss Violet was sitting forward on her seat, legs gracefully folded to one side nibbling on gingerbread. All eyes turned toward her. She felt she was desperately trying to avoid a trap. It was all very well disrupting a political meeting or putting strong views in a college debating society, but in the drawing-room of respectable people, over fine bone-china cups? And she didn't want to embarrass Grace. Was it possible she had been brought here by way of entertainment? A variety act? What she'd said was true – nothing new about her views; after all Sheffield was where the first women's suffrage society had formed, back when her granny was a girl.

'I do believe there is something very different about women that makes us quite unsuitable for political life,' said Mrs Potts. 'For one thing we have few opportunities of developing a sense of honour. We are more trained in cunning and artifice. Don't you agree?' There were nods, and Miss Violet smiled, coyly. 'Those are the skills we have honed, rather than masculine ones of brilliancy of intellect or profundity of the soul, which are unattractive in the female. Depth of thought has never been something we have developed on any subject. We are rather more governed by our emotions.'

Elsie was struggling. Little bubbles were exploding in her head like hydrogen shown a spark.

'And it is those very virtues that make us unsuitable for the vote,' added the creation in blue chiffon. She had a narrow nose, on which her lorgnettes perched precariously, and thin lips so tightly pursed as she was listening to Mrs Potts speak that she struggled to get them moving as she spoke. 'The majority of women are not sufficiently well qualified to focus a correct opinion on the plethora of subjects required. They would seriously outvote those men who were. You only have to observe the ignorance of the majority of our sex. And, what is more, women cannot act as soldiers or policeman or sailors, so why should they have a voice on the laws which govern these people?'

Elsie squirmed. 'I'm not sure I agree.'

'But you must see that the sexes are so very different. We women lack the sense of proportion, that men have, that is essential as a good voter. I am more than content that my husband can exercise his vote in my best interests.'

Mrs Potts resumed: 'And the suffrage riots prove the point. They are too emotional, too irrational. Until such a time as women prove that as a whole they could use their vote for the better, it should not happen. Mrs Yelverton is correct. The vote is not a right but a responsibility vested by the state in those best fitted to use it. I trust Mr Potts to use it sensibly, much more than I would trust myself.'

Elsie felt all eyes were on her again. As if she was being goaded, like a peaceful bear being set on by dogs, to make it fight. But like the bear she was chained and not free to fend off the attacks. She was furious with Grace for bringing her. She looked towards Winifred Channing who smiled at her and gave her a little nod. Had she just given her approval to respond?

'But... '

'Do continue, Elsie,' said Winifred Channing.

'Well, surely the exact same arguments apply to many men who currently have the vote. They're not in command of the facts – they just vote on their emotions – responding to the whipping up of contempt by one side or the other. How many men truly understand the arguments on tariff reform or the Irish question? And if some women are ignorant, even though I would contend they are as capable as men of knowing what is best for their futures and those of their children, is that not because we do such a poor job educating our girls? Is that not an argument for better education, for fairer education for girls? And who is it that cares more about the education of their children? Is it not the mothers?' She spoke calmly and without raising her voice to the shrill tone that her emotions were demanding. She was pleased with how she thought she had come across.

Winifred was nodding. The others were not quite sure how to react. Miss Violet shuffled in her seat. She looked as uncomfortable as perhaps she would if she had broken wind.

'The women who break the law – break the law of order cannot be given the right to have a say in the law?' said the creation in blue chiffon.

Elsie looked to Mrs Channing and again only read encouragement.

55

'But for centuries men have done the same, have they not? The chartists did not politely seek permission to have the vote. The Corn Laws were not changed through polite letter-writing to the Times. And there is not the same bitter condemnation when men go on strike and break the law.'

The anti-suffrage ladies sipped their tea. Grace stared at her hands. Winifred Channing smiled. 'Well that was most interesting, ladies. Now you must come and see the latest acquisitions in my Japanese woodcut collection. I'm really rather pleased with it.'

Winifred took Elsie to one side as she was about to leave.

'Thank you ever so much for coming. That was most uplifting. Quite frankly those three have been frightfully annoying and I needed someone like you to knock them down a peg or two – I could never have done it, you see – you find all the right things to say. It was quite marvellous. You must feel free to call round for a chat whenever you like.'

Grace barely spoke to her on the way back.

***

On Saturday after work Smith put a down payment on a smart looking, dark grey raincoat – he'd wear it when they went out on Monday. He hoped for rain so that he could show off its weatherproof coating.

'Where did you get the money for that?' Elsie said, when he came in.

'It's smart ain't it? Does tha like it?'

'I asked a question first. I've got the rent man coming round later, and I've had to buy bread on tick and I owe Nelson's for last week – and you're chucking money away on a coat.'

'Look, don't worry. Here's twenty shillings, and a bit more, for in the tin.'

'Have they paid you extra? You've not had a rise?'

'No. I just came into a bit of money that's all – so that's all sorted now. Ease off.'

He sat in his chair after dinner on Easter Monday and lit a cigarette while Elsie went up to change. He reckoned he could sell twice as many coupons before the weekend's matches, which would bring him over four shillings extra – he'd soon have his new coat paid off. Imagine spending over two weeks wages on a coat? She'd go spare if she knew.

Elsie was wearing a charcoal grey skirt pulled in tight at the waist and a white blouse with her hair fastened up and a feathered hat perched on her head to match the skirt.

'Will I be all right with only a shawl over my shoulders, or do I need a coat, do you think?'

Smith started getting his boots on.

'Don't know. Why don't tha go outside and see?'

She went out and came back in again.

'I'll just wear a shawl, I think. Does this one suit?'

Smith looked up at her. He noticed she was wearing the fancy necklace around her neck.

'Where did tha get that?' The words came out without him giving chance to form them.

'What?'

'Tha knows – the necklace. I've not seen it before.'

'No, it's new.'

'So, who bought it for thi because I presume I didn't?'

'I don't know, Smith.'

'What's that supposed to mean?' She was being unnecessarily coy.

'I mean I really don't know. It was just delivered to the shop.'

'Then why's tha wearing it?'

'Because it's nice, and because I've nothing else like it.'

He stood up and faced her. 'Because a lover bought it for thi?'

'No.'

'Then who?'

'I've told you. I don't know.'

'Who is HP?'

'I don't know what you mean.'

'I saw a man's handkerchief in thi drawer with HP on it.'

'You have no right to go through my things.'

'Did he buy it for thi – that bauble? Take it off.'

'I have nothing to be ashamed of.'

'Take the bloody thing off!' He grabbed it and pulled. The chain broke easily. He threw it onto the floor and it slid under the sideboard. She moved as if to retrieve it.

'Leave the bloody thing there.'

Elsie turned and ran upstairs. She pulled her hat off and threw herself face down onto the bed. He was such a brute, so boorish! He had hurt her. She felt her neck. There was no blood on her hand, but it felt sore. How could he? She did everything for him, looked after him, and this was what she got. No trust. No respect. She wept into the pillow.

There was a gentle knock at the door and it was opened.

'Come on, Else. We said we'd call and get them at one.'

'I'm not coming.'

'Look, I'm sorry. I believe thi that tha don't know who it were from.'

She didn't move. He lay down next to her. She felt his breath. 'I'm sorry, Else. I didn't mean to hurt thi.' She felt his lips on her neck. 'I'm sorry. I just got jealous. I want to buy thi stuff like that myself. I love thi, Else.' She felt his weight, then he climbed off and she felt his hands move up her legs, and fumbling at her undergarments. She froze. 'No Smith, don't.' But he did not heed. He pulled her half-off the bed. And she again felt his weight on her and his flesh. 'I love thi, Else. Forgive me.'

'I'll be downstairs. Don't be long.' She was still lying face down on the bed. Still wearing her gloves.

'At least bring me a jug of water.'

He reappeared a moment later, with the water. 'We'll not be too late if we're quick.'

She changed into a blouse with a high neck and went down.

'I really don't know who bought it and I'm sorry I put it on. You're right, I shouldn't even have accepted it in the first place. I had no right to bring it home. As for the handkerchief I was going to give it back. Someone lent it to me – an act of chivalry, that's all. I washed it and starched it, and was going to give it back.'

Smith smiled at her. 'Come on, let's go. We were going to go for a drink first but we'll have to go straight there now.'

They called round for Charlie and Grace. Grace gave her a peremptory 'Good afternoon, Elsie' with no more than a polite smile then walked on with Charlie. She was horrified by what they might have read in her face, and her flustered appearance, the least of which was from having to keep up with Smith striding to make up time. Oh, she was wretched! She felt sick, and now Grace was shunning her for what she no doubt perceived as having been shown up in front of her "anti" acquaintances with whom she would have liked to have been intimate in the hope that success was something you could breathe in.

Smith and Charlie hurriedly bought sixpenny tickets and they arrived at their seats just in time for the start of the film; though not early enough to avoid annoyance and tutting from the other holidaymakers. The film was *Zigomar* and for periods took Elsie away from her troubles – the scenes in Paris and in the Moulin Rouge of Esmée being carried on a sort of bed covered in jewels, then dancing in white veils as flames flickered and coloured lights appeared from the projector as she danced faster and faster, until she collapsed exhausted on the floor. Then the evil Zigomar set fire to the place and there was chaos. There were various attempts to catch the villain made by the hero, culminating in the robber plunging from a mountain top in the Alps.

They went for a drink afterwards. 'Are you all right, Elsie?' said Charlie. 'You don't look your usual self.'

'No, I think I might be sickening for something. I think I should go home.'

Smith looked at her as if expecting her to make her own way, before realising that meant he had to hurriedly finish his pint. 'Sorry. We'll get off then. See thi tomorrow, Charlie.'

'Well that was all a bit queer!' said Grace, after they'd left.

'Poor Elsie. She was out of sorts.'

'She's stuck up, that one. That's what it is. Thinks she's a cut above, with her suffragette ways and her cleverness.'

'That's not very fair.'

'Isn't it? You should have heard the things she said at Mrs Geoffrey Channing's h'afternoon soir-ray – shameful the way she treated respectable ladies. Using her fancy words.'

'She's not well, Grace. That's all. Anyone could see that.'

'Ooh! You don't think she's... do you? It'd be about time. If she ever unclamps that tight...'

Charlie got up and went to the gents without even looking at her.

CHAPTER EIGHT

Elsie wrote to her old college for an invitation to the Whitsuntide reunion. She discarded several drafts before getting the tone just right. She was desperate to go; it had built up in her mind as a thing of immense importance and her first attempt at opening lines seemed deranged in their pleading and oaths of allegiance to the old place.

For the next few days she anxiously awaited the post, and when an envelope arrived with a Lincoln postmark she strove to suppress her emotions. On informing Smith that she was going to her college reunion his response was: 'How will tha get there?'

'By train.' She knew he had been asking her where she would get the money, exerting control, but she wasn't going to answer that.

'How long will you be gone?'

'All weekend.'

'In that case I might pop to Staveley to see Mother. It would be miserable here on my own, and at least I'll get some decent snap.'

***

How strange it was to be walking up Steep Hill again. Was it really only three years ago? It seemed like yesterday, but also a lifetime away. Several other young women, and some older, had got off the train at Lincoln, but she had not recognised them, if they were even there for the same reason. How she regretted not having put greater effort into staying in touch with more of her friends. She had corresponded with Kathleen who was living in Bristol, and her best friend from college, Flo, who was still teaching in Nottingham, but the rest had fallen to the slayer of best intentions.

She paused to get her breath.

'Aieee!' There came a shriek from over the road. 'Elsie!' And she was rushed by a whirling thing in skirts and a hat and was enveloped in a big hug.

'Agnes! Agnes Maxwell. How are you? Oh, I'm so pleased to see you.'

'Not as much as I'm pleased to see you. And it's Mrs Agnes Hinton now. Oh, you look just the same. I didn't know you were coming. Oh, how wonderful.'

'I left it a bit late, and I've lost touch with so many people. You're married then?'

'Yes, to a schoolmaster in the village. Only a month ago.' Agnes wiggled her finger in front of Elsie. 'I see you are married too.'

'Yes, for nearly two years now.'

'Any children?'

Elsie shook her head. Another young woman joined them from over the road.

'Do you remember Millie? Mildred Hall,' said Agnes. 'She was in my year. This is Elsie, my "mother." She helped me such a lot when I first arrived here. I was such a shy, homesick little thing – I don't know how I would have settled in without her.'

'Yes, I remember you, Millie. You were very good at art, I seem to recall. You did all the stage decorations for the plays.'

'Yes, that was me. I wish my *mother* were here too: Violet Searsby?'

'Oh yes, Violet. I'd forgotten about her.'

'She's in South Africa now, running a school.'

'Are you teaching?' asked Agnes.

'No, I had to give it up when I married.'

'What a waste,' said Agnes. 'You'd have been such a good teacher.'

'I think I was becoming a good teacher, yes.'

'They let me stay on because it was such a small village and they couldn't get a replacement.'

'Look, have you two had anything for lunch yet?'

They talked of old times, swapping stories of funny incidents: of getting into trouble for messing about when on laundry duty, and of midnight feasts and how they used to put a slice of cake or some grapes outside the doors of the tutors so that they would leave them alone. Agnes and Millie chatted on about their teaching practice in Hull, when they lodged amongst the fisherman, and of the hubbub in the streets down by the fish dock: carts and crates banging, singing and shouting, barrel organs and fiddles.

They established themselves in their rooms – Elsie's was in the house of one of the governesses, at the top of the hill – and arranged to meet in an hour outside the cathedral. She unpacked her small suitcase and lay down on the bed staring at the ceiling wondering at the passage of time.

Elsie's eyes were trying to take in the magnitude of the cathedral facade when Agnes and Millie turned a corner with two others they had latched onto. They went inside to renew their friendship with the venerable old lady. They sought out the imp and the funny and grotesque carvings of man and beast on the choir screen.

They were drawn towards the college by their impatience, far too early for the official reception at six-thirty. They were not the only ones – groups of young women were engaged in excited conversation, transported back to their days as first years.

As they approached the recreation ground Elsie burst into tears. A cuckoo was calling over in the trees – a sound which took her right back to her last summer there – to when, as a second year, she had welcomed back Kathleen, her own "mother" to a reunion.

'Are you all right, Elsie?'

'Oh yes. Did you hear the cuckoo? I'm just so happy to be here again. I've not heard one since I left. I wasn't sure I'd feel at home here any more – like I was looking in from the outside – but instead I feel I really belong.'

'Well, those cuckoos only remind me of being woken too early. And if it wasn't them it was the cows bellowing like elephants.'

As they wandered about, Elsie stopped to shake hands with others and before long had separated from Agnes, Millie, and friends. She delighted in news of her old friends, of teaching jobs, of courtships and babies. She made lots of promises to stay in touch, felt privileged to be treated as a peer by former governesses who were arriving for the reception.

The first years had done a splendid job in decorating the corridors and the common room where the reception took place, and the lecture hall had been transformed into a fairyland for the operetta put on by the second years, to which they were summoned by the bell at seven-thirty.

It was the usual affair, with fairy kings and queens, entourages of dancing fairies, jesters and princes, singing and tomfoolery. Like the one they had put on as second years. The evening flew by and culminated with an impromptu procession around the college and grounds, with favourite songs from college days being struck up by the boldest of them and joined in by the rest before they broke up and went their separate ways to their rooms.

On Sunday morning Elsie walked to the early service and morning prayers at the cathedral with a young woman who had a room in the same house and who had left college only the year before. On arrival, Elsie was pleased to see Agnes and to be able to shake off her escort; she had irritated Elsie. Just when she was feeling a real sense of belonging, that they were all part of the college, whether past or present, and all working with the same aims, this flighty young woman made seeming attempts to trump anything Elsie said as if laying claim to a greater stake of the college than Elsie by the recency of her experience. *Oh we didn't do that; we did this.*

Inside the great building Elsie's heart soared upwards with her voice, joined by the voices of all those other wonderful strong women. It leapt and tumbled round the great stone columns and up into the vaults of the roof.

She stayed behind afterwards and found a quiet chapel to herself. She could not face the mundaneness of speech.

She felt dizzy when she emerged into daylight and had to steady herself against the wall. She was surrounded by ghosts – she saw Smith touch his cap to her, laughing and being nudged in the ribs by Charlie as they hung back after the service. She headed through the Exchange Gate and up Castle Hill. They were there in the castle grounds in their uniforms fooling about. She heard his gentle voice, felt his arm through hers. Saw his smile. She ached to have that man with her again, right here. He was a good person, but things had taken a wrong turning. Perhaps he should have stayed in the army; perhaps he was better suited to that than working his fingers to the bone in a smoky, dingy workshop. If only they could be a bit more comfortable, if her boy had survived, if they had somewhere like this again.

She felt exhausted by it already, and yet she knew this to be, in some way, a pivotal moment in her life, a rare chance to reassess, to envision the past and future, a moment she would look back on with gratitude or, if she let it, regret. She had an obligation to her past self, to that timid little first-year Elsie, to her future self and to her college – to those who had worked selflessly to help her improve herself and to her comrades who believed in her.

She rested after dinner back at the house, then returned to the college with renewed enthusiasm to talk to those she had missed and to explore old haunts: dormitories, classrooms, the library, and to present an image of enthusiasm and encouragement to the current students at afternoon tea and at Chapel in the evening.

On the Monday she joined in the hockey match between current and past students, and cheered the tennis tournament to its conclusion. In the evening, after dinner, in the converted first-year classroom, she danced until nearly midnight. When it came to Auld Lang Syne, with her hands linked to others, the tears rolling down her cheeks she could do nothing about.

She went down the hill to the station in the morning with a sense of having found something in herself. She left the light, the greenery, and the peace of one of God's cities. The train pulled into a dominion which seemed lost to him – colourless and close, belching sparks and smoke, hammering and thumping to the beat of Vulcan. As she waited for her tram she could taste the gritty air and feel the very earth vibrate as dragons inside the iron works breathed fire and slammed their tails on the ground.

Weary but resolute footsteps took her up Grimesthorpe Road towards home.

She pushed open the door to find that although he had also been away for most of the weekend he had somehow succeeded in turning her home into that of a slattern. She hung up her coat and put on her apron.

Smith seemed pleased to see her when he came in, but she was not sure that was for herself, or because it meant he would be provided for. Whatever the reason, he was much more tender towards her than usual that night.

As he sat up in bed smoking, he said: 'Me and Charlie have received our orders for our training – so it's not just you that gets to go away.'

***

The firing range was only a short train ride away over the border into Nottinghamshire. Charlie and Smith were in uniform either side of the window watching the countryside pass by, and being watched closely by a small boy who was sat in the corner of the compartment next to his mother.

'I wish we were going for longer. I fancy one of those camps like the Territorials get to go on for a week – proper manoeuvres and marches, camping and the likes.'

'Yeah, but they only play at it. I'd rather get practice with a charged Lee Enfield than a pop gun or a broomstick.'

'Yeah, true enough.'

'A chance to show if you've still got it.'

'Oh, I've still got it. Can't wait to get my hands on a smelly again.'

The small boy chortled. 'What's a smelly, Mister?'

'Arnold! Manners!' said his mother.

'Short magazine Lee Enfield, son.'

'Is it smelly?'

'No. It's just what we call it: S-M-L-E – smelly – see? The best there is.'

The boy's eyes widened. 'Can I see it?'

'What?'

'Your gun, mister.'

Smith laughed again.

'No, we're not allowed to just carry them around.'

'Have you ever killed anyone?'

'Arnold, that's not nice,' said his mother. 'Come on, it's our stop coming up.'

'Sithee, Arnie,' said Charlie, with a flicker of an impish smile.

The boy waved. His mother shot a cold look at Charlie and jerked her son away. They stifled a laugh until the train door clunked shut after them.

They were issued with rifles and instructions and went out onto the range, starting off at two hundred yards firing five rounds whilst lying down, then kneeling behind sandbags, and progressing back until they reached five hundred yards, tallying up the points allocated to them for each round as they went.

Smith was pleased with his overall score of seventy-four, especially when he learnt he'd pipped Charlie by a few points.

'Took a few rounds to get used to the little lady that's all,' said Charlie.

'That's just you all over, that.'

'No, seriously. Once I got to know her she was fine.'

'Yeah, that's what I mean – you have to show them who's the boss, that's all. Take control. Not be so eager to pander to their little whims. Once they're in line, all's sweet.'

'We are still talking about rifles here aren't we?'

'Of course. But you're right: it's better when you've got one on individual issue. You develop an understanding. Get to know her and how she feels. Look after her, and she looks after you back. They're all the same, they all have their own little ways.'

'Rifles, right?'

'Yeah. What did you think I was talking about?'

CHAPTER NINE

Stakes were raised for parliamentarians: bombs went off at Lloyd George's country house, and destroyed one of the many residences of Arthur Du Cros. Liberals break the law of the Lord, suffragettes the law of the land.

Mrs Pankhurst's trial and sentence to three years penal servitude for inciting the bombing meant huge crowds at the monument as various speakers denounced the tyranny of the State.

From her granite pedestal Queen Victoria looked down on her former subjects as they agitated and debated.

'This is no more than a thinly disguised attempt to silence us – to say to women that our domain is not the public one but the private one. But we will not leave our towns and our country to be led solely by men while we wait at home like good little ladies!' Molly strained her voice to make herself heard over the voices of affirmation and the hecklers.

'What you need is a husband!'

'Oh, do shut up. Let her speak. Go on, miss.'

'Mrs Pankhurst will not be that easily silenced. She is on hunger strike – it is the only weapon left to her.'

Elsie thought she could detect a look of disdain on the face of the old queen. This monarch whose outlook on womanhood was so antipathetic in every respect to the views she was now being forced to listen to day after day. Elsie couldn't help but smile.

After she had finished her turn Molly came over to find Elsie.

'JP's going to be speaking at the Temperance Hall on Sunday.'

'What, are you going to liven things up for him again?'

'No. Not this time.'

They were joined by Jack and Henry. Henry greeted Elsie with effusiveness. She observed his eyes drop to her neckline, followed by a tiny upwards twitch at the corner of his mouth. As if she needed confirmation. She had looked under the sideboard and even fished around under it with a knitting needle. But the necklace had gone.

'I was just telling Elsie about Pointer's meeting on Sunday. I've had a better idea than a standard bit of heckling. Let's go and find somewhere quiet to talk and I'll tell you about it. I need a drink after all that shouting.'

Jack and Molly walked ahead; Molly taking Jack's arm.

Poor Henry struggled to find something to say having received a "Yes, thank you" to his question of "Are you keeping well?" He walked along beside her, furtively glancing at her. He eventually came out with: 'I don't think she'll have to serve three years – Mrs Pankhurst, I mean.'

Now Elsie found herself tongue-tied. 'Don't you think so?' she said.

'No. I expect there'll be a long game of cat and mouse, don't you?'

'I suppose that's the best way to try and control her.'

On the Sunday evening, as it was going dark, a young man walked up Stafford Road – a pleasant but unremarkable suburban street near to the Duke of Norfolk's park. He stopped a hundred or so yards farther along and leaned against a lamppost. Two women could be seen heading in the same direction a moment later and nodded to another man perched on a wall as they passed. They came to a house with a small front garden, enclosed by a wall mounted with wrought iron railings. They stopped. One went up to the front door and removed a little bottle and a paintbrush from her bag. The other woman crouched by the front wall and also got out a small glass bottle. Half a minute passed. Their work done, they carried on down the street and one of the women took the arm of the man who had leaned against the lamppost and flashed a row of white teeth at him in the gloom. They were caught up by the other man and got onto a tram into town.

Joseph Pointer MP returned home, pleased with how his meeting had gone. He paid the cabman and, feeling in a good mood, gave him a tip.

It had all been very orderly – those vile women did not show, the questions had been well balanced and the debate constructive. How to push aside the millionaires of the Liberal Party and stop narrow Toryism and their calls for restrictive trade and conscription. He particularly liked his line about the Liberals stealing the clothes of the Labour Party while they were bathing. He smirked to himself and smoothed the ends of his moustache. Then he saw something unusual in the faint glow of the lamplight. Looking closer he saw writing on the front garden wall: "Votes for Women." And – dash it all – on his front door. And on the wall next to it. And underneath the window!

***

Following Mrs Pankhurst's trial it felt everything was finally coming to a head. Molly and Miss Schuster returned from a trip to London HQ with some new, more effective test tubes for making a mess of pillar boxes; and raids were made on His Majesty's mail outside the Town Hall, on Bow Street and High Street.

Spring's gentleness hardened into summer and straw boaters, re-emerging from gentlemen's wardrobes, were dampened and prodded back into shape, and frivolity replaced practicality on the heads of ladies. A bomb failed to go off at St Paul's Cathedral; then a few weeks later the nation was rocked by a woman throwing herself under a horse. The act of a deranged member of the monstrous regiment, proving that votes for women as a concept was as dead and buried as she now was. Or: it was an act of heroism by a lovely woman on behalf of the oppressed whose lives were devoid of meaning, whose existence was as enchained as slaves in all but a literal sense, on behalf of future generations and their rights to a say in their lives. Representing Sheffield, Molly and Miss Schuster joined the thousands who marched through London to ensure her passing was marked as the momentous occasion that it was in the life of the nation.

With the end of the football season, Smith felt the drop in his income. Within the space of a few weeks he'd come to rely on the extra four shillings and eightpence; not that it had gone towards paying bills, but it was his freedom money – money she didn't know about. That way she could have his wages, but the extra was his to add to the three and six he got from being an army reserve, which he'd always regarded as uniquely his. He was good at cards and usually reckoned to be in credit, and he ran a little crown and anchor dice set up at snap time which brought in a few bob. The Skyring was proving irresistible too, but he was careful – he had money in his pocket now – if it went it went, he wouldn't tap into the housekeeping tin unless it was an emergency. But he sometimes made a bit extra. There was nothing like the excitement of the ring, the sense of danger, the thrill of doubling your money.

He met Spud Murphy up there now and then; kept in with him for when the football coupon business started up again.

'If you needed a bit of extra work, come and see me,' he had said. 'I'll introduce you to my gaffer.'

At the shop one evening there was a discussion on the meeting that was being organised. They had secured a speaker from London who had been involved in the hunger strike at Holloway. Molly was working out a plan with Mary for publicising it. They would chalk pavements and print a small handbill for distribution at the monument and for handing to visitors at the shop.

'Let's write down our ideas,' said Molly.

'Yes,' said Mary. 'Something about the government being too arrogant to back down and treat women with respect, so they bring in their Cat and Mouse Act. Letting hunger strikers out on licence then arresting them again at the first opportunity. That takes courage: to keep going and keep getting arrested. I know I couldn't do it.'

'No, me neither,' said Elsie. 'It's a propaganda war. People have to understand what is actually happening. If they only read the newspapers they'd believe the police behave like perfect gentleman faced with a very trying situation – that it's our sisters that are the serious threat to the security and prosperity of the Empire. That forcible feeding is all very civilised: like getting a naughty child to eat her cabbage.'

'Are you getting this down, Mary?' said Molly. 'We should use that: not like getting a naughty child to eat their greens. Did you see that cartoon saying what they would do with suffragettes? It suggested they be marooned on a desert island, and one of the pictures was of a lion having eaten a woman. When you protest that it suggests that women be subject to transportation for wanting representation, or killed by being fed to lions, you get accused of being a humourless old spinster. Can we show that for what it is?'

'You're not allowed to show emotion. Because, if you do, somehow all that proves is that you can't be trusted with the vote.'

'I'll do some work on it tomorrow, shall we do an hour or so's selling?'

When they headed out towards the monument, Molly addressed Elsie and Mary. 'I wanted to let you know before everyone else got to find out: I'm moving on.'

'What do you mean? Leaving?'

'Not quite yet. I've resigned from the organiser's job.'

'Oh no. Surely…'

'It makes sense. All the Fulwood lot have had enough of me – they can run the shop as volunteers from now and that will put paid to the young men helping us out that they so object to. The lease on the shop is due to run out soon anyway.'

'But what will you do?'

'Oh, I'll stay on and help the committee, but I've got a post in the Medical Supply Association. I have always wanted to become a nurse; this might give me a way in.'

'Oh, you don't want to be a nurse,' said Mary. 'You end up as a servant to a lot of men: doctors who think they can treat you worse than they treat their domestic servants, and by patients who want you to be their mothers. You get all the horrible jobs and none of the credit.'

Elsie was subdued. She knew that Molly was leaving – despite what she said. Her heart was elsewhere – with Jack, or a new career, or with socialism, rather than just women's suffrage. She had increasingly been looking wider and adopting the arguments of socialism about changing the fundamental way that politics was organised rather than just achieving votes for all. Enfranchisement is just a battle in the war, it's not separate, she had said. Elsie was sad for the cause – that the short-sightedness of the ladies of Ecclesall and Fulwood had made Molly turn away; but more than that, she was sad for herself. She wouldn't see as much of Molly now, as she drifted away. The shop, and life, would be much duller.

In the week before the pilgrimage they chalked pavements to advertise their meeting, with women on watch to alert the chalkers to the approach of the police should it be necessary.

Eleanor Pendlebury was to be the speaker – she had been held in Holloway for six weeks and forcibly fed after she went on hunger strike. Molly was also going to go on the platform to speak to the Prisoners' Temporary Discharge for Ill Health Act – The Cat and Mouse Act.

Elsie used her chalks to good effect – representing a cat with long claws grabbing a mouse by the tail and the words "hear the truth," and "deeds not words." Her green, white and purple "votes for women" design she could now complete in a matter of a minute or so with a few deft flourishes of her chalks – it was becoming something of a trademark.

The great pilgrimage was a lacklustre affair. Several thousand people gathered on waste ground at the bottom of Snig Hill to listen to a bland, local dignitary from the Liberal party, well respected for his blandness, deliver a bland message about bland but respectable ladies. Some of these ladies, however, bordered on the dangerously radical by borrowing the penchant of their more militant sisters for wearing rosettes and ribbons. This put the plainclothes policemen slightly on edge as they patrolled ready to pounce at the slightest hint of assertiveness. Elsie and Mary amused themselves by rolling their eyes at the speeches and doing theatrical yawns to each other. As the meeting broke up they distributed a few handbills advertising their meeting for the following evening.

On the evening of the meeting Smith went out straight after his tea, so she didn't have to justify herself to him. She quickly tidied up and left the house to its empty self. They had not really been talking much anyway over recent weeks – other than exchanges of information necessary, or expected, in the running of a house. There's tea in the pot. I'm off up, now. Your snap's in the bag. Your shirts are ironed. Pass me the relish when you've finished with it. Can you empty the mousetraps. You'll have to replace the newspaper on the back of the privy door, I used it up. I've put twenty shillings in the tin. I've paid the coal man for half a hundredweight. I don't want owt for tea, ta: we stopped for fish and chips on the way home. Mrs Devlin called round for you – her Millicent's bad again. This royal wedding's got to be a good thing – whenever cousins get together for family weddings there'll be no falling out. What's that? King George in Berlin. Pass it me when you've finished with it. Is there any more pie left? Bloody bomb in Westminster Abbey now. Old Mr Hinchbrook from number eleven's funeral is on Thursday.

There was a large turnout for the meeting. Henry was on the door with one of his friends to keep away any troublemakers. He smiled and offered his hand.

Elsie settled into her seat next to Mary. She was glad to sit down – she felt a little dizzy and nauseous. She'd been a bit headachey for the last few days but had resisted going to the chemist for aspirin. She would have to, though, if it carried on.

'Breaking those windows at Swan and Edgar's was my first militant act; and my last.'

71

Eleanor Pendlebury's voice was not strong – but the hall was quiet: everyone mesmerised by the small, dignified woman on the platform, so every word was heard. On the lapel of her jacket was pinned her medal of valour.

'My health is not what it was, therefore I leave that for others to take forward now, but I can still share my testimony.

'I let fly a pebble from my catapult and the effect was quite dramatic, I must say. Those windows are very large and the whole window simply shattered and fell – I had only expected to make a hole in it. It was quite thrilling, and strangely beautiful – something that, by definition, you could not see, turned for a split second into a thousand diamonds.

'I was sentenced to six weeks in prison and went on hunger strike halfway through. I was terrified at first, but eventually the thought of living with the shame of not having done my bit – for the rest of my life – became stronger than my fear. I could not leave the fight completely to others because of my cowardice or the constraints of my position in society. It was the only protest left to me, to protest against being held as a second class prisoner along with committed criminals, when our cause is a political one and Irish political prisoners are afforded the privileges of first class.'

She paused to take drink of water. There was not a sound as they waited for her to resume.

'Being forcibly fed was the worst experience of my life and I was subjected to it a dozen or more times. It is nothing short of torture designed to break us – to break our minds, and our bodies, as mine has been broken, so that we give up the fight. But we will not.'

There was a ripple of applause that spread then quickly waned.

'There is no surrender.'

The restraint broke and the hall broke into loud applause. Mrs Pendlebury waited for quiet again.

'For those of you who have not had the pleasure, let me describe the procedure for you.'

Her voice faltered. She sipped at her glass again.

'Wardresses and a doctor descend on your cell – the number depending on how enfeebled you are. The first time I was honoured by the attendance of four wardresses to hold me down. These women – I swear that some of them take pleasure from this task, as do most of the doctors, who supposedly have a code of ethics – were unnecessarily brutish and rude.

'The doctor arrived with an assembly of apparatus – tubes and pumps and straps and steel instruments of various sizes and shapes, and a jug of liquid – this was usually beef tea or some milky concoction, but you could never tell what it was as it by-passed your mouth.

'I was made to sit on a wooden chair – a wardress held my feet, one held my arms, another tilted the chair backwards, and the other pulled my head back in her big hands. "Please don't force my neck, so," I said. But anything I said was ignored.

'They fed this disgusting tubing up my nose. It did not look new – I retched as they put it to my nostrils – it smelt not just of indiarubber, but of vomit.'

There were cries of anguish and disgust around the hall. It quietened again.

'The pain was excruciating – in my nose and throat and in my breast. The doctor's ruddy face and mutton-chop whiskers were above me, and I swear he was smirking. "Saves the risk of being bitten by the little vixens," he joked to his associates. I felt I was suffocating, I was drowning, struggling for life, but I was held tight as I struggled in panic.

'As the liquid filled my stomach I convulsed as my body tried to reject it. As I bent double in pain they wrenched me straight again.'

Mary looked at Elsie with an expression of horror on her face.

'That, I'm afraid, was not the worst of it. After a week or so my nasal passage would no longer take the tubing – it was inflamed, and the agony as they tried first the one then the other nostril was indescribable. So they gave up. They pinched my nose closed and forced open my mouth, inserting a steel gag, which forced my jaw apart farther than it naturally went. I was held down as before, and the pinkish-orange tube went into my mouth. The doctor standing over me: his face big and red, with beads of sweat on his brow. I was disgusted. Outraged by the procedure; that they take possession of women's bodies this way.'

Mary grasped Elsie's hand. Elsie gave her hand a little squeeze back. She looked at her: her eyes had filled with tears.

There followed a discussion on the Cat and Mouse Act, and Molly talked of how it was being used as a weapon to silence people – with conditions attached to release, preventing them from activism on threat of re-arrest, or for the authorities to avoid any responsibility for the health of their victims caused by forcible feeding going wrong, through infection or carelessly inserting tubes into windpipes.

'This is why we need to do more than walk politely to London. They do not listen to polite voices. Only power has influence. They say that militant protest disqualifies women from being able to vote, but look what happens to the oh-so-polite women's suffrage societies – they wouldn't say boo to a goose, and still get pelted with eggs and tomatoes as they march. We heard yesterday their calls to restore faith in the suffrage movement – to show that they are not too emotional to be trusted with a vote – that by being law abiding they will have great influence. And yet these respectable ladies are still derided and pelted with rotten fruit. So much for that touching faith in their womanliness.'

'That was terribly upsetting, wasn't it?' said Elsie, as she headed up towards the tram stop with Mary. 'That poor woman.'

'I know. I'm sorry for being such a ninny.'

'You're not. That you empathise with other people is one of the things I love you for, Mary. You put yourself in their place and share their pain. You imagine things very intensely.'

'It wasn't that so much as...'

'What do you mean?'

'I am not imagining that well. Oh, Elsie...' She started to weep again.

Elsie stopped and held both her hands.

'I'm so silly.'

'You're not. What is it?'

'It... it brought back some horrible memories. There was this man – he was a friend of the family – I was only young, not yet a woman, and he did things to me, Elsie.'

'Oh, Mary. You poor thing. Come on I'll take you home.'

'No, there's no need.'

'I insist.'

'But it is so out of your way. You might miss the last tram.'

'Then I'll sleep on your settee if needs be.'

She returned home at mid-morning the next day having stopped at the butchers for two cutlets for tea.

Mary had been in no fit state to be left on her own. She had no one else she could turn to – no family nearby, and her landlady, a widow in her fifties, was kindly, but not exactly a confidante. They had talked until quite late, Elsie trying to put aside her own sense of fatigue and her nagging headache. She had not slept well on the settee in Mary's room either.

She put the meat in the safe in the cellar and got water on to boil for the washing before going upstairs to wash and change. As she removed her drawers she noticed some light spotting, even though it was not yet that time of the month, then as she went about her tasks she became conscious of a tenderness in her breasts. Could it be true after all that time waiting? She counted back – she was well overdue. She had feared after the birth of her son that something had gone wrong with her, that she would remain barren, but this gave her renewed hope. Of a sudden, life had a new meaning. Would she tell Smith? Not until she was certain. But oh! She was.

As she pegged out the washing she imagined her pride in hanging out small garments, of small shirts or socks next to Smith's large ones, while he slept in a cradle in the corner of the yard, or played with a wooden train on rails she had chalked on to the flagstones. But she must not think like that. It was too miraculous. And yet it seemed to happen all around her with no sense of a divine hand at work. But that was it, it was all His work that people just took for granted; she promised to Him that she would never be guilty of that.

It was a lovely day and white clouds drifted across blue sky, and the washing fluttered on the line and was dry by mid afternoon and put in a pile ready for ironing. She opened doors and windows front and back, pulled out rugs and gave them a good beating, and swept the floors.

By the time she had potatoes and spring greens on to boil it was as if she had emerged from the dry, dark interior of a forest into the light and air of the meadow beyond. She fried the cutlets in lard and glanced up at the clock. He would be home any minute. She tested potatoes, drained them and put them in a covered dish in the lowest part of the oven. She checked the clock again and took the pan off the heat, placed the cutlets in the same dish and made a drop of gravy from the juices in the pan and the water drained from the vegetables. Plates were put to warm and she sat at the table. Half an hour passed as she waited. The dinner was spoiling. Still she waited. She heard footsteps in the passage and a shadow passed over the window. The door clicked open.

'You came home then?'

'I'm sorry. I had to take Mary home and then missed the last tram. Sit down I'll get you your tea.'

She picked up a cloth, went to the oven and got the dish out.

'I wondered what story you'd come out with.'

'It's not a story.'

'And you expect me to bloody believe it? You bloody liar.'

The dish clattered onto the table as it slipped from her hands. 'Smith, please…'

'It's a bloody disgrace. Who were you really with? Who is he? I'll…'

She looked up at him. 'I was with Mary!' she shouted defiantly. 'She was not well.'

He raised his hand.

She braced herself. 'You have to believe me, I had to…'

He lowered his hand, and covered his face.

'What will people say? You know there are already rumours?'

'Don't be ridiculous.' She was shaken by his remark. Her challenge was unsure.

'Ridiculous? It's you defying all sense of decency. Come here.' His eyes were wild. He moved to the side of the table. 'I said come here, damn you!'

She moved towards him slowly. He grabbed her arms by the elbows and pulled her towards him.

He put his nose in her hair, sniffed at her neck, her breasts and pulled up her skirt and knelt before her sniffing like a dog. She couldn't help humiliated tears, her knees from shaking. This wasn't supposed to happen today of all days. He stood back up and kissed her on the mouth so that she struggled to breathe.

'Go on then, put my food out.' She fetched the plates, head down, avoiding his gaze.

'Have you any beer in?'

'No. I'll mash some tea instead.'

He was rough with her in bed pulling at her breasts with his teeth.

'Smith, don't. They're sore.'

'What do you mean? Why?'

'I think I might be expecting.'

He stopped and looked at her, right into her eyes, his expression changeless. His hardness softened, his lovemaking became slow, tender, considerate.

CHAPTER TEN

Blackburn beating Liverpool by six goals to two and the United beating Derby five-three away on the opening day of the football season were results that no one had predicted, so it was a good day for those running the football coupon business.

As he entered the Hussar with his takings, and to collect coupons for the following week, a party was in full swing.

He was greeted by Murphy. 'Smith, what you having? The boss is buying the rounds tonight. I'll introduce you. Murphy picked up the pints off the zinc and handed one to Smith.

'Cheers.'

A smartly dressed young man was sitting by the fireplace. He was holding forth – recounting some anecdote, surrounded by a group of men, like disciples, shining faces held under the young man's gaze – waiting to laugh at the right moment. Smith hung back from the circle, waiting.

'And so I said to him "I'll tell you what you can do with your chicken. You can shove it up your fat arse." '

Everyone burst out laughing and the young man sat back and smiled, taking a long pull from his beer tankard. Murphy stepped forward. 'George – can I introduce you to Smith here. He's the one I was telling you about – who's on the railways. The old soldier.'

'Oh yes. I remember. Sit down, Smith. How's the business going?'

'Yeah, good. I'm happy to be up and running again now the season's underway. To be honest the extra cash is welcome.'

'Always is. You boys don't earn much for what you do, either; so I gather.'

'You gather right.'

'Wife and kids to support?'

'Wife – a kid on the way.'

'Good man. If ever you need anything you come and see me, yeah?'

'Thank you, Mr...'

'Mooney. But we're all mates, so call me George.'

'And thank you for the drink.'

'Pleasure. We took a lot of money and paid out very little this week so it's worth celebrating. We'll have weeks when we barely break even so we make our hay when the big beautiful sun's high in the sky.'

Smith smiled. So this was the boss. He'd heard the name before, spoken in whispers, like the owner of it was a dangerous hooligan, but this man didn't fit the image. Instead Mooney was one of those people you couldn't help but like – good-looking, with a strong jaw, sparkling blue eyes and neatly trimmed hair. But more than that he made everyone feel important. Made you feel good about yourself – like some of his magic rubbed off on you. He was wearing a well-tailored Harris Tweed suit that must have cost the best part of eighty shillings; twice what Smith had laid down for his coat.

'I've a little job for you, Smith. You'd be doing me a big favour.'

'Of course. What is it?'

'We've got a little job on later with any luck. Some sorting out to do and could do with a few good lads with us just in case. They'll be nowt to it.' He reached inside his jacket and pulled out a silver crown, which he popped into Smith's top pocket. 'Here, have this for your trouble. Stay here – enjoy the evening. We'll give you a shout when we're ready.'

Smith wasn't sure what he'd just let himself in for, but soon got drawn into a few games of nap, and, as the evening drew on, was well up on what he'd walked in with – even discounting the five shillings he'd being given. And he had had his fill of beer without having to pay. Towards eleven o'clock the door of the pub was flung open. Smith looked up from his cards and saw a young lad enter. The lad picked Mooney out of the throng and went over to where he was sitting with Peter Winsey, the one who handed out the football coupons.

There were a few nods, and chairs and stools scraped back. Murphy tapped Smith on the shoulder. 'Come on we're off.'

'They're in the Castle Hotel,' someone said.

They headed off towards West Bar. Smith counted nine including himself. A few peeled off at the urinal near the cabman's shelter, then came running up to rejoin them, after.

They were met at the bottom of Snig Hill by another runner. 'I think they're about to leave,' he said, panting.

'Let's be ready for them, lads. They'll be heading down Water Lane to get home. Pete: you and me will deal with it unless there's a load of them. You lads just hang back unless you're needed. Rigby and Jonesy, you go up the hill and follow them down.'

Smith and the others followed Mooney, left by the Grand Theatre. It was becoming clear to Smith what the sorting out was – it was no ordinary business transaction. Murphy marshalled the reserves at the top of Millsands, while Mooney and Winsey waited around the corner where Water Lane met Bridge Street.

A couple of minutes later, three men could be seen coming down Water Lane. Murphy signalled to the other two, hidden over the road. 'Come on,' said Murphy. 'Let's just step over the road so they know we're here.'

As the three men emerged onto Bridge Street, Mooney and Winsey stepped out. The men looked back up the lane but could see the other two, Rigby and Jones, blocking their escape.

'You let me down badly, Mr Crisp. Very disappointing when someone tries to cheat me,' said Mooney. And without waiting he knocked him down with a right hook to the jaw. Winsey then gave him a kicking whilst he was down. Smith winced as the blows fell on his body and once on the side of his face.

Of his two companions, one froze and stood there helpless; the other made as if to run but was dealt a blow to the head by Rigby and went down.

'Good evening, gentleman,' said Mooney. 'We're done for the night.'

Everyone walked away. There had been no shouting, no raised voices at all. It was all very businesslike. As Smith headed down towards the bridge he looked back and saw the two men raising themselves off the ground: at least they weren't dead.

He'd nearly paid off the coat now. Perhaps a new suit would be good as well? Something a bit more classy. No. There were more important things to be saving up for now – they'd kept some stuff they'd put by from the last time – up in a trunk in the box room, but there were bound to be other things. No child of his would go without.

A couple of weeks later when he went to collect football coupons, Peter Winsey wasn't there, another man was doing it instead. Smith collected his two dozen coupons and, seeing Spud Murphy leaning against the bar, went to have a chat.

'Where's Pete?'

'Didn't you see the paper? Gone away for a bit with George. Them bastards went squealing to the police about that business the other week. Just a month each. They'll live to regret that: it's breaking a gentleman's code. Next time he'll not know who's done him. Left us a bit short-staffed. You don't fancy a bit of a management job do you? We could do with a bit of help up Scaith Wood of a Sunday – keeping order, looking after the money – that sort of thing.'

Smith leaned his head to one side, making a non-committal sucking noise.

'You don't have to. It's all very friendly, only the odd drunk who doesn't want to pay out. It's just a kind of outdoor pub – a bit of cards, tossing ring, dice games and whatnot. Stops folks getting bored of a Sunday if church ain't their thing.'

'How much does it pay?'

'It's on a percentage; but maybe twenty bob if the weather's fine, and the clients turn up. From about two while ten. We meet up here for about one, beforehand.'

'Sounds good to me. Count me in.'

***

For the second Sunday in a row Elsie went alone to evening service at All Saints. She felt awkward; wondered what people would say as she walked up towards the church gates. She greeted a few neighbours on the way in, but they didn't remark on her being unaccompanied. He hadn't said where he was going, other than that he was helping a friend out with some work, and she hadn't pressed him. He had, after all, been making an effort to get on in the last few weeks: not challenging her on what she was doing, so it would seem perverse to go looking for conflict.

She enjoyed the service; it was one of her favourite times in the calendar. Just to be able to join her voice in song with others was so uplifting. "Bring thy final harvest home, Gather thou thy people in, Free from sorrow, free from sin."

The only thing marring the occasion was a funny smell. Like meat that had gone off. She wrinkled her nose and looked around her to see if she could see the culprit so that she could perhaps shuffle farther away.

She was glad to get out in the fresh air – on Sundays it wasn't too bad usually – fewer chimneys belching out their filth. And there was a stiff breeze blowing down off the moors.

When she got home she found the stench had followed her, and there was a dampness between her legs after walking. She went upstairs and found dark staining on her combinations. It was the source of the smell. It was not normal. Her heart started racing, she felt hot, and dread rose up through her. She felt sick.

She washed and changed and rinsed her clothes. Then she set about getting some supper ready for when Smith returned. She set out some bread and a small pot of dripping, with a nice layer of jelly underneath, on the table, filled the kettle, ready, turned the gas light down low, then went up to bed.

She woke when she heard him come in, clattering, into the house, whistling as he went about mashing some tea.

She pretended to be fast asleep when through half-open eyes she saw his huge shadow travel up the bedroom wall, cast by the candle he was carrying. He got quietly into bed and left her alone.

She got up first the next day and, as she was placing coals from the bucket on to the remnants of last night's fire to get it going again, she felt a trickling down her leg. She got a cloth and wiped off a lot of blood, rinsed the cloth in the scullery and cleaned herself up.

Smith came down in a cheery mood when he smelt the bacon cooking. The stench was so strong to Elsie – revolting.

'That smells good,' said Smith. 'I'm ready for that. How was the church service?'

'Nice. The harvest decorations were beautiful.'

'Shame I had to miss it. Still we had a good day – I've put another five shillings in the tin. Why don't tha go and buy a nice bit of steak, and get thisen a new hat or summat. Baby stuff maybe. You'll need all sorts no doubt: napkins and whatnot.'

'Thank you. I might.'

She nibbled some bread and butter and sipped her tea while Smith tucked into his breakfast.

'Tha don't look none too good: a bit peaky. Not overdoing it, are tha? Nice bit of liver for tea – get a bit of iron in thi.'

'I'll see. I'll just go and get dressed then get your snap ready.'

She took it easy for the rest of the day and, other than popping round to the butchers and cooking the tea, did little other than sitting and reading.

The next morning she woke in a lot of pain: an intense aching across her abdomen. Smith had already gone down and she heard the fire being raked and plates being put on the table as he whistled "When I take my morning promenade." She lay still, staring at the curtains, with a crack of light shining through.

The pain eased and she sat up on the bed. The pad she had between her legs was soaked. She removed it, put it in the chamber pot to deal with later, and quickly dressed and went downstairs.

'Morning, Else. Feeling any better?'

'A little, perhaps.'

'That's good. Tea's mashing.'

As she helped get breakfast the pain started again. She felt a sudden urge to urinate.

'I'll just nip across the yard.'

She bolted the privy door behind her and sat down. She felt pressure in her abdomen. There was a lot of blood not urine. She pushed down and passed something – looking down she saw placenta and cord – and a lot more blood. She pulled the chain in horror to make it go away, then regretted what she had done.

The pain eased. She cleaned herself up as best she could, pulled the chain again and went back inside.

'Tha took thi time, tha got the trots? Tha does look a bit ropey I must say.'

'I'll go back to bed. Perhaps you can call by Mrs Devlin's on your way to work and get her to come round.'

'Old Dame Devlin? Is everything all right?'

'Yes. I need to rest, that's all.'

The room was closing in on her as she lay there with an old blouse rolled up between her legs. She had heard the door slam closed and Smith's boots going down the passage. The pain came anew. She felt pressure again, like she really did need to urinate this time. She got out of bed and got the chamber pot and squatted. Something slid into the pot.

There lay a tiny baby, only an inch or so long, but with perfect, little legs and arms. That boy in the sailor suit of her imagination, taken away from her so cruelly. It brought back all the pain of the last time: seeing her boy, baby George, so perfect and yet so still. She howled with rage and hurt, and tears rolled down her cheeks and dripped off her nose onto the tiny figure.

Mrs Devlin found her several minutes later sobbing, hunched over the chamber pot.

'What is it, Elsie, love. Pass it here. Oh, my lord! You poor thing. Let me deal with that. Oh, you mustn't.' She took it and placed it on the floor. Get back into bed. I'll get you some water and get you cleaned up.'

'What will I tell Smith? Oh, Mrs D...'

'Don't go worrying about that, dear. I'll get you sorted then I'll go and get our Maud to come round to ours, and then I'll come back and stay with you till he comes home. I'll get his tea and everything.'

'Do we have to tell him?'

'Of course. You mustn't hide it from him. He has a right to know. Come on, lie down I'll get some warm water.'

She slept for some of the day and Mrs Devlin made her beef tea. She was dreading Smith's return as the day wore on. She heard his boots up the passage, heard the door click open and him shout: "I'm home," as he sometimes did. Then it went quiet and stayed quiet. She heard the oven door and the cupboard close. What seemed like an hour later his footsteps creaked up the stairs and the bedroom door pushed open.

He crept forward and sat on the bed, still.

She turned her head to look at him. 'Is Mrs Devlin still here?'

'Yes, she said she'd wait a bit longer and tidy up.'

'Did she...'

He nodded. Tears welled up in his eyes and he brushed them away angrily with the back of his hand.

'I'm sorry, Smith. I...' She couldn't stop her own tears.

'Dun't matter, lass. We'll try again.' He took her hand. 'Tha'd best get some rest. I didn't mean to upset thi. I'll just be...' He pointed to the door and left her.

Mrs Devlin came up again and sat with her for a bit until she was calm again. 'It's just nature taking its course. It wasn't meant to be.'

'But why? Why does God...?'

'He knows what's best. Have faith and it will happen. You mustn't think bad things.'

'What did you do with...?'

'I dealt with it properly. Don't think about. It's all over now.'

But it wasn't. Not really. Even though she gained in strength and returned to her former self again, her body still hadn't finished reminding her of what she had lost, as it went about the process of ejecting any traces of what had nearly been.

Her brother Thomas's wife, Louisa, came round to help out and keep her company. She was grateful for the distraction. Louisa tried to avoid the subject of children, but Elsie couldn't bear the falsehood of the situation and asked her questions about their John and Annie.

'In fact I'd like you to bring them round sometime. I've not seen them in a while. I could perhaps make some little cakes for them and they could come round for tea one day.'

Her brother came over one afternoon after his early shift with the intention of walking back with Louisa later. They all sat at the kitchen table talking over various plans for Christmas, and whose they'd go to and when. Louisa poured more tea. 'I'll go and straighten the bed.'

'You not want another, Lou?'

'No. Thank you. I'm all tea-d out today.'

Tom looked at her and smiled. 'So, you all right then, sis?'

'Yes, Tom. Don't fret about me. Your Louisa's been wonderful. You can have her back now. To be honest I've been selfish having her here when I don't really need her. You are very lucky – she's so warm-hearted and such good company.'

'You forgot her steak and kidney pud. That's the real reason I married her.' He looked at her and smiled a half-smile. 'What about Smith?'

'What about him?'

'How's he taking it?'

'Oh, he gets by. It shook him a lot but he's got his work and he copes by keeping busy: going out with his mates. And he's got some sort of work on the side too. Bringing in a bit extra.'

Tom looked at her again, then down at the table. 'Do you know what he's been up to?'

'How do you mean?'

He shuffled about on his chair and stirred more sugar in his tea.

'Thomas Green. I've known you since you were a baby. You can be straight with me.'

'Well, I've heard he's been mixing with a bit of a rum lot.'

'No. I don't think so – not Smith.'

'People have been saying he's involved with the Mooney gang… I've maybe got the wrong end of the stick. I don't want to worry you; only maybe you should just… I dunno, but thought you're better off knowing. I've only heard he's helping out with some gambling business – not anything more troubling.' He looked at her; she looked very pale. 'I shouldn't have mentioned it. Sorry, sis.'

84

'No. No, you were right. I'd rather know. You don't suppose he has been caught up in anything more serious, then? No... that couldn't be. He's not like that. He just likes his cards and a flutter every now and then.'

'You're right. I'm sure.'

CHAPTER ELEVEN

One Monday evening in November, Smith went round to the Hussar as usual to collect his football coupons. He was now selling between forty and fifty a week, making at least four shillings for himself, with extras on top for other bits of work – managing card schools, or doing work as a piker at the new tossing ring at Tinsley. Then there was the occasional win on top – or loss, in which case he'd have nothing extra to show for his efforts.

When he got to the Hussar it was quiet.

'They're round at the Norfolk Arms,' said the landlord. 'It was getting a bit hot in here with the Constabulary. Lost me a lot of business. But daresay they'll be back.'

Round at the Norfolk Arms, Smith was greeted by one of the pikers on the door, on the lookout for the approach of polished boots.

It was busy inside, with money changing hands on cards and dominoes. Smith sorted his business, then joined one of the tables. On every side the accents were Irish – he could have been in Dublin. There was some talk of the weekend's game; United getting the better of Chelsea, and of their hero, Billy Gillespie, but mostly they concentrated on the hands they had to play.

On an adjacent table, George Mooney raised his voice and the pub went quiet.

'No one does that to me, McGarry.'

'Ah, now. Give over will ye. What now big man?'

Mooney flipped. 'Outside. Now.'

They both headed out, and a small, excited crowd followed. Smith had money on the table and a decent hand, he looked about him, the others at his table showed no sign of wanting to leave.

Five minutes later the pub filled up again.

'What happened fellas?'

'Mooney got a bit peckish – took a chunk out of McGarry's ear.'

'Whist! He no?'

'That he did. Off to the hospital, so he was.'

Smith went for another drink. A man came in the pub and joined him at the bar.

'You're Elsie Green's fella aren't ye?'

Smith nodded.

'I thought I recognised ye. Bill Cavill...' He held out his hand. 'I used to live next to the Quinns. The Greens were just down the street. Then they all moved up in the world. I'm still mates with Tommy and Paddy. I've seen ye around, someone said ye married into the clan. You've a good 'un there, so ye have. Fancied my chances wi' her myself at one time, so I did. But she was a class above, that 'un. No wonder she went for a fine fella like ye.'

Smith laughed. 'Nah. Just reckon she kissed a frog thinking I'd turn into a prince.'

'What ye having?' Cavill lined up a couple of pints of Jubilee stout.

'Ex-army, someone said ye were?'

'Still in. On reserve.'

'Good man. I'm a sergeant in the King's Own – well in the Special Reserve anyhow. Brings in some money. Am not long back from training up at Hunmanby. Ye ever been? What a crack that were. We got complaints from the locals in the evening. Just high spirits, so it was. Ye ever see action.'

'No. Only the odd skirmish in Ireland.'

'Some round here think bad o' me for being in the army for that very reason. Here, did you see the fight outside?'

'No, I was in the middle of a game.'

'Bloody disgusting – not a fair fight at all, you know. Mooney was losing. His mate jumps in and then Mooney bites his ear right off. Blood everywhere.'

Smith finished his pint. 'Thanks for that, Bill. I'd best be getting back.'

'Give her a kiss from me, eh?'

As he was about to leave, George Mooney entered with someone Smith had seen around but didn't know.

'Now then, Mr Mooney,' said the landlord. 'I think it'd be best if you went home now and save any further trouble.'

George turned to go but then noticed Cavill sitting in the corner. 'I hear you're after reporting me to the Polis, Cavill? Were you backing McGarry in the fight and sore about it?'

'I don't want nothing to do wit' ye, Mooney. I'll let ye get away home.'

Smith saw Mooney swing at Cavill, turn and leave, replacing some object back in his pocket.

Cavill was doubled up, holding his mouth with blood pouring between his hands. His mouth caved in. Smith decided to leave as well.

***

Smith was inside the firebox of a 3835 Class when the foreman shouted him from the footplate.

'There's someone to see you, Smith, lad.'

'Tell them they can bloody well wait, I'm not finished. I ain't crawling in and out – once I'm in, that's it.'

'It's a policeman.'

'I don't care if it's King Bloody George his sen, I'll get this lot shovelled out first – if he wants he can allus come in and talk to me in here.'

Ten minutes later Smith emerged coughing and covered in sweat, soot and ash. 'All yours.' His teeth and eyes flashed white in his dirty face. 'Sorry to keep you.' He held out his hand to shake hands with the policeman, delighting in the man's dilemma between appearing rude and getting filth all over his clean hands.

'Were you at the Norfolk Arms on Monday evening.'

'Which Norfolk Arms do you mean. I know of at least six.'

'Tenter Street.'

'I might have been.'

'We're investigating an assault that took place there. Did you see it?'

'I didn't really see much.'

'You're an army man aren't you? Like the man who was roughed up. He's in a bad way. He might not be able to carry on his army service. You need to make a statement. I've squared it with your gaffers – you'll not lose any pay.'

'Go on then, so long as there's a sit down and a cuppa in it.'

The policeman wrote out a statement in the boiler inspector's office and Smith signed it. He admitted being in the pub at the time and having talked to Cavill. Yes, he had seen George Mooney enter, and that he had invited McGarry to step outside, but, no, he had not seen the fight. He had seen Cavill bent over, covered in blood with his mouth smashed in. But it was too much to expect him to admit to seeing Mooney strike him.

'What do you expect from me? To sign my own chuffing death warrant? I suppose you know who George Mooney is?'

On his way home from work the next day, as he was about to turn the corner into Danville Street, two men came from nowhere, one grabbing each arm.

'Let's carry on walking shall we?'

'What do you want?'

'Just a friendly chat.' His arm was fair yanked out of its socket. 'Now – you going to cooperate?'

'Yeah. Let go of us.'

'As long as tha don't do owt daft.'

Smith looked at them; he thought he'd seen them around somewhere – up at Sky Edge or Scaith Wood.

'Is this about George?'

'Just keep walking.'

They got out onto the rec at the back. Some kids were kicking a ball about in the growing gloom. He had nowhere to run, and there was no one to help. It was too dark for anyone to even make out what was going on.

'Cigarette?' One of the men held out a packet of cheap cigarettes. He was tall, pasty-looking, more gaps than teeth in his mouth and a beak-like nose. Smith took a cigarette and pulled out his own matches.

'Thanks. What can I help you with.'

'We've got a spot of bother. People have been talking.'

'But I've not said owt.'

'We know you spoke to the coppers and have given a statement. That wasn't very clever.'

'Yeah. I had to. They know I was there. But I didn't say owt in it. Didn't point the finger at George.'

'That's not we've heard.'

The other man, dark, thickset, ugly with big lips and a thin scruffy beard, spoke: 'You might want to consider withdrawing it.'

'How can I do that? Don't be daft.'

'Say you thought it over and remembered that you weren't there after all. Have a think about it. We'll come back for another chat – see how you're getting on.'

Before he could react he was punched hard below the sternum and dropped to the ground. He smelt the mud and grass as his head made contact with the wet ground. Then there was a sharp pain in his back from the toe of a boot. He lay still for a few seconds unable to react, before realising he was alone.

Elsie noticed him wince with pain when he got out of his chair later.

'What's the matter Smith?'

'It's nowt. I just got a bit of a bump at work. There's no room inside those bloody fireboxes. I caught myself on summat.'

She fussed around him and wanted to take a look at his bruising, fetch the arnica tincture.

'Nay, lass. It's nowt.' But he enjoyed the attention. 'Tha don't fancy an early night?'

'No, Smith. Not yet. It's still too early. I don't want to go through it again.'

'But it's been ages now. Is there owt up with thi still?'

'No, but.'

'Well then. Come on. There's nowt to lose.'

'No, Smith.'

'There must be summat wrong in thi family, that's what.'

'That's cruel, Smith.' She couldn't hold back her tears. 'Don't you understand? After what I've been through... that's unfair.'

He picked up his newspaper. Why had he done it? Said that? He knew before he'd opened his mouth it would end up like this – like it had been inevitable all evening.'

'I sometimes wonder why you ever married me,' she said, picking up some sewing.

'Aye. Happen as not.'

CHAPTER TWELVE

Molly Morris left Sheffield and went back to Manchester. Then Mary's father in Renishaw fell ill and she left too. And so the joy Elsie found in the WSPU disappeared. When she went along to the shop now it was largely out of a sense of duty, and for want of doing something.

Miss Schuster tried to get Elsie to take on extra responsibilities, but at times it seemed mere drudge. Without the sense of hope of progress it was hard to feel inspired. No matter what they'd tried, the drawbridge remained up. The hopes of a few years before: of a settlement in Parliament were gone. They had raised the stakes and seen no response; to keep on raising them was impossible. Of course, it was their destiny to prevail, Elsie knew that. The twentieth century was different; the old Victorians would die out and be replaced by modern Georgians with new ideas. Perhaps the new year would somehow provide the events to clear the deadlock – open people's eyes and hearts to the justice of their cause.

1913, however, didn't give up easily. Its autumn had been so mild that some wily folk knew fields where mushrooms could still be found, or hedgerows with blackberries that the devil had not yet claimed for his own.

Christmas Eve was fair and Elsie and Smith went to church in the evening, but the next day broke to a steady drizzle as if the very day was rebelling against last century sentimentalism of blankets of snow thrown over landscapes and rural idylls, rosy cheeks, and fur coats.

Smith appeared pleased when he peered out of the curtains over the greasy slate roofs; the reason becoming clear later, the weather seeming a validation of his choice of gift for Elsie: an umbrella. Even after that triumph he wasn't finished as he presented her with a box of half a dozen soaps. Elsie gave Smith a silver-plated cigarette case, with his initials: *S.O.* engraved on the cartouche.

They went round to the Quinn's for Christmas dinner with a variety of small gifts for the youngest members of the clan. There was a dozen or so of them packed into the small living room, not everyone being able to sit at the table for dinner – some doubling up on chairs and variety of crates and stools being used as perches. Smith fidgeted all through dinner and excused himself after the goose course – not waiting for any pudding.

'Are you leaving, Smith? Are ye not going to the divine service with your wife?'

'No. I've got to go. I agreed to meet up with Charlie – there's a match on at Bramall Lane this afternoon.'

Once Boxing Day was out of the way, winter came rushing in. New Year's Eve was a snow carnival on the hilly slopes around the city; its steep streets became lethal toboggan runs, with excited children slaloming round lampposts and foolhardy grown-ups – mostly successfully.

Smith carried on selling football coupons. The heat he had felt back in November cooled. He had held his nerve and ridden the storm – he stuck to his story: that he had given nothing away, that the police were no longer interested in him. One or two stuck up for him: Spud Murphy and Peter Winsey – to them he appeared loyal and brought in useful trade. And besides, Mooney himself was no longer around – he'd not been seen for months in the city. It was denied he was on the run from the law – he was simply expanding his empire in the Midlands, working the racecourses, doing deals. While he was away, others seemed to be benefiting. Smith wondered just how much Mooney was really in control. He'd even taken to siphoning off a little himself; instead of returning unsold coupons like he was supposed to, he took to saying he'd used them to light the fire. That was sometimes the case, but one or two he ran privately.

In April the news came that Mooney had handed himself in. This caused hilarity because in truth he had been spotted by a keen-eyed sergeant down at Bower Spring who took up chase to execute the warrant that had been out for him since November. Mooney, in one last desperate attempt to seek mitigating factors in his defence, had run panting into the police station, arriving shortly before his pursuer.

The next day when Smith got home there was an official letter waiting for him. On opening it he found a witness summons for the Magistrates' Court at the beginning of May. The full force of the significance struck him then. The last few months had been no more than a lull before a storm. His choice was to go to court and perjure himself – deny having seen Mooney in the pub with Cavill, and so betraying a fellow soldier as he looked on. Or, tell the truth or risk being tricked into saying the wrong thing by a smart-arse solicitor and get his leg's broken – or worse. He had to think fast because Mooney's associates would be about to get very interested in the list of witnesses. They would be round to look for him again – but what if they couldn't find him – either Mooney's lot or the police?

'What was in the letter?' Elsie asked as he emerged from the scullery drying his hair.

'Oh nothing. Just a thing from the Battalion about training.'

'I'm off out to a committee meeting tonight.'

'Right you are.'

That gave him time to think. He sat smoking a cigarette after tea. After Elsie had left he went upstairs, got his kit bag out, emptied it into the wardrobe and refilled it with his clothes and other things he would need.

He wrote a note, propped it up against the teapot on the table, put on his boots and coat and left with his bag over his shoulder, out into the night.

Elsie wasn't late back. She thought that Smith had gone to bed early or had gone down to the pub. It was dark downstairs and up. She lit a candle inside the scullery door then the gas lamp when she got into the living room. She filled the kettle enough for a cup of tea and put it on the ring to heat whilst she washed and dried a couple of pots. She got a biscuit out of the pantry to have with her tea. The kettle started to sing so she went to get the teapot off the table. Leaning against it was a piece of paper. She unfolded it and read: "Sorry Else it's no good I've had to go. Left some money on the side to tide you over. Smith." So, had he finally left her? Rejected her? Left the dry desert for greener pastures? The way he'd treated her over what had been nothing – his suspicions over the necklace – and all this time it was it him seeing someone else? And now eloped?

She couldn't give him what he wanted: that had been clear for quite some time. She sat at the table and put her head in her hands.

Over the next few days she made excuses for him when people asked – that he was away on army training. People would believe that. There was a growing sense of unease across the country; though of course no one believed it could ever come to anything. The Germans were not so very different from us.

Someone came round from his work. No, she didn't know where he was – she couldn't lie to him because Smith always cleared it with them for army training. The man lifted his hat to wish her good day. His hair was thin on top and plastered over his head. He went away tutting and muttering about things being "irregular" and having left them "in the lurch."

Then a policeman came round and she dreaded the worst – but he did not have any news of Smith's demise – only wanting to know why he hadn't answered a summons.

'What has he done wrong?'

'He is expected in court again next week to give evidence. Tell him he needs to attend or we might issue a warrant for him.'

What was he up to? A witness summons arrived, then a few days later she was scared witless by an even more insistent knock on the door and threats from two men, not just aimed at Smith but at her.

'You'd best not be lying to us. If you know where he is you'd better tell us or it will be worse for him and you.'

'I haven't seen him for a week now.'

'You expect us to believe that?'

'It's true. He's left me. I promise.'

'You'll not mind us having a look round then.'

They pushed their way past and searched the house, from box-room to cellar.

'How dare you! I'll fetch the police.'

'Oh, do shut up. If you're telling the truth we'll be quick.'

She followed them, outraged.

'See, I told you. No boots, no razor. Nothing. Are you even going to tell me what he is supposed to have done?'

'Nowt yet, maybe. But if he does do, it'll be very serious for him. You can tell him that if you see him. He'll know what we mean.'

The procession of enquiries continued with Charlie calling round. Someone she welcomed speaking to at last.

'It's good to see you, Charlie.'

'Have you heard from him?'

'No, but we found this posted through the letterbox.' It was a plain envelope with fifteen shillings inside. 'He's obviously working somewhere.'

'But where is he staying, Charlie? Has he left me? Is he ever coming back?'

'Course he's coming back. He's just lying low for a bit, I reckon.'

'The police were keen to see him. And two hooligans came round looking for him and threatening him as well. It's that gang isn't it?'

'I can't see Smith doing anything so daft as to get caught up in something like that.'

'I'm not that naïve, Charlie. There's something you're not telling me. What have you heard?'

'It's probably nothing, you mustn't worry. It'll be some mix up. You're all right for money now though, yeah? Well, if you need any help just come and see me.'

She tried to get into a routine of getting up, doing jobs, doing work for the WSPU, going to church. She caught up on lots of little jobs around the house, but, with only herself to make it untidy and only her laundry to do, she soon found herself idle and having to go out for walks to avoid spending too much time with her worries and frustration. She took in laundry to make Mondays more useful, but she still lacked a purpose, felt she was existing, not living. Life had to have a goal, had to achieve something, or it was a sin against creation.

She felt her prayers were answered when a letter arrived from Mrs Channing.

My dearest Elsie,

I hope you do not mind my having inquired as to your address in order that I might write to you. I do not wish to presume, so forgive any intrusion and please feel no obligation towards me; however, I heard recently, through my charitable work for the Cripple Aid Society, of a position which made me think of you. There is a little girl, very capable in some respects, who is not allowed to go to school because of her misfortune. It seems most unfair, when she would benefit so much from an education. Her mother has tried her best to teach her but has other children to look after. Through supporters of the society we have a small fund to pay for her teaching at home. I thought this might be of interest to you: a teacher who has been prevented from teaching, and a little girl who has been prevented from going to school! If you are interested, please call round and I should be delighted to furnish you with details.

Sincerely yours,

Winifred.

Elsie felt like putting on her boots and rushing round straight away, but a sense of decency kept her fidgeting around the house until after dinner.

Mabel Jackson was a charming little girl of eight years old. Life had taught her to be patient and understanding and the importance of being loved – and she was: by her brothers and sisters, even though she could never keep up with them or join in their games. She could get along slowly on crutches. But she helped by keeping the younger ones entertained by playing with them on the floor, or by reading to them. To them she was just Mabel, with wobbly legs and a funny way of talking. That's just the way it was – no less loved than a cloth bear with a button for an eye, and a leg that had been sewn back on wonky.

However, once outside her own house, people treated her as mentally deficient because of her slurring, and a nuisance because of her ungainliness.

Elsie, too, underestimated Mabel when she first met her. She pitched her lessons too low, and Mabel was so thrilled to have a teacher that she didn't want to appear in any way ungrateful. However, Elsie soon started to see there was nothing wrong with Mabel's mind, that she was in fact bright and rebellious of thought in a way that excited Elsie. It became a challenge to see how far that mind could be set free from the constraints of the body it was in. Her handwriting was awful, but only because her fingers wouldn't quite do what her brain willed, not from lack of attention, effort or idleness as she had seen in certain children before.

Elsie borrowed books from the free library and got hold of illustrated magazines. They read aloud and Elsie patiently worked on Mabel's speech to improve it. She started with the Tales of Mother Goose, but soon they were exploring desert islands, the jungles of India, chasing white rabbits and having adventures with pirates and crocodiles.

The early summer days were warm. Too warm for many in the city. For those who shovelled coal into furnaces, for those who rolled white hot lumps of metal into red hot plates or bars, for those who heaved and turned the metal with tongs as forge hammers beat out Vulcan's tune.

The air was dusty and dry, the streets filthy with soot and the crushing by wheels of dried lumps of horse dung; people stinking of sweat, sewers and drains emanating foul stenches of fermenting contents. Small children shed clothes and conventions and ran through the courtyards with paper water bombs. Queues snaked round the corner outside Sutherland Road baths as people looked for a much sought after respite.

Somewhere far away, a foreign prince, or duke or something, was shot when he was going for a drive through streets where what he stood for wasn't universally appreciated. What do you expect from such people? Hotheads! A shocking event that grabbed attention momentarily, before thoughts turned again to whether a few days at the coast was affordable – Mablethorpe or even the south coast?

Two days into July, as people headed home from work, dark clouds gathered, sparked and rumbled. Hail rattled down onto vehicles and hats, sending people running for cover. Then rain fell to cleanse the streets and pavements, lashing roofs and umbrellas, along gutters and down hills and gullies in torrents, lifting drain covers in spouts four or five feet high.

Elsie got by without Smith. Money arrived from him via Charlie and envelopes passed hand-to-hand by men who worked on the railways. He was over Chesterfield way from what Charlie had found out.

'Is there still no message from him?' Elsie said as she poured some tea on one of his visits.

'Nothing. He must be safe and well though.' He shook his head. 'It's a strange business. Keep your chin up.'

'Oh. I am doing – as best I can. This bit of teaching helps.'

'Look, me and Grace are off to the pictures tomorrow night – you should come.'

'Thank you, but I'd rather not be a gooseberry.'

'Don't be daft.'

The smell of fish pie filled the kitchen one Monday teatime – she'd done enough to last a couple of days and had some runner beans to go with it. She put the pie onto the table and went into the pantry under the stairs for a new bottle of relish. When she came back into the living room she nearly dropped it. Smith was standing there in his work clothes, just like he used to.

'Best get another plate out, lass,' he said. 'I'm not a ghost. See.' He stamped his feet. 'Tha looks like tha's seen one though. Going to give us a kiss?'

She stepped up to him and he pulled her in and kissed her passionately.

'Put me down. You're covered in muck. Get yourself washed and changed and I'll get you some tea.'

He went into the scullery and after a couple of minutes of splashing at the tap shouted: 'Gerrus a towel with tha?'

She fetched one from upstairs. He was standing in the scullery, hair dripping wet, in just his shirt: long shirts tails hanging down; not hanging straight down, though: there was a bulge at the front.

'Ta, love.'

She ignored him. 'Shall I take your bag through. Are you stopping?' she said, with a hint of sarcasm in her voice.

'No, leave it. I'll sort it later. And I am stopping. Tha don't get rid on us that easy.'

They sat down to eat. 'I've no beer in.'

'I'll go round to our Charlie's in a bit. Tea'll do.'

'So where have you been? Have you been keeping all right?'

'Not bad. At mother's mostly.'

'Why didn't you write or let me know?'

'It were best not. I upset someone — it were summat or nowt really, but if they'd known where I was... And if tha didn't know tha didn't have to lie, and there was nowt to wheedle out of thi.'

'I wouldn't– . You should know that. Credit me with a bit of nous.' He was mixing mash and beans to stick to his fork. 'I think they might have been here once. Right after you left. Two big ugly fellas.'

'That's why — best that they thought I'd gone for good, and far away.'

'But is it safe now? The police said there was a court case?'

'Yeah, it's not a problem. The law got its man — I didn't have to snitch on anyone. So all sorted. Back to normal.' He returned to his food.

He would be all over her when he got back from the pub. Back to normal.

*

Something was in the air — like before a thunderstorm, when you sense a change in the air, your skin tingles, and fine unpinned hair on the head of a girl rises upwards, and the birds are stilled and stop singing. In pubs and workplaces there was talk of the Triple Alliance –

not of Germany, Austria and Italy but the railwaymen, the miners and the transport workers – all working together. This would be an irresistible force to change the ownership of wealth, to create an annual universal franchise, to take power out of the hands of the corrupt and greedy and give it to everyone. There was talk, and fear, of revolution. Fear of people with no respect for property, fear of a mob intent on theft, fear especially of war in Ireland where a through-the-looking-glass struggle for power was being played out. Fights broke out in the pubs around Scotland Street and the Crofts as rival factions played out a proxy war.

All across Europe the old order felt under pressure, so to avoid turning inwards they were taking the age-old stance of looking for people not like themselves to blame. The enemy without to contain the enemy within.

When educated Sheffielders read of Vienna issuing Belgrade with an ultimatum it was a long way off. But somehow within a week Germany had declared war on Russia, and then France, and was invading neutral Luxembourg, probably on the way to Paris. Europe a-blaze. But Europe is not us they said. We're not duty-bound to intervene. We must work for peace.

Five days later and those voices were heard no more. No one wanted to hear questions and doubts. To try to understand, or even discuss why, wasn't patriotic, as men queued up to sign and a great mobilisation got underway. They were not angry at those who claimed a right to rule, no questioning of the rights of aristocrats to send the working classes and peasants into the furnace for the sake of their pride and vanity. No. They were not angry – they waved the flag and cheered and sang their songs. True Britons – by Jingo! We've got the ships, we've got the men, we've got the money too.

Smith answered the call to reservists, polished his boots, Brasso-ed his buttons and cap badge and left. Elsie did not join the crowds outside Hillsborough barracks when the Foresters mobilised, she did not sing Rule Britannia or join the throng to cheer anybody who appeared in uniform. She did not wave from the station as the brigade headed off to war. Instead she watched him cross the yard and go down the passage.

He had kissed her on the cheek and said: 'I'll see thi, then. I'll miss thi. But we'll be back for Christmas. See if we're not.'

'No. No, you won't.'

'What? Why won't we? We'll send them scuttling back where they came from – everybody says.'

She went inside and closed the door. Bloody Christmas! That's not what she meant. She meant he wouldn't miss her. Or only for one thing. Even then she wasn't sure he didn't get that elsewhere.

She sat down and wept. She wept for the girl who had let herself be wooed and flattered and who had been carried into this house that damp autumn evening, nearly four years ago, so full of hope. And she felt sick with dread. This was not another Empire Day pageant at Bramall Lane. Could they not see that? She could not bear to see the faces of those men, those boys. How many would return?

CHAPTER THIRTEEN

At last Smith was able to get his head down. The incessant babble had stopped as the fading light imposed the sort of calm that the sergeant major had long since given up on.

As the sounds of the brass bands had faded away across the Solent and the swell of the ocean grew, the day that had started with an orderly embarkation descended into chaos as men, whose feet were more used to contact with solid muck, tripped over comrades and equipment to head for the side to relieve themselves of their rebellious breakfasts. The SS Georgian was no Cunard or White Star liner: but for the absence of cow pats you would have had it down as cattle transport rather than a conveyance for the Empire's finest. There was no prospect of wandering about on deck to stretch your legs or relieve the boredom, you stopped where you had landed on the deck you were assigned to and tried your damnedest to protect your territory so that you had space to stretch out or curl round your pack.

The swell worsened as the steamer emerged into the Atlantic.

'We should've just hopped over the Channel, never mind bloody Fritz – they'd soon of legged it when we faced 'em.'

'Don't be daft, if they make it to the ports first, we'd be sitting ducks.'

'I'm none so sure as our generals know what's going on really. First, they send us up to Edinburgh for fear of invasion, then change their mind, then we're off to *Boo-loin* but they bottle out of it.'

'Shut thi rattle. Tha turn'll come soon enough.'

Smith managed to hold down some bread and water despite the smell of the sea, fags, vomit, oil and grease, and won a bit on games of pontoon.

They had reached shore at St Nazaire and joined the queue of boats waiting to unload their cargo of men, trucks, wagons and horses.

The movement of the boat was gentle now they were enclosed in the bay; clouds rolled overhead drawing a veil over the occasional star that tried to look down.

Charlie had made use of Smith's thigh as a pillow and his head had already gone heavy. That was the experience of the old soldier for you

– waste no time when the opportunity for sleep arises. It was like a game of spillikins: lying next to him, the other way up, resting his head on Charlie, was Curly, or "the vicar" if you wanted to wind him up since he was a fiercely non-conformist man. Ginger's head was nearby – with the woolly hat he wore at night: the one his mother had knitted him. Resting on Ginger was Smiler, so called because of his appalling teeth, like headstones – and their absence – in an abandoned graveyard; but still he boasted more girlfriends than anyone else. No matter what, you couldn't help but like Smiler. Tucked up next to Smiler with his arm over him was Murphy, or Spud – no relation to Mooney's mate – but all that clan ended up being called that, east of the Ards Peninsular.

'You asleep yet, Smith?'

'Fuckin' 'ell. I was till you woke us, Ginger.'

'Sorry.'

'What's up?'

'Nowt...'

'Well, fuck off to sleep then.'

'Right you are.'

'Smith...'

'What?'

'Sorry for waking you.'

Smith didn't want to listen to any more doubts or anxieties, hopes or fears. He just wanted to get on with it, not think, not look back, not look forward. There was no point in dwelling on it; you couldn't do anything about it. What will happen will happen. He didn't like all that layering of emotions and scheming on top; old men piling on their safe version of patriotism, their opinions parroted from their newspapers; women adding their sense of loss, or unsatisfied desires, their discontents with husbands and their hopes of better things from their sons; brothers and sisters, their rivalries and jealousies; politicians, their ambitions and prejudices, their greed and their arrogance; the dukes and earls with their heritage turning this into a rally to the flag, to wrest back control from the industrial masses, to reassert the hereditary principles; the Irish, seeing this as an opportunity to strike while attention was elsewhere, to align with dark forces, and bugger the consequences for everybody else. Never mind what the hell the Hun thought they would achieve! No. It was time to get it over with as quickly as possible.

Some very welcome sausages were brought up on deck in the morning while they waited for a berth at St Nazaire.

'When I signed up, I'd never imagined that most of a soldier's life was spent waiting, sat on his arse,' said Murphy, standing up and stretching, his eyes closed towards the rising sun.

'Good job yours is such a fat 'un then, in't it?'

In daylight, the size of the operation became apparent. They were just one of many ships in the harbour or unloading at the quayside. A thousand of the Foresters plus a couple of thousands of Yorkies and the Durhams making up the 18th.

A few locals had gathered to stare at this invasion of their little town as they made their way down the precarious looking walkway that had been manoeuvred to the ship's side. Someone tried to set it bouncing.

'You are now guests in someone else's country – start behaving like soldiers or you'll regret it very quickly.' It was Captain Parkinson. You didn't mess with Parky.

They assembled in the vast square next to the quayside and took their orders to march to the encampment just outside the town. A letter was read out by Lieutenant Colonel Crofton-Atkins from Field Marshal Lord Kitchener in which they were exhorted to show themselves in the character of a true British soldier, to be courteous, considerate and kind, because they were sure to meet with a welcome in France and Belgium and their conduct must justify that welcome and that trust. '… so keep constantly on your guard against any excesses. In this new experience you may find temptation in both wine and women–'

'I sincerely hope so,' some nearby ventriloquist quipped.

'– you must entirely resist both temptations, and while treating all women with courtesy, you should avoid any intimacy. Do your duty bravely. Fear God. Honour the King.'

As they marched through the town the locals gathered to cheer.

'Let's give 'em a song then, boys.'

A round of *God Save the King* struck up, followed by *Tipperary*. Some women held out flowers, others postcards of the town with stamps ready stuck on, or little paper parcels of biscuits. In return they got a smile, a wave, a "Vive la France," a blown kiss or a hastily pulled off button or badge. As they headed out of town, others were coming back in to meet their train.

The camp was huge – thousands of men sprawled over all the fields surrounding the town, outnumbering the townsfolk five to one, being shipped in by the thousands and rushed cross-country packed into trains.

Their first priority was to get water boiled in the dixies for a mash which the French biscuits were ideal for dunking in.

'This war malarkey is not so bad after all,' said Smiler.

'That's it – just a big camping holiday, ain't it, Smiler? Anyone ever told thi what a first-class blubberhead tha can be?' said Charlie.

'Oh, yes. Quite frequently. That's exactly what Minnie said when she kissed me goodbye. And what Edith said when she pushed me out of her nice warm bed.' The full glory of his teeth was put on show.

The camp was a source of great attraction for the Nazairians – French tobacco was swapped for Woodbines, *gallettes au beurre* for shortbread. Unfortunately, not many of the locals had read Kitchener's letter and at tea-time produced bottles of *cidre bouché* or even local white wine. A football was soon pulled out and a couple of teams involving local children were arranged.

After a night stretched out under a warm Breton sky, they fell in and marched back to town singing: *Where are the boys of the old Brigade, Who fought with us side by side? Shoulder to shoulder, and blade by blade, Fought till they fell and died! Who so ready and undismayed? Who so merry and true? Where are the boys of the old Brigade? Where are the lads we knew?*

They passed shops with their awnings down, with smells enough to make you weep wafting out from cafes and boulangeries. Spontaneous choruses of *Allons! Enfants de la patrie, le jour de gloire est arrivé* broke out from onlookers as they marched with smiles over the cobbled streets to the Place de la Gare.

The first stop came at midday at Châteaubriant where a treat awaited them. The local women had set up trestles at the station loaded with long French loaves, cheese and tomatoes. They gave postcards to *les Tommies* on which to write a few words home; they, in turn, mostly remembered Kitchener's words and smiled and offered a few "mercy bowcoups." Smith took one from a shy young girl – it had a picture of the chateau on the front with the stamp stuck sideways on the picture at the top. He scribbled a few words. It struck him how French the name "Danville" looked.

As the train rattled and groaned through the French countryside, those who had windows to look out of saw orchards of cider apples, brown and white dappled cows grazing in gently sloping meadows, willows dipping down to lazy rivers and spires of great cathedrals. Those sat on the straw of cattle trucks saw rifle butts, khaki backsides, or flashes of light and green through the slats of the truck, light enough to play cards from if you were sat towards the edge.

Of Paris they saw very little but railway sidings to the south where they rested and were treated to bully beef and potato stew. That night those Parisians fortunate enough to live near the railway would have heard an unusual refrain drifting over the rooftops and through the shutters of open windows, in a language they could not make out, *certainment pas l'anglais ça*: several hundred Yorkshire voices from Redcar to Rotherham, from Scarborough to Silsden, combining in singing Ilkley Moor.

The city was no longer under immediate threat of invasion from the Germans. They had been pushed back: it was said by reserves rushed to the front in Paris taxis. The Foresters were to join that push across country. The German master plan had failed, and perhaps it *would* all be over by Christmas.

The Foresters detrained at Coulommiers the next day, and, having unloaded their equipment, began the march to the front. They were billeted at Doue – some in barns, some in the church, others in their bivouacs.

'Get some kip, boys,' the sergeant said. 'The hard graft really starts tomorrow.'

He was not wrong. From six in the morning until nine at night they marched in a long line, half a mile front to back: men, horses, wagons and medical officers' carts. The decent weather they had been enjoying, having decided it was no longer befitting of the times, had departed, leaving the field to near constant, heavy rain that soon had them longing for home. Any illusion of a late summer holiday was over. From Chateau Thierry they set off again for another day's march, more rain coming down.

'I can't get any wetter, so it don't really matter any more,' said Ginger.

'Yeah. Thi mother would gi' the Colonel a reight good telling off, if she knew,' said Smiler.

'Aye. She would an' all.'

At Chacrise they were given a day's rest before an early start for the Aisne, to where the enemy had retreated and taken a stand.

As they advanced and the daylight grew, they saw more signs of what had gone before: a beautiful orchestrion in ruins having been dragged out of a hotel and used as the centre piece of some bacchanalian fete, surrounded by tables draped with now scorched tablecloths. Farther on, piles of bottles and an occasional, still smouldering building.

'Look at what those bastards have done: set fire to it for fun.'

'When the wine was looted, no doubt.'

They stopped at Dhuizel, and fell in, where they were addressed by General Sir Horace Smith-Dorien, a Forester, but also commander of the II Corps that had been involved in beating back the Germans from the Marne. Their division was to be divided, with the brigade joining the 1st Corps under General Haig. They were on the move to the front, to provide much needed reinforcement for those who had fought at Mons and marched in retreat: a distance twice as far as that they had just covered. They were to relieve the first battalion of the Black Watch at a place called Vendresse.

As they approached the Aisne they heard their first sounds of battle – big guns firing, like the rumble of thunder in the distance, getting louder as they advanced.

Someone started a refrain that was picked up by others and spread to the whole column as they marched: *It's the Soldiers of the King, my lads, Who've been my lads, Who're seen my lads, In the fight for England's glory, lads, When we've had to show them what we mean: And when we say we've always won, And when they ask us how it's done, We'll proudly point to ev'ry one of England's soldiers of the King!*

They crossed the river on a pontoon bridge standing next to the bombed remains of the old bridge, and began their ascent up the side of the valley towards God only knew what.

They made their way through a wood and out the other side when a buzzing sound grew louder and louder – they drew in their necks like tortoises. There was a flash and then the air was shattered and a cloud of earth, vegetation and thick black smoke rose across to their left. Trees uprooted and shattered. They staggered as the ground shook, and their eardrums were assaulted.

'Stop worrying, lads. It won't hurt you – not now anyway.'

'Must be a Wednesday striker, couldn't hit the back of the net from ten yards, that one!'

They practically had to crawl into the trenches. As they did so the Black Watch headed out.

'Nice afternoon for it, Jock.'

'Yous'll have to keep your heeds down, boys.'

'You've done a shit job here, fellas. Call this a trench! It's more like summat I dig for mi tatties.'

'Well, aye, big fella. Let's see you do better, eh? Be seein' you, boys.'

They spent the rest of the day trying to tidy the trench up. The reason it was so shallow became clear: the ground was solid – a mass of rocks that, even if they could be shifted at all, took a lot of working out with a trenching tool.

Ginger stood up to stretch. 'My fucking back's...' He didn't finish his sentence. Smith looked up to see him staring ahead as if he'd just spotted something in the sky. Then he fell forwards, face down in the muck with blood pouring from the back of his head.

'That's why you keep your bloody heads down fellas!'

'Fucking hell, get him out of here!'

Smith helped carry him back down the trench to where stretcher-bearers took over.

Before night fell they were relieved by the Gloucesters and headed to the reserve position at a village called Troyon. Smith had seen the first of his mates go down, killed instantly. 'The sneaky bloody Hun,' he muttered to himself. This was now personal.

He was already wide awake when the others started to stir around him. His first waking thought was of how much blood had poured from the back of Ginger's neck.

As they washed and shaved from water drawn from the well at the farmhouse, sounds of rifles echoed round the valley, coming from the ridge above. It was cold and the sky was an unrelieving grey. Rain occasionally turned to sleet.

Not much was said between them, one or two trying to make light of it, but then the sounds of artillery silenced them as they imagined what was happening beyond the trees.

They were placed on standby: 'The Boche are trying to retake our positions. The rest of the battalion are resisting – we may be needed to provide support. Stay ready.'

The wait dragged out.

'What are we waiting for? We should just go and stick it to 'em, not sit here.'

'There's not room for us all up there in those trenches. We'll get to go when needed.'

They sat and played cards or poker dice, trying to block out the sounds as if it were no more than idle chatter at the table while trying to read the newspaper.

The call came late morning. The West Yorkshires were coming under heavy attack from the right flank where the Germans had occupied trenches they had taken by driving out Moroccans who had fought back several times to no avail against the better equipped foe.

The heavens opened as they approached the line and it was clear that a serious situation confronted them. Casualties were being stretchered away – rainwater running pink down the road leading to the ridge. The Germans had driven the West Yorkshires out, inflicting heavy losses firing along the line of the trench, and capturing many more. They were now threatening to do the same to the Durhams who were next along the line. The remaining company of Yorkshires were regrouping.

Smith's company were given orders to move across country along the side of the hill to a position by a small copse from where they could advance to retake the trench. They thought the trees would provide cover but a machine gun started up and bullets seemed to ricochet in all directions – like the trees themselves were attacking them. Ahead Smith saw Lieutenant Milner go down, his body jerking in a macabre dance of death as it was riddled by bullets.

He squatted down behind a tree and steadied his rifle, fired off seven shots and dropped another five into the magazine.

'We move on towards that hedge, men.'

Smith looked round – D company were moving around to the right hand side. He reloaded again and on the signal ran across the boggy field. A spray of bullets took the tops off all the ragwort and nettles away to the right, moving in his direction. He dived into a small dip just as the spray whistled over his head, then he was up again, the air alive all around him. Someone who was running beside him was suddenly no longer there, and he flung himself at the foot of the hedge next to Charlie.

'Parky's gone down,' Charlie said.

'Dead?'

The answer had to wait for a pause as they reloaded. 'No, just his leg. Never heard someone so posh use pit language like that. "Fucking Kaiser! Bastard Germans! Take no prisoners! Shoot the lot of the fucking devils." '

'What now?'

'Wilky's over there – watch for his signal.'

As D company came round the side, Smith and the remnants of A moved forward, firing on the German positions.

The Germans retreated back over the ridge.

'They didn't fancy six inches of Sheffield steel!'

The Foresters cleaned up the trench, finished off a few lamed Hun and pushed the dead ones over the top, covering the faces of their own. They steadied themselves for the counter-attack. The Durhams and the East Yorkshires were driven back into the trenches away to the left by machine gun fire and shrapnel.

A shell went screeching overhead.

'What the fuck!' They all dropped. 'Where the bloody hell is our own artillery? We're just sat here while they bomb the shit out of us from a mile away.'

As the ground shook, a thick cloud of black smoke rose over towards the hedge.

'I had a girlfriend who made that sound,' said Smiler.

'What sound?'

'That shrieking.'

'What you mean…?'

'When I was showing her a good time.'

'Mucky bugger!'

'What was she called?'

'Dolly.'

'We're under attack from Delirious Dolly, boys!'

For the rest of the next two days they held their position – trying to make themselves as comfortable as they could in their muddy little ditch, trying to keep their heads down, alert at every little sound, praying that Delirious Dolly wouldn't find them. Then they moved back to reserve at Troyon again to regroup. They had lost forty-eight men including four officers, and there must have been three times that wounded. The Germans tried several more times to pierce the line over the next few days, though Smith only ever heard the fighting going on away to the left or right. His days at the front were spent working in shifts, hacking at unyielding rocks in the trench bottom, widening and deepening it and increasing the parapet height, or on sentry duty.

Night Patrols were sent out to see what could be learnt of the German positions. Over the top of the hill was an old sugar factory which gave a good vantage point over the plateau and valley. They were well ensconced in there and it was hard to see how it could be attacked.

When they next pulled back to the reserve position they were told to get ready to move on. They headed east across country, coming under shell fire soon after they set off, adding seven to their tally of wounded. They were billeted in the relative safety of a village, and, as they waited in reserve, new officers were appointed to replace their losses.

One afternoon they were told to get their heads down and sleep if they could, but rest if they could not, because they were moving out.

'Where to Sarge?'

'I'm sorry Private Stainforth, did General Haig forget to consult you? Then I suggest you get one of your subordinates to send him a wire. Now piss off and do as you're told.'

'Yes, Sergeant.'

They set off after nightfall heading west and it soon became clear to anyone with their wits about them that they were not alone. They passed other battalions grouped in fields taking a break, or saw other roads running parallel, thronged with men and vehicles. And their billets along the route showed signs of recent occupation. The BEF was on the move. They were told to stay under cover during the day to avoid being spotted by German aeroplanes. The rumour was that they were leaving what was now a stalemate along the Aisne to the French and heading back towards the North. Some said closer to supply lines, others to defend the Channel, and others thought there was a plan to try to get round the German lines to the north or reinforce the Belgian border. For two whole nights they marched by moonlight along country lanes and through forests until they reached Compiègne on the ninth of the month. En route, the commanding officer Crofton-Atkins fell by the wayside, as did one of the majors. Taken to hospital it was said, though there seemed nothing much wrong with them.

'They just can't hack modern soldiering.'

'Not like in my day, old sport. Hand to hand combat with swords. All very gentlemanly, eh what?'

'None of this splattering a man with one of Dolly's presents so there's nothing left to bury.'

At Compiègne the battalion received reinforcements to replace those they'd lost.

'What's our new Captain like?' Charlie asked one of the long service men.

'Wilkin? – old "Wally-Willy"? He's all right. Served in South Africa under him. Decent. Fair.'

'And about bloody time they've got the same kit as us now. Might have well as carried bloody big signs over their heads saying "shoot me first." '

CHAPTER FOURTEEN

Elsie struggled to make ends meet. She had applied for her twelve and six Separation Allowance and queued for hours to register with the Soldiers and Sailors Families Association, but that did not result in any money, only being sent away and told that someone would pay her a visit.

'You would think it was coming out of their own pockets, wouldn't you?' the women complained.

'I was in the queue yesterday afternoon as well and got nowhere. They sent us back home when they shut up shop and said we'd have to come back.'

'My Bert left us ten shillings. He's gone off to fight for his King and Country and they grudge me money I'm entitled to. I've never wanted no charity, but now that ten shillings has run out what am I to do? How am I to feed the kids?'

Elsie felt grateful for the few shillings she got from teaching Mabel, and for the small amount of money she had saved from before she got married. She waited for a visit from the SSFA but none came. Fortunately the initial shopping basket madness at the start of the war had died down – people had rushed to the shops to buy flour and sugar. Women saw queues and had to join them – what would they do if the shops ran out? If everyone in the queue got served the shelves would be empty.

Sugar, even the cheap stuff, went up to five pence a pound; flour went up to two shillings a stone. Sensible shopkeepers refused to sell customers more than the normal weekly amount, and only sold to their regulars.

Wherever you went, whomever you talked to, there was only one thing on people's minds – the war. Fear overwhelmed the credulous – they believed the Germans would sail up the Humber any day. Others sought to combat their fear with knowledge, and to master every tiny fact of military tactics – cutting out the maps from the newspaper and devouring every detail, marking German advances and taking reassurance from reports of their having been checked and repulsed. They nodded sagely when the town of Liège was mentioned, as if it had been as much within their knowledge as Doncaster or Bradford.

'I reckoned on Leedge being well defended,' they'd say.

'Aye. Happen the Kaiser's been sent scuttling.'

Then they fell back on their unwavering conviction that, if needed, a hundred thousand strong British Expeditionary Force could repulse the million Germans.

Old Birkinshaw the barber, who lived over the road, and who had spent time in Hamburg and spoke a bit of the language, regularly held forth and was regarded as a bit of an authority on all such matters.

Soon everyone spoke of Heligoland as if it were somewhere they were familiar with from annual holidays, and of the superiority of Grand Fleet over the High Seas Fleet as they would of the Wednesday drawing Grimsby in the first round of the Cup.

Elsie was drawn towards the newspapers like a moth circling an oil lamp. She didn't just read about so many troops in Belgium in the abstract, she felt the pain of those who loved them, of the mothers who had given birth to sons whose beautiful bodies lay ripped apart. Each soldier to her was a loving father or husband whose families would first grieve and then go hungry. Then she read of British soldiers fighting. They became boys she knew from school with limbs blown off and lying in agony. She tried to ignore the news but couldn't stay away. Of Smith she knew nothing. He could even be dead already, one of the five or six thousand that the newspapers were already reporting as dead. The *Guardian* said it had it on good authority that the Sherwood Foresters were already in Belgium.

Five or six thousand! But they were being told not to worry because Germans were being slaughtered in greater numbers and their morale was so low that they were in open revolt. But then elsewhere it said that Germans were bayoneting the wounded to save the trouble of taking prisoners and cutting off fingers and hands of Red Cross men.

Then a postcard arrived from Cambridge saying that they had been up and down the country and were now getting ready to leave. They were all bored and itching to get at the Hun. So not dead yet, after all.

Many people took comfort in the mantra: "business as usual," mouthing it as they hurried along like so many white rabbits checking their pocket watches. "Leave it to Kitchener" they said – Kitchener, the man you heard of everywhere, wanting to take half a million boys to throw into the war. And they queued up for hours to answer the call to teach those blasted Germans a lesson. They leaned against walls sharing cigarettes, picnicked on the pavements, waited till the door closed and they were turned away, then came back the next day undaunted.

Everywhere the flags of the allies fluttered over doors and were draped over shop displays to vie with each other for patriotic customers as if by the very act of purchasing a bit of leg meat from Sturgess's or a potato from Goddards you were hastening the defeat of the mad Kaiser.

Elsie tried to numb herself from it all, telling herself it would somehow all work out for the best. That the Germans would be taught a lesson and that something good would emerge from it – that people would be kinder to each other, would realise that no one really wins in a war. Business as usual; what else was there?

She sought out company – the women of the WSPU used their skills to organise knitting circles, where they sat and talked and drank tea and turned balls of khaki coloured wool into cardigans, knitted socks or fashioned sleeping helmets out of flannelette for the troops. When men go to war, women knit. They organised collections of food and clothing for women whose husbands had enlisted and who hadn't yet received their Separation Allowance. She even welcomed Grace into her home when she came round to see if Elsie had news that she did not, about Charlie and Smith. They had almost identical postcards from a place called Chateaubriant.

Elsie's read:

"Arrived in France. Everyone pleased to see us. Good bread and coffee. Heading out West now,

Smith"

It was postmarked the 14th of September.

Charlie's card did not say much more; though it started: "To My Dearest Wife" and ended: "Give the children a kiss from their Daddy. I'll be back before you know it,

Your loving husband,"

***

The Second Battalion of the Sherwood Foresters got onto trains heading north through Amiens to Abbeville and Calais, where they would have been a day's march from Blighty, if the Channel could only have parted like the Red Sea. Then they were on to St Omer where they detrained and were billeted at Arques just outside the town. A short march from there took them to where a couple of hundred lorries awaited, for the luxury of being freighted to Hazebrouck, the officers heading up the convoy in buses. All the BEF seemed to be converging on the town, along with quite a few ambulances coming the other way.

They disgorged from the lorries into a large, cobbled square surrounded by old buildings with a bandstand in the middle.

'Hey lads! Remind thi of Paradise Square?'

'Gi' o'er will tha.'

They sat in the square and ate bread and cheese, and a barrel of apples had been obtained from somewhere. Then they headed to their billets scattered around the town: churches, and various Communal buildings.

The day broke wet and grey and didn't let up as they fell in and started marching towards Vieux Berquin. There were sounds of fighting up ahead where some Germans had dug in. While the Foresters were held in reserve, they were entertained by an aerial fight between two aeroplanes wheeling across the sky. Smith fancied his chances with his Lee Enfield, but was told to stop being a silly beggar.

'That's the future though, ain't it? Ruling the skies like we rule the seas. No mud and shit up there.'

The Durhams had taken a heavy hit – quite a few ambulances went by as they marched forward again. The church in the town had been badly damaged by shelling. As they made their way towards Steenwerck, a couple of miles from the Belgian border, which was to be the HQ of the 6th division, they passed groups of French and Belgians with nothing but small bundles of possessions on their backs, trundling a cart if they were lucky, a wheeled barrow or baby's perambulator. They looked tired, bent and dishevelled as they trudged away from their lives. Small bleary-eyed children stumbling along holding hands with big sisters, or hugging a wretched looking doll.

'Poor buggers. Look at 'em. That old lass has got to be older than my nan – and she lost her eldest in the Crimean war she's that bloody ancient.'

'Yeah. Poor buggers. Vive la France! Vive la Belgium!'

The result was not like at St Nazaire: only a glance sideways and a sign of the cross over her chest.

At Steenwerck, Smith and his company set to, digging in at the edge of the town and putting up trip-wires, barricading roads and preparing buildings for defence. Now, their billets were abandoned houses that they carefully broke into, in the perhaps vain hope that there would some day soon be something for the owners to return to.

After lunch on the second day they were given orders to head to Sailly-sur-la-Lys, where they were to hold the bridgehead for the engineers to replace a bridge that the Germans had blown up.

They set off at about seven and they soon lost all sense of direction in the pitch dark. They had to keep a steady pace because it only took one to fall out of step and everyone was cursing as they tripped and bumped into the man in front.

'If I'd've been carrying a pint, tha'd've been a dead man, Smith.'

'It weren't me, it were that lummox, Spud, in front.'

To help them they met up with a French guide, a cavalryman who had been amongst those driven out by the Germans earlier that day.

' 'ere, does tha reckon this Froggy knows what he's doing? I'm sure we've marched past here before.'

'I can't see nowt. I'm not got bat ancestors like thi. Could be going round in circles for all I know.'

The greatest excitement came as they were heading down the bank to set up position. There was a stifled yelp followed by a loud splash, and a commotion.

'What the bloody hell's going on? Is it a Jerry?'

'No. It's the captain – he's gone arse over tit into the water.'

'Is he all right?'

'I can't make it out. Think someone's gone in to drag him out.'

'He could've sunk with the weight of all that kit. "To Mrs Wilkin. Regret to inform you that: Captain W Wilkin died whilst heroically paddling in a river. Lord Kitchener expresses his sympathy." '

They settled into position whilst the engineers went about filling the gaps in the bridge with farm wagons and spanning them with ladders. They then crossed gingerly in the middle of the night.

'Careful where you step lads, I've heard a rumour that the water's quite deep in places.'

'Aye and it's that wet sort of water, if the Captain's owt to go by.'

There was not much German resistance at Sailly – the church was set on fire by the Germans and some rifle fire came from the houses over the river, but they were soon dealt with or decided to flee. The Foresters took up position south of the town to defend the crossing, were joined by the rest of the Brigade, and pushed on towards where the Germans were said to be entrenched west of Lille. They were to join with the others of the 6th division and the 4th, forming the IIIrd Corps under General Pulteney, spreading out to hold a line twelve miles long. They slept well that night, having had no sleep the night before and only a few hours the night before that.

On the Sunday evening the Foresters moved to the village of Ennetières to relieve the Durhams who had spent the day making the deserted village defensible. As the last of daylight faded, Smith and his company moved quickly into the shallow trenches dug into fields on the far side of the town, stumbling and cursing as they tried to make their way over unfamiliar ground.

'Let's set to then, fellas, and see if we can't turn this into a palace by morning.'

Their arrival was greeted by the German line a few hundred yards away as bullets whistled overhead and thudded into the low parapet above where they stooped. This was added to by machine gun fire and the occasional shell bursting. More than once that night they had to rebuild the parapet and clear the damaged areas of silenced or moaning casualties. All they could do was hope and pray. That initial shock of seeing Ginger's life depart so suddenly had been displaced by other more horrific images, each time the brain adjusting to a new starker reality, in a permanent state of numbness. Taking cover when a shell whistled in became an instinct – to flatten oneself to the Mother Earth, to cling to her, to press one's limbs into her folds as the roar and thunder raged across one's back, assailing the ears, as clods rained down and the storm of fragments of metal flew. Then it passes and he wipes mud from his eyes, flexes his limbs, closes his fists, realises they are still there, that any pain is only bruising, gets up from the earth's bosom and carries on.

The Germans decided it was time to sleep when the early hours of the morning arrived, and shelling stopped. Smith snatched a couple of hours of sleep sitting on the floor of the trench while others took their shift. As day broke and they dipped into the dixies that were brought along the trench, they started to realise how exposed they were. The village jutted out towards the enemy line with them stuck out furthest on the eastern side of the salient, 'A' company on the southern end and 'C' round to the north, with a machine gun section up near the road to the left. The day was spent digging and repairing the trenches – a much easier task by daylight, again being sniped at and shelled, with the occasional response from an eighteen pounder that had set up on a hill on the other side of the village.

They were not permitted much by way of sleep as shell fire continued throughout the night.

The next day dawned slowly – the light being held back by a dense, cold, barely falling drizzle hanging over all the fields in the still air. They came under heavy fire seemingly from north, east and south, hitting their position and the village where the battalion headquarters had been set up. The stretcher-bearers were kept busy; all the rest of them could do was sit tight.

'Target practice, boys! They're coming.'

They steadied themselves against the parapet. The grey figures of the German infantry seemed to be materialising from the fog itself at a distance of about seven hundred yards.

'What's thi accuracy at half a mile like, Smith?'

'Fifty-fifty maybe?'

'I'll give thi three to two odds on each Fritz then.'

'Let 'em have it!'

'This is like tin cans on Smithfields fairground.'

'This one's for Ginger, you bastards!' Smiler shouted.

Still they kept coming. Artillery rained in. Though German casualties were higher, the Foresters lost many and 'B' Company coming up from reserve were soon exhausted. Men were falling all around and there was no time to get them out. The best any of them could hope for was assistance with a tourniquet; others gently moaned: 'don't mind me, I'll be reight,' as their life drained away. But at least their ammunition could be put to good use. Smith now had two rifles on the go: his own and another for when that got too hot. He was getting better with the extra practice, fumbling less on reload, adjusting his sighting, better with each shot. He had lost count of how many. He heard gunfire coming from right next to him; he turned and saw two spiky-helmeted figures falling over the parapet away to his right, down the trench.

'Howay lads, looks like you've got a spot of bother.'

'The Durham's are here fellas! Glad to see you boys. It's been getting a bit hot.'

There was a lull and the Germans pulled back to regroup.

The lions at the front were roaring, but the donkeys brayed back at Divisional HQ. Major Leveson-Gower, the Brigade Commander was worried about being surrounded and wanted to pull back to the other side of the village where a defensible line could be formed – there was a huge gap between his brigade and the 16th to the south. He had a written message sent to Captain Wilkin in the trench to start to draw back and communicated this intent back to HQ. They hee-hawed back that the line was to be held. Captain Wilkin had barely refolded the piece of paper telling him to retire, when a breathless runner came down the communication trench: 'Brigade orders – on no account to withdraw.'

A further attack came. By 4:40 p.m. they found themselves being attacked on three sides from Germans who were, in places, only fifty yards away.

'What the bloody hell's happened to our Emm Gees? Looks like they've beat a retreat. Leaving us to it.'

They were running out of ammunition and only one of the two maxims was still working. Everyone's rifles were caked in mud and the bolts were jamming. As light started to fade they fell back.

'I've still got ammo. I'll cover!' shouted Smith.

'I'm with you,' said Charlie.

'Me too,' said Curly. 'The old boys, back together again!'

They kept reloading and firing ten or more rounds a minute. Germans falling but more coming on. They started to run out of ammo again.

'Come on let's leg it!' shouted Charlie.

They turned and fled, at times tripping over or stepping on arms and legs of fallen men as they fumbled in the darkness. As he reached the village, Smith was alone except for prone figures dotted around where they had fallen. He picked his way through the rubble of fallen buildings, heart pounding in his chest, moving as quickly as he could as the panic rose. He felt drunk, couldn't see, couldn't hear – like his ears were under water; didn't feel he was all there. Not his body. Not convinced he was heading the right way. He blundered into some telegraph wires festooned across the street and fell cutting his hands on broken glass that covered the paving. He cursed and got back to his feet.

Ahead, he saw a group of men.

'Good to see you,' said Captain Wilkin as he came panting up. 'Is Jepson still with you?'

He shook his head.

'Whitham?'

He breathed deeply, but didn't answer.

'Right lads let's scarper, back down the hill to regroup.'

They half-marched, half-ran out of the village. Ahead they could hear horses hooves disappearing up the road.

'Fuck this! I'm ditching this pack – I can't keep up with it on my back.'

'Me too – and this bloody coat. I'm lathered.'

It was dark when they reached the crossroads – trees on both sides of the road added to the gloom. Smith reckoned there were just over a hundred of them – no more than half of the company. Through the darkness they saw some troops arriving from the road to the south.

'Thank God for that! It's 'D' Company.'

'No. It must be the 16th.'

'*Hände hoch! Es ist vorbei.*'

Some tried to run down the other road but only ran straight into some more Germans coming that way, others tried to turn and fight, and felt the bayonet.

'It's no use, lads, it's over for us. Drop your weapons.'

'*Los. Für Sie ist der Krieg verloren.*'

They were surrounded. Smith half thought about going out fighting but something stopped him. Something at the back of his mind said he had to carry on; weren't there things back home he had to put right? He threw down his gun, clattering to the ground along with others.

CHAPTER FIFTEEN

They were rounded up and, at the point of a bayonet, were marched for two hours.

Smith was heading towards something with the others it was a football ground Bramall Lane on a winter's night he was being jostled in the crowd then it all went blank and he was falling he woke to a swift kick in his back *Steh auf, du Schwein.*

He'd been captured. He carried on into the night.

They were surrounded by a pack of dogs or wolves his head hurt a bang went off was it a shell or gunfire he lurched they were in a column several hundred yards long German voices on both sides there was the sound of Granny's old clock ticking and the smell of something cooking on the range Elsie was dressed in white floating she vanished he sensed Charlie somewhere nearby *Got to keep going, old boy* he stumbled and dropped onto one knee as someone behind bumped into him 'Soz, mate' he felt a rifle butt in his side sent him into the mud *Up you get old boy.*

At Lille the officers were separated out and taken away. The rest spent the night locked in a church with sentries by the door, at the altar and one in the pulpit. In the morning they were told to fall in by Captain Wilkin and were counted: just short of three hundred. The captain had evidently had a much more pleasant night than they had – he had somehow managed a wash and a shave, unlike them: begrimed, stinking and stubbly from not having been near washing water for two days. Wilkin wished them all well, and told them not to blame themselves for what had happened – they'd had no choice.

The officers were taken towards the station.

'They're off to the first class waiting room, like as not.'

When it came to their turn, they were put onto a train without so much as a drink of water. The trucks they were pushed into had previously transported horses. It took no amateur sleuth to work out what kind of beast of burden had preceded them: they had not even been swept.

'The bastards have done this deliberately!'

They kicked it all into a pile in the corner and for two days and nights they travelled, suffocating in the stench, only able to sit down in shifts, they were packed in so tight. The pile of horse muck had to double up as their own latrine.

As the train trundled slowly through the night a lonely whistling of the refrain of the *Soldiers of the King* was heard in a nearby carriage. Probably Murphy, Smith reckoned. Everyone listened; no one spoke; lost in their own thoughts.

Once over the German border the train stopped at every station for the locals to see the freak show – jeer at the *Englisch schwein*. The stations were bedecked in black, white and red flags celebrating the great attack. They saw a mannequin, at least they hoped it was, in khaki, swinging by its neck from a rope. They had not eaten for days and had had nothing to drink. At more than one station they asked for water and were refused; they begged a woman with a Red Cross armband for a drink. She approached with a bowl: '*Wasser?*' She threw it over them.

'You fucking bitch!' someone snarled.

'Who was it who said we'd be all right, that Germany was a civilised country?'

Late on the second night they were woken by shouting.

'*Raus mit dir, du Schwein!*'

They had to jump down from the truck, there being no platform.

Outside were a couple of hundred Germans with burning torches.

'Looks like they've got us a welcome party together, boys.' Smith recognised Smiler's voice. At least he was here.

'Oh, is there a marching band? Lord Mayor, and children waving little flags? Didn't think so.'

They were marched past more people who had turned out to see the spectacle; they were spat at, and, if they told the perpetrator what they thought of them in return, were kicked by soldiers or had torches thrust into their faces.

They were marched through some gates of a compound surrounded by a wire fence and made to stand near a brick building. Those that still had them were made to hand over their greatcoats. Small enamel bowls were thrown at their feet and they were pushed through the building, where they each got a cup of something resembling black coffee, but which tasted nothing like it. But it was warm and wet so it was consumed – it would have been if it was bilge water. They stood expecting to be fed too, but instead were pushed and shoved towards what looked, in the dark, like mounds. They were little more than trenches covered by tarpaulin with a few steps down, cut into the earth. They were prodded with rifle butts and bayonets and pushed inside. Most were so exhausted they settled down and slept on the mud floor. Smith slept deeply. Charlie kept him company in the night, slapped him on the shoulder, raised his hat to Elsie, but there was also darkness and ravens circled.

When day broke they emerged to try to make sense of their surroundings. It was a large camp surrounded by wire fences and wooden sentry turrets. There were rows of wooden huts as well as their own luxurious accommodation: "tamboos" they called them.

Smith and Smiler went to speak to a Frenchman who was leaning against a hut talking to Murphy.

'What's the score then, Spud?'

'Well it's not looking so good. My little Froggy friend, Emile, here, says we ain't getting no bread today, 'cause that only comes every three days and we missed the delivery yesterday.'

'They can't do that to us, surely? There's rules about this ain't there?'

Emile looked at them and shook his head.

'So where are we then?'

'Où est-ce que nous sommes?'

'Hamelin. Tu connais? La où il y avait le joueur de flûte.'

'Non. Quel joueur?'

'L'attrapeur de rats.'

'Oh! The Pied Piper. It's that place with the Pied Piper.'

'Well, he left quite a few rats behind – they were all out to greet us last night.'

'So, when do we get fed?'

'On mange à midi, n'est-ce pas, Emile?'

'On ne mange pas. On bois plûtot. Il n'y a qu'un espèce de potage – même un espèce de tisane de choux.'

'What did he say?'

'We get some sort of soup, but he calls it cabbage tea.'

It was no exaggeration. They had to fall in with their metal bowls and queue for a small cupful of "coffee" in the morning – it was said to be made with burnt barley or acorns. Some sort of soup was indeed served at twelve, in which it was rare to find anything floating: potato or cabbage, never mind meat. There was a greasy scum on the top of it from some unknown source. The coffee was served again at around five, then they had to be back in their tamboos and stay there until morning.

In those early days, when bread was scarce, they sold what they could to the French and Belgians who had a bit of money – their boots, their buttons, the clothes off their backs, in order to raise a few pfennigs for a small bread roll. Smith looked for Elsie's silver cigarette case to sell, but he no longer had it – lost or stolen somewhere on the way.

Some were reduced to walking around just wrapped in a blanket, shuffling round looking for scraps of anything vaguely edible. They'd follow dixies of soup being carried to other parts of the camp in the hope that a bit might slop over that they could lick up off the ground; a bit of orange peel or discarded cabbage stalk became treasure. They would even dip into the pigswill bucket for anything solid.

***

Thirty day's march and an ocean away, Belgian refugees arrived in the town, as did soldiers lucky enough to be badly wounded rather than killed. Crowds gathered at the train station to welcome the heroes before they were transported to one of the many hastily set up emergency hospitals.

Life had to have a purpose; but Elsie could see none. Not for her. Not for so many people around her. She could write to the college friends she had renewed acquaintance with, but what was there to say? She went to church, she prayed, but there was little comfort. From the pulpit the words were not of supposedly Christian countries trying to destroy each other but of God being on their side in a battle against the evils of Prussianism, and that men should not fear signing up because they were fighting for God as well as for King and Country.

Towards the end of October she returned for lunch one day to find an official looking envelope had been posted through the door. She had been expecting it. What more did she deserve? She sat down and took out the dusty pink sheet of paper.

Sir or Madam

I regret to have to inform you that a report has been received from the War Office that (No.) 1875 (Rank.) L Corporal (Regiment) Sherwood Foresters was posted "missing" on the 20th October.

The report that he is missing does not necessarily mean he has been killed, as he may be a prisoner or temporarily separated from his regiment.

Should he subsequently rejoin, or any other information be received concerning him, such information will at once be communicated to you.

I am Sir or Madam

Your obedient servant,

Officer in charge of Records

That meant they just had nobody to identify, she knew that. Blown to pieces. She hadn't loved him enough. In fact lately she hadn't loved him at all, and he hadn't loved her. She wondered if that had made any difference – are you more likely to survive if you know there is someone who truly loves you? Would you think that bit faster, care just that bit more if you knew there was someone who needed you to return? She had given up on him ever returning, and now here it was confirmed.

To make matters worse Grace came round clutching a similar letter.

'Oh, I'm so sorry, Elsie,' she'd spluttered between her tears.

Elsie sensed that she was relieved to find out someone else had received bad news as well; that her pain was lessened by knowing it wasn't something that fate had intended for her alone.

'But perhaps it's easier for you not having been so close as me and my Charlie.'

'I think you'd better leave, before you say anything else we'll both regret.'

'Oh, Elsie... I didn't mean... it's just that Charlie loved me so much – and what am I to do now?'

'Please just go.'

She had sent Grace away sobbing down the passage, feeling even more sorry for herself at having been snapped at. She wondered, though, whether Grace had a point; or was it actually the other way round? Did Grace at least have the comfort of knowing she was loved. Smith liked the idea of love, had thrilled in the challenge of winning her hand, liked the idea of having a good-looking wife, but little more.

She went to see Louisa the next day whilst her brother was out at work and she poured her heart out as the teapot was kept topped up.

'I can't even start to think what I'll do now. What have I got?'

'Us. Your brothers. Your cousins. And there is still hope – it only says he is missing. You know what he's like – maybe he will turn up and things will be better between you, having endured this. It must be chaos out there, keeping tabs on everyone, with battles going on. Record keeping can't be easy.'

'People sometimes say they know when someone has died – someone they are close to. Even if it happens a long way away. I felt Smith was lost to me a long time ago. If we ever had a connection it mostly died with baby George, and then entirely last year. I don't know what I can do. I've still not received an allowance. What will they do now? I'm in that big house on my own with no one. I won't be able to pay the bills – especially with how everything is going up – even if I get an allowance. Twelve and six doesn't go very far these days.'

'Don't you worry. I'll have a word with Tom. There's always room for you here.'

'No, there isn't. Where?'

'Well, there's the front room: we never use that.'

'No, I wouldn't want to impose on you.'

'Think it over. I'll speak to Tom. It might make sense. You'd be able to help us out too.'

'Anyway, I don't need to decide straight away. I can manage for a bit. But, thank you.'

CHAPTER SIXTEEN

In Hamelin, cheekbones and ribs started to protrude; arms became too thin to carry much weight, legs too weak to stand for long.

One dinnertime, a rumour went round that there was some extra soup. A queue of sorts formed near the cookhouse. Smith, Murphy and Smiler joined it in hope rather than expectation. The queue swelled.

'Ey up: every language under the sun going on here: French, Dutch, Rusky, Arab, even Cockney.'

The crowd started to sway forwards just like behind the Shoreham Street end when a corner was being taken.

' 'ere gi' o'er shoving will yer!' said Smith.

'Nah. It's not me. It's this Rusky.'

'Well, get 'im to gi' o'er then, eh?'

Murphy gave the Russian a bash on the head with an enamel bowl, denting both. The tovarisch sank gently to his knees.

A dixie of soup then appeared, being carried by two Germans. The queue turned into a mob. A guard raised his gun and shouted everyone to get back. Those at the front couldn't move, as they were pressed forward by the crowd. The guard fired into the air. What goes up must come down, and there was a cry of alarm – the bullet had hit a Russian in the shoulder. In the panic that followed the shot, the dixie was knocked over. The crowd melted away leaving the Russians to carry their comrade to the hospital.

They had no choice but to adapt and survive, or go mad – some men just sat all day staring into space.

There were no latrines: only a pit with two poles suspended over it, across by the perimeter – the use of these facilities became one of the sights that the good citizens of the town would stroll out to take in on their Sunday constitutional – like a visit to the zoological gardens – to see just how savage and uncivilised their enemy was.

There was a single tap on the parade ground for all the prisoners: Russians, French, Belgians and North Africans. Smith, like the others who had not yet given up, had to wash in his small enamel soup bowl out in the open.

Before long the camp's wildlife moved in to welcome the new visitors – soon they were all crawling in lice and scratching at sores, adding further discomfort to that of the dysentery.

Lice hunting became a favourite pastime. It gave them a purpose, a distraction. But it was a losing battle. Unlike them the lice had a constant supply of food and ideal living conditions: unwashed bodies, beards and hair that hadn't been trimmed for weeks on end, clothes that hadn't been changed since capture.

In the tamboo, in the bunk next to Smith, was one of the Durhams who had also been captured at La Vallée. He had ended up with 'D' company and had held out in a house surrounded by Germans for an extra day, until they had exhausted their ammunition. His name was Cornelius, but he was known to everyone as Darky, by virtue of his jet-black hair and dark complexion. He had a small New Testament, though he couldn't read very well. He got Smith to read to him. 'Read me that bit about nations rising up against each other. It might make some sense of all this.'

'Where is it?'

'Matthew, I think.'

Smith flicked through. He vaguely remembered it from the Boy's Brigade.

'Here it is: "And ye shall hear of wars and rumours of wars: see that ye be not troubled: for all these things must come to pass, but the end is not yet. For nation shall rise against nation, and kingdom against kingdom: and there shall be famines, and pestilences, and earthquakes, in divers places.

All these are the beginning of sorrows." '

'Is that what's happening now, Smith? Do you reckon?'

'I'm damned if I know. We need my mate Curly here.'

The landsturmer who made up the majority of the guards at the lager were mostly old, bitter and twisted, holding the Tommies personally responsible for their own sons being killed or stuck in trenches on the Western Front; those who were not old were still bitter and twisted, facing being sent to the front, or having been conscripted and feeling repulsed by those louse-infested, stinking swine they had to guard.

Punishment was handed out freely, usually summarily by the butt end of a Mauser or a well-aimed boot. Resistance meant unleashing a frenzy; fall to the ground and they'd behave as a pack and wildly aimed kicks, from which some never recovered.

There was a more specialist punishment that Smith soon experienced.

A cart of supplies entered the camp one morning while Smith and Cornelius were idling about by the wire. There were crates of potatoes on the back and only one guard, so they sloped up to the side of the cart opposite from the guard and relieved the cart of a couple of potatoes – one for each pocket. The driver saw something out of the corner of his eye.

'*Donnerwetter, meine Kartoffeln!*'

The Sentry rushed at them with his bayonet. They backed off and raised their hands, and another guard came and searched them. One of the German sergeants then arrived. The *schwarze Schwein* was taken away and Smith was led to the pole. His hands were tied behind it at above head height and then he was left for nigh on two hours. He blacked out several times, the pain in his neck and shoulders was so intense. By the time he was released he could no longer stand. He was carried back to the hut by Spud and Smiler. Cornelius received the same, only getting roughed up a bit as a warm-up.

The Red Cross visiting the camp was a cause for excitement. They handed out postcards for sending home with basic details to fill in: name, rank, regiment and whether injured or not. Smith filled it in and addressed it to home.

'*Raus, Schwein.* Outside.'

They were fallen in. A Belgian acted as an interpreter for the *Feldwebel*, the camp commandant, or "fieldwobble" as he was more commonly known. There were some words of German spoken to the Belgian.

'This old bastard wants you who have been builders in your lives to help build new huts.' He turned to the fieldwobble.

'They will come and ask your profession before army.'

The interpreter went down the line with a German sergeant.

'What did you do?'

'Tell him I was a clown,' said Smith.

'Pardon?'

'You know in a circus? Red-nose, big shoes.'

The German raised an eyebrow and moved down the line.

'A professional billiards player,' said Smiler.

'What is that?'

'It's a game with balls and a cue.' He mimed a potting action.

Cornelius said he was a painter.

'*Ah! Ser gut,*' said the German.

'...of rocking horses.'

'*Wie bitte?*'

'*Ein Schaukelpferd.*'

A look of confusion passed over the German's face.

There were several tea tasters, a whisky taster, an icer of buns, numerous men of independent means, a hangman, a butterfly breeder, a button inspector.

There was a short conference in German, then the interpreter said: 'This pig says you are all pigs and they will choose. He says you have also not been obeying order to salute German officers. You will do so as you go past to your tents.'

They fell out and marched past the fieldwobble with a salute which involved the thumb being inserted up the right nostril. Several received rifle butts in their ribs in return.

Smith was selected the next day by dint of not being one of those who fainted when they were forced to do drill on the parade ground. Just three months before, but a lifetime away, on Midsummer Common outside Cambridge they were an impressive unit: stretching their arms and bending their legs in unison. Now some could barely raise an arm.

Just lifting a single brick was an effort, it took three of their skeletal bodies to lift a three-by-two that they could have once swung with one arm. However, they were generously rewarded with an extra half-slice of black bread per day.

Compared to the tamboos the huts were luxurious. Wooden floors, long rows of double tier beds and straw-filled sacks for mattresses. Plenty of places for vermin to hide. Over the door had been chalked the words "Gott strafe England." Words they were familiar with, words heard as regularly as "how do you do" back home.

'Why does tha think they hate us so much, Smith? It's the Belgians and French get all the cushy jobs, and get first dibs at the food,' asked Spud.

'It's because of Mons and Marne – and Aisne. We slowed 'em down and stopped 'em. Stopped 'em getting to Paris within a week.'

'But the French and Belgians? Isn't our king a cousin of Kaiser Bill?'

'Yeah, but we weren't supposed to get involved were we? They expected a little resistance from the French, but expected them to fall into line. We were supposed to let them get on with their little games and not interfere. They are spoilt brats who try to steal humbugs off their little sister and have their legs slapped. They don't hate their sister for squealing about it, but they resent the backs of their legs smarting.'

The huts also had a stove, which proved useful for cooking as well as staving off hypothermia. Black bread was made slightly more palatable by resting on the stove first, but the best was when one of the Belgian cooks, peeling potatoes, was persuaded to throw the peelings out of the window. Some ate them raw, stuffing their faces with them and their pockets, but Smith had the idea of taking some of them to the hut and placing them on the stovetop. Soon the hut filled with the aroma of baked potato – it was the best thing they had eaten since capture.

When a German photographer visited the camp offering to take a picture for five pfennigs to send home as a postcard, he was turned away by the guards: it would have been bad for the reputation of the Kaiser – they all looked like tramps dressed in shirts that had been worn for over two months, paper trousers and clogs. But a transformation was about to take place.

'Hey lads who fancies a shave?' Cornelius entered triumphantly waving an old knife. 'I found this when I was chucking the rubbish into the cart and I've sharpened it up a treat on a bit of stone. What do you reckon?'

They had all recently been issued with a small ration of soft soap so lined up for a shave – of sorts – painful, involving many oaths being uttered, with more ripping than razor-like action. But with only a slight loss of blood they were transformed from a bunch of Robinson Crusoes into something approximating to civilized beings.

One morning Smith went for his constitutional. They no longer had to use the latrine pit, but Smith still liked to walk around via the perimeter to get a sense of his surroundings, to see if there were any weaknesses in the fence that might provide a chance of escape – he couldn't see that there was. He held conversations with Charlie – but it was a bit one-sided. Charlie would have known what to do. Men were being taken away to the coal mines or salt mines which was a near certain death sentence. Better to die trying to make a bolt for it than helping the German war effort raising coal for fuelling their ships or their gun factories. Over at the other side of the fence a woman was standing, staring at him, looking pained, sorrowful. She was the same age as his mother.

'Hello, Tommy,' she said in a German accent.

He looked back, blank-faced.

'I am so sorry. I wish I could help.'

A sentry came running over, raised his gun at her and moved her on.

Smith watched as she was pushed away.

'You bastard. Raising a gun to a harmless woman,' he muttered. The whole of his reality had been shifted, and he didn't know how to react. For months he had viewed all Germans as the same.

CHAPTER SEVENTEEN

Elsie had never felt more alone. It wasn't that she was missing Smith exactly – not for himself, and that in itself made her feel bad. She ought to be the grieving widow, sitting at night cradling a portrait of her husband, but that wasn't it. Her sense of grief was no less, however: for loss of the man who had courted her, if not the man he had become. She'd still loved the man he had been in those summer days walking through the castle grounds in Lincoln: so charming and yet with a streak of rebellion, of desire for change.

She hated returning to a house that would always be empty – only her presence, not the prospect of anyone returning. And always, everywhere she went, never far from her conscience was her dead son: flashbacks at night-time to the tiny baby in the chamber pot as she woke in a sweat, re-living it, or at strange times of the day. She wanted to be out of that house, to get away from its memories, not to have to return home to its coldness, not to have to work out whether it was even worth lighting a fire – balancing the economy of coal against the price of buying bread rather than making it herself, and of counteracting the penetrating autumn damp.

Her visits to teach Mabel had ceased – another victim of the war as sources of funding dried up – and she soon tired of the knitting and sewing groups, no longer being stimulated by the conversation of the women. They only had one thing on their minds but now none of them would give voice to it, as with the superstition of not mentioning the horned gentleman, or a long-tailed gentleman by name. Fear was corrosive and ate away at everyone's spirits; hope cowered next to it. Her former acquaintances in the WSPU no longer talked of suffrage or exciting events of the day. Instead conversation reverted to anecdotes of offspring, or what was on at the pictures. And it bored her.

She headed home via the monument, in want of mental stimulation. When the Salvation Army had done their hectoring best to save a few lost souls, a young man stepped up. As he turned and started to speak she saw that it was Henry.

'Out in France our brothers and sons and husbands are dying. They stagger back to their trenches holding onto their innards only to be shot through the head. Our soldiers are killing others in the same way – it is mass slaughter. And for what purpose?'

'To teach the Hun a lesson, tha pillock!'

Henry carried on ignoring the heckler: 'It is at the bidding of kings and politicians who say they have authority over us.

'These same rulers, who in peacetime exploit us and steal from our labour, send us to war in khaki to kill other workers who are equally exploited by their rulers, while they remain at a safe distance in their mansions adorned with their fancy ribbons and medals.

'We are told to march to the drum, to fall into ranks and obey. To charge with bayonets raised when all it takes to plough them down is to turn the handle of a machine.'

'Tha's a coward – a bloody shirker that's all!'

'Boo!'

'But ask yourselves what is behind this? We are being told to fight to protect a failed capitalism – greedy beasts of nations who want to go on devouring unchecked. A Germany jealous of its neighbours' conquests.'

'Bloody nonsense!' A bottle was thrown and struck Henry on the head and Elsie saw him go down. A policeman stepped up and pulled him off the platform to cheers from some of those who had gathered round. Elsie pushed her way through: 'Excuse me. Excuse me.'

The policeman had Henry by the arm.

'Please, Constable, can I be of help?'

'No, Miss. I don't think so.'

'Look, his head is bleeding. Let me attend to him. I'll make sure he goes home afterwards. He's surely allowed to speak his mind?'

'Not any more. Under the Defence of the Realm Act it is illegal to spread rumours that might cause alarm.'

'But he wasn't spreading rumours. Only giving an opinion. You should be arresting the person who threw the bottle at him. Isn't that assault? I wouldn't want anyone to get the wrong idea about one of our hard-working police constables, P.C. 231.'

'Very well. Just get him out of here.'

Molly would be proud of her, she thought; wherever she was…

Henry got out his handkerchief and dabbed at the blood that was trickling down the side of his face. 'It's all right, it's nothing.'

'Come on. We'll go and find somewhere to sit down until you recover.' They headed down Fargate. 'Is your head badly hurt? Let me see.' He stopped and took his handkerchief away from where he was holding it. It was still bleeding.

'I think your cap cushioned most of the blow.'

'It's nothing.'

'Still, we'll get a cup of tea and get you cleaned up.'

'What have we come to Elsie?' he said, once they had settled into their seats. 'Everyone has become so full of hate.'

'They have – even Germans who we counted as friends just a few weeks ago are being attacked – like the butchers on the Common.' She poured the tea. 'You are very brave to question it all.'

'There are still some speaking out. People who believe it is not too late to put an end to all this, if we can establish communication between socialists of all the countries involved in this ghastly mess. If word can be passed on from rank to rank to get them to lay down their arms and refuse this fight between the capitalists.'

'But surely no one wanted any of this to happen?'

'No. It's true that no one single person... except for some deranged German barons. But everyone has stood by and watched the slide into war. It is not the rich who will suffer – the capitalists will not loosen their grip on wealth and power – it is the working people who will end up paying in gold, and with their lives.'

'Men like my husband...' She looked down at the table.

'Elsie. I am so sorry... What a pig I have been. I didn't once stop to ask how you were. I forgot your husband is a reservist.'

'*Was.*' She looked into his eyes and gave him a thin smile. 'Don't apologise. He went to war willingly, as others cheered and waved their flags. I had not loved him for some time.'

'May I ask what happened?'

'Oh. All they say is that he is missing in France somewhere. It's all I know. But everyone knows what that means really. Just they haven't found a body.'

'I'm sorry. And those things I said...'

'No. You are right to tell the truth. But do you really think that Germany could have been stopped?'

'Yes. It had been building for decades. Carpenter called it an insane commercial and capitalistic rivalry – making money out of ever-increasing arsenals – and England no less responsible than the others, he said.'

'Surely not?'

'All it took was a trigger. That mad vanity of Prussian jack-booting. Desire for expansion to stop workers at home from revolution. The whole economic model is built on growing more and more. Germany lacked an empire to exploit, to keep on ever increasing its profits. So it burst its bounds – breaking through its borders.'

'And Russia too – looking to maintain its hold over Servia?'

'Yes. Yes, that's it. Exactly. And a route to the sea. As well as access to oil.'

Elsie's heart was racing. This was the first she had heard a proper explanation for what had happened. Throughout the country the narrative was that the Germans were mad, evil, or both. She smiled at Henry.

'You look tired,' he said. 'How have you been keeping?'

'Oh, you know. Muddling through. It's been hard and I've had little money coming in. I've only just been given an allowance – it's not much but at least I can afford to eat now, if not pay the rent.'

'That's another thing – they expect soldiers to rush to war on a shilling a day – with no guarantees for their families, while others make large profits. To fight *their* war for a pittance, like in peacetime they work for a pittance.'

'The main thing though is that I am bored. I'm doing a little bit of teaching, when I can find it, and helping out with the Aid Committee, but I still spend too much time on my own.'

Henry's teaspoon tinkled in his cup as he stirred his sugar.

'I've had a thought,' he said. 'My cousin, Lilian – Lily – is looking for somewhere to stop. She was in service up at Ranmoor, but left and is working at Cockaynes now. She's in digs but wants somewhere nicer. Perhaps the company would do you good? I think you'd like her. It would also help with the bills. I'll get her to call round.'

Elsie moved into the smaller back bedroom to let Lily have the larger room – it only seemed right since she had agreed to pay half of the rent and half of the gas and coal bills.

They got on well. Lily was only a few years younger than Elsie and breathed life into the house as soon as she stepped into it carrying a small pile of gramophone records. Henry was a few paces behind her carrying the gramophone itself.

'Is that yours!'

'Of course. My prize possession,' said Lily. 'I wasn't going to let that travel over on the cart – well, it's not exactly mine – not yet –

more of it belongs to Wraggs than me, still. But I've only another year or so of payments to make on it. It's wonderful though – worth every penny. I'll show you.' She put on a record and wound it up as Henry pushed the chairs to one side.

'Steady on. What are you doing?' said Elsie.

'We need some space. You can't sit still to this.'

'This one's called Sailing Down Chesapeke Bay,' she said, as she placed the needle on the record. 'It's my favourite.'

The most wonderful sound of accordion music came out, and Henry and Lily were soon twirling around the room bumping into chairs and tables as they danced. Elsie sat and watched. They played it again.

'Come on, up you get,' said Lily.

'No, I don't… You carry on.'

'You can't escape that easily,' said Lily.

Soon Lily was leading Elsie round the room.

'My turn,' said Henry. 'It's nice to see you laughing,' he said, as he swayed her side to side and glided around in the tiny space.

***

Elsie had tea on the table as soon as Lily came in from work one evening.

'This can't go on,' said Lily. 'Nice as it is to be looked after. But it is intolerable. Henry led me to believe you were a modern woman, and here you are looking after me like a good little Victorian wife.'

Elsie's face fell. 'But I thought…'

'Oh, I'm only joking, you silly thing.' Lily laughed. 'I'm sorry I didn't mean…'

Then Elsie smiled. 'Of course, if you don't want it, I'll take the plate away.'

'Don't you dare! Pass that plate here. I would fight back a dozen Zulus for one of your chicken and mushroom pies.'

They sat down to eat.

'You make a very good point though. Have I fussed round you too much?'

'Oh no. Only a little. You've been ever so kind. But you must let me do some of the work – I don't need looking after. I was in service don't forget. I'm used to looking after others.'

'But you are working, and I've nothing else to do.'

'Well, that's the problem, isn't it?'

'It is, yes.'

On Monday, Elsie took their washing round to her sister-in-law, Louisa's. She had taken to doing this to cut down on the cost, and for the company.

The week before she had seen a notice outside the steelworks: "SHORTHAND TYPIST – young man wanted to work in office." The notice was still there, pinned up on the door, looking rather dusty and weather beaten. The tragedy of it struck her – that the young man they were looking for was probably somewhere in North Yorkshire being put through his paces, fed and drilled to get him into shape to send him off to France to be killed.

The next day she got dressed up and went round to the steelworks, and as boldly as she could walked into the office. The clerk at the desk looked up as she entered.

'I've come about the job.'

'I'm sorry?'

'The job, as a typist.'

'But...'

'I see you've not managed to fill it, so I thought I'd offer my services.'

He looked a little flustered. 'If you just wait here, miss.'

He came back a few minutes later and sat down, not looking at her, busying himself with the contents of a ledger. Elsie stared at him. Then the door opened and a man in a dark suit, spectacles and heavily macassared hair entered.

'I understand from Mr Martin that you are enquiring about work.'

'Yes, I saw the notice.'

'And you will have seen we were looking for a young man.'

'Yes, but you appear not to have found one.'

'But we need someone with certain skills.'

'I can type and do shorthand – I learnt at college.'

The man sighed. 'Please come through.'

She followed him down a dim corridor with a polished wooden floor and into a room where he introduced himself as Mr Turner, the sales office manager.

'Do take a seat. I have to confess we have had an advert in the *Telegraph* for a week or two. It is a sad state of affairs. Have you any experience?'

'Only of teaching. But, as I said, I learnt to type at college. I had a friend who had a typewriter, she taught me and I learnt shorthand too. And I have kept my hand in: I have been taking minutes at meetings and typing them up.'

'Very well, shall we put it to the test?' He dictated a letter about steel stock. She didn't know some of the words but managed to get something down.

'There is a typewriter down the corridor.' He led her farther down the corridor to another office where two boys, who looked no older than seventeen or eighteen, were sitting at desks, heads bent over their work. At an empty desk was an American typewriter and Mr Turner asked her to type out the letter and return it to his office. She was a little slow and painstaking, but got through the letter with only minor mistakes.

Back at Mr Turner's office he let out an involuntary sigh as he looked over her work. She tried not to give way to her sense of triumph.

'Of course you realise you'd be the only female in the office other than Mrs Jannock who brings the tea round.'

'That doesn't worry me. I would look forward to making more of my skills and being of use.'

'We'll only be able to pay you fifteen shillings a week.'

'That will be fine.'

'Very well then. Needs must. Beggars can't be choosers and all that. And you have typed that perfectly adequately. Could you drop it off at the post room on the left at the end of the corridor on your way out? When could you start?'

'Tomorrow?'

He smiled his first smile.

When she got home she trod on a plain postcard as she pushed the back door open. She picked it up. Across the top was the undecipherable word: *Kriegsgefangenessenglung*. She turned it over and read the printed words:

> Fill up this card immediately.
> I am prisoner of war in Germany.

Below that, in Smith's writing, were his name, his rank, and regiment. She looked closer. Next to a box printed: "Sound," he had written: Yes. Printed across the bottom was: Do not reply to Limburg. Await further instructions.

Elsie wrote to her mother-in-law in Staveley to update her. Twice, his mother had written short, rather pathetic letters asking whether there was any news. The mother had never given up hope – unlike the wife – to whom the word hope had never fitted. She knew it was not right. It was a serious flaw in her character and morality, but there it was. She had never had hope that he would survive. She believed he would not, and she did not really miss him. She found the plaintive letters from his mother an annoyance. That too was a flaw in her character. She had nothing against his mother, it was just the fact that she thought her son some kind of angel that made her resent and pity her.

CHAPTER EIGHTEEN

As the end of the year approached their rations increased. They were given a three-pound loaf per day between eleven men, the cutting of which became an almost religious ritual to ensure each man got his fair share. Knives were of course *verboten* along with almost everything else so they had to be careful to hide it away again after use. The loaf was cut and the man who cut it numbered the slices from left to right or from right to left. No one was allowed to see, each calling out which number they wanted.

They even saw something resembling meat – a stinking stew – some big chunks that someone said was horse. Bones were found in it, and an attempt to identify the animal made – it was small. Murphy who had once worked as a butcher identified what he was sure were leg bones: bigger than a rabbit, but smaller than a lamb.

'What the hell is it then?'

'Who knows? German sausage dog?'

'It's awful, but I'm still eating it.'

Parcels from home also started to get through. These were searched thoroughly by the guards, who would even go so far as to bayonet each package and tip all the contents: tea, sugar, coffee, cocoa, all into their bowls – what a strange brew it made, but it was still better than the coffee the Germans dished out.

None of the Russians received parcels from home, so when nice white bread arrived in a parcel they would often give their black bread ration to the Russians.

At parade one morning snow lashed their faces, whipped by an easterly wind.

'All Irish Catholics are to fall out,' shouted the Belgian interpreter.

'Should I say I'm an Irish Catholic, do you reckon?' said Murphy. 'My name is Irish after all.'

'No. Stay put – with us. You don't know what they are up to.'

The Irish we're all ordered to get their things and marched out of the camp.

One of the Belgians said he'd heard the Germans talking about trying to turn them over to their side.

'That's a load of bollocks is that. They might be rum 'uns, but they'd never do that, they're our mates.

Several others were counted out and ordered from the English huts and made to go to the Russian's huts and some Russians were moved into theirs.

'There we see how you like to share your allies.' The guard laughed and left.

'The bastards have done that out of spite.'

It took a while for it to settle. As well as being less insistent on washing, the Russians liked to have all their windows closed – stinking away in a warm, damp fug, whereas the British favoured ventilation. It was a running battle, which eventually was conceded to those with the power of food parcels.

Spirits improved along with improved rations – and the arrival of tobacco. Smith received an ounce of twist, a small tin of Wilsons' snuff and a knitted vest from his mother, some socks from Elsie and half a packet of broken biscuits mixed up with a packet of tea. The socks eased the discomfort of wearing the Zuider Zee clogs – his boots having long been confiscated.

***

When Henry found out that Smith was still alive he asked, 'Can I still come round? Does this change anything?'

'Why ever would it?'

'But how will it look?'

'Who cares how it looks. Mrs Grundy died with the old century. Who cares these days what she would have said?'

'It was less Mrs Grundy than the police I was thinking of – they are snooping on the wives of soldiers, and getting their allowances stopped, they say.'

'What rot! You come round to visit your cousin, do you not?'

She knew he didn't. She knew that was just an excuse. But the truth was she looked forward to seeing Henry. He cheered her up with his infernal optimism, with assertions that good would prevail, that socialism was inevitable once this current crisis ended, that what they were witnessing were the death throes of a doomed economic model, that power would slip from the grasp of kings, kaisers and archdukes. That the people would take over.

142

'Have you heard from him recently?'

'No – but I don't suppose he gets to do what he wants.'

'At least you know he's alive and being looked after. Also, it means certainty for you that he will survive the war, doesn't it?'

She stared at the fire. 'I've sent him a parcel – tea and tobacco, socks and biscuits.'

They sat quietly.

Henry broke the silence. 'Is your work still going well?'

'Yes. It is so much better to be busy and productive – to feel you have achieved something.' It was the truth – she had not felt so content for a long time – despite the constant dread, as of a huge dark ravenous beast somewhere over there, just over the next hill, devouring bodies and crunching on bones. The office had got used to her being there and saw that she was helpful, good at what she did and efficient, making their own jobs easier in the process.

'You seem to have a different disposition anyway.'

Silence fell again. Henry said, 'I was wondering…'

'What?'

'Do you think the three of us should go to a pantomime?'

'Oh, but isn't that for children?'

'Of course not – you're never too old to laugh. And the children only ever go to the matinees. We'd go to an evening performance. We could even borrow some children if it makes you happier. Or we'll go and see a different show if you'd rather. We're all working hard and need to let our hair down.'

She smiled at his boyish enthusiasm. 'Oh, very well then.'

Curtains up for the Hippodrome was at nine. In truth, Elsie would have preferred to go to see Dr Coward conducting the Sheffield Musical Union's performance of the Messiah at the Albert Hall, but she bowed to appeals for something more "jolly." Only a few years separated them but still she felt she was appeasing the children; so much living in those few extra years that she felt middle-aged.

They went for a drink beforehand at the Barleycorn just down the road. The news had been dominated by the bombardment of North Sea towns from German ships. For the first time in a thousand years, English civilians had been killed on English soil by invaders.

'So many more funerals today, and they've already buried dozens. That it is somewhere I have been, like Scarborough, seems to make it so much more real,' said Elsie.

'And old people and women and children too,' said Lily.

'Baby-killers.'

'I just don't understand. Why would they do that? It's not the same as soldiers fighting soldiers.'

'But it is what they did in Belgium, too,' said Elsie. 'It's hard to think of them as human.'

Henry took a swig of his beer. 'That's all part of how the warlords try to get their way – to stoke conflict. If you dehumanise the enemy, make it a battle of good over evil. Everyone invokes God as being on their side. God save the King. Gotte, Kaiser, Vaterland. Before this started we rubbed along with Germans quite nicely. But to get Tommy to fight Fritz they have to get them to hate each other. Myths of devilry build up on both sides. Churchill is very eloquent but he is really playing the same game. He said: "Their hate is the measure of their fear: its senseless expression is the proof of their impotence, and the seal of their dishonour." '

'But what do the Germans gain by bombing Whitby Abbey, and people's homes – killing hundreds of innocents?'

'I suppose they think that stoking fear in civilians will get us to bring our troops home, to leave the European mainland to their whims.'

'Oh come on you two! You said we were going to let our hair down. You're not preaching to the crowds now. Let's forget it all for the evening. Let's go and immerse ourselves in magic and princes and princesses, shall we? I won't hear another word on that other thing, and, if I do, I'll scream till your eardrums burst.'

'You're right, coz. Sorry. Bottoms up.'

Elsie sat between Henry and Lily. The curtain went up to a scene in a fairyland forest glade, and once the murmur of excitement at the magically lit scene died down the audience were rapt, as fairies twirled and danced.

But there really was nowhere to escape the war. Allied flags were paraded in a march, and Florrie Forde's Prince Charming was tinged with jingoism as she sang: "soldiers, fellows, across the sea, over in Paree, happy as could be." It was a song that Elsie had heard belted out at just about every family gathering in the last few years, with Uncle Quinn hammering away on the old stand-up piano, so she knew all the words to the chorus as everyone joined in: "Shure we're Irish,

144

and proud of it too! And we all like a hullabaloo. We've all come over to see the fun, every mother's son of a gun."

But still Elsie felt she was being pulled from the mundane, from the darkness of the auditorium to the light of the stage, and let herself walk through palace gardens and fairyland, as she laughed at Pickles and the antics of the Ugly Sisters and forgot that Prince Charming was played by a woman. There was still a beast over the hill, but for now it didn't matter.

At the palace ball Prince Charming and Cinderella sang a duet: a song well known to everyone.

Ever since we have met
I have longed for the day
When at last I could call you my own.

Elsie sensed that Henry was looking at her. She kept her eyes fixed on the stage. A sensation rose up from deep inside her, up her spine, and she had to take a deep breath.

So now if my secret you know very well
That you are the one I love best
There's a nice little spot the sweet story to tell
So I like very much to suggest.

She felt the warmth of his hand gently close around hers. She half turned to look into his scared eyes, and tried to smile, though her lips quivered.

Meet me where the lanterns glow
And softly come and go
Like stars above you
Let me whisper in your ear
And try to tell you dear
How much I love you.

Elsie tried to join in the chorus with everyone else but her voice caught in her throat and the scene in front of her blurred.

She pulled her hand away at the end of the song.

The final scene in the palace came all too quickly, and they applauded as if by doing so they could avoid being dragged back to Christmas 1914. People rose to their feet with a sigh, and strolled out into the cold night, arm in arm, singing their favourite tunes, trying to prolong the magic.

Elsie behaved as if nothing had happened. But she knew it had.

CHAPTER NINETEEN

On Christmas Eve, Smith could not get out of bed. He had spent the night alternately shivering and burning up with fever. His throat was red raw and he was having difficulty breathing. Cornelius tried to get him up to help fetch the coffee but he couldn't speak. They returned with a stretcher and carried him out of the camp accompanied by a guard to the local hospital.

He was examined and told to open his mouth: he retched as the doctor painted the inside of his throat with iodine. He was put in a bed that was no less flea-ridden than the ones in the camp and that is where he spent his Christmas – drifting in and out of delirium.

He was ordered back to the lager as soon as the swelling in his throat had subsided, trudging back through half an inch of snow, walking like an old man, each foot before the other an effort.

They bade good riddance to 1914 with as much spirit as they could muster. They tried to teach some Russians some of their songs with little success, then the Russians sang one of theirs – a sad dirge. Their friend Peter said: 'It about man who drive horse in snow and died, he be bury in snow, and comrade, he give his ring, ring of man, for wife, for her to find new husband.'

'Bloody hell, Pete! Tha's reight cheered us up there, lad. Don't you blokes have any cheery tunes?'

' 'ere this will cheer you up. I've written it mysel',' said Murphy.

In a passably good tenor voice, he sang, to the tune of Sons of the Sea:

'One day there came to Hamelin, on a morning cold and still,
The remnants of a great Army, captured close to Lille.
They were taken by the Germans, in the middle of the night,
After sticking to the trenches, through a stern and bitter fight.

They wish now they had fought on, though they could not have hoped to win,
For the remnant of that army now starve in Hamelin.
Ah, it is sad to see the men's faces, once so plump and red,
Now so thin and pale with hunger, they can but crave for bread.

Here you see a British soldier, wolf a load of spuds and bran,
After selling belts and braces, or any bit of kit he can.
Here you see a British Tommy, with his boots and buttons gone,
Dipping in a swill tub for his breakfast, eating stuff a pig would shun.

Now you people there in England, feasting on salmon from a tin,
Send a bit to Tommy, for it's scarce in Hamelin.
Tommy won't forget you when he draws his army pay,
You'll be there to call him hero, you who stopped away.'

One of the Berkshires in an adjacent hut had managed to keep his watch hidden in a smuggler's pocket that he'd sewn into his shirt tails. His hut was charged with letting the others know when midnight arrived. They sang *God Save the King* and competed to out-sing *God Save the Tsar* coming from the other end of the hut. This was followed by *Auld Lang Syne* and *Rule Britannia*. They were about to move on to another rendition of the Hamelin song when a guard appeared and put a rifle through the window: '*Ruhe da drinnen!*'

'Looks like the party pooper's arrived, boys. Here's to these bastards getting it shoved up their fat arses in 1915!'

'As eloquently put as ever, Smith, old son.'

The New Year brought about a change of scenery: Smith, Cornelius and Smiler were taken by train to a camp a couple of hours or so to the south. They saw normal life from the train window: farms and towns, hills and woodland. To eyes accustomed to compacted muck, fences and barbed wire it was painful.

They arrived at another camp much like the other in most respects, except one – the degree of organisation of work.

They were awoken at five o'clock by blows to the toes and soles of the feet by rifle butts or the flat side of bayonets and given a breakfast of potato gruel; then divided into working parties.

Smith and Cornelius were given spades and other tools, marched up on to the moors and given instructions by an interpreter on peat cutting – the German peasant, who was demonstrating, making it look very easy. Some of the prisoners set to, clearly having done it before. The new recruits were started off on stripping the top layer of turf ready for cutting a new trench.

They were worked for four hours without a break and if they slowed down or stopped from fatigue they were shouted at and beaten with the sticks that each of the guards carried. After a short break for soup, cooked over a fire by two Belgians, it was back to work again.

In the afternoon, cold rain fell and soaked them through.

'I'm damned if I'm doing this to keep German fires burning,' Cornelius said.

'What can we do though?' said Smith.

'I could take one of these buggers' heads off with a spade and make a dash for it.'

'You'd be shot before you could reach the trees. Let's just do the minimum to get by, eh?'

'You know, Smith: how much I regret surrendering? Just chucking down my rifle rather than taking out as many as I could with my bayonet before they shot me.'

'That would have done no one any good – not you, not your family, not the war. At least here were tying up guards and soldiers, keeping them away from the front.'

'Some blokes say we've done our bit. It's just not true. That *bit* was far too short. Just let me at them.'

'No, Darky. And that's an order from a Lance Corporal.'

Cornelius carried on digging for a bit.

'I've done this before, you know – peat cutting. On the moors in Yorkshire.'

'I thought you were from the North East.'

'No. I'm not really from anywhere.'

Kein Geschwätz. Arbeitet!'

It was late when they got back to the camp. More potato gruel for tea with half a slice of bread that they had to carry back to their hut in the dark, trying not to trip. They ate in the dark then settled down on their bunks, there being nothing else to do in the darkness.

'I meant what I said about not having done my bit you know.'

'Yeah, I know. Let's not do anything rash though. Time is something we have got.'

Parcels from home had been held up after their move. The backlog arrived on consecutive days. Smiler got one from his mother: and sat and stuffed his face with fruitcake. Afterwards he gave a big belch and announced: 'You know what? It makes me bloody mad.'

'What's that, Smiler?'

'Not a bit of baccy in that parcel! No consideration.'

The very next day he opened another parcel: copies of the parish magazine, some clothes and several packets of Woodbines. He lit up, even though it was verboten in the huts.

'You know what? It makes me bloody mad!'

'What is it now, Smiler?'

'Bloody baccy for a starving man!'

They spent several weeks cutting peat, taking small satisfactions from making the cuts irregular so they didn't stack very well, and making the trenches ragged looking. If a suitable stone was unturned they'd strike it to blunt their tools.

They were then moved to a job canalising a stretch of river – part of it was to be bypassed by a new canal that they were having to dig alongside the river. Smith and Cornelius learnt a few tricks from the French prisoners. As long as you looked purposeful you weren't pulled up. So, if you marched past swinging a spade, the guards believed one of the other Germans had given you orders. This way you could have a nice easy day cutting steps into the riverbank that were of no use to anyone, or scraping the sides of the new canal that didn't need scraping, then leaning on your spade in the spring sunshine until another guard came past when you again looked busy. This way a few cushy days passed.

As the days lengthened there was more time for leisure in the evenings. Someone who was a dab hand at mending shoes back home made a decent cricket ball by stitching some leather around a tennis ball, someone else fashioned a bat from a piece of wood that was "lying around" and brought back down a trouser leg. The parade ground was flat enough for a wicket after a bit of groundsmanship, so teams were formed: army versus navy, and large crowds gathered to watch on Sundays.

There was even a small shop set up on the site run by two local women, the *zwei dicke damen*. There you could buy a pipe, bits of material, mouth organs, buttons or postcards. It was even possible at the right price to place special orders: an old Kolbe piano accordion was obtained that needed a bit of mending with strips of canvas and glue. This addition, and other instruments, soon led to the formation of a half decent camp band, which greatly increased the quality of the entertainment on offer.

***

'Hey Smith. Keep watch for me; I've got an idea.'

It was approaching knocking off time and the light was starting to fade. Smith busied himself on the bank hacking vaguely at some undergrowth and keeping an eye out. Cornelius jumped down into the canal with a pick. It was a section where the river ran close to the dry canal and would eventually be broken through on completion.

After a while he scrambled up onto the side sweating and panting. Come on let's head back: must be nearly knocking-off time.'

'What were you up to?'

'Oh, just a bit of digging. Did you ever get told that story about the little Dutch boy who put his finger in the dyke? That was what gave me the idea.'

In the middle of the night everyone was woken by shouting.

'*Aufstehen! Raus mit euch!* Pumpers, pumpers! Men to go out *und pumpt wasser!*'

A small, drowsy, very grumpy working party was rounded up. Smith looked across towards Cornelius.

'Darky?'

There was no reply, but in the dim light he could see a broad grin: white teeth in the black frame of his face.

The days stretched out, punctuated by parcels arriving with soap and jam, news from home. Grey prisoners' uniforms arrived onto which yellow paint was daubed down the sleeves and trouser legs, so that they looked nothing like civilians, were they to escape.

Quite a few books were available – New Testaments, and the Book of Common Prayer were easy to come by, as was Robinson Crusoe and Treasure Island – not falling victim to the guards opening parcels and censoring them, unlike Punch magazine with its cartoons lambasting the Germans. Some books got through only by dint of having their covers ripped off, largely out of spite. There were also itinerant booksellers who arrived at the camp – one popular book was Baedeker's Guide to Northern Germany. It took a while for the guards to work out that it wasn't the highlights of German *kultur*: its fine building and treasures, that were the attraction, but the much copied maps contained therein, showing the routes to the borders. By the time it was *verboten*, hundreds of prisoners including Smith had secret maps hidden away just in case.

Hands became calloused and backs hardened from days spent digging, carrying timber, or laying railway tracks. They also buried their dead.

One man was killed by a wagon on the railway where he was working. Another known as Kipper, a trawlerman before the war, a member of the Royal Naval Division captured during the defence of Antwerp, had slowly been going off the rails, sitting on his own, reading the same letter over and over, muttering and swaying like an Arab in prayer. Then one morning he was found in a pool of blood having hacked at his own throat with a piece of tin can.

One day some new Russians arrived at the camp dragging a sack behind them.

'What's in the sack, Smith?'

'I don't know, but by the size of it and the weight I'd say another Rusky.'

'Poor bastard. And the rest of them don't look none too great either.'

Later, the guards came round with an interpreter saying that the Russian who had died of a fever would be buried in a sack unless money was raised for a box.

'I don't suppose he gives a bugger what he's buried in.'

They raised a small collection and handed it over.

That night there was singing coming from the guards hut.

'I bet those bastards are having a booze-up on the money we raised.'

CHAPTER TWENTY

Henry had fallen into the habit, when he wasn't on shift, of calling round to the house for his tea – it made sense, they all agreed, to share their meals, being cheaper that way. It was the end of September 1915; they had cooked on the range, given the seasonal chill in the air.

'Well, fancy missing all the excitement,' said Henry. 'I knew nothing of the visit until I heard someone talking about it on the way over. So did you just bunk off, or were you allowed out?'

'We were given an extended lunch break,' said Lily. 'He travelled back through the town on the way to the steelworks. Everyone was out, waving whatever flags they could find. And I've never seen makeshift bunting go up so fast. Still, there's a war on and we can't be expected to put on a show like we did when King Edward came.'

'I remember the old Queen coming in ninety-seven. That was really special,' Elsie said. 'Town was so beautiful.'

'And do you wemember her Corwonation gwandma?' Henry simpered.

'Cheeky 'aporth! I was only six – you were around then too.'

'But *far* too young to remember it.' He got a slap on the arm in return.

'So he didn't visit the most important steel works in the city, then?'

'What ours? Don't be daft. Only the big boys. But those of us in the office were allowed out to see him drive past – there were loads of school kids out too, on Carlisle Street, singing for him – very sweet. Seeing as no one knew he was coming they put on a good show along the route, nonetheless.'

'Thousands there to see him off at the station, by all accounts.' Henry reached in his jacket pocket and pulled out a feather. 'This one looks like a swan's feather. Another for the collection. I'll have enough for a bloody pillow, soon. Where do they get them from, eh? Can you buy half an ounce of white feathers at the market?'

'Can't they see you have an "on-service" badge?'

'They don't care what work I'm doing – all they see is a fit, young man not in uniform like their husbands or sons. They don't stop to think who'd keep the country running. They imagine boilers run themselves.'

'It's not fair.'

Lily changed the subject. 'I thought I'd go and see Aunty on Saturday after work, and stop over to keep her company. Are you coming?'

Henry's eyes flicked to Elsie. 'No, I can't. I'll perhaps run over in the week. I've said I'll work late on Saturday: they're a bit short.'

As the autumn rays filtered through the curtains on Sunday morning, Elsie turned over in bed, away from the light in an attempt to stay asleep amidst the warmth of her dreams, but gradually the cold day imposed itself on her. She opened her eyes to see Henry smiling softly at her, his bright blue eyes sparkling. She smiled back.

'Good morning, princess.'

'Good morning. Have you been awake long?'

'A little while. But you looked so peaceful. I didn't want to wake you.'

She smiled.

'Serene, even. Did you know you sometimes smile when you're asleep.'

'That's only when I'm dreaming of you, dearest.'

He leant over and kissed her gently. 'I am a lucky man. For so long all I could do was dream. I tried not to. How I tried – it was all so impossible after all – ridiculous.'

'No. Not ridiculous.'

'It was. All my wishes placed on the impossible. A stupid boy, denying himself the possibility of ever meeting anyone else. No other girls could hold a candle to you.'

'But it wasn't *so* impossible was it?'

'No. Somehow. But one day Smith will return and...'

She put a finger to his lips to stop him; then followed it up with her own lips. He rolled over onto her.

'Be careful, won't you.'

'I always am, aren't I?'

'It probably doesn't matter anyway,' she murmured, as she held him tight.

*

The gloomy days of November were endured: damp, foggy, and that sort of cold that penetrates however many layers you put on; nights when anything that could double up as an extra blanket was brought

153

into use until the covering weighed you down so much that you could barely turn over in bed.

Elsie hadn't seen Henry for several days. She wrote a brief note to him at his lodgings suggesting he came round one evening when she knew Lily would be out, since she wanted to talk to him.

They sat down at the table and Elsie poured the tea.

'What's that?' she said, indicating a khaki armlet bearing a red crown on his jacket sleeve.

'I've got news for you as well, but you go first. What did you want to talk about?'

'No – you tell me your news.'

'I've attested,' he announced without any note of conviction in his voice.

'What do you mean, Henry?' said Elsie. 'I thought you'd already registered.

'Yes, but I decided to do it under the new Derby scheme. It is clear to me that conscription is coming, when they will take free will away from you. I cannot live with that risk – I'd rather be a volunteer than press-ganged, rounded up like a coward. I'm not a coward.'

'What has changed? You are so opposed to this war?'

'I am. I've not enlisted. Just been put on a list of those willing to serve if called on. My fate will be decided by my employer. If they need me then a tribunal can decide.'

'Does that mean they'll send you to France?'

'Not necessarily – there are other things I could do that wouldn't need months of training – but the chances are my work will keep me here – it's essential work to keep the trams supplied with electricity.'

'But your pacifism? Wouldn't you refuse on those grounds?'

'I wouldn't say I was a pacifist. Socialists have always upheld the right of nationalities to defend their existence, to resist domination. This is a terrible, pointless destruction. That hasn't changed. But what I now have to accept is that peace will only prevail once one side wins. There will be no workers' uprising to stop it, no soldiers laying down arms. That was naivety on my part, or youthful optimism. It will now run its course until one side is on its knees. I might as well help speed that up if needs be.'

'But, Henry…'

'It's true though, isn't it? And no one has God on their side. The war is against God. But if Germany were to win it would look to subjugate the other nations – that is what so many of their generals have said and written. We would all be under the Prussian jackboot. We socialists would defend our political rights if our own government sought to remove them, so we should defend them – our rights, and those of other nations, against a Germany seeking domination over Europe. It is their avowed policy to be a power stretching from the Persian Gulf to the North Sea. They are against the interests of labour and democracy.

'I can't take being labelled a coward any longer, Elsie. I won't be the one who skulks around cursing everyone, condemning them all as fools: even those laying down their lives to defend our country.'

'I think that is very noble, Henry. You must do what you think is right.'

'I'm sorry, I've rather gone on a bit. There was something you wanted to talk to me about?'

'Oh, it was nothing. I only wanted to talk to you, that's all. I've missed you.'

'I've missed you too. I wish I could just move in, then we could see each other all the time, but it is impossible.'

'I love you Henry. I do so wish things were different.'

'You know how much I love you too. I always have.'

'Come here you soft 'aporth.' She kissed him; losing herself in him. She couldn't tell him her news. Not now. It didn't seem right. She had no right.

The war that was supposed to be over by Christmas raged on through another. In France, Greece and Turkey, Persia and Africa.

The week before Christmas, Henry answered notice papers he received, and queued at the Corn Exchange with hundreds of others to find out whether he was to be called up. It was all very confusing. He was told to let his employer know straight away, so that they could submit the correct forms to the recruiting office. He was in limbo until the New Year.

Elsie was starting to make plans. She wrote to her friend, Mary, who was still nursing her father in Renishaw, explaining that she needed to talk to her.

'I'm afraid I can't leave my father's side,' she replied. 'He is not long for this world, now. But if you could find a way to come over, I would be delighted to see you.'

Christmas was subdued that year. And at her uncle's house an effort was made for all the children of the family to carry on as normal, to not transfer their worries and black clouds to wiser souls in smaller bodies, who could not even imagine evils such as were being carried out in the name of their futures.

Everyone complimented Elsie on how well she looked – how clear her complexion, how she had a healthy glow.

'I've been eating well,' she said. 'Having a little more money coming in helps, and work suits me; it takes my mind off things.'

'Have you heard from Smith recently?

CHAPTER TWENTY-ONE

In the *lager*, Christmas of 1915 was different to the previous one. They had, by then, found ways to get hold of schnapps from civilians who came into the camp, or from prisoners who worked outside; there were parcels of food, musical instruments and preparations made for festivities that were long remembered.

The hut shook with the rhythm of wooden clogs dancing, and then, as with any good night out on the town, the evening finished with a few old scores being settled in a punch up. The guards who tried to enforce lights out at nine o'clock were given short shrift and decided to back off. The party ended an hour or so later when reinforcements arrived from the guardhouse with loaded rifles.

No one was feeling particularly fresh the next day when they paraded. The interpreter spoke: 'The commandant is very unhappy at last night. For a week you will be in bed by seven and no lights no talking. Also if anyone finds his cat, that man will get a reward. His cat is missing. He is unhappy at that also.'

There were mutterings and questions. The story going round was that the Russians had eaten it for their Christmas dinner. The Fieldwobble's *Muschi* was well fed – approaching the size of a large Christmas goose. For days after, the Russians were greeted with miaouws. There were knowing smiles and replies of: '*Da. Verkusna,*' and a rub of the belly. The English were not quite sure if they were having their legs pulled.

***

Elsie took advantage of the works being on shutdown over Christmas and New Year to travel over to see Mary. There was a soldier in her train compartment staring out of the window the whole way there, avoiding any eye contact with his fellow passengers. At his side was a wooden crutch – his left leg was missing. She tried to not look at him but found herself drawn to thinking about who he was and where he was going. He was not much older than her. She looked out at the passing landscape and occasionally glanced at him; if he did make eye contact she would smile at him, let him know that she cared about him. Then she caught a glimpse of the side of his face that he had turned towards the window: horribly scarred and his ear was missing He had every right to his privacy. She looked back out of the window at smoke hanging low over rooftops in the still damp air and drifting through a nearby copse.

It was a short walk from the station up to where Mary's father lived in the cottage where he had grown up, and raised a family in. It presented a gloomy aspect to the little lane that Elsie turned down – off the main street – the roof was uneven, the walls standing in defiance of their lack of cement, window panes that were cracked or blocked up with cardboard, and wooden frames that were creviced and bore a closer resemblance to driftwood than squared timber.

She pushed the door open and went in, with a gentle: 'It's only me.'

Mary emerged from the back with a smile lighting her face. She took Elsie's hands. 'You look lovely. I wish I could say the same for me.'

And it was true, she looked pale and drawn, her hair lank and lifeless, clothes rather dowdy and shapeless – not like the Mary she knew – vivacious and fashionable. There was also an ugly bruise across her cheek.

'You'll have to forgive me. I have little call for getting dressed up these days, and they'd soon get spoilt if I put my nice clothes on. The most I can manage is to nip out quickly to the shop when he's asleep. If I'm not there when he wants me he gets agitated and upset.'

'I'm so sorry, Mary. Have you no one to help you?'

'Not really – other than Mrs Dawes from over the way who pops in occasionally. And her son runs errands for me.'

'I should have come over sooner.'

'There's no need. I manage. Come on; take your coat off. I'll put the kettle on and you can tell me everything I've been missing.'

'What happened to your face?'

'Oh, it's nothing. He caught me when he got upset. He didn't mean to but he doesn't really know what's going on sometimes. I was just trying to change his shirt.'

The little kitchen was very cosy and like stepping back in time, like something straight out of Adam Bede. It had an uneven flagstone floor, door jambs and walls out of vertical, an ancient, scrubbed wooden table, the top of which resembled gently rolling countryside and chairs that creaked and settled alarmingly when you put your weight on them.

Pale winter light filtering through the small glass panes competed with the fire in the range for brightness. There was no gas-lighting, never mind electricity.

'So, what was it you needed to talk about?'

'I'm in trouble, Mary... I'm pregnant and don't know what to do.'

'But... is Smith...?'

'No, he's... in Germany still.'

'Oh, I see... Then who...?'

'Henry, you know... who used to come in the shop.'

'Does he know?'

'I came very close to telling him, but it looks like he's leaving to join up.'

'What? Henry? Joining up?'

'He's coming round to thinking it is the only way to save democracy in Europe. That the only way out of this is a purging – for humanity to fall so low it becomes reborn and rebuild a better society from the bottom. He's very troubled by the whole thing... has become very gloomy and grimly determined... thinks he just needs to see it through, no matter what. He is profoundly affected by people suggesting he is a coward all the time.'

'But you must tell him.'

'How can I? What good would it do? It would upset him even more, and we can't do anything about it, can we? Smith can't ever get to know. No one must ever know. If I told him it would only be selfishness on my part, to make some sort of claim over him – but it's simply futile. I'd put him in a position he could do nothing about. I can't add to his worries, needlessly.' She stared into her teacup. 'There is also a very practical point: if anyone finds out I'd lose my allowance. I have to give up work soon anyway before it starts to show, and then what would I live off? I couldn't go cap in hand to my family. They'd surely disown me. I'd end up in the workhouse. But, anyway, the chances are I'll lose it – it's what happens with me. And the problem will be solved.'

'You can't say that. It is a sacred life you are talking about.' Mary's brown eyes shone bright, the brightness swelled then spilled over her lower lashes.

'I'm sorry, Mary. I've just had no one to tell, to talk to. I don't know what to do.' She hung her head and wept also. There was one thing she would not be able to share with anyone, not even Mary – especially not Mary. It was her shame and hers alone. Early on she had tried to get rid of the baby. She shuddered, thinking of her conversation with the herbalist about "obstructions." He was a small man with sharp rodent-like eyes, who had shuffled about behind his counter weighing out herbs he took from tins on the shelf behind him: dried pennyroyal and feverfew. The concoctions had made her sick, with no other effects. There was also a woman who lived up Attercliffe, well known for her fortune-telling, but also for some pills she could dispense. She went by the name of Mucky Millie. Elsie went round one drizzly evening, hunched under Smith's umbrella, a shawl wrapped tightly around her head and covering most of her face. She handed over a shilling for a single pill that looked like a large silver bullet. It was so hard to swallow and made her violently sick almost straightaway, and the next day she could not leave the house, having to make numerous trips to the privy. After enduring such illness she expected her period to return, but it did not. She was now deeply ashamed of what she had tried to do. Mary's tears confirmed that.

'Don't worry. We'll think of something,' said Mary.

'What about you. Have you heard from your Robert?'

'He's not *my* Robert any more.'

'Why, what happened?'

'Oh nothing much. That was the point, nothing much ever really happened. Now he's gone off and enlisted and didn't want me tied to him so we agreed to call it off. He still writes, but just as friends. He's in training at Cannock Chase. There's talk of getting ready for a big push isn't there.'

'I'm sorry, Mary. You've got enough troubles of your own without adding mine as well.'

'Nonsense. Besides I am sure troubles don't follow the normal mathematical rules of addition. Come on, you can help me get father's dinner ready, then we can spend the afternoon coming up with a plan. There's some paper somewhere – I find it always helps to write things down and make lists.'

It was a few weeks into the New Year when Henry received his orders to mobilise.

'At least I avoided compulsory conscription,' he said. 'I'm off on a jolly adventure, Elsie,' he said. 'Off to sail the Seven Seas. I'm to be a stoker on a ship – it's doing what I do now, no training needed, straight in at first class stoker. Once you've seen one boiler you've seen 'em all. I'm off in the morning.'

'So soon?'

'Yes. Shall I call round on my way to the station?'

'No. I've got work in the morning. We can say goodbye properly after tea. Lily is off to the pictures with her pals.

Henry put his coat on and left at the same time as Lily that evening; then he waited until she was round the corner and crept back.

In bed, Elsie lost control of her emotions as she felt Henry's weight on her.

'I'm sorry, Elsie. Shall I stop?'

'No. No. Don't. Carry on. I'm just a silly.'

'No. No, you're not,' he murmured as he dried her cheeks with his palms. 'You're the most perfect creature there is.'

She looked deep into his eyes, twinkling in the candlelight. 'There's no need to stop, it won't make me pregnant.'

'Are you sure?'

'Yes. I know. Show me how much you love me, Henry.'

***

He settled his cap on his head and smiled at her.

'I'll see you soon then, Elsie.'

'Yes. Do take care.'

'Get yourself back in the warm.'

'Yes, I will.'

'Goodbye, Elsie. And thanks.'

***

A month or two later she spoke to the office manager and handed in her notice saying she had to go and look after an elderly aunt.

Mr Turner received her notice reluctantly. 'I don't know what we shall do to replace you. It is getting harder and harder to find people with experience, and ability. And, I must say, you have surprised me more than once with your ideas for improvements. Are you sure you won't change your mind?'

'No, sir. I am so sorry to have to leave you in a predicament, but it cannot be helped.'

'No. You must help your aunt if she needs you. I understand.'

'Perhaps if she gets well, then I could call in and see if you have any vacancies? I'd be willing to take anything on, to help you out.'

She told Lily she was going away to help an aunt convalesce. 'I'll send you what money I can for the rent. In the meantime, I can let you have half a crown.'

'I might have a friend at work who could move in if that would help? She's up from London and is in awful lodgings in town. You'll need your allowance for yourself, especially if you're not working. I can manage here.'

'That would be marvellous, Lily. A weight off my mind – and company for you too. She is welcome to my room; then when I come back, I can make up a bed in the front room if she wants to stay on.'

'You will write to me?'

'Yes, of course. And I want to keep hearing all the latest gossip from the millinery department and the staff restaurant.'

'Ooh, that reminds me! You'll never believe what happened today in gentleman's outfitting...'

The following week, Elsie had packed a bag and was travelling back to Renishaw. She was to sleep downstairs – Mary's father never left the upper floor. She would help by looking after Mary, whilst Mary looked after her father. And she would await events.

CHAPTER TWENTY-TWO

In spring several men were moved eastwards to another camp – farther from home, deeper into Germany. After spending a day or two there, they were marched to a nearby village and from there they were dropped off at various farms in the surrounding countryside. Smith was the last to be dropped off – the farmers chose Belgians, Italians or Russians in preference to the Englander. The last farm was a run-down looking one – the farmer just as bad: ancient and cantankerous. He did not want Englisch schwein. The guards allowed no choice. It was the Englander or no one.

The old man showed Smith into a yard with a woodpile and gave him an axe.

'Hack. Muss hack.'

The old man and his manners revolted him.

'Nicht verstehen,' he said.

The old man snatched the axe off him, placed a log upright, swung the axe like a twenty-year-old and split it, thrusting the axe back at Smith. The old man disappeared across the farmyard.

Smith did a bit, then rested and looked round. The farmhouse windows were dirty and cobwebby. The whole thing needed re-pointing: it would be full of mice or even rats the state it was in, and the roof was little better. There was a figure at an upstairs window that pulled back when he glanced up. He took off his jacket and split a few more logs then looked up again. Yes, he was being watched.

He worked for a bit longer before going over to the farmhouse door and knocking. He waited; then turned the door handle, pushing it open. It opened into a kitchen. He poked his head round the door.

'Hello?'

He heard a clatter and saw a young woman backing away from a mixing bowl she had dropped onto a table.

Smith held up the palms of his hands. 'No. Don't. I don't bite.'

He mimed drinking. She looked at him open-eyed, frozen. He goofed around like he was dying of thirst clutching his throat: '*Wasser! wasser!*'

A flicker of a smile changed the look of fear on her face, softened it. She was the one he'd seen upstairs. She had long dark hair, tied up, brown eyes set in natural shadows. She moved round the table keeping those eyes towards the door, picked up a cup and filled it from a jug – her long grey skirt whispered as she moved. She put the cup on the edge of a small table near the door and backed away.

Smith laughed at her. 'Look, I'm nice, me. *Freundlich*.' He half entered the room and picked up the cup.

'*Ich heise* Smith.'

She lowered her eyes.

'Here's where you tell me your name. *Wie heisen sie?*'

'Anna.'

'Pleased to meet you, Anna.'

'Pleased to meet you, Smiss.'

'You speak English?'

She smiled, colour returning to her cheeks. 'No. Only little. You muss... Vater.'

He understood, finished the water and backed out.

How strange he felt – to have a girl smile at him. That had not happened since... since St Nazaire.

He didn't exert himself; the old man came back into the yard several times and scowled at him, clearly expecting the work to have been finished on each return.

At dinnertime he sat at the table in the kitchen at the far end from the girl and her father – like he was contagious. The bread was chewy but wholesome and the stew actually contained some meat. He watched them as he ate, and threw in the occasional remark to break the silence.

'It's not bad for the time of year, is it?'

Anna looked at him, then at her father, before lowering her eyes again.

'I said it's not bad for the time of year is it you rude ol' bugger.'

Anna flashed a look of rebuke at him. He immediately felt guilty and took it no further.

He must have had her late in life – the dirty old sod. What was he sixty? seventy? You never could tell with these weather-worn peasants. Skin like chewed leather. He speculated where the mother was and whether there was anyone else in the household while he finished off his dinner.

***

Elsie's ordinary clothes, even the more ample ones, were starting to no longer fit her. Mary got out some of her mother's old clothes; ones she had never had the heart, or the need, to clear out. They were not the height of fashion – especially a traditional peasant smock that her mother wore in the garden – but they were comfortable and roomy.

In her letters to Lily she deliberately omitted her address, just writing "Derbyshire" on the top. When she had sat down with Mary to work out a plan they considered the dilemma of what to do with Henry – he would be sure to write to her at Danville Street, and if she gave away her new address he might try to visit if he was on leave. He was stationed on the Firth of Forth – so, with a railway pass, could be home the same day. They had both decided it was best that he never knew. Elsie had to let him go. The war would not go on forever, and Smith would return. They only had to keep up the deceit for a few more months.

They had decided the best thing was to arrange a private adoption involving as few people as possible. Mary said she knew someone at the church she went to in Spinkhill who might be able to help. It was an abstract concept at first and Elsie was convinced she would miscarry anyway, which made it even more so. However, one evening as she was sitting reading she felt a kick as the baby moved – inside her was a healthy, living being making itself known.

As the days grew longer and the frosts less severe, her relationship with her baby developed. She got to know its habits: when it slept and woke, when it hiccupped and its love of singing. Her baby's favourite song seemed to be "In Haven" – a songs she once sang at a concert in Lincoln, though she struggled for breath when trying to hold the notes. Tears rolled down her cheeks as she sang: 'Closely let me hold thy hand, storms and sweeping seas and land, Love alone will stand.' She hoped he was in a haven somewhere and not fighting against, and being tossed around on, a hostile grey sea, where it was hard to see where the water ended and the sky began, fearing an even more hostile enemy. But the song never failed to still the baby.

Mary's father liked it too, so Mary said. He thought his wife was downstairs in the kitchen and it brought him peace. Elsie did not see much of him – he became too stressed when it was someone other than Mary at his side. His shouting and raving became, to Elsie, just another of the sounds of their strange, little household – a different reality from the mad world outside, cut off it seemed in time and place.

They ate simply but well on their small income; Mary's father had worked on the local estate up until his illness and was given a small pension in return. In addition, Mary had managed to maintain her father's small cottage garden throughout, with some help from a neighbour. At first, when he could still get about the house, sitting in it had been a great comfort to him.

Elsie kept an ear open for sounds upstairs whilst Mary popped out one morning. She stood at the back door and felt the warmth of the sun on her face as she closed her eyes. A chair placed outside the back door step was about as far as she had roamed – she was in self-imposed exile, a bird in captivity, but it was not an incarceration so much as a cocoon. It felt as if it could go on forever, but there was someone who had other designs, who was already getting ready to shatter the spell, already manoeuvring to create a different reality.

Mary returned. 'I have some good news. I have spoken to Mrs Wheeler, who I mentioned to you. There is a young couple she knows of – very respectable, quite well-to-do. They're unable to have children – desperate to make a family.

'I know how that feels,' Elsie muttered.

'They're willing to take your baby and give it a good home. They don't want anything in return, and are even willing to give you five pounds as a goodwill gesture.' Elsie burst into tears.

'I don't want to sell my baby, Mary. I don't want to let it go at all, but won't sell it!'

'That's all right, Elsie, love,' said Mary putting her arm round her. 'You won't have to sell the baby. You don't have to take any money. I know it's hard. But, what else can we do? We've been through it all.'

'It's not fair. It's too cruel. I can't bear it.'

'Don't you worry about it. Everything will work out for the best, you'll see. From what I hear, the baby couldn't have a better home – parents who have the means to look after it and who will really love it. You mustn't worry.'

CHAPTER TWENTY-THREE

Smith planted beans, got soaked to the skin, cut – very badly – the first hay of the year with a scythe: just because he had some idea how to forge and grind one didn't give him any advantage in using one, and any rate this was inferior German steel so, if he made a hash of it, it wasn't his fault – and it wasn't his hay. He skived as much as he could get away with. He breathed lungfuls of fresh air and washed in cold clear water. He had some nights on his straw filled mattress when he felt rested at the end of his sleep, when the dreams hadn't returned or woken him up in a cold sweat.

Slowly his nerves were soothed a little. Slowly also, the old man, as well as his daughter, realised that Smith's horns were not so pointed, and that he was not going to strangle them as soon as he got an opportunity.

He snatched the odd conversation with Anna when her father was out of earshot. He helped her draw water from the well – something straight out of Grimm's Fairy Tales in Smith's eyes.

'Do not be cruel to Papa, Smiss. He is old and has much unhappiness. My mother, she died when I was young.'

'Did he bring you up on his own?'

'With his cousin – my aunt: she who taught us English. She lived in your London and came back when my mother died. My brother Manfred he was killed at the war, in West.'

'That's not my fault. You should not have started it.'

'We are not responsible. It is not the... low people who start war.'

'Ordinary people.'

'Yes – ordinary people. It is kings and counts and governments.'

'But your countrymen supported it.'

'Yes, that is so. But they are lied to. It is no good. So you won't say any bad things to Papa?'

'For your sake, no. But he clearly hates me.'

'He does not hate you. He – I don't know – an Englander killed his son – he has long been told that Englanders want to...' She ground her fists into her palm.

'But it was your Kaiser who...'

'I don't argue, Smiss. I try to... I see you are not bad man.'

'Well, thanks for that.'

She looked him in the eyes. Then looked him up and down. She touched his arm. Smith shuddered – it was like an electric shock through his body.

He stepped away.

'What is it? Smiss?'

'Nothing.' How could he tell her? No woman had laid a hand on him for two years.

'Your shirt is *schmutzig*. I will find you one of Manfred. This, I wash and *flicken*. Vater must never know from where it comes. You promise?'

'Yes. Thank you.'

On a fine day Anna came out into the field to help collect the hay. Smith was handed a wooden rake by the old man and the single word *Harke*. Never a *bitte* or *danke*, so he never got Smith to do more than a half-hearted job. It just made him more entrenched: it wasn't his hay, wasn't his farm. Anna and her father forked the piles onto a cart.

At dinnertime Anna produced some bread, and Smith took his ration and went to sit on his own by a tree for some quiet. He was sitting smoking when Anna came up.

'Papa says it is time to work.'

'He'll have to wait until I finish my smoke. Would you like one?'

She looked back up the field.

'Go on. He can't see us.'

She sat down and he lit her a cigarette and handed it to her.'

'You have sad eyes, Smith.'

'Wharr abaht thine? None too chipper neither.'

'I sometimes don't understand you.'

'Your eyes aren't happy either, I mean.'

'Does anyone have happy eyes in a war?'

'I suppose not.' He studied her face. He thought she flushed a little.

'Don't stare, Smiss.'

'Sorry. I'm just not used to seeing a female face up this close. Not since...'

'Do you have a girl in England?'

'Once. But... '

'I didn't mean to...'

'What about you?'

'My Hans... at the start of the war in France.'

Smith thought of all the German lives he'd have on his tally when the great day of reckoning came. He took a drag on his cigarette and narrowed his eyes. 'I'm sorry.'

'It's not your fault – there, your eyes are sad again. Come on we should try not to be sad. Let's work. Work is good.'

***

Elsie was the first out of bed, if only the second to wake: the baby woke before her and was yawning and stretching as it greeted a new day. It only took a slit to open in her consciousness before the need to use the chamber pot ended any hope of getting back to sleep; and, on top of that, her back was aching and the narrow bed in the parlour became unbearably uncomfortable.

She dressed and went through to make up the fire and scooped some water from the bucket to fill the kettle. Out in the garden it was still and quiet – one of those spring mornings where everything was wet with heavy dew, waiting for the sun to rise and warm the air.

She heard the creak of the stairs and Mary appeared in her dressing gown – her face expressionless, reflecting the cold grey dawn outside.

'He's gone,' she said.

Elsie knew immediately what she meant and went to give her a hug.

'When...'

'In the night. A noise woke me and when I went through I thought he had stopped breathing; but then it started again and I knew he was near the end. I've been sat with him waiting for the daylight to return. I wondered if it ever would.'

*

It was the first day of June. Elsie was in the house alone while Mary was out putting some of her father's favourite blue delphiniums on his grave. Dawn had been beautiful and the sun was now finding its warmth. She placed a wooden chair in a small sunny spot next to the honeysuckle, placed her hands over her large belly, turned her face to the sun, felt its rays on her eyelids. When she opened her eyes a robin was sitting on a rock a short distance away. She kept very still as it hopped across to another rock then fluttered up on to a twisted branch of the honeysuckle a few feet from her. It looked at her and she smiled.

169

'Good morning, sir. What is it?' It turned its head. She blinked in the sunlight. And when she opened her eyes it had gone. She looked around but it was nowhere to be seen.

A fortnight passed. The baby seemed to know it was time. Mary had negotiated staying on at the house for a few weeks by paying rent in advance; the landlord was kind but there were other workers on the estate who needed to be housed. But both of the women were steeling themselves for change. Mary suggested that Elsie move upstairs for the birth, but she would not – she was used to the little parlour with its ticking clock, the creaking sounds, the cardboard patches flapping at the window panes when the wind blew and the scurrying sounds at night.

Elsie hadn't wanted anyone else there. The thought of it becoming a public affair, gossiped about – made more real by being spoken of by strangers – horrified her. She and Mary had built this bubble of unreality around themselves and that was a small comfort at least. Mary had planned and prepared with military precision. She had found out about various complications and what to do, she had written notes and lists and lined up her clean towels and string, sharp scissors and carbolic. But it had gone well.

Mary placed the little towel-wrapped bundle on Elsie's breast, kissed her on the forehead and went to the kitchen.

The baby's hair was dark. She smoothed the still damp tufts. Its eyes seemed to stare and it moved its mouth. She was sure it was recognising her, seeking her out – it looked into her eyes and shattered her heart.

'Hello, little one,' she whispered. 'You are the most beautiful thing I've ever seen.' Her tears wetted the baby's head as she kissed it. 'I wish you would remember me. Always carry in your heart the knowledge that you were loved so much from the very start.' She unwrapped the towel and placed the little girl against her skin, felt the perfect, tiny hands against her chest. Those eyes seemed to look into hers again, and there followed a grimace. She put her to her breast and surrendered to the surge of love, so strong that it could have melted guns and blunted bayonets if unleashed.

The baby girl fell asleep and she sang: 'Kiss my lips and softly say, joy sea-swept, may fade today, love alone will stay.'

CHAPTER TWENTY-FOUR

Smith felt frozen in time – he did not want to think of the past, could not think of the future. This war that was supposed to be quick and decisive was three years old already. If you believed the Germans then it was nearly all over, that England was on its knees, but he saw around him with his own eyes the evidence, and everyone talked of it back at the *lager*: young German boys off to the front because there were no more men, prisoners parcels being robbed and fought over by Germans because they had no chocolate or cigarettes, the black market price of decent boots was sky high – and he had given Anna half a used bar of soap that she treasured like it was gold leaf. That couldn't be a country winning a war.

As harvests came in they were moved around to other farms, working in gangs – one day digging potatoes, the next picking beans. What should have been a reasonable potato harvest turned out to be less than expected when the Burgermeister inspected the stores. All had seemed to be going well when he visited the pickers in the fields. But, once his back was turned, for every potato picked for the Kaiser one was planted a little deeper for King George or "*une pour le Kaiser, et une pour le Roi Albert*" – or "*la Republique.*"

One hot summer's day Smith went with the old man up onto the moors where he was shown how to cut heather – this for taking back down to the farm for bedding for the cattle. Anna had wrapped some bread and cured beef in a cloth and sent him with a bottle of coffee. He soon got bored and went for a little walk to straighten his back and for an early dinner break. The moorland reminded him of Derbyshire: purple heather and birch woods, small rocky outcrops, boggy areas with cottongrass. He took off his boots and cooled his feet in a small mossy bog. He did a bit more work in the afternoon then headed back at around six. Anna was waiting for him at the farm entrance, reading a book. 'Did you work lots?'

'Yeah. Fair bit.'

'Back again tomorrow?'

'Yeah. No rest for the wicked.'

'I do not think you are wicked, Smiss.'

He smiled and shook his head, waving over his shoulder as he headed back to the *lager*.

The next day he was again given a small rake and scythe and sent back to the moor. As dinnertime approached he went to get his snap but realised he'd forgotten to bring it. 'Oh well, I've gone for longer. Wonder if there's any bilberries anywhere? At least I'll get some water.'

He went off to look and found a small river. It was just too tempting. He was sweaty and grimy and he'd not felt the freedom of swimming since visiting the baths at Sutherland Road. He hung his clothes over a tree at the water's edge and slipped and slid his way down the bank, before deciding to creep down crab-style towards a gravel bank at the edge of the cold water. A few yards in it was just deep enough to swim and the flow was such that with a certain effort he could maintain his position – going nowhere – or he could give up and float downstream before getting to his feet again and tentatively wading back up on the rocky bed of the stream. This beat cutting heather. It certainly beat life in Hamelin or getting shot at.

'Smiss, are you there? Is that you?'

'No! I mean yes, but…' He sat down in the water so that only his head was above the stream. 'You are bad. I brought your bread. You forgot it? You should work. Come out.'

'I can't.'

'Oh.'

'Turn your back, and promise not to look until I say.'

'I promise.' She headed a few steps up the slope and turned her back.

'I'm getting out now.'

'All right.'

Clambering up the grassy bank was easier than getting down. In his concentration to keep his footing he did not notice Anna quickly glance his way, nor her shoulders shaking as she suppressed a giggle at his pallidness and his somewhat cold-diminished state.

She walked back up to the heather with him.

'What will I tell father? You've have not much cut.'

'Tell him what you like. It's not my heather. They're not my cows. I am a slave don't forget.'

'You are not. You go too far.'

'What?'

'You go too far. Your words.'

'Exaggerate.'

'Yes, exaggerate. You exaggerate. Always. And the opposite. Why? When something is good you say it is "all right" or "not bad," when you are well you say you "have been worse," or "all right from neck up" – what that means? When you are sick or sad you say you are "fine." I don't understand. '

'I suppose I do do that. It's perhaps a Yorkshire thing. And it's "from t'neck dahn" not up: sound, but not reight in t'head, kinda thing. I'm pulling your leg.'

'What? What is the relevance of my leg?'

'Oh, it doesn't matter.'

'You must do more work. I must go or my Papa wonders.'

'He might think you've been carrying on.'

'Carrying on? Carrying what? *Das Heidekraut?*'

'Heather.'

'Yes, the hezza.'

'What's tha on abaht?'

'Wass?'

'Ne' er mind, eh.'

'Wass?'

'Go on. See you later. Wiedersehen.'

He worked quite hard the following day, and at dinnertime decided to go for another swim before he had his snap – he deserved to have a cool down after such unwonted exertion.

The afternoon wore on, and he was considering finishing early and taking a slow walk back when he saw a horse-drawn cart pulling up the track. It was not being driven by the old man but Anna. He stopped, leant on his rake and watched her approach: she moved in time with the cart as it bumped over the path. She raised a hand in greeting.

'To what do I owe the pleasure?'

'*Ich verstehe nicht.*'

'Nothing. How do you do?'

'Very good. Have you worked hard today?'

She jumped down from the cart.

'Papa was called to an important meeting in the village. I said I could instead. I come to take the hezza back. You help?'

They turned the cart around and Anna put a nosebag on the old horse. She fetched two forks from the back of the cart and they

173

started to load it up, working quickly without speaking. They soon had a cartload.

'*Danke schön, Smiss.*' She touched him on the elbow. He pulled away.

'Why you afraid of me?'

'I'm not. It's…'

She took both his hands and held them tight. He hung his head, and from somewhere deep inside him a sob rose up, something that took him by surprise.

'You poor boy.' She touched his cheek and he convulsed. His protective layers, his armour, built up over years, fell around him as the sobs broke over him. She pulled his head onto her shoulder and held him. His knees buckled.

Slowly his tears subsided and embarrassment and disgust came over him as he regained himself.

'I'm sorry,' he said, lifting his head. 'I had no right. I'm sorry.'

'No. Do not be. I am happy I can be your friend.'

He looked into her dark eyes and was confused, scared. He made to get to his feet but she kept her hand on his shoulder. Her face was flushed from the last heat of the day and their efforts loading the cart. Strands of hair had come loose from under her headscarf and clung to the sweat on her forehead and at the back of her neck. He breathed in her scent, brushed the hair away from her forehead.

She folded her arms around him. They lay down on his jacket and afterwards he again sobbed from the release, from an emotion so strong, from a love – right there and then – like he could not recall, but also from his shame. Anna comforted him like a small child.

When he arose the next day he was full of anxiety. His head was a whirl with images of Anna. She had filled his dreams. He could still smell her on his hands. How would she receive him? Would she be ashamed, or angry with him for what had happened?

Instead, she promised to bring the cart up again in the evening. It meant he had to work at least hard enough to produce a load – not a work incentive he was accustomed to.

Then later in the week she came again and suggested that he take her to his swimming spot. She sat on his knee in the water and he felt her warmth. The effect of the cold water on her body was something incredible to him.

He was up as usual at five thirty the next morning ready to head to the farm. He got ready and lined up for the march to the farms with the other prisoners. Instead of just the usual elderly *landsturmer*, the *feldwebel* was out. He walked down the line with one of the guards and picked some men out.

'You. You. You. Go with.' Smith was the last of the ten chosen.

They were shown to a cart waiting outside the camp gates and told to get in.

'Où est-ce qu'on va, camarade?'

'Don't ask me. Working together on a farm perhaps.' This was not the first time a gang had been put together.

It was not until they pulled up outside a small station that Smith realised that this was not the usual day trip. The train they were put on took him farther and farther away from Anna.

They were taken to a large farm and locked in a barn fitted out with bunks. In the afternoon they were in the fields cutting wheat alongside locals who assiduously shunned them, and guards all too willing to exhibit their vicious streaks.

For weeks they brought in crops, operated threshing machines, heaved straw into barns. They were made to hoe fields, or lift root crops.

The accommodation was poor and Smith found himself covered in lice once more, relying on sporadic food parcels again to keep body together now that he was back on black bread and thin soup.

CHAPTER TWENTY-FIVE

Some stopped working, but Elsie carried on after the buzzer went off and the arc lights went out – she still had enough light with the incandescent bulb over her favourite Drummond lathe to see the base-ends of the eighteen-pounder shells and to make sure they were true. People still went to and fro in the semi-darkness, pulling trolleys, clinking shells, each lathe had someone stood by, base-ending or pipping the shells, boring and cutting threads. She called her lathe, Bessie – Bessie Drummond. She sang to Bessie and Bessie sang back as she brought in the tool and removed the outer skin of steel to make it bright and shiny.

She and Bessie had an understanding – one that could only exist between two females; her traverse was a bit temperamental but shouting at her and cursing her like the men did wouldn't get the best out of her. Elsie coaxed her along and produced twice as many shells in a day as her predecessor, Bert. Bert who had originally shown her what to do before he left for France. But she had learnt properly by teaching herself, not thanks to him. The fitter Charles, though, was someone she could get along with – rather aloof and condescending, but he was not as rude and sullen as some of the others, so that went a long way with her.

Then the remaining lights went out and they were plunged into darkness. This was not the first time, so Elsie picked her way slowly over to the gangway.

'Are you there, Mary?'

A voice came back. 'Yes, over here. I'll come towards you. I'll strike a match.'

'Is that crate still there?'

'I think so. Yes, it is. Come on.'

They found each other's hands then sat back to back on the crate.

'What time is it, Mary?'

'Well, we had dinner about... what? ... an hour and a half ago? So... two-thirty-ish?'

'So, perhaps another three-and-a-half hours to go.'

'Yes. Could be a long night. The longest of these has been five hours, so George said.'

A song was already being stuck up by some of the girls: 'Dear face that that holds so sweet a smile for me, were you not mine, how dark the world would be.'

Then they heard the thump thump of the anti-aircraft guns over on Wincobank Hill and everyone went quiet, lost in their own thoughts.

How far away that last spring now seemed? It almost seemed like a dream. At least that is how it felt in her head – her heart knew truer.

She was taken away in a brand new rush basket. That middle-aged woman with a pinched mouth, clearly wanted to get it over with as quickly as possible, no fuss or nonsense. How her body had ached

Her milk seemed to take weeks to dry up despite the cups of sage tea – her tears would never dry, her heart would never heal. Every day she woke to a sense of loss when she realised she was alone.

Her grief had been compounded when she had got back to Sheffield and Danville Street.

'Where have you been, Elsie?' said Lily when she'd stepped through the door.

'You stopped writing? You never gave me your address. I needed to write to you.'

'I'm sorry. I just couldn't,' said Elsie, bursting into tears. 'I wanted to, but I couldn't.'

Lily started to cry too, and they embraced.

'I've got some bad news, Elsie.'

Elsie pulled away to look Lily in the eyes. 'What?'

'It's Henry. He didn't make it.'

Elsie sank into a chair.

'His ship... it went down. No survivors.'

Ever since she had not been able to get visions out of her head. They came during the daytime but were worse at night. There were explosions and cold water, oil and fire pouring in on her in the darkness, and her baby being ripped away from her by the sea.

'Are you all right Elsie,' said Mary. 'You shivered. Are you cold?'

'No. I'm fine. Mary... there's something I've never told you.'

'What's that?'

'You'll think I'm a bit soft.'

177

'I won't.'

'I think Henry came to see me.'

'What do you mean?'

'I was sat in the garden at Renishaw when a robin came and sat with me. About the same time that his ship was lost. Silly, isn't it? Just a coincidence.'

'That's as maybe. But it's nice to believe it – so I believe it.'

'To think we'd end up here, eh?' It went quiet again outside. 'But it honours his memory, doesn't it? – he had decided it had to be brought to an end as soon as possible with our side the winners, so that's what we're doing: throwing our all into eleven or twelve-hour days or nights. It has become a question of mathematics, hasn't it? If we can produce three or four hundred shells each day, how many Germans can our boys kill with each of those, and how many Germans do we need to kill to get them to give in?'

'Elsie, that's horrible.'

'But it's true, isn't it? That's all it comes down to. Who can obliterate the other side the fastest. Henry's just one. There will be millions of Henrys before this ends.'

One of the girls over in counter-boring started singing "Meet Me Where the Lanterns Glow." Sometime last year, Henry had bought the record of the Haydn Quartet singing the song and played it on the gramophone – back in the days when the war had not really affected them, and its only impact on her had been Smith's absence.

Henry had mentioned the song in one of the letters he had addressed to them both. How painful that had been – to bring him to life temporarily in their reading?

'I'm looking forward to being back on days again next week,' said Mary. 'I feel so tired. In fact I'll just rest my eyes for a bit.'

Elsie was left to her ghosts.

CHAPTER TWENTY-SIX

When all work in the fields was done, once ditches had been cleared and roofs secured, there was another shake-up; Smith was moved and crossed paths with Cornelius again.

'All new Englanders outside.' Their names were called out by the interpreter along with some Russians: 'Get your kits and come.'

They were marched to the station and onto a train. After travelling across country they came to a small station, and from there a long walk took them to another camp where the huts were made from corrugated iron.

'Looks like a pig farm, Darky.'

'Probably was – ach, chuck some barbed wire around it and there you go. Ready for the English *Schwein*.'

They were pushed into one of the sheds and the door bolted behind them. There were no bunks in this place – they slept on the floor.

Smith introduced himself to a young lad called Ellis he pitched down next to.

'You'd better keep your voice down in here. The sentries are bastards. Worse than anywhere else I've been. Got everyone quaking in their boots they have.'

'What's that accent? Cornish?'

'No, I'm from Canada, mate. Don't tell anyone – especially the Hun. Well, I'm half Scottish but you're best off being fully Scottish round here than Canadian – they hate no one more than us. Regard us as some sort of mercenary they do.'

'I know. I've seen how they treat you boys.'

Smith learnt how he'd been captured at St Julien near Ypres after having witnessed a gas attack.

'Clouds of greeny-yellow fog drifting towards us. I'll never forget those men I came across in that trench. Faces red, suffocating on fluid in their lungs, vomit everywhere.'

They stood in line and the camp commandant came down the line feeling their arms: '*Kräftig – für den Steinbruch.*'

'What they say, Smith?'

'*Kräftig* is strong. And *stein* is stone. So *steinbruch* must be stone-break – quarry, I guess.'

'Oh shit. That's not good.'

'*Seid still.*'

They were nearly all selected for the quarry. They were lectured on hard work, and punishment, and fallen in to march to the *steinbruch*. The work involved loading up small trucks with stones on the narrow gauge railway, and getting regular beatings off the guards for not keeping up. Cornelius took the lead by carrying two of the smallest stones per trip to put in the truck – at that rate it would have taken him all morning to fill it, rather than the matter of minutes expected. Smith followed suit. As he bent down to pick two more up he felt a pain in his head. The guard had thrust his revolver into his temple: 'You must work.'

'You want to get a long one of those, and get to the front, you cowardly bastard.'

They worked a bit harder. Next it was Cornelius's turn. A guard kept kicking him to work faster. He finally gave him a shove and Cornelius fell over onto a heap of stones. He sat still for a second or two, frozen; then he rose up holding a rock over his head and moved towards the guard who was frantically trying to get his pistol out.

Smith saw what happened. sensed the switch being flicked in Cornelius's head.

'Put that bloody thing down, you suicidal bastard!' he ran up shouting, and grabbed the rock off him.

'No German's going to knock me about.'

'Your turn will come; not now.'

Young Ellis who was nearby also jumped up and stood in the way of the guard, got him to cool down. Then a few more prisoners gathered round.

'You're pushing us too hard – we're only supposed to work till six, not seven.'

'Ja. Ja. Back to work. Work to six.'

'And no more kicking.'

'Ja. Everything forgotten. Work to six.'

They went back to work until a little later when the Feldwebel appeared with a Belgian interpreter and gathered all the prisoners together.

The interpreter spoke: 'The German pig says you're not working hard enough. That is the problem. If you work harder, no more beatings and you get *fleische* two times each week.'

Then the Feldwebel pointed at Cornelius. 'You – *mitkommen.*'

He then spoke to the guards and one of them pointed at Smith with his pistol.

'You – *kommen.*'

Ellis walked up to the feldwebel, opened his coat and tapped his chest and said coldly, 'Put it here, you German bastard. Put it here.'

'Get back, Ellis. There's no point your getting a bashing as well.'

Then some of the others stepped forward.

'Altogether, lads,' and it was the same: 'Put it here! Put it here!'

The sentries tried to restore order, tried to single out Smith and Cornelius but couldn't. The others kept grouping round them.

'Ja. Ja. Back to work. All is *vergessen.*'

Back at the camp, spirits were high.

'I'm glad you Brits came along,' said Ellis. 'Everyone here's been too cowed to stand up for themselves. All it took was a bit of a stand.'

'Victoire, camarade!' said one of the Belgians.

Smith wasn't so sure.

They were woken in the morning with the usual rifle butts on feet. As the guard approached Cornelius he sat up in bed: 'You do, you bastard, and I'll have you.' The Guard moved on and hit the next man instead.

After they'd been round the hut, two of them came back to Cornelius and ordered him to remove the urine bucket. As Cornelius bent to pick it up a guard struck him with the flat of his bayonet, the other kicked him in the backside. He picked up the bucket, contents slopping over the poor Belgians whose bunks were near the door and rushed at the sentries. One ran from the hut, the other hid behind the stove and was trying to get his pistol out.

Smith and Ellis again calmed the situation down.

'Put the bloody thing down, Darky, you mad-eyed bastard.'

The German made his escape.

They all filed out of the hut to wash in the yard and lined up by the tap. Two guards were waiting by the door to give them a kick on their return: they backed off when Ellis snarled at them, Smith copied him and escaped the treatment as well. Back inside, the doors were bolted.

Then they realised Cornelius wasn't back. Smith rushed to the door but it was no use.

'Ah, kaput – mijn vriend.'

When they were falling in for work they saw blood on the parade ground – lots of blood.

'Anyone going to go and break rocks for the German war effort lads?'

'Nah. I'm done.'

'Right – no one picks up any tools when we get there.'

They marched to the quarry then stood still refusing to move.

'*Los, and die arbeit.*'

'No. No work.'

There was shouting and shouting back, but no one moved. They were marched back to the camp, the guards in a filthy mood.

They lined up against their hut, stony-faced, with a guard up on a raised bank covering them with his Mauser. The Feldwebel came out and stood facing them, then paced up and down. Guards rushed off to the village, returning with the Burgermeister, his shotgun under his arm.

'So you will not work?'

Several of the prisoners spat on the floor sending him into an apoplexy. Then the reinforcements arrived from the village – old men armed with poles, hedge-stakes, and pitchforks.

'Bloody hell, lads. Look at that lot.'

Some of them forced a laugh. The prisoners were pushed and prodded into a compound surrounded by barbed wire, with sentries training Mausers on them.

'Here you stand until you work.'

Minutes turned into hours. Lunchtime came and went and still they stood in silence.

The Feldwebel came. 'You will work now?'

There was no reply. He spoke to a guard, who returned dragging Cornelius behind him. He looked dazed, was covered in blood and his skull was red raw where they had nigh on scalped him with a bayonet.

'So you will not work? He would not work. This is what is no work.'

Smith looked at his feet. He couldn't bear to see what had happened to Cornelius. It would haunt him. One by one they were asked if they would work and one by one they replied with a sullen: yes.

The next day Smith and Ellis were taken away and sent back to the main camp they had been in before. They went straight into solitary confinement. They found themselves in adjacent cells – six feet by six, made of wood. It was easy enough to communicate through the thin partitions.

'I'll see if there's anyone on the other side,' said Smith.

He tapped. 'Anyone there?'

'That you, Smith?'

'Darkie? How you blowing?'

'Been worse. Head all bandaged up, but at least I'm getting fed. Sending me away for a trial apparently – food for a condemned man no doubt.'

The rations in solitary were water and black bread, but one morning when Smith was led out for a wash and to use the latrines, Smiler was hanging around. He gave Smith a nod and when the guard wasn't looking tipped tea into Smith's empty wash jug and some white bread went into his enamel bowl, which he covered with his towel.

They occupied their time fantasizing about escape – discussing the odds of making a run for it if they were sent back to the canal or the moor, or of whether there was a way through the fence at night, or jumping from a train if they were transferred again.

After ten days Smith and Ellis were sent back out to work again – Cornelius left behind, still awaiting his trial.

CHAPTER TWENTY-SEVEN

Life was a succession of long shifts at the projectile factory punctuated by occasional trips to the cinema with Lily and her friend Betty or, at the end of a night shift, she went with Mary up into town for coffee and a toasted teacake. Materially, life was very comfortable – she was earning far more than she could spend, especially when on piece-rate at four and three-quarters per dozen. Some weeks, when Bessie was behaving, she could make the best part of fifty shillings.

It was nice to share the house with Lily and Betty – it meant she often had company to take her out of herself. She also liked continuing her new habit of sleeping downstairs, feeling closer to the earth.

She enjoyed stretching her limbs out between cool sheets, tired after standing most of the day. That feeling of drifting away from the mundane. Footsteps passed by along the pavement outside... Footsteps coming towards the park bench on which she sat... flowerbeds laid out with yellow and pink... the spring sunshine on her back...

Something disturbed her sleep. She emerged from unconsciousness with a sense of unease. How long had she been asleep? She couldn't see the clock in the darkness. There was a vibration – *zum zum zum* – like a traction engine was moving down the street, or a threshing machine.

Then an almighty bang and glass shattered all round her – louder than ten simultaneous claps of thunder. There was a scream from upstairs. She threw the bed clothes back and glass fell to the floor. She grabbed her boots from under the bed and crushed glass underfoot as she went to the bottom of the stairs.

Betty was at the top, ghostly white in her nightdress: 'Lily!'

'I'm fine. I think.'

Elsie rushed up the stairs. They found Lily still in bed; pieces of window glass on the counterpane glistening in what little light filtered through the billowing curtains.

Again the night was shattered by an explosion and the walls shook. There was a deep rumble somewhere above then a thud.

'Oh my God! Oh my God!' Lily muttered, rigid, not daring to move.

'It's all right Lily. Let's get you up. We need to move fast.'

They sat her up, shook glass to the floor. There was another huge bang – Elsie went to the window. A dark shape like a big black cloud was moving across the starry sky, travelling in the direction of the city. 'It's a Zepp. It's quite close. We need to get out down the cellar.'

'I'm not being buried in the cellar,' said Betty.

'Let's get out into the open, then.'

'I think I'm bleeding.' Lily's palm was wet and dark.

'Let's get you downstairs.'

They lit a candle and examined Lily – it was a cut over her ear. Elsie wrapped a bandage around her head.

'Are you sure you won't come down the cellar.'

'No chance. I'm going to see if anyone needs any help.'

'We'll all come, then.'

They put on coats and hats and went out into the street. They weren't the only ones. People were gathering at the entrance of the court over the road – people coming out covered in plaster dust, looking scarcely human in the gloom.

'Is everyone all right?'

'Fred Stratford got hit, someone said. The bastards!'

Betty and Lily guided people away from the scene and helped with getting the children washed and tea mashing. Elsie went through into the yard at the back and had to climb over a pile of rubble and bricks. The air was acrid and she could taste the dust. The back walls had been blown off, leaving the houses looking like an open dolls' house after a peevish brother had attacked it – furniture was up-ended and thrown across the rooms, bedclothes were strewn about and a water pipe trickled over bricks making them glisten in the starlight.

One of the neighbours came out of the house.

'Is everyone out?' she asked.

'Yes. I think so... I was just checking... apart from old Mr Stratford, that is – what's left of him.'

There was another loud bang, and another in quick succession down past the end of the street.

Some slates slipped and crashed at Elsie's feet.

'We'd best get back out before it's too late.'

An orange glow over the rooftops beyond Grimesthorpe Road shone on the faces of people out in the street. More explosions followed, getting farther away. A mother comforted her two children, wrapped in blankets. Elsie recognised Mr Harrison, an acquaintance of Smith.

'Is anyone hurt?' she asked.

'No, thank God. They were both in the back bedroom. There was shrapnel embedded in the walls over the bed, but they were both untouched.'

'If you want to come round to ours I'll get the fire lit. We've lost some windows but it's not too bad round the back.'

'Thank you.'

Mrs Harrison was singing quietly, 'Praise God from whom all blessings flow, Praise Him all creatures here below.'

It was a song that would be heard again before the night was out.

The Harrison children were put to bed in Betty's room where the windows remained intact. Elsie started to clean up.

She only had a short doze in a chair that night before going out to make more shells to exact revenge for all those killed.

They learnt of one family who lived nearby: mother and father, two daughters and two little granddaughters who were sheltering in their cellar with two neighbours. All eight were killed; buried in the cellar. The overall toll was at least twenty-four killed outright, with several others not surviving their wounds.

After that night, the city was on edge – the belief that the Zeppelins would never reach so far inland had been shattered. Every air-raid buzzer became a cause for extreme anxiety, if not panic, and sent people scurrying for open ground – for the parks, recs, or graveyards.

'If they gerrus there, at least it'll save 'em the bother of carrying us ovver, an' save t' price of an oak box,' said one her neighbours, Mr Jebbison, whom she met on the way up the road one dark evening at the end of November.

*

At the works, things became more organised – across the city those in charge of armaments' production saw a need to keep the souls and bodies of their workers together. They provided canteens to ensure they had at least one good meal a day, committees set up to organise variety evenings, teams representing various works competed against each other in swimming and hockey. Elsie got elected to the women's organising committee. The newsletter carried an appeal for players for a women's football team. "No experience necessary. Speak to Effie Sayles in the threading department." She discussed it with Mary at tea-break.

'Perhaps I should join the choir instead. After all I know I can sing.'

'But you're always singing – at least once a week in church. You should do something different. I would but I'm useless at sport – I've no coordination – I couldn't even get skipping in the playground right. Not like you.'

She attended the first football training session at the rec on Scott Street. Mr Grimes, a foreman from the grinding shop, was to be their manager. He split them into two teams and watched them chase the ball around for five minutes before stopping them and calling them over.

'You are like a gaggle of geese chasing a bloody meal bucket. No discipline. Spread out. Pass the ball. I know you're slipping all over the place in your work boots, but if you applied a little *nous*, you might not have to chase around so much.

It was true. They did look an ill-disciplined bunch. Only one or two in proper boots; most of them in their work gear: long skirts flapping around, an assortment of hats for keeping their hair out of the machinery, and not much of a clue. They tried to spread out and pass, and succeeded to a degree. Elsie even managed to score a goal. A ball had bobbled in front of her and she'd whacked it as hard as she could and was quite amazed to see it fly on target into the bottom corner.

'Right. Well done, ladies. Some of you have potential, at least.'

As she made her way home afterwards something happened to her that hadn't happened for a long while. It took her by surprise; crept up on her. She smiled and laughed to herself. It was a sense of euphoria – a natural and unexplained happiness.

CHAPTER TWENTY-EIGHT

On her way home after her shift, Elsie saw a queue forming outside a grocer's shop on Ellesmere Road. She went to join it. She recognised a neighbour just in front of her.

'Good evening, Mrs Hughes?'

'Ey up, love? Come to join the party?'

'I thought I should at least see.'

'You do right, love. Hawleys have just got some tea in, so they say, so I thought I'd pop along. But then I get here and someone says it's butter. Either way, I'll stop and see.'

'Well, we ran out of tea last week, so it's worth a try.'

'So, how are you keeping, love? Heard owt from your fella?'

'I'm not so bad, thank you, Mrs Hughes. And no, I've not heard from him for a few months. I don't suppose it's easy.'

Mrs Hughes shook her head. 'Well, no news is good news, as they say.'

'What about your eldest?'

'I had a letter from him Monday, last. As good as can be expected. But I do worry. All the time. You do, don't you? You get a letter and think: that's good he's safe, then a day passes and you worry again, then a whole week where you don't know owt and you're feeling just as sick again until another letter, and so it goes on. Any sign of this queue moving? I can't see over the tops of these hats. Will you hold my place while I go and see what's happening?'

She came shuffling back a few minutes later.

'Aggie, her from number fifty-one, on t'end, says it's definitely butter, but then another says she's heard it on good authority that it's only margarine. By the way. How's things at your works? All back to normal now the strike's ended?'

'Yes, thank goodness.'

'Well, I'm glad. Shameful it had to come to that. It dishonoured our boys out in France.'

'Yes, but...'

'Oh, don't get me wrong. I think they were dead right. My Edward said so much in his letter – he's not out there fighting so that the government and bosses can roll back everything that workers have fought for since the days of old King George.'

'I agree…'

'To go back on an agreement was shameful of that Lloyd George. They just want to turn our men back into serfs again. Tugging their forelocks. Yes, sir. Anything you say, sir. But we won't have it. No. A war that ends in subj… wotsit –'

'Subjugation?'

'That's it – is not worth fighting. It's all very well bringing in lasses like you, and I'm sure you do a grand job, but they want dilutees everywhere to bring down wages.'

'You're absolutely right. People can blame the engineers, say it's not patriotic – but they use that as an excuse. Is it patriotic for the Government to prolong a dispute – hold out for weeks on end to try to starve men and their families back to work on wages that don't support a family. They claim the country can't afford it and blame the war, but it's a choice. The rich choose not to share their wealth.'

'Well said, lass. I knew you were a good 'un. Saw you up the monument handing out papers before the war. I can't be doing with stupid flag-wavers that have not even tried to think things through.'

It was already light outside when Elsie and Mary came off shift. They joined the little streams of women merging into one vast river at the works' gates and spilling out into the road. Already the sun was up and starting to chase away the night-time's dampness, leaving an assortment of wet geometric shapes on roads and pavements where its rays had not yet reached. Steam and smoke billowed out from chimneys and vents, up into the sunlight.

'I'm famished; don't know about you?' said Mary. 'Shall we treat ourselves?'

'I don't know. I'm a bit tired.'

'No you're not. What you need is a change of air. Come on. I'm going to go home, get changed and go straight into town and have a slap up breakfast at Cockaynes when it opens, and you're coming with me.'

'Oh, go on then. You've twisted my arm.'

Elsie transformed herself as best she could from munitionette into something approaching elegance – at least as far as her dull lifeless hair that smelt of cutting fluid, broken fingernails and stubborn traces of black in the cracked, hard skin of her hands would allow. She got out her best frock, fingered some lavender water through her hair and pinned it up, and was reasonably pleased when she checked the results in the mirror over the sideboard on her way out.

She was still early, so decided to walk into town. As she passed under Wicker Arches she saw the elephant approaching, its head bobbing up and down as it pounded the dusty street, trunk limply swaying. Elsie stopped at the curb's edge to watch her pass. So big, so powerful. Her eyes pricked and tears welled up as the beast came near – saw its sad eyes. Such a beautiful creature, dignified and dutiful – doing her bit for the country, even though it wasn't hers. Her long life spent so far from home. And yet she just got on with it, worked hard. She smelt its scent and wanted to reach out and touch its wrinkled flanks as it passed, then looked on in horror as the man riding behind struck her on the side with a cane.

She walked slowly towards the bridge. People made jokes about her: 'as as big as Tommy Ward's elephant' they said, or, if someone was carrying lots of shopping, 'done up like Tommy Ward's elephant.' Instead she should be a symbol of dignity and resolve to see this war through.

She was still very melancholy when she reached Angel Street. They spent a small fortune on their breakfast.

'There's no food shortage for those that can afford it, is there?' said Mary.

'No, it's true. They say that there are people with vast stocks of food up in places like Ranmoor.'

'So come on, then – what's up? You've not been terribly good company lately.'

'Oh, I don't know, Mary. Just like everyone else: I'm tired. Tired of it all dragging on. It's nearly three years now and there's no sign of an end to it. In fact, it's hard to retain hope, given what we hear of what's going on. And, oh... I don't know...'

'What you need is a break. A holiday. Let's go to the seaside.'

'No, Mary. We can't.'

'Why? What's stopping us?'

'Well, there's work for one thing.'

'Oh, stuff that! There's the bank holiday coming up, anyway. It will do you good. Even a couple of nights away. Where shall we go?

Blackpool? There's the Pleasure Beach, the Winter Gardens, the circus – and it's safe from bombing.'

'No. We should go to Scarborough. Support them. They need it most. If I'm going, I'm not running away from the war; simply getting a rest. And it's more peaceful and beautiful than Blackpool.'

'Very well, then. Scarborough it is.'

Mary bought an ABC Railway Guide before Elsie could change her mind and bought an *Independent*. Then in her eagerness to get everything planned she sent a telegram to the owner of a boarding house on the South Bay who was asking four shillings and sixpence for full board.

They worked Saturday morning and set off straight away. There were due back on nights on the Monday.

They arrived in time for tea and went for a walk on the Esplanade and through the South Cliff Gardens to the Spa and beyond to the new bathing pool with its water chute. Elsie breathed deeply, the air such a contrast to the soot and smells of home. They watched the holidaymakers relaxing, laughing, and children playing as if life were normal. They stopped to listen to some music at the Spa, then went down to the foreshore where cool evening winds and saltiness were blowing off the sea.

'Shall we head back,' said Mary. 'I'm ready for an early night.'

The next day they caught a tram and went boating at Peasholm Park and in the evening went to a concert at the Floral Hall having strolled around Alexandra Gardens. On their last day they visited the castle, wandered around Boyes department store and made a few small purchases, then drank tea in the cafe. The day passed too quickly.

'I'm going to go for a little lie down before it's time to go, said Mary. 'All this sea air makes you sleepy. And I'll be back on my grinder tonight.'

'I'll stay out a bit longer,' said Elsie. 'I intend to eke out every last minute. This was such a good idea of yours, Mary. I might pop down onto the sands.'

'Well, in that case, I might leave you to it. See you in a bit.'

She stood for a long time looking out over the beach which was starting to empty. The bathing machines had been pulled back up the beach. Away to her left stood the cliff with the castle walls standing watch; and nestled below that, the old town with its chimneys and harbour, sadly depleted of its trawler fleet. What brave men they must have been to face both the sea and the submarines in those small boats. There was not much sign of the damage done by the bombing, except that the lighthouse tower no longer stood over the harbour where she remembered it.

She sat on the sand, unlaced her boots and felt the cool sand on her feet. She headed down to the water's edge and hitched up her skirts as the cold water lapped at her feet. She let the sound bathe her mind and closed her eyes. She lost her sense of vertical, felt she was a flimsy thing swaying with the breeze and the murmuring waves. She had to open her eyes again; they were drawn to the line between sea and sky. Somewhere out there, hundreds of feet down was the Black Prince. And Henry. His body reclaimed by the sea. His atoms spreading through the whole ocean. She reached down and dipped her hand in the cold water and raised it to her lips. She tasted the salt. Salty drops from her lashes fell and added a tiny amount to the sea's volume.

She turned and walked back up the beach. She too had now said goodbye.

CHAPTER TWENTY-NINE

As their third summer of captivity came to an end, and they started to steel themselves for another winter, more men were sent to the mines. The stories from the coal mines were bad enough, but, with what the salt mines did to your skin – bringing you out in suppurating blisters, the rocks ripping your skin to shreds – and the effect on your lungs, it was regarded as a death sentence.

There was a thriving black market – money changed hands on games of cards or crown and anchor dice.

One time, Smith wiped out a Belgian at Crown and Anchor.

'Right then, Ludo. What are you going to do about it? That's five marks you owe me now.'

'I get you something comrade. What you want?'

'Can you get me a hat?'

'What hat?'

'Just an ordinary felt hat, like a German wears.'

'Yes, Smet. I can get. Give me a chance to win back. I add nice shirt if I lose, yes? Ten marks is one shirt. Credit?'

'Right, Ludo you're on.'

'*Allez. Un mark sur trèfle.*'

'Here goes. Ah, Ludo. Too bad. Two anchors and a diamond.'

'*Ah! Godverdomme!*'

Smith was put to work on some new huts that were being built to expand the camp – a much more cushy job than the quarry or work on the moors, so he actually put in a shift to hang onto it. He also had other motives.

One evening, Smith was visiting the latrines before locking up time. A workman was up a short ladder replacing a pane of glass. His toolbox was on the floor, and, as he went past, Smith bobbed down and carefully and soundlessly removed a screwdriver. Then on the way back out, as the workman was scraping the window frame of old putty, he deftly removed the workman's jacket that was hung on a slightly protruding nail, folding it and slipping it under his own jacket.

Before lights out he checked his new acquisition and found a permit in the inner pocket as well as a box of matches and some tobacco. He folded it all back up before anyone could see him and when the lights were out hid it at the bottom of his palliasse. He waited, expecting there to be a commotion and a search, but it never came – perhaps the workman was scared to confess that he had been so careless.

A week or two later a rumour circulated – one of the Belgians was convinced there was about to be a large number of prisoners removed for the mines. He'd overheard Germans talking about the desperate need for more workers, because of people being sent to the Front. Smith decided it was time to act. He spoke to Ellis.

'You're not going to wait to be sent to the salt mines are you, Ellis?'

'Why? What you mean?'

'Do you fancy trying a home run?'

'You bet. What's your plan?'

'I'll explain later, but tell me a bit more about growing up in Canada and surviving in the forests...'

On Sunday he had had so many trips to the latrines that his friends had started calling him Trotter. However, he'd been carefully stashing things behind a panel concealing a water tank using his screwdriver to remove the retaining screws.

He spent Monday taking every opportunity he had to rub dirt on the remnants of the yellow paint on his trouser legs and scraping at it with stones so that by the time he finished work it was only on very close inspection you'd notice it. As the guards were about to change he had another trip to the latrines. He went in as an English prisoner. He again removed the panel, took off his prisoners' jacket stuffed it in and pulled out the one he'd hidden in there. He pulled on his hat after bashing it into shape, and filled his jacket pockets with other items: a German book containing a pencil sketch map copied from Baedekers onto the back page, a small stash of marks, a match box containing a magnetized piece of razor blade attached to a horse hair which when suspended swayed to the north, Oxo cubes, chocolate, biscuits and a razor.

The guards changing shift meant that no one knew who had gone into the latrines so when a German workman emerged it was not remarkable. He set to "fixing" things. Several guards walked past unmoved as he unscrewed and levered off the brackets of a drainpipe.

He pulled his hat brim down and proceeded to carry the length of drainpipe on his shoulder round to the back of a hut. Ellis was waiting around the back looking anxious.

'Nicht sprechen,' said Smith.

A pile of rubbish lay on the ground, left from the refurbishment of the Feldwebel's hut, including a filthy piece of carpet ripped up off the wooden floor. Smith picked it up, got Ellis to hold the end then rolled him in it. Earlier in the day he had dumped a workman's barrow there: a simple one-wheeled contraption that had been made in the workshop out of wood and a cracked wheel from a quarry tub. He lowered the somewhat fatter roll of carpet onto it and arranged some bits of timber and his length of drainpipe around it to take the eye away from the strange carpet roll. He also picked up an old sack containing an enamel pot and some other bits that Ellis had brought with him. He set off towards the gate. He tried to wheel the barrow effortlessly despite the extra ten stone of Canadian lumberjack – he walked past German guards avoiding eye contact, past comrades who would have recognised him if they had seen something other than a German handyman trundling a barrow. No one else knew what the plan was – it was safer that way.

He reached the first gate and dropped the barrow down and rested his aching arms. The sentry came out. Smith flashed the workman's permit. The sentry made no effort to inspect it and just said a vague: 'Schön,' as if it was all an inconvenience to him.

Smith saluted, keeping his face as much as he could under the shade of his hat brim. The sentry unlocked the gate. Smith picked up the barrow and trundled it to the gate in the outer fence and waited until that was unlocked and opened, then picked the barrow up again and continued on the first steps to freedom. He risked a glance behind at the barbed wire and sentry posts. The gate was being locked again. He suppressed an urge to pick up his speed, but instead carried on trundling slowly down through the village – he was grateful for the kind gradient, as the effort of pushing the barrow up a hill would have been too great for its apparent load. He was passed only by an old Frau shuffling between two houses.

He continued through the village and out the other side where the ground levelled off. He paused. He looked around. Some rooks cawed over the way, heading to their evening roost in a small coppice across the field. It was a still evening. Dampness in the air. His breath visible from his exertions.

'It's clear. Let's have you out.'

Between them they got the barrow over the hedge and threw the carpet and other rubbish into a ditch, retaining some of the dry timber. They got their bearings then struck out across the field in the remaining light. They had to put some distance between themselves and the camp whilst there was some daylight remaining and couldn't risk travelling by road – Ellis in particular stood out as a prisoner. He produced a hat from his pocket and turned his trousers and jacket inside out to conceal the yellow stripes but that just made him look odd. His stripes, though, had been sewn into the prison uniform and with a bit of patience and daylight could be turned into something resembling a workman's clothes by unpicking it with his contraband pocket-knife.

When night fell they emerged onto the country lanes heading west.

Dawn found them in a small wood, in the early hours of the morning. They had a small fire going which now glowed without much smoke. Ellis had gathered handfuls of things from the woods to which was added a couple of potatoes they had lifted from a field.

'Are you sure those toadstools aren't poisonous?'

'I'm fairly sure. I've done this before. But there's always the worry that everything in this country is poisonous.'

Smith gave half a smile.

'Don't you worry, mate. It'll be fine.' He ripped leaves off nettles, adding bits of dog-rose hip, and some beechnuts, then threw in an Oxo cube.

They took turns with the one spoon they had, dipping into the pot. It was hot and made Smith feel truly alive.

'This is the best thing I've tasted since I left England. You are a genius.'

'Thanks.'

They continued in silence. This young Canadian was almost young enough to be his son, but they were truly equals – there was a connection. In reality he knew little about him and Ellis knew little of his own story, but there was no one he could call a better friend. It was as if they shared a single thought and a single purpose.

They slept through the day on beds of leaves and travelled by night. The next morning they were within sight of Osnabrück. The plan was to go by train to Rheine – less than twenty miles from the Dutch border.

'I'll be glad when today is over, mate.'

196

'Me too. It was bad enough walking past some doltish sentry without trembling never mind sitting in a train just feet away from nosey civilians.'

'All we can do is try to avoid conversation. Avoid eye contact. I'll let you do the speaking – you sound more German than me.'

'Chuffin' 'ell!'

'There you go: sounded like perfect German to me.'

Smith practised out loud: 'Zwei Tickets nach Rheine, bitte. Zwei Tickets nach Rheine, bitte. Zwei Tickets nach Rheine, bitte.'

'All right, mate. That'll do. You're getting on my nerves now.'

As they walked into town they felt like all eyes were on them. Ellis went first, some thirty yards ahead of Smith. That way if one of them got rumbled it gave the other a chance.

The station was very German-looking – not a friendly, welcoming place – imposing spikes like off picklehaube helmets either side of a stone coat of arms looming over them.

Smith went up to the ticket office window, reciting his lines in his head.

'Zwei Tickets nach Rheine, bitte.'

He listened hard to the clerk telling him the price, which he roughly knew from talk around the camp. He handed over some coins. He took his tickets, passed one to Ellis and turned to go through the barrier. There was a tapping at the glass. He had been found out. He looked at Ellis. Could they run? There was another tap on the glass: the clerk was pointing to the change he hadn't picked up.

'Danke schön.'

They had to work out what platform they were on; there was a wait of thirty minutes or so until the next train. They felt it would be safer where there were fewer people so went on to the platform to wait, but then they thought they stood out even more in their scruffy clothes and scuffed, English-looking boots. Ellis pulled out the *Frankfurter Zeitung* they had bought from a kiosk and leant against a stanchion for the canopy. Smith got out his book that had the map in the back: poems by Goethe – Goaty he called it – and pretended to be engrossed: especially when a German officer approached. He continued to walk past them.

The wait seemed much longer than half an hour. They got into a second class carriage hoping they would have the compartment to themselves but no sooner had they settled than two soldiers, a young woman and an old man got in. Ellis pulled his newspaper up over his face and Smith buried his nose in his book. The old man sat next to him and spoke. Smith nodded and said, 'Ja.' Ellis helped him out by nudging him to point out something in the newspaper to which he nodded and raised his eyebrows then he shut his eyes and pretended to sleep.

As people came and went at stations, Smith watched them through half-closed eyes. As they approached Rheine they shared the compartment with an elderly woman and the two soldiers who were still there. Smith was now keeping a look out for the station. The woman was studying them. Her expression was disapproving – but they probably didn't smell that sweet after sleeping out in the woods despite their efforts to wash and shave. And to be fair they were still crawling with lice. Smith couldn't imagine wanting to travel with someone like him before the war.

'*Wie viel Uhr ist es, bitte?*' said the woman.

Smith caught the word "Uhr" – he revealed an empty wrist, shrugged and looked out of the window. The woman muttered something and spoke again.

One of the soldiers spoke, but Smith broke into a bad fit of coughing which he made last until the train pulled up onto the platform. They couldn't get off the train and away from the town fast enough. They hid in a hedge just outside the town until nightfall, then looked for a forest – Ellis kept them moving west by looking at the stars and the razor blade compass. They reckoned by Smith's map that they must be about ten miles from the border.

They walked across fields, ate biscuits and chocolate and spent the rest of the night in a wood. They didn't go farther the next day – just checked that their spot was sufficiently safe from neighbouring farms, raided a field for beets and worked out their next move.

They needed to reconnoitre the border, so set off again the next night. Dogs barked as they snapped twigs underfoot or stumbled in the darkness near to farms. They discussed what they would do if challenged – would they run or stand and fight? They didn't know, but they were poised to spring at all times; every moving shadow made them tense, every night-time noise was, to them, a soldier or a *landstürmer* with a shotgun. This heightened state of alertness was exhausting. They knew that anyone turning them in would get a reward of twenty marks.

As dawn approached they holed up in a patch of brambles – the best cover they could find – not easy to get into and not conducive to good sleep. That was it then – they had run out of food having eaten their remaining biscuits and a couple of manky apples each. They were too near the border to risk a fire – it was no more than a mile away and was undoubtedly patrolled. The next night they would push for Holland.

They crept out of the brambles an hour or so after nightfall and set off, avoiding roads, getting clods of soil stuck to their boots making it hard to walk. They got nearer and in the moonlight saw lines of barbed wire. They laid low and watched – they could make out a sentry moving with a lantern. Their hearts sank.

They both knew exactly the mind of the other man. After a moment Ellis grasped his shoulder and whispered, 'Come on – take heart. We can still do it. We just pick a spot, then when the sentry's past it we get under the wire.'

'If it's like the wire in the camp there's no chance.'

'We've got to try; we've come this far.'

Once again it was the young Canadian who had stiffened his backbone. They watched and waited – there seemed to be a good ten minutes between the guard going one way then coming back the other.

They were by now covered in mud; wet, cold and exhausted. The guard went past once more. They heaved themselves up from their prone position for one last push for freedom. Smith's whole body ached, his head was throbbing, his lungs bursting as they ran, keeping low, towards the border. They were confronted by a simple fence of iron stakes and barbed wire. Smith wrapped sacking around the bottom strands and pulled it up to allow Ellis through. Then Ellis did the same for him. He was fighting back the panic and the wire ripped at his jacket, but they were through – they tumbled into a trench and had to clamber up the other side – Smith giving Ellis an old-fashioned bunk-up like he'd done many times as a kid – jumping jennel walls and into gardens to scrump apples. Ellis pulled him up the other side. It had clouded over. They couldn't see where they were going. A loud clanking noise rang out in the night – they had contacted another fence rigged up with tin cans like cowbells. Smith pulled at his leg which was caught fast – if only he could see where. The pain seared through his calf. The more he pulled the more the bells clanked. Ellis made a whimper like he was suppressing pain. He too was rattling the cans.

'Oh god! Oh god! Oh god!' Ellis was panicking now.

'All right, lad. Slow and steady – we're all right, try not to struggle – try to free yourself slowly.'

Smith ripped his trousers, felt pain in his hands as they scrabbled in the wire, his jacket snagged too. He lost his footing and fell, sending the bells clanking for what sounded like hundreds of yards. The clouds parted, he struggled to unsnag his jacket and get to his feet. Then he started again on his trousers now he could at least partially see.

'Halt!' a voice shouted from the darkness.

'Smith, help me! Oh god!'

There was a flash, and the crack of gunfire. Smith leapt and fell backwards tumbling over, pain searing through his foot and his leg as he fell back into the trench. Bullets rattled overhead as he lay stunned, looking up at the night sky.

He got to his feet and saw a dark shape slumped and motionless over the wire. He retched but nothing came up.

'*Gib auf, Tommie!*' He held up his hands. Captured a second time.

CHAPTER THIRTY

Back at the camp Smith was taken to the hospital hut. He was stripped and examined. His legs were badly lacerated, as were his arms and hands. He'd also taken a bullet on his right foot, slicing across his toes. He screamed as his boot was removed, the dried blood and matter sticking to his wound. He passed out as the camp doctor, without chloroform, got out his scissors and trimmed his toes – removing smashed bone and rent flesh.

He was put into prison clothes and clogs, and thrown into a cell to await sentence. The cell was dark and low; only bread and water rations, with soup every fourth day.

At night he battled with wire, snaking up and wrapping round his limbs and across his chest. Fear rose up in his throat, in a scream that never came, merging with sobs from Ellis. He'd kick out as something gnawed at his toes – only to wake up in pain as his foot struck the wall of his cell. During the day it was as bad: Ellis bent over a pot of stew, his face in concentration, lit up by the embers of the fire. Grinning at him as he emerged from the roll of carpet like a kid on Christmas day. Did his people back in Canada even know how brave he was? If only *he*'d been shot too, then he'd have been spared this hell. He curled up in a ball and begged for it to end.

He knew nothing of his trial but spent a further fortnight in the cell before being released back to the hut with the others. Smiler had gone, Darky had gone – and Ellis. He knew many of them – they all wanted to hear his story, but he wouldn't talk about it and soon they ignored him. Instead of a hero, all they found was another nutter wrapped up in himself.

He couldn't walk properly, so was put on parcel duty – sorting parcels for inmates, taking beatings from the Germans for not cooperating and supplying them with their share of treats and cigarettes.

***

Elsie worked hard at the factory out of a sense of duty, but played football for her own happiness. The team had improved; having boots with studs meant they could stay upright – they got proper jerseys and shorts and matching bonnets. They learnt combinations and positions. They stuck to their roles and relied on each other to stick to theirs – each part of the machine having a function. They learnt to push the ball out to the wings, to whip in crosses. And Elsie learnt to time her forward runs to beat the defence. She was quick and could anticipate the ball before it was released. When Mr Grimes got out his blackboard and started chalking circles and arrows it started to make sense – even the offside law.

That next goal became a hunger – she needed it to make her happy.

There had been nothing like the sense of anticipation she experienced before that first proper game in the South Yorkshire Ladies' Football League against Hadfields. College hockey hadn't come close. She could only describe it as fear. There were hundreds of people gathered to watch – she almost wanted to run away, but something kept her there. A desire.

When just before half-time she picked up a cross right in the space she had run on to, nudged the ball on, away from the centre-half, slowed time down, looked up, picked her spot and let the ball fly, she knew the outcome. She saw the goalie stretch and fall in the mud, saw the net ripple. Her team mates grinned at her and patted her back. A strange sound came from her throat – a shriek of unbounded joy unlike anything she had ever uttered before. They didn't win the match but Elsie didn't care. She just looked forward to the next games against Vickers B and the YMCA Ladies with that same mixture of fear and craving.

***

Smith was moved across country; this time to a forest where they were made to fell trees and carry them to the sawmill, or on easier days to plant saplings. The forest work was even more gruelling than anything that had gone before – there were no opportunities to skive off. Here, there was not just the occasional visit from a lazy guard or a cursory enquiry from the host farmer. At the sawmill and forest there was constant supervision and regular beatings when slacking was perceived or sullenness exhibited.

He existed from day to day. His physical wounds healed, though abscesses had to be lanced, and he had spent time back in the hospital with a fever. He learnt to walk again with only a slight stutter in his step, and a pair of old boots sent by his mother were better than the clogs that chafed at his scarred toes with every step.

If anything, work in the sawmill was worse than being out in the forest, though working in the boiler room feeding the furnace was at least warm. In the mill they had to carry timber all day long, to and from the saws whose deadly blades rattled round making one hell of a din. Dust lay inches deep on the floor and on every surface; the air was so thick they could chew on it, they breathed it in and their huts at night resounded to coughs and wheezing. Smith was one of only a handful of Tommies; the majority were Russians, plus a few Italians, French and Serbs.

He received a parcel containing half of a fruit cake – he knew where the other half had gone – it was not the first time. There was a tin of Zam Buk, some cigarettes, a packet of tea and some socks. It was from someone back home, but there were no clues left to say who had sent it.

As he sat on his bunk that evening smoking he became aware of a young Russian staring at him. He held out the remaining half of his cigarette. The young Russian didn't need asking twice, he practically snatched it from Smith's hand. Ungrateful sod, he thought. He watched his cigarette being savoured, the boy's eyes closed, the smoke held back and treasured, then released slowly. It was smoked right down to the very end, and only then did the Russian speak. 'Spacibo, tovarisch. Spacibo. Menye zovoot, Grigory.' He offered his hand. 'Smith.'

They talked for a bit in broken Russian and English, Smith having picked up a bit of Russian along with other languages.

Grigory was only seventeen. He said something about his mother and grandmother, spoke of the beauty of his home and his farm, of his trips hunting, and collecting mushrooms: at least that is what Smith reckoned *griby* was from the gestures. Grigory went to his bunk and dug out a small musical instrument from underneath. 'Tee lyoo-bish musicu?' The little instrument was made from a tin can, carved pieces of wood from the mill, and strung with electrical wire. He tuned it and the sound it made was quite beautiful, a bit like a ukulele. As soon as he struck up a tune he was joined by some of his comrades and Smith was treated to Russian folk songs. He found himself smiling for the first time in a while, and sharing round a couple more cigarettes and joining in when he had learnt the words to the chorus.

Smith found himself working alongside Grigory in the mill a few days later. He was carrying a large wooden slab over to a bandsaw with Grigory at the other end. There was a jerk then suddenly Smith took all the load, and turned to look for where the lad had got to. He had apparently vanished. When he went to investigate he saw the poor Russian lad's trouser leg had carried into a belt drive, pulling him in, quickly wrapping him round a pulley until right before Smith's eyes all that was left of the lower half of his body was a mushy mass of flesh, blood, shattered bone and cloth. He'd barely had time to cry out before he'd gone – his dying eyes burned into Smith. His lips formed the word *matushka*.

***

Elsie dropped her sugar ration cards round at Hawley's grocers before heading to the conference at the Montgomery Hall. Her old umbrella was scarcely up to the job, such was the wind and rain; she didn't want to arrive looking like a cat that had climbed out of the canal, she wanted to look the part – serious-minded, representing all the hundreds of women from the works, the very epitome of the unanswerable case for extending the franchise to those who had responded to the call to work and who now would help mould the future. She was relieved to not have to wait long for the tram.

There was a buzz in the hall when she took her seat towards the front. Men as well as women delegates still stood in little groups, smiling and gesticulating. Shop stewards jabbed the air with their lighted cigarettes to emphasize the veracity of the point they were making, women spoke into each other's ears, nodding and nudging. Up on the stage was a table and chairs. Sitting alone and making notes on some papers in front of her sat Sylvia Pankhurst. She was without a doubt the most beautiful of the family; though, many would probably disagree. Christabel and her mother had a more classical beauty perhaps, but Sylvia's compassion showed in every feature – in her almond eyes, and the shape of her mouth. There was not a trace of pride in her features, none of her mother's or Christabel's conceit, nothing sharp or self-serving; instead the suffering of others was reflected there.

'Hello, I'm Sarah,' said a woman settling into the seat next to her and tearing her away from her reveries. 'Don't I know you from somewhere?'

'I'm not sure.'

'I do! You scored that penalty against me a fortnight ago. I play in goal at the NPF.'

'Oh, I'm sorry – of course! You look so different.'

'So do you, but I make a point of studying my opponent's face when there's a penalty – looking for clues and hints at character that might determine whether they'll shoot high or low, blast it or place it. It clearly didn't work – you sent me the wrong way!'

Elsie laughed. 'I'm so sorry. Nice to meet you.' She offered her hand.

'Ooh, we're about to start.'

How different it was from a meeting before the war – it was no longer a demand for suffrage that was debated – there was an assumption that the franchise bill would be nodded through. That battle was already won, by all their struggles and sacrifices. This was about what they would do with their new-found votes.

Despite everything, there was a feeling of optimism; they dared to look forward to a better world after the war. The first motion was moved by Mrs Fisher, the wife of the MP for Hallam: 'That a wide and considerable advance in the national system of education is one of the most urgent needs of the day.' It was argued that women voters would take a keen interest in education of their children. 'Some people regard education as an undue interference in the lives of children and subsequent work, but I cannot help but feel that too much thought has been given to the industrial side and not enough to the human and citizenship aspects of education.'

'It is because we bring up our children to be merely earners – that is a key reason why they are so deplorably backward in education,' said the seconder.

The debate went on: whether industrial injustices should be tackled first, that they mustn't flinch at the cost of reform, and that the Education Bill was only the start of it. Elsie wanted to get up and speak, felt she had something to say about not stopping married women from teaching, but her courage failed her.

They went on to debate equal pay for equal work and then Sylvia proposed a motion: 'That this conference is of the opinion that some system of endowment of motherhood should be established in this country in the near future.' She spoke with passion of her experiences in London of children dying from preventable diseases because of poor nutrition and living conditions not fit for animals. 'We will never have a healthy race of children so long as women are expected to be working at machinery during a very critical period.' She also picked up on an earlier suggestion that education would only make children look up to their superiors. 'I would prefer to express it this way: on the contrary, a good education system will make our children realise that they have *no* superiors.'

There was huge applause. Elsie rose to her feet and shared a big smile with her new goalkeeper friend.

*

She stayed behind after her shift to help out with preparations for the Christmas party. She was tired and went to the canteen for her dinner and for a rest before they were due to start. She queued for her food. Addie dished her out a bowl of stew.

'There you go, love… Hang on… I'll just…'

She fished out another chunk of meat and added it to the bowl. 'You need to keep your strength up, love. All that running around. I enjoyed the last match – you were terrific. Showed those Empire Mills girls a thing or two.'

'Thank you, Addie. It's good to be able to entertain you all. But I do feel guilty.'

'Why ever's that, love?'

'Well, I only do it for my own pleasure – it seems strange that so many people come along to watch.'

'We don't mind why you do it. We're just glad you do. It's nice to have something to cheer about.'

'Are you helping at the party later? Yes, here all day, love. Go on, sit down, before it goes cold.'

Elsie went to find the table that Mary was sitting at.

'I'll have to stop reading the paper,' Mary said, nodding to the folded newspaper in front of her.

Elsie read the headline: *2 M German Troops Massed Along the Western Front,* it read.

'That's only part of their five and a half millions, so the rest of the article says,' Mary added.

'But that tells you nothing about how well equipped they are and what their fighting spirit is like. And the Americans have now joined us.'

'About blinking time too.'

'Did you see the tank in Fitzalan Square? Imagine if you were a young German boy and saw that coming towards you? I went in for a look.'

'Did you buy a bond?'

'Yes, for ten pounds.'

'Ten? Elsie that's a fortune.'

'I can afford it. We need this to end. Everyone has to make sacrifices. What are you helping out with, tonight?'

'With the wounded soldiers' teas in the gaffers' mess room.'

'I'd best be getting over to the men's canteen – I'm supposed to be helping wrap presents for the children and then we've the stage to decorate for the entertainment.'

The women chatted as they wrapped presents, donated for the children and soldiers, and placed them under the tree. Preparations had been underway most of the week: rehearsals for the choral society, making paper chains and decorating the tree and wrapping presents, but as expected there was always a last minute rush. There were books and playing cards, boxes of Wrigley's spearmint, and cigarettes for the soldiers – she had sent a box to Smith with similar items in, but with additional things like soap, Oxo cubes, and a tin of Harrison's pomade: standard items for soldiers.

People started to arrive at about five o'clock – some children were overawed and clung to their mothers, others, unused to being in a big room and not under supervision of teachers, couldn't contain their excitement and started running around and playing games before being reined back in again.

After they had had their tea they gathered round the Punch and Judy show, sitting cross-legged on the floor.

Wounded soldiers came through to watch too – some in wheelchairs, some on crutches. They gathered to one side, not wanting to intrude too much, not wanting to play the role of Banquo's ghost, to remind the children of the reality. Elsie spent as much time watching the children laughing and pointing and shouting at Mr Punch's naughtiness as she did watching the puppets. She also couldn't keep her eyes off the uniformed figures on the far side, many of whom were also predominantly watching the children – as if their very lives and unblemished youthfulness was something they were trying to absorb, to fill voids in their souls.

After the Punch and Judy there was a conjurer who had real baby rabbits, and pockets that seemed to hold all sorts of unfeasible items. One little boy looked on open-mouthed as the conjurer asked him to look into the breast pocket of his Sunday-best jacket that his mother had made him wear, and found there a bar of chocolate. He was even more amazed to discover he could keep it.

Father Christmas then arrived ringing a bell and went to sit by the tree and the children all queued up to receive a present. Elsie went to help Father Christmas, who was really Bert from quality control.

She pulled out presents suited to the children, whether boy or girl, tiny tot or prematurely-installed man-of-the-house, using a cleverly devised system of dots and crosses on each present.

One little girl, perhaps about five years old, hung back.

'Come on. Don't be shy, said Bert. 'What's your name? Let me see... you're Millie aren't you? I hear you've been a very good girl.'

Her eyes opened wide at the confirmation of Father Christmas's omniscience. The fact that Millie's mother, Emma, worked in threading and lived only a street away from Bert, who used to drink at the same public house as Millie's father was all by the by.

She crept up to him and he gave her the present that Elsie passed him. Little Millie stood as if transfixed, not wanting to move aside for the next child. Bert smiled at her and wished her a happy Christmas. Still she lingered. The queue behind her jostled.

'Father Christmas,' she whispered.

'Yes, Millie.'

'Will you please bring my daddy back?'

'I will try my very hardest.'

Elsie had to turn away to hide her face. How Bert had managed to reply she didn't know.

Once the children were all taken home, the second half of the entertainment started with a magic lantern show featuring photographs taken around the works, and everyone trying to spot themselves. Then the choral society sang a few favourite glees such as: "In the Hour of Softened Splendour," and afterwards, a comedy duo from the milling department did impersonations of the works' manager receiving a visit from the Factory Inspector and from the man from the Ministry of Munitions. It probably didn't mean much to their guests and visitors but the mirth it caused amongst the employees made up for any puzzlement on their part.

The evening finished with a cleverly choreographed performance of *Hitchy Koo* with the singers all in different coloured costumes, holding hands and rotating, ducking and interweaving. *Oh, every evening hear him sing, it's the cutest little thing, got the cutest little swing, Hitchy Koo, Hitchy Koo.* Everyone joined in. The nonsense of the song was just what was needed by way of antidote and was sung and whistled by many on their way home.

As Elsie walked to church the following day, snow was falling over the city – thick white flakes clumping together as they fell, making everything look pure and muffling the air, bringing a sense of peace. She looked skywards as the dizzying flakes fell onto her face, caught on her lashes and pricked her eyes.

Elsie's sense of unease built as the New Year opened. There were more strikes as other workers held out for increases to match those of the favoured few on munitions. Twenty thousand were on strike across the East End. The country again seemed divided. Could the war ever be won without a clear idea of the values being fought for: freedom, or freedom to exploit others? The strike was settled by paying the rates demanded, and work recommenced.

She craved the release that playing football allowed, but Mother Nature had other ideas. No one was to get respite by playing games while ever she was being defiled by their bombs from the North Sea to the Mediterranean, from the Baltic to the Red Sea and beyond – 1918 started with a storm raging across the city, bringing down roof slates and chimney pots. Then she sent her snow in icy blasts, whipping down off the moors and drifting up against cracked window panes and draughty back doors, destroying umbrellas, sending hats spinning off into filthy roads, and dispatching the feeble and the weak. She locked root crops tight within her frozen soil for weeks on end, and made pitches unplayable. To add to this, U-boats sent thousands of tons of potatoes, grain, tea and sugar to the bottom of the ocean with their ships and crew. Necessities of life ran out: chips, beer and a right good mash of tea.

Tea and butter joined sugar on ration, and shops closed when meat ran out. Queues formed and alarm spread.

News from France added to that alarm as German Stormtroopers advanced into France, inflicting huge numbers of casualties and taking many prisoners. Elsie had no time off. When not working, she was volunteering at the Vestry Hall in Burngreave where a communal kitchen had been set up to share food and save money by economies of scale. It became a great comfort to many and a way to support each other and keep up morale. No one took time off at Easter, such was the desperate need to replace munitions lost in the German offensive. Besides it was better to keep busy. She could not afford to stop and think. If she did her heart would surely break. Somewhere a little girl was walking and talking, opening birthday presents and laughing and smiling and calling someone else mummy. If she concentrated on the spiral of swarf coming off the singing shell, or kneading the bread and sifting the flour, she could make it go away.

By the summer, everyone could afford to take a breath. They had been sorely tested but had survived – there was a sense that the Germans had rolled their last dice. Mary and Elsie could once again afford a few days away and went to take the waters at Matlock.

CHAPTER THIRTY-ONE

In the spring, Smith's work had changed to a nearby brick factory. There was a change of mood amongst the guards. 'You are losing, Tommy. We are marching to Paris. Your little army is being blown to hell. Ha ha.' He had heard it all before: London being bombed, Kitchener killed, England starving to death as the wonderful *U-boots* sank ships. But now it seemed that Russia had left the war – that was the talk of fellow prisoners. First rumours had circulated of events back home. Then new prisoners arrived with tales of revolution in Moscow. Fists flew as sides were taken and arguments were fought out. So now Germany had only one front to fight on.

Smith started to contemplate never being released – of being enslaved to this bunch of bastards forever. He hated them – his hatred consumed him. It didn't help that he knew deep down that they were not all bad: because even the good ones just let it happen. He wanted to strangle his gaolers one by one. But he was nothing but a coward. A coward who let himself be captured. Twice. He should have fought to the end. Charlie would have, even Ginger. But not him. All bluster. All he could do was imagine strangling them. He'd never do it. Gutless bastard.

Then one day, when he was shovelling coal from a barge he passed out – he had been unwell for a few days, suffering from headaches, a bad throat and congested lungs. The doctor diagnosed *die Grippe* and he was put into a hospital.

The hospital bed was only marginally cleaner and less infested than in the camp but Smith was beyond caring – he was barely conscious most of the time.

His nose bled and he started to cough up blood. He knew he was dying. He should have taken out some Germans when he went. Not like this.

In his feverish dreams he drowned in mud, pouring into his throat, he tore at his flesh which fell away from his bones in putrid lumps, large birds landed on his face and pecked at his eyes. He was shelled, and mud, rocks and body parts rose into the air and landed on him, he became tangled in wire, and lay down with a woman who turned to corpse beneath him covering him in pus. And he was always trying to reach something, but being beaten back down.

Someone poured water down his throat. Bitter liquid. He slept more calmly.

Eventually it subsided and he sat up in bed. He was brought white bread and soup by an Italian prisoner, working in the hospital. He didn't speak, had one eye, one arm and a horrific facial disfigurement, and went about his duties with diligence. The next day Smith was shipped back to the camp to make way for others going down with the same illness. He learnt that they had already buried five. It was still not yet his time.

If it had still been winter, it might not have been as bad as at the sawmill. There, the icy winds had whipped through the doorless buildings – designed for ease of movement of wood, not for the comfort of *schweine*. But now, in the warmth of the summer he found himself trundling carts of clay bricks into an oven still hot from the last batch, or burning under the sun out in the yard where bricks were stacked – shredding their skin on the sharp edges.

He was shouted at for not working fast, blamed for his debilitation, his loss of strength. He no longer fantasized about picking up a shovel and splitting a guard's head open with it. He just took it and tried to stay out of trouble. He despised them, but he despised himself more. People came and went: English, French. He was civil but avoided getting too chummy with any of them. He was apart from them. No one could be relied on. You got chummy with someone, they just let you down. *Dieu et mon droit: Fuck you Jack, I'm all right*. That was the well-known motto. Hope was not an emotion that coursed through him as it once had. Hope for what? Even when trying to escape it hadn't been a destination that drove him on, or a concept he ran towards – it was no more than a certain cussedness: not wanting to be mastered and fear of being sent underground. He contemplated his own death, since his existence was so apparently pointless and wondered what it would feel like to fashion a noose for his neck and swing, like others had. He was too cowardly a bastard, even for that.

*

Across the *lager* something was changing. The guards were sullen and less disciplined – some picking a fight with prisoners without any build up, others not bothering to keep prisoners in check, not insisting on salutes, not enforcing lights-out, and even being polite. It was no longer: "Be quiet schwein!" but: "Comrades – please. It is lights out."

Rumours spread that Turkey had left the war, then Austria.

One morning on parade the camp commandant addressed them: 'Gentleman – ' A huge roar went up. No one heard another word from him. They didn't need to. He had said all they wanted to hear already. They were no longer *schweine* or *schweinehunde*. None of them were going to listen to him ever again.

Guards were posted on the gates with machine guns trained on the men. There was fear that there might be retribution, a rampage, but there were negotiations and reassurances and they stood down.

Allied flags were found from somewhere and hoisted in the camp. Alcohol was procured and a party commenced that lasted beyond what used to be lights-out. Smith was not amongst the partygoers although several tried to sweep him along. He was subdued; he could barely stand never mind dance and jig about. He could not explain or understand why he felt so anxious. He knew he should be glad. He'd made it through when so many others hadn't, but he just felt empty. He felt like he was outside in the snow looking through a window at a scene of a shiny-faced family at Christmas.

The next day men went strolling out of the gates round the town – seeing what they could buy with their money.

***

She was with Mary. Oh! and there was Miss Duncombe, her English teacher from college. She tried to wave. It was a queue for sausages, or jam or something. She was so very hot – she had been queuing to use the plunge pool in Matlock, not queuing on Attercliffe Common, and yet there she was, but bare-footed. Why Attercliffe anyway; it was a long walk back? She needed a drink, there was something in her mouth, like kapok, she tried to spit it out but couldn't. She was so thirsty. Church bells were ringing and a boy was shouting about the war. Was that steam buzzer from the factory? A gun fired – a big one, an AA gun. It must be an air raid. Zepps. There was a hand on her forehead.

'Oh, Mrs Harrison? Is everything all right?'

'Don't trouble yourself, dear. Don't speak – you were just dreaming.' Elsie relaxed.

'Right let's get you sat up. It's time for your medicine.' Mrs Harrison unfolded the paper wrapper and stirred its white powdery contents into a glass of water. 'Here drink this – it'll make you feel less feverish. It did wonders when Mr Harrison had the flu.' Mrs Harrison held the glass to Elsie's lips. It hurt her throat to swallow. 'I've made you another jug to drink – I want it all gone by the next time I'm here this afternoon. It's got Enoch Colton's blackberry vinegar in it, and some herbs he swears by. Now shall we get you up for a wee?' She helped Elsie up and steadied her over the chamber pot. 'Right, back into bed with you before you get cold. We need to keep you warm. I'll get you a clean bonnet, this one's damp. You really ought to have a fire lit in here.'

Elsie settled back into bed. The bells she had heard in her dreams rang again and she could hear a piano playing.

'What's going, Mrs H,' she murmured.

'Oh, that. The war's over, dear. So they say. That'll be old Mr McNolty on his piano – they were threatening to drag it out into the street and start a party. I'll go and tell him to pipe down. I'll just go and empty this.'

She returned. Elsie had no sense of how much time had elapsed.

'I've warmed you some beef tea and pobs. Can we get this down you?'

Elsie let herself be spoon-fed like a child.

'Right then, I'll be back in a bit. Get some rest. That's the best healer. Are you warm enough?'

In her delirium there was no distinct boundary between awake and asleep. How long had she been in bed? What day was it even? She ought to be in work. She'd missed too long already. Germany had to be taught a lesson. She was climbing a grassy slope that carried on getting steeper until it was almost vertical and there were no hand holds and she feared falling all the way back, never making it to the top where she wanted to lay on her back in the sun. It was over – a car horn sounded, and she heard the national anthem being sung. She had her football boots on, and on the grassy slope were her team-mates, kicking the ball up the slope – it wasn't so steep now – and the ball kept rolling back down. She was running after the ball and breathing hard and sweating. Then she fell. A boy shouted. People were cheering. Someone had scored. Was it her? No. She was sad. It was over. Mrs H returned. 'Have some more fairy powder Elsie.' It went dark outside. She sat on the grass in the park, the band was playing. What was the tune? It was that one by Holst that always made her cry. Henry was holding her hand, but she could not move or turn to see him. Henry went. She was sad, but happy. Deeply sad. She was on her own. There was someone – she was lying down – she couldn't move her limbs – someone watching her – none of her body would move, like everything was made of lead. She tried to cry out, but her voice wouldn't work. She was suffocating. She tried again to scream.

'It's all right, Elsie. Just a dream.'

'Oh.'

She felt Mary hold her hand.

'What...' she cleared her throat and swallowed. It still hurt. 'What time is it?'

'About six?'

She waved in the direction of the drink on the floor next to her low-level bed. Mary helped her sit up a bit and gave her a drink.

'Mrs Harrison said to give you some more powders too. You look a little better. You've been sweating it out – you're soaking. I'll get you changed. Do you feel up to getting up and going and sitting in front of the fire in the living room while I get your bed changed? Both Lily and Betty are out but I've built the fire up a bit?'

'What day is it?'

'Monday.'

'Shouldn't you be in work?'

'Maybe. But who cares. The war's ended – didn't you hear?'

'I think so.'

'Nearly everyone walked out from the works and into the street. We've been up into town. Everyone was there. Sorry – I don't want to trouble you – I should let you rest.'

'No, tell me.'

'There are so many flags out – hanging from every window and lamppost. I've even seen dogs go by wearing flags. The Cathedral bells are ringing and the churches are all full of people. We've done it, Elsie. We've come through.'

'Not everyone.'

'No. I'm sorry. I didn't... Oh, I've upset you. Here, have this handkerchief. ' Mary squeezed her hand. She sobbed.

'Don't worry, Mary. I just felt he was so close to me before I woke up. I'm just feeling sorry for myself – it's this flu.'

'I think you're past the worst of it now. Hopefully.'

Elsie smiled at her friend. 'I must count my blessings. Tell me some more about what's going on out there.'

'Well, town is all lit up for one thing. I'd forgotten how it looked at night…'

Life at the works was changed overnight. When work restarted on the Thursday, after the workers' almost spontaneous holiday, they found that not everyone had returned. Elsie did a few hours but was sent home again by the department manager.

'But I'm perfectly all right now,' she insisted.

'That's as may be, but you don't look it. And we don't want to risk anyone else catching it – it's not like there's a war on, is it? Don't come back before Monday.'

***

More prisoners arrived at the camp from the surrounding farms and work camps, awaiting repatriation. One or two others simply walked out of the camp and tried to make their own way home: there was talk of being home for Christmas – this time for real, and some of them couldn't bear the wait.

Smith wandered round the camp, then wandered back the other way – there was no one to tell him what to do so he didn't know what he should do. He supposed there was nothing to stop him going out to see Anna, if he could find his way there. He'd have to walk a long way or get a lift – but that was impossible – and by now she had probably forgotten him. He'd be embarrassed to just turn up, especially looking as he did now – a skeletal Ben Gunn, covered in lice, with stinking breath. It wouldn't be fair on her, and he was ashamed of how he had treated her. No, it wasn't possible and it would serve no purpose. He was going back to England. Why risk upset after all this time?

Life in the camp went on around him as they waited patiently and filled the hours with what entertainment they could: music and plays, games of bingo and cards.

***

The work at the projectile factory gradually ran down, as men started to trickle back to their old posts and production scaled down and changed.

Worst of all the ladies' football team never played another match. Then Elsie too lost her job and found herself with time on her hands.

She threw herself into working for the Labour candidate for the General Election. She might have just missed out on her chance to vote but that did not stop her persuading those women who were old enough to use theirs for change.

The Labour candidate, Mr Jones, was the only one telling the truth and it shocked her how hard she had to try to get people to open their eyes. Persuading them to attend the open air meeting on the waste ground in Gower Street in December was a challenge – only the committed would take it up. Couldn't they see that Lloyd George was playing games? Plunging the country into an unwanted general election – claiming he had won the war whilst denying soldiers who were sent out, supposedly to fight for democracy, their vote? The coalition was afraid of them.

When Christmas came, plenty of money was spent. They ate and drank as much as they could afford, and their digestion would tolerate. They pulled homemade silent crackers and shouted "crack." They wore, and felt daft in, home-made paper hats, as in happier times, and read aloud and applauded the little rhymes that the children had written. They tried to make it like it was in the old days.

But it never would be again. One of the Quinn boys had not yet been de-mobbed, one would never see again and couldn't hear much either, such was his proximity to an exploding shell, and the youngest had perished just weeks before the Armistice.

'At least you'll get your Smith back. Have you heard from him?' She shook her head. She tried her best to smile in gratitude for their kind thoughts.

***

A few days before Christmas they started to depart. Smith did not fight his way to the front so was not on one of the first trains. Spirits were high as they left the gates and waved and blew ironic kisses at anyone who watched them go. They sang all the old songs. Old men and women glowered at them – the same ones probably who'd spat at them and spouted filth when they arrived as prisoners. On Christmas Eve Smith reached Hamburg where an ocean liner awaited them.

As they waited to board, a German guard had started bawling at them to get in line. A Royal Navy officer stepped up and raised his voice: 'Sir. You will stand aside and crawl back to your hole. I am now in charge of these men. You, sir, have no authority, and no right.' There was a big cheer and for first time they felt truly safe. It was real freedom.

On board there was, added to this, the *taste* of freedom – soft white bread so fresh it must have been baked on board, buttered and piled on plates, and tea with fresh milk. It was all Smith ate – anything else was too rich – too much of a challenge on his digestion and his remaining teeth.

Christmas day was spent on board. He was assaulted by it all: the rich and copious quantities of food, the raucousness at the table, the singing. It was all right for them, but what about the others who should have been there: Charlie, Ginger, Curly and Ellis. And what about Smiler and Darky? What had been their chances of making it through? It was indecent to celebrate. He nibbled at a bit of pudding and custard.

They each got a parcel containing cigarettes, a pipe and tobacco, toffee and chocolate. Smith took these up on deck and looked for a quiet spot out of the breeze and away from the soot of the funnels. He was not alone. The darkness was punctuated by red glowing cigarette ends of other broken men for whom it was all too much.

The first sight of England was a line of cranes and warehouses. Smith went up to see when someone shouted "land ahoy!" He struggled to get a view past the ranks of men eager to see home. Every vantage point was taken – men shinning up poles and climbing onto lifeboats in order to get that first sighting. He caught a glimpse of a tall tower sticking up on the horizon, but then gave up trying to see past the jostling crowd.

'It's Grimsby lads! Can't you just smell the fish?'

'I'm going to eat fish and chips every night when I get back.'

'No. My missus's steak and kidney pud.'

'Roast beef and Yorkshires.'

'Nay, bonny lad: pease pudding and ham in a stottie as big as your smiling face.'

'I'm glad we didn't go to Dover. It feels better just slipping in the back door nice and quiet like.'

'I'm going to do that – and be sat in my chair by the fire when my missus gets in – see the look on her bonny face.'

As they sailed up the Humber they were surrounded by destroyers, steamers and fishing boats blowing sirens and foghorns. On shore, factory buzzers were sounded, bells rang out from churches. Quietly slipping in the back way it was not. It got louder as they approached Hull. As they disembarked they were met by women – veterans of every recent disembarkation.

'Has anyone seen Michael Jones of the King's Own?'

'Lance Corporal Thomas Carruthers – my husband – Northumberland Fusiliers?'

Some held up photographs of men in uniform or portraits taken on wedding days.

Smith fixed his eyes on the feet of the man in front. It was pitiful. Smith resented their presence, their openly worn grief, their pathetic faith and forlorn hopes. They made him sick.

Other women, assisted by the Boys Brigade, administered to the living. They were each handed a copy of a handwritten letter from King George welcoming them home. Smith stopped to read it – it was about right, he thought – it talked of their miseries and hardships, said that they had been uppermost in their thoughts.

Others gave out homemade buns in paper bags and set out cups of tea on trestles. Some passed newspapers to anyone who wanted one. Telegraph forms were freely available to those who wanted to let wives or mothers know of their arrival.

Smith was not alone in being overwhelmed. Many who were voluble on board were now subdued and felt their burden of shame dragging at them. These civilians, overly keen women and old men, jingoists who seemed to think that something good had happened, repulsed him. Nothing had been won. It had just ended and they were too stupid to see that. He wanted to get away from them. It would have been better, kinder, to let them slip in unnoticed. They had been captured. They had grovelled in the camps, lost all dignity, been reduced to animals. Theirs was not a war to be proud of.

A local brass band played God Save the King as they were taken to the station and boarded trains to Ripon. Others' onward journeys were made in motor ambulances lined up at the dockside. The last to disembark, when the crowds had melted away from the dockside, were carried silently down the gangplank in coffins.

***

The camp at Ripon was a blessing to Smith – his life was regulated again, decisions taken away from him – he was fallen in and they were taken to a shower block where they shed their old prison clothes, which were taken away to be burnt. They were given soft carbolic soap to comb into their hair. They shaved and showered and were given a completely new uniform, kit bag and coat. They were fed well – there was as much bacon and eggs and porridge for breakfast as they wanted. There were rumours of men having died from overeating – their starved bodies not being able to take it – so Smith was cautious – he wasn't what he used to be. He was checked over by the MO – he weighed in at seven and a bit stones – he had once been ten and a half.

The processing took some time and some of the men grew restless – forms to fill in, back pay to be sorted, travel passes, I.D. He was asked whether he wanted to apply for an army pension – he'd have had to wait for a medical board to convene. Or he could take the two pounds payment and sign to say he wasn't suffering any disability.

'I can't be bothered to be honest, sir. I've had a bit shot off my toes, but that's nowt to be honest. Some decent grub and I'll be right.'

'Good man. That's the spirit.'

They didn't want people hanging around longer than they needed. Every day there were more arriving. He was given two months' leave.

Two days before the end of 1918, Smith was on a train heading for Leeds, where he was to change for Sheffield.

CHAPTER THIRTY-TWO

Elsie had spent the afternoon with Mary, going to see Mary Pickford in the matinee of *How Could You, Jean?* at the Don Picture Palace. If anything it had been a bit disappointing. Everyone had talked about it since it had come out, but it wasn't as good as the other Mary Pickford films they'd seen.

She would fry a chunk of rump steak and add it to some stew she had left over. Both Lily and Betty were staying with their families until the New Year so the house was quiet.

The kettle started to whistle while she was reaching into the corner cupboard for a bowl.

'All right, I'm coming. Stop your whistling.' Then there was a sudden frantic banging on the back door. She went to unlock it to find out what the matter was.

As she turned the lock, the door flew open, knocking into her, and a khaki figure rushed in. Vomit sprayed everywhere as the figure heaved – aimed inaccurately at the scullery sink. It also splashed onto her. She stood horrified as another stream of vomit emerged from the crouching stranger.

'That's better. Should've opened the bloody door sooner.' She recognised something in the voice. The man uncurled himself and wiped his mouth with his sleeve and looked at her.

'Well, tha gonna welcome home the returning hero?'

She looked at him as he took off his cap. His eyes were dull and sunken into his face, his skin was dark, flecked and blotchy, his brow furrowed, his cheeks hollow, and several teeth with missing, his hair no longer thick, golden and well-kept, but thinning, messy and dull. He had aged fifteen years in just over four. What she saw in front of her was an emaciated, disgusting old man, stinking of vomit.

'Don't move – get that coat off. She retched as she took it off him. 'And those trousers.'

'Steady on, lass, I've only just got in t' door.'

She didn't reply. She got a cloth and a bucket and started to clean up.

'Go and sit down, and for God's sake don't throw up again.'

She wiped and rinsed and splashed Jeyes fluid around.

She was finishing off when she heard a crashing sound. Smith wasn't in the living room. There was another crash from upstairs. Shouting. She rushed up the stairs. In the front bedroom he had swept all of Lily's things off the dressing table, and had tipped the contents of a drawer onto the floor.

'Where the fuck's my stuff? What a bloody way to treat a soldier fighting for king and country. It was hard to make out his words as he slurred through his missing teeth.

'Stop it. You've no right.'

'That's it. No bloody rights. Lost bloody everything, even my rights.'

'Just stop it. You can't expect everything to stay the same for four years. I've had to make do.'

'Bet you bloody have. Bet you moved a bloody fella in soon as my back was turned.'

'Oh, yeah. Who do you think this lot belongs to?' Lacy undergarments and bottles of scent, a hair brush and hand mirror littered the floor. 'These are the things of a good friend – without her help with the rent you wouldn't even have this house to come back to. So how dare you.'

'You bloody...' He staggered towards her but she pushed him hard in the chest – she met no resistance, it was like brushing away a fullback in the box. He stuttered and fell. He slumped against the bed; trouserless, ridiculous. He grasped his knees, buried his head, convulsed.

Elsie was quite taken aback at his reaction. 'Are you all right? Smith?' It was the first time she had used his name for... she didn't know how long. There was no reply. He rocked backwards and forwards. Her emotions went from disgust to pity. This was not Smith – what could have happened to turn such a man into this? But she could not bring herself to comfort him: this stranger.

She tidied up and put the drawer back. She left him there and went up the ladder to the box room, to the trunk where his clothes were, and pulled out an armful of mothball-reeking trousers, a jacket, shirts and undergarments.

He was still sitting in the same place, but looked up as she entered. 'Here, I've got some of your old things. You can get changed now. Here's some trousers and a shirt.' He pulled himself up to his feet with an effort, grasping the bedstead.

'I'll go and put the kettle on. I'll leave you to it. But don't touch anything. It's not yours. I'll explain when you come down.'

She changed her own clothes and mashed some tea. She watched him limp over to the chair, his misshapen jacket hanging off him, his trousers pulled in at the waist like he was wearing a cheap suit picked up from the pawn shop after never being reclaimed.

'I'll get them to move their things out when they get back after the New Year.'

'Who's they?'

'My friends, Lily and Betty.'

'They shouldn't be here. I don't want them here.'

'How was I to know? I didn't know when you'd get back. I didn't even know you were still alive.'

'That would suit thi, wouldn't it?'

'I've not heard from you since before last Easter.'

'Funny that.'

'Was it really that bad?'

'You don't want to know.'

'I still sent you parcels.'

'You wasted your money.'

'I'll get your things washed tomorrow.'

'The house was empty when I my got back. I didn't have a key, so I had to go somewhere warm. I guess I'm not used to beer any more.'

'You could have gone to a neighbour's.'

'And have them stare at me and interrogate me?'

'I'll make you up a bed in a bit. I've got some stew for tea, or I could do you some scrambled eggs and toast. Would you prefer that?' He nodded.

After tea she tidied all of Lily's things into the back bedroom and hung the rest of Smith's clothes back in the wardrobe. She couldn't bring herself to move her own clothes from the chest downstairs in the front room – the thought of sharing a bed with him made her shudder, but when she came down he was asleep in the chair, so she put a blanket over him and left him there and went to her own bed in the front room, pushing a chair up against the door handle as she closed the door.

She found him in the morning asleep on the rug by the fireplace – like a dog.

It was a great sadness to her when Lily and Betty moved out in the New Year. How was she to occupy the days stretching out in front of her with nothing to do but worry about the presence of Smith? He said he couldn't be doing with feathers and mattresses, so she was spared that at least for now; but could she really share her life with this old man, a stranger who would not talk, except to ask for things – for a newspaper, or cups of tea. He would not go out himself – he just sat. At night-time she would hear noises coming from the living room as he muttered in his sleep or emitted strange words, and grunts like a wild beast asleep on the hearth rug.

She helped Lily and Betty carry their things down – Smith sat staring at the fire, ignoring them, not even looking up as they passed, and they glanced sideways at him, like some guard dog you had to avoid making eye contact with for fear of rousing it. After they had loaded their boxes and other things into the van, Lily came back for her gramophone.

'I've left you the records that are yours, Elsie.'

'I have nothing to play them on.'

As the gramophone exited the living room it was like a soul leaving a body. She remembered the music and the laughter: Henry whisking her round, bumping into furniture, giddiness and excitement, and the hours that sometimes followed upstairs. She forced a smile for Lily.

'Thank you so much for everything, Lily.'

'It has been such a pleasure, despite everything – the bombs and the food shortages, the times we had no coal. It has been one of the happiest times. I will miss you so. And your pies.'

'I'll miss you, too.'

'Well, I'll see you. Do take care, Elsie.'

Elsie noticed Lily's eyes flick to the window, to where Smith could be seen, sitting in the living room.

'We must have a night out soon.'

'Yes, we must. Say goodbye to Betty for me.'

'I will. No need to come out.'

She closed the door on so much more than a cold afternoon in January.

'What gives them the bloody right to demand anything?' Smith said delivering a backhand blow to his newspaper.

'Who is making demands?' Elsie looked up from where she was wiping the linoleum on her hands and knees.

'The Hun: Count von Summat-or-other, making demands at Versailles. This German paper apparently reckons somehow that the German people weren't to blame; that they were misled into thinking they could win. As if that lets 'em off. Christ almighty! They hated us – wanted to crush democracy and now they think they can make demands when they lose. We shouldn't have signed the Armistice.' Elsie looked up again. 'We've been too nice – we should've carried on marching right into Berlin.' Elsie went back to cleaning the floor.

He had tried to make sense of it all. He'd kept all the newspapers in a pile and kept coming back to things – it took a long time to work through it. He read about Spartacists in Berlin, and revolution in Moscow, of British troops now in Russia, an ally, to protect oil fields for the capitalists according to some. The people's peace or a profiteers' truce. The bloody, greedy bastards! Look what they had done to him.

And then he'd feel guilty. Millions had been slaughtered. God only knows how many? Fifty times the population of the city, or more? That could not even be conceived of.

He read of British prisoners who were taken to the Russian front and made to dig graves in the frozen earth to bury the German dead. Some prisoners then had frostbitten feet amputated. The same private in the West Yorkshire Regiment told of Lansdorf Lager where a hundred a fifty Rumanians died of starvation – "their legs no thicker than my wrist." "Every fortnight they used to whitewash us with powder which took off the hair from our bodies. They said it would keep us free of lice." What right had he to feel sorry for himself? What right? Selfish bastard.

He'd throw the paper onto the floor and sit and stare at the fire, watch the little devils spitting and blowing their trumpets, the pulsating oranges and yellows, the smoke rising and falling, twisting and turning.

'Why don't you get yourself out of the house. You can't sit there all the time? I'm sure Tom Harrison would be pleased to see you, buy you a drink or two.'

Tom Harrison! Was that the best she could come up with? Shirker Tom Harrison with his perfect kids. She was right though, he couldn't stay in all the time. He put on his coat and hat.

'Do you need some money?'

'No.'

He went out into the dark street. He had no plan of where to go. He wandered down the street, turned right, turned left. He couldn't go in a pub where there were memories. He could just head back now, perhaps. No.

It was as if nothing had happened: laughter from behind drawn curtains, cosy fires, complacent bastards. He pushed open the door to a pub that he didn't remember, ordered half a milk stout and went to sit in the corner. Here it was the same. People laughed and joked, someone played the piano. Except there was a man opposite, also sitting on his own, a pint in front of him, not looking at anything in particular. An ex-Tommy. He had that look – those eyes had seen things too. People talked too much, rattled on about nothing. Look at her, there? They had all had a good war – like Elsie. She was just the same, if not better – untouched, unsullied by it all. They didn't want to know, and, even if they said they did, they could never understand. And what was the point? He wasn't going to satisfy their curiosity. Let them stare. Let them feel uncomfortable that he and the other man sat and reminded them of what life was really like. What death was like. What people were really like.

Those missing years had been filled in his mind with rumour and conjecture, stories told in the *lagers* by those who had not got themselves captured so early on as he. It would all be forgotten as the world went back to making money. But was anyone any the wiser? Was the world a better place?

But he was still alive and the world still turned and that was all anything came down to in the end. Who survived. Those who didn't were no more than dead ends in family trees.

She'd often hear Smith pacing about in the night. She heard him cry out sometimes – it woke her with a start – it was like a fight was taking place in the bedroom.

He had come back from that trip to the pub slightly drunk and she had put the kettle on, made him some toast and spread some dripping and jelly on it. They had sat at the table sipping their tea.

'Where did you end up?'

'The Norfolk Arms.'

'See anyone you know?'

'No.' He lit a cigarette.

'Busy?'

'Not really.'

What else was there to say to a man, a stranger who didn't want to talk? How was Germany? What was the weather like? Did you know I played football, and was good at it? I loved it. Miss it. I had a baby you know. We were bombed by a Zeppelin. I worked in a munitions factory turning shells on a lathe, and enjoyed it, and earned some good money, despite everything; more than you took home before the war. Why do you limp?

He stubbed out his cigarette in his teacup.

'Right I'm off to bed. I'll try sleeping upstairs now. You should too.'

She looked at him. 'At least in the back bedroom,' he said. She hoped her sense of relief wasn't visible.

'You can't stop down here, no more than I can. It's not right. What would people think?'

'Do you not want me to come in with you?'

'I would disturb you. I don't sleep very well. It's probably best not.'

'Yes. Probably.'

He got up and limped to the door.

'Smith?' He stopped and turned.

'What are you going to do with yourself now?'

'How do you mean?'

'I wondered if I should try and get a job. I've –'

'No. I'm to support you. I've got some back pay. I'm not broke. And I suppose when my leave's up I'll get de-mobbed and go and ask for my old job back.'

He was at it again now. Walking up and down in the room – rhythmically. Thump, thump, thump, creak, pause, thump, creak, thump, thump, thump, pause, thump, thump, thump, creak, thump. Back over the same floorboard.

She was lying there, counting the thumps, waiting for the creak. There was no way she could sleep. She lit a candle and crept onto the landing. The door clicked as she opened it. Smith cried out – like he'd seen a ghost.

'Are you all right?'

'You just startled me.' He sat back on the edge of the bed. 'I couldn't sleep.'

'What is it that's troubling you?'

'Nothing… It's nothing – I'm just not used to it yet.'

She saw in the candle's glow his white feet sticking out from the ends of his pyjamas. His right foot was shorter than the other. Several toes were missing. She tried to act as if she had not seen and went to sit next to him. She placed her hand on his thigh, felt him flinch as she did so.

'Best get back to your bed,' he said. 'You'll get cold.'

'Try to get some rest, Smith. Good night.'

CHAPTER THIRTY-THREE

He had only been back at work a few weeks and now here he was at lunchtime, sitting in the pub with nothing to do for the rest of the day. What did they expect? That they were going to get the same man back? After they had sent him to war, got him shot at, nearly blown to bits, then cast into hell itself for over four years.

He'd come home with his body marred, but that wasn't the problem. Was it a surprise he couldn't concentrate? Or that he had been found asleep one morning? When you've woken up in the night having seen the head of a man you were talking to explode, or you stepped on a body that split open and maggots poured out and crawled up your leg, or the faces of devils appear out of the fog? They'd be tired too. He was pretty useless though, it was true. Poor time-keeping. "I'm sure you haven't had the easiest of times – it's not been easy for any of us – but you must see it from my perspective," the workshop manager had said. Pompous bloody fool! – not been easy for any of us! No bloody idea. Thinks he knows what it was like out there. They all think it was the same as a scout camp with a bit of added peril. All a jolly jape – songs round the campfire, bully beef and biscuits all round and the inconvenience of a bit of mud to brush off your trousers. So long as you avoided the bullet yourself it was all right in the end. Nice clean deaths like gentlemen: a tiny hole in the chest and a "well this it old chum – toodle pip." No blood and snot and crap and entrails and splattered brains. No fear and sobbing and madness. No scooping of miscellaneous body parts into buckets. No gas, no stench of death, no rib cages crawling with rats. Well, fuck him and his job. "You must see that I've got engines to turn around – or I'll get into trouble. I tried warning you. I have been more than patient." Bloody shirker who's had an easy war, that's what. "But we can't carry dead weight," he said. That expression hit him like an anvil swung on a crane's rope. Dead weight – that's what he was. "First you forget to replace wash-out plugs. That's bad enough. But then you swept the tubes, then thought you'd steam through again – you could have killed the bar-man at the other end – scalded the poor bugger to death. You're a bloody fool."

There was hardly anyone in. It was nearly chucking out time. The woman behind the bar had hung a towel over the pump and looked over at him as she polished the glasses and hung them up. She half-smiled at him as if to remind him to finish off his drink and go — buxom: almost compulsory behind a bar.

He wasn't even a proper man any more. He'd seen the look of disgust on Elsie's face, and who could blame her? He disgusted himself. He wasn't even half the man he'd been before the war. He'd surprised himself by what he'd seen looking back at him in the mirror. His looks were just one thing the Hun had robbed him of. But she had shown him some signs of... if not affection, at least a little warmth. As if she had been at least in part ready to pick up some sort of relations.

'If you would like to come into bed for a bit you can,' he had said.

They had lain there and she had held his hand. She had put her head against his shoulder. It was mechanical. She didn't love him. At best she sympathized with him. Images of Anna came into his head, images he tried to drive away. It was no use. It was impossible. He'd turned away and shortly afterwards he felt the bed move and creak as she slipped out and back to her own room.

He supped up and extinguished the stub of his cigarette.

'I'm going straight to bed,' he said, when he got in. 'Don't bother getting me up in the morning. I'm not well.'

'Drunk, more like.'

'What if I am? It don't bloody matter. Not like I've got a fucking job to go to, is it?'

It was early on Saturday morning when there was a knock at the door. Smith looked up at Elsie from his paper, and she went to answer.

'Grace. How are you? It's been a long time.'

'Yes. It has. I trust you're well. I heard Smith was back, and I thought...'

'Yes?'

'Is he in?'

'He is, but... just a second.'

Elsie went in. Smith had left the room. She found him in the front room.

'It's Grace. She'd like to see you.'

'I can't. I don't want to see her.'

'I don't think you can avoid it, Smith. Don't you owe it to Charlie?' His eyes flicked to the door and then to the window. He took a deep breath.

'Come on, and sit down. I'll make some more tea.' She held back and let him go through the door first, followed, and went to invite Grace in.

'Come in, Grace. I'm sorry to keep you waiting out in the cold. I'm afraid a lot has changed.' She lowered her voice to barely more than a whisper, 'Go easy on him.'

'Thank you. Yes, a lot has changed.'

She watched Grace as Smith got to his feet to shake her hand. What a fake smile she wore – a smile that covers up what you really think.

'Do sit down, Grace,' said Elsie. 'Can I get you a cup of tea?'

She took the kettle off the range and quickly brought it to boil over the gas ring. Grace was hardly changed. Rationing had not made her lose any weight. If anything she was even plumper than she had been before. Elsie had seen her a few times since – on the opposite side of Spital Hill or in town, but had pretended not to see her or had ducked into a shop doorway.

'It's good to see you back, Smith,' she said.

Smith tried to smile without opening his mouth. It was what he did now, ashamed of the state of his teeth.

'I heard you were back at the depot. And I thought...'

'I'm not there any more.'

'Anyway, I thought... It's just... I don't know anything... what happened, I mean. I had a letter from him and then nothing. Then a missing-in-action letter. I just wondered... I sometimes think... sometimes hope. Despite everything... ' She was now weeping quietly and profusely, dabbing at her eyes with a handkerchief.

Smith's eyes were fixed on the rug in front of Grace's feet.

He looked up at Elsie and nodded towards the door at the stair foot.

'I'll pour the tea and take mine in the other room,' she said.

She closed the living room door behind her and went into the front room. Then she crept back and listened at the door. She had at least developed a feeling of protectiveness towards him – her vows meant something still. She still had a duty. He needed her to look after him.

'What did you want to know, Grace?'

There was such a tone of resignation – of defeat – in his voice.

'I don't know. Is there any chance…'

There was silence. Then a little sob from Grace.

'We had to retreat – we were so overwhelmed. Me and him hung back to let the others get a head start.' Elsie held her breath. 'Then we turned and fled too. At least that's what I think I remember. I don't know what is true and what I've made up. It's been round my head so many times.'

It was quiet again.

'I was up in the village, and then… and then he wasn't there.'

'Didn't you go back for him?'

Silence.

Grace's voice again: 'I'm sorry. I didn't mean to…'

'He was a hero, Grace. *My* hero. My mate.' Smith's voice was broken now. 'He was a better man than me. He never would surrender. He never… '

There was a scraping noise, and an animal noise, like she'd heard in the night.

Elsie peeped round the door and saw Grace backing away from Smith in horror. He was on the floor curled up like he was having some sort of fit. She rushed in.

'I think you better leave now. You've had your answers.'

Grace grabbed her handbag and got away from the scene as fast as she could.

Elsie sat on the floor next to Smith, got a cushion for his head and put her hand on his shoulder.

She sat with him for a long time until he gradually came back.

He sat quietly for the rest of the day. She read *Treasure Island* and bits of the Gospel to him. It seemed to calm his nerves.

CHAPTER THIRTY-FOUR

He didn't get up the next morning, complained of a headache and feeling tired. It was true he didn't feel well. He pulled a blanket up over his head and tried to get back to sleep when Elsie had come into the room to see if he was getting up for breakfast. He knew he shouldn't be lying there feeling sorry for himself – he didn't want to be, not really, but what was the point?

She brought him up a cup of tea and a newspaper.

He dozed a little.

She came back in at dinnertime. 'You've not touched your cup of tea.'

'I fell asleep.'

'I've made some shepherd's pie. I'll fetch you a fresh cup of tea.'

'No need, I'll drink it cold.'

She put a pillow behind him and he sat up. She moved the still folded newspaper off the chair onto the side of the bed. 'I'll pop the paper where you can reach it. I'll be downstairs if you need me.'

He tried to go back to sleep when she had taken the plate away but couldn't. He picked up the newspaper and flicked through it. It was all pointless. Nothing was going to change – it was already forgotten; same old crap, none of it mattered, nothing amounted to anything worthwhile. What did you gain from reading it? Was he really any the wiser? Did it prove anything or make things better? Who was he kidding? What did he have to build, to create, to be able to say "that was worth the effort"? Wasn't that the point – to leave something behind when you've gone? Something that people will remember you for? Having made things better, improved something? If you only made things worse: what then?

As the sun went down he nodded off with the fading light in the bedroom. He awoke again when he heard voices downstairs. A man's voice speaking low – speaking to Elsie. He got up and opened the bedroom door so that he could listen, but couldn't make it out. The door downstairs opened and light from the living room lit the stairs.

'You're up. I thought I heard the boards creak. We've a visitor. Morris Simmonite? Says he used to work with you at the depot. I've told him to call another time.'

'No, it's all right. I'll come down.'

'Are you feeling better, then?'

'A bit, yeah.'

Elsie made herself scarce in the scullery when he came down.

'Good to see thi, Morris. It's been a long time.'

'Nearly five year. I was back at Brightside and heard tha were around – thought I'd look out an old mate. But I don't want to disturb thi, if tha's not well.'

He saw Morris' eyes taking in the sight before him. 'It's fine, tha's not. Does tha fancy a drink?'

'Yes, all right. Shall I get thi missus to put the kettle on?'

'No, I meant a proper drink.'

'I thought tha weren't well.'

'Might do me good to get out of the house.'

'Elsie said tha'd had a bit of a rough time,' Morris said, when they got sat down with a couple of pints.

'Not as bad as some, but not exactly a holiday neither. What about thi?'

'I guess the usual: Dardanelles, France, the usual shit.'

'Yeah, I heard.'

'Bad do.'

'Yeah.'

'Someone said about... '

'Yeah.'

'Bit of a bugger that. He was a good bloke.'

'The best. I don't suppose Tom...'

Morris shook his head. 'Passchendaele.'

They both sipped their beer.

'Look, if tha fancies a bit of a flutter any time, I still do the Skyring most weekends. It's just the same as the old days. I'll probably go up Saturday afternoon after work. Meet some of the lads at the Golden Ball first.'

A little shiver ran through Smith at the mention of the ring. 'That would be good; I'll take thi up on that.'

'That was nice of him,' said Elsie when he got back.

'Yeah. Good to see him again.'

'You feeling better then?'

'Yeah. I'll get up in the morning.'

'What are you going to do?'

'Look for a job, I suppose.'

He spent the next morning wandering from factory to factory: anywhere that might need someone who knew how to work with metal and with tools, but posts were already filled they said. He crept back for his lunch, then brooded by the fire.

In the following days he trudged the streets in wider and wider circles asking if there was work for a fitter. He was met with sympathy, and looks of pity, but they were having to make changes, shift production, and were not looking to take people on right then, or still weren't sure about men returning to posts they had been promised. Call back in a few weeks, they said, and we'll see.

Then when the dinnertime buzzers went he'd find the nearest pub to wash down a pie or a bread cake and a slice of haslet or brawn. There he'd stay until closing, by which time he'd mutter: ah, fuck 'em all, and head up into town for something to do, when he couldn't face returning to the house.

He'd chuck a penny into the blind fiddler's hat or watch people go by in their fancy carriages and fancy hats, leaving their drivers waiting outside. Shop windows promised a better life of made-to-measure worsted suits and felt hats, of furs and shiny leather boots, of musical instruments, gold watches, chains and fobs, mahogany furniture and electric light fittings. It had not been a bad war at all for some folk.

She'd had something on her mind all evening. Waiting for the right moment, he could tell.

'Which firms have you tried?' she asked. 'Perhaps you've not managed to talk to the right person. Could you not look for something other than a fitter's job? Or might you have to take whatever is going in the meantime, work your way into something better?'

'I'm not doing some shitty labouring job. I'm time-served. And I don't need advice. I know what I'm doing. Besides, it's not as simple as that. Anyhow, tha knows nowt about factory work. Here, have this if it's money tha's worried about – ten guineas. Happy? That might keep thi off my back for a bit.'

'Where did you get this?'

'It's mine, if that's what tha means. It's back pay from while I was on holiday.' He knew he was being spiteful and pushing her away after

235

she had been trying to be good to him, but still he did it. He didn't really understand why. He couldn't control his resentment.

He had a pint or two that evening then wandered down towards Newhall Bridge. He pulled his collar up and tucked his head into his muffler. He wasn't sure if it was still there. What a bloody fool. People moved around in the war, things had changed, businesses of every sort came and went. The house still looked the same. He stood outside on the opposite side of the road. He should go home. But something held him back.

A man came out, pulled the door behind him and looked up and down the street and walked away. Smith crossed the road and knocked on the door. He waited and was again about to leave when it opened a chink and a face peered out.

'I was wondering about some business.'

The door opened and he entered a dark hallway.

'Sit yourself down,' she said. He sat on a small wooden chair. She loomed over him, arms folded. 'I don't recognise you, you've not been before.'

'No.'

'What is it you're after?'

He cringed. 'I've got money. I don't know. Just someone nice, y' know.'

'Ten shillings, up front.'

'Ten?'

'What do you expect? First time discount?'

He took the small roll of black and red Treasury notes out of his jacket pocket, and placed one on the table. She tucked it into her ample cleavage.

'Wait there.'

He was kept waiting; his throat dry, armpits dripping, despite the chill in the hall. She returned and led him upstairs and into a bedroom.

'There's a washstand there if you need it. I'll bring Violet. Take your shoes off.'

He sat down and removed his jacket and shoes. It was quite warm, a small fire smouldering in an iron grate. The room was lit by an oil lamp with the wick turned down low. The furnishings were sparse: a small table with a bottle of some sort of brandy and two glasses, a cane chair, a Japanese-style screen in the corner, and thick drapes over the window. He was ashamed and disgusted at himself. But he needed this. He just couldn't stand being judged. Perhaps he could lie down with someone as disgusting as himself.

The door opened and a girl came in. She was not at all what he expected – she wasn't dressed like a tart, her face wasn't painted to cover up marks or to hide her age. She was pretty and very ordinary.

She looked at him and gave a half-smile before disappearing behind the screen.

He heard rustling noises and she returned wearing a long silky robe – an oriental looking thing in crimson and green. She wafted towards him.

He closed his eyes and rubbed his hands over his face.

'I'm sorry,' he said.

'What for, love? We all have needs. We've all got to make ends meet the best we can. Relax and let me take care of everything.'

He took a deep breath.

'Can I get you a drink?'

He nodded. She poured two glasses from the bottle on the table, then, clutching them both, sat on his knee.

She downed her drink and put the glass on the bed and started to unbutton his shirt. He closed his eyes and breathed in her scent – a mixture of rosewater and the musky smell of the female body. A shudder ran through him. He swallowed the alcohol and she took the glass off him.

She did things to him that should have been distasteful, but she didn't seem to mind. Ran her fingers over his damaged toes. She didn't seem embarrassed at anything, didn't pass comment, didn't flinch when he dared to be bold and touch her warm skin. She was extremely professional about the whole transaction.

He apologised again afterwards, apologised for his stupid tears, and she laughed for the first time.

'Don't be silly. It's good to be of service to an ex-Tommy.'

She got dressed quickly.

'How did you know?'

'It's obvious, love.'

'Yes. You're right. Can I see you again?'

'Of course; though I don't work every evening.'

'Speak to Mrs Mappin about it. See yourself out when you've dressed.'

CHAPTER THIRTY-FIVE

'Now he's got a job he's in a much better mood,' said Elsie as she picked up a sugar cube with the tongs and plopped it into her tea. She had met up with Mary in town on Saturday afternoon. 'How's your new job going?'

'It pays the bills. It doesn't compare to munitions work though – less money and... well, it was just... fun, somehow, wasn't it? All those girls working together and singing, and we had some laughs, as well as some tears. But the office is very serious – certainly no laughing allowed. Typing away all day. But, I've got some other news too.'

'Good news?'

'Yes. Yes, it is. Bob's back.'

'Bob?'

'You know: Robert. Except he calls himself Bob now.'

'You mean, *back* back.'

'Yes. He needs me, Elsie. After everything he's been through, like Smith needs you – but it's more than that, he's different.'

Elsie looked down at the tabletop, then into Mary's eyes.

'He's changed in so many ways. He's grown up... into a different man... with depths he never had before. He wooed me all over again with a passion the old Robert never had. I guess he knows himself and the world now, like he never did before.'

'That's wonderful news, Mary. I always liked Robert.'

'So, what is it Smith is up to now?'

'He doesn't say – other than some sort of sales agent or something – going round factories and places. He goes about in that awful coat of his – the one that cost a fortune before the war – did you ever see it? I can't think that makes him look business-like. But he's bringing some money in, and he's getting out of the house and meeting people again – he's not just sat there like some brooding presence.' She dunked a biscuit in her tea. 'You'll never guess what he's done – he's only gone and bought a gramophone. It was delivered the other day – I was telling them to take it away, that they had made a mistake, that we'd not ordered one.'

'Oh dear, how embarrassing. But it's good isn't it, having a gramophone in the house again?'

'No, it's not. He knows nothing about music.'

'I remember you once saying he had taste in music?'

'Did I? When?'

'When you first told me about him – when you met him in Lincoln.'

'Ah – what I now realise is that Smith is quite a convincing bluffer – or I was willingly taken in by him. *You* decide whether he has taste in music: one of the records he got is that awful *Land O' Yamo Yamo* thing.'

Mary broke into song in a squeaky voice: '*In the land o' Yamo Yamo. Funicula, Funicula, Funiculi...*'

'No! Stop it! Seriously. He plays it over and over again and it drives me insane. I even find myself singing it at odd times. I swear I'll take the poker to the blessed thing one day. And then there's that Marion Harris *After You've Gone* and her awful American squalling and drawling. In fact, there's nothing he's bought that I like, really. But what can I do?'

Mary laughed. 'Can't you get something different to play?'

'Not really. How can I justify spending three or four bob on a record? I've got my old ones hidden away in the loft but how do I explain those? Anyway, he sees it as his gramophone. Do you think he'd let me put on a string quartet record?'

Smith was standing outside the Wellington waiting for the dinnertime rush. He had a view up and down Brightside Lane and across to Upwell Street – ever vigilant, you had to be, not just for coppers in uniform but some sneaky ones in plain clothes. You could usually spot a copper a mile off though.

They liked to stay ahead. Mooney wasn't daft. The other week when a plain clothes copper was giving evidence against a runner that worked over Darnall, Mooney had got them all down into the public gallery at the courthouse so that they could take a neb at the copper and would recognise him if he came sniffing around. Interfering bastards that's what they were, more bothered about losing taxable income than upholding morals. Stopping working men having a bit of fun, that's all it was. But not only working men, the unemployed too. For some of them, winning a tenner or even twenty on a treble was their only hope of ever having any money to spend on anything. And there were returning soldiers with back pay and miners with their Sankey money. On a good day he was earning the best part of ten shillings on commission. He'd fallen on his feet.

' 'ere mister.' A boy of eleven or twelve came up to him: scruffy breeches, moth-eaten looking jumper and a threadbare cap perched on his head. 'Mi dad says can we have sixpence on Toadstone for the three forty-five at Hurst Park?'

Smith took the money, looked around him and fished in his inside pocket for the slips, pencilled one in, tore part off and gave it to the boy.

He'd lost all of the money he'd had in his pocket that first afternoon back at the Skyring: best part of five quid, but he'd also met some old faces: Spud Murphy and Peter Winsey. Even George Mooney himself was there with his brother and a few others, smoking cigars, sipping beer from bottles and slapping each other on the back. It was so busy that there were two rings operating side by side.

He'd seen Murphy first and nodded a greeting to him. Murphy stopped and looked for a second or two and, when he realised who he was, it was like he'd met a long lost brother, such was the vigorous handshaking and friendly punches on the arm.

'Smith, good to see you, fella. Holy Mother of God but you look like shite. You had a rough one didn't you, to be sure.'

'Could have been better. You know. And not feeling very chipper – lost big tonight, so I don't feel too good about that.'

'Well, if there's anything I can do for you, you've only got to ask, so you have. Wasn't it the railways you worked on?'

'Yeah. Not now though. They got rid on us. On the scrapheap. No room for an old soldier.'

'That's bad,' said Murphy blowing cigarette smoke out of the side of his mouth. 'I was just going to ask if you fancied a little commission on the side, like in the old days, but maybe we can do better than that for an old pal. I'll ask around. Catch you in a bit. Don't go away?'

He caught up with Morris on the edge of the ring.

'Who was that?'

'A fella called Murphy, who I knew before the war – you never meet him? Did a bit of business with him back then.'

The buzz of being back there! The camaraderie, tinged with fear of stepping out of line. Your heart pumping blood through your veins as you waited for the coins to fall. The sinking feeling of losing outweighed by the joy of scooping up a big win.

It had started off well; cautiously – a sovereign at a time and he'd been up to a tenner. His rival, a short, knuckle-dragging miner, by the looks of him, had come in with ten on tails against his heads. He'd felt so sure of it, felt this was his luck turning. But it didn't. He'd tried to claw back some beer money with his last six shillings but had lost it all. Not even enough for a tram back into town. Everything crashing back down around him again. He watched a few games and saw Morris win back what he'd started with.

Murphy found him and they withdrew from the ring.

'I've spoke to the gaffer. He passes on his regards, but he's a bit tied up with some business, otherwise he would have come across and said hello in person. The good news is that we can offer you some work, if you're up for it. Come down to the Eagle Tavern at West Bar on Monday and we'll get you sorted.'

A factory buzzer sounded, then another. Yes, Smith was back in the game. He'd got a good little patch to keep him busy – his old railway depot – the lads from the gasworks, and Cyclops, and the streets between, as well as a fair few streets around Brightside. Then at weekends he was earning ten bob a day as a piker at a new tossing ring at Parkwood Springs – nice and difficult to get to except on foot and a good vantage point to keep a look out for approaching trouble.

Right then, Smith, old lad. Look lively, customers approaching.

CHAPTER THIRTY-SIX

He still had a belting headache – but it went beyond just his head: his neck and shoulders and back were sore too. He must have slept funny – that and the however many pints of stout and whiskeys. Mooney had a reputation to uphold as a good payer and a heavily backed favourite winning in the National had been the worst possible result. No big payouts but lots and lots of them.

Smith's jacket pockets weighed him down – the breeze that was picking up wouldn't blow him away given all the ballast he had. He smiled to himself. Mooney had sat in the corner of the pub counting out little piles of coins for all the runners; then, the unpleasantness over, had started to drown his sorrows and insisted on everyone else doing the same. Smith had been happy to do so.

He wasn't one to go with the crowd, piling money on the favourite. He had fancied Rubinstein at thirty-five to one. He put a fiver on it – his winnings from the previous day's programme, backing Santa Cruz in the Spring Cup at ten to one, on a ten bob bet. Imagine if poor Rubinstein had stayed in the race! It had been going well up to the last fence apparently – he'd made it over but then collapsed and died. He'd also lost a guinea on Snow Maiden: pipped to the line by a short head in the Union Jack Stakes. He should've done it the other way round put the guinea on Santa Cruz. Bloody Liverpool!

He'd perhaps been getting over-confident – felt like he was getting inside knowledge, reading form and ground, not picking entirely on a hunch or superstition. That was for mugs – like that fella who'd chucked all his pawn tickets on Daphne at five to one just because he'd had a dream about his mother – and that was his dad's pet name for her or some such nonsense. A hard lesson. Fancy having to explain that to the missus: that she couldn't have her Sunday best back, that she'd have to go to Chapel in her rags or stop in the house. Only himself to blame. Smith had tried to do his best by him; told him to back Santa Cruz instead. Even obliged him by taking pawn tickets instead of silver.

It was worth keeping close to Mooney – if he shared a tip with you it was usually based on something sound, whether honest or not –

probably not. He smiled again. He had connections, did Mooney – he toured the courses. That was a more sensible approach – curb his own enthusiasm and self-belief. No such thing as a poor bookie.

A shower cloud came over so he went into the pub, got a beer and sat in the corner waiting for his customers so that he could repay them their stakes plus the little extra that Piggott and Poethlyn had earned them.

He swung by the chippy for a fishcake and chips for his dinner – she had said she was stopping out for her dinner then off to the bloody circus, with that Mary and her fella, like she was some nine-year-old. Did he want to come too? Did he heck as like. Let her stop out if she liked. He wasn't going to beg.

He ate straight from the newspaper, sitting by the remnants of the morning's fire, listening to the clock ticking on the mantelpiece. He wiped his greasy fingers, then gave *After You've Gone* a quick spin on the gramophone, sitting and tapping his foot against the fender.

He picked up the poker from the hearth and weighed it in his hand – part of the companion set he'd once made himself and given to Elsie as a birthday present. He'd found a spare bit of rod lying about the workshop at the depot and had hammered it into shape and bent the end into a nice handle. He wiped it on the hearth rug – might be a useful precaution just in case of trouble – there had been rumours of a new Gas Tank Gang forming from Neepsend, getting jealous of the new business up at Parkwood Springs – felt that that should be their territory. A bunch of kids who needed to learn a bit about life, as well as some manners, according to Spud Murphy. He put it in his inside coat pocket, newly adapted for such eventualities – use of a needle being a skill he'd learnt on his holiday. He headed up the street so that he could skirt round the bottom side of the cemetery where they said the bomb had landed, past Christ Church and the laundry then up the hill to the ring to be detailed for the afternoon's duties.

A goods train rumbled overhead on its way to Bridgehouses as Elsie went under the arches. She was curious to see what Robert was like after all these years – a man who had succeeded in getting a ring on her best friend's finger, when before she had been so unconvinced.

She found them in the foyer of the hotel standing together in intimate conversation. She stopped, not wanting to interrupt, but Mary saw her and gave an excited little start and came skitting across and grabbed her by the arm. She held her left hand up to Elsie's face and wiggled her bejewelled ring finger.

'It's not a real diamond, of course, but it's nice isn't it?'

'It is, Mary. I'm really happy for you.' Mary's lip quivered, she was teetering between crying and laughing, but Elsie smiled and her friend mirrored her. 'Oh, come here.' She gave Mary a hug.

'So, Smith isn't joining us?'

'No.'

'That's a shame. It would do him good to laugh.'

Elsie replied with a flat, half smile. 'Come on, let me go and congratulate Robert, I mean Bob. He doesn't know how lucky he is.'

Bob was leaning against the panelling of the foyer, smiling at them as they walked over arm in arm. He held out his hand; it was dry and rough and swallowed hers up in its gentle grasp.

'Good to see you again, Elsie.'

'You too, Bob. I was just saying: you don't know how lucky you are.'

'I think I do.'

'Well, good. I should think so. You won't take her from me will you?'

'Of course not. In fact we'd like you to feel part of our family. And before that you'll be bridesmaid of course.'

'Of course. If you tried to suggest anyone else I'd scratch their eyes out.'

'Oh, Elsie! What are you like?'

'Shall we?' said Robert, indicating through into the hotel.

'Bob has booked a table for lunch.'

'Do we need to get tickets for this afternoon?'

'No, he's got that sorted too, haven't you, Bob?'

'How much do I owe you?'

'No need, Elsie. It's my treat.'

'No, I must.'

'Put that away. It's my way of saying thank you for looking after my Mary.'

Over lunch of potted meat sandwiches and cake, Elsie reflected. She wondered if her and Mary had changed as much as Bob. Probably not. Men changed so much. Some entered their twenties still looking like boys, before metamorphosing into men. Sometimes the effect was negative – something charming about the boy disappearing into the ugliness of manhood, but in others the effect was positive – from gawkiness and unappealing immaturity into something rather attractive: from repugnant naivety to a depth of character that both drew you in but also instilled a little fear of the unknown. Bob had an assertiveness that Robert never had – he was now a man of the world: lines around his eyes and across his forehead were the lines of a story. A well-trimmed moustache. His eyes no longer only reflected light but burned themselves. She felt a little pang of jealousy towards her friend.

A waiter nearby dropped a plate, clattering and smashing onto the floor. It didn't just make Bob jump, he was almost under the table. He shook it off quite quickly and carried on as though nothing had happened – a quick glance left and right to check whether anyone had seen his apparent cowardice. Elsie sipped at her tea. She had seen this all before.

The afternoon had brightened up. The shower clouds had blown over – Smith felt some warmth in the sun on his back as he turned up towards the woods where the tossing ring operated.

There were three main pikers needed: one at the intersection of the tracks up from Douglas Road, one at the Rutland Road track and one over by Shirecliffe Hall. They were to do an hour or so each in rotation before someone would come and relieve them. Runners were to be stationed a bit closer in, within signalling and whistling distance of those on the outer edge.

For the first hour he kept vigil over the track by the hall and didn't see a soul – it was not an obvious route for anyone wanting to head up to the ring – unless the toffs of Shirecliffe had developed a strong interest in gambling on the fall of ha'pennies rather than stocks and shares. It still needed watching though – if he'd been in charge of a bunch of detectives or a rival gang, this was the back way from which he would approach unseen.

He alternated between chewing on a piece of liquorice root and smoking cigarettes to pass the time. After a while someone came down to take his place so he walked up to the woods, grabbed a bottle of beer and watched a few rounds before he had to get back to work. It was starting to get busy now the afternoon was wearing on: they were two or three deep around the toller – a bit of a showman in a brown velour hat: a foreign-looking thing that Smith did not approve of: far too Teutonic.

He finished his beer and was sent down to the track up from Neepsend. He emerged from the woods on to the hillside and picked his way through scrub and heather towards the main track down. The warmth had gone from the sun now, as it was dipping down towards the smoke that hung over the hills and the valley. He exchanged greetings with the runner posted at the top of the path and skidded a bit as he descended the broken track towards the piker at the bottom.

'Nah then, Bill. How's it going?'

'Starting to get a bit parky now. Is it busy up there?'

'Pretty much. Should be a reasonable pay-out tonight.'

'Right you are. I'll get off then. See thi in a bit.'

'Yep.'

Smith lit a cigarette and looked out over the valley from the vantage point – across to the hills at Wharncliffe and Stannington through the smoke and haze, rows of houses climbing the hillside opposite, glimpses of river reflecting light within the vast amphitheatre, and the works down at the bottom with its vast gasholders and chimneys churning out smoke and steam. He took a drag on his cigarette. It could be worse.

He watched the progress of a man wearing a billycock hat as he climbed the path up from the road – another one who regarded their headgear as a sign of being a bit of a cut above. He nodded to him as he approached. It was all that was needed – both knew each other's business, respected the rules and customs. They came in dribs and drabs – sometimes in twos or threes. Sometimes with a: 'how do' or an: 'a'reight,' sometimes just a glance, but always an acknowledgement of his status.

It felt like the chill air was rising up from the valley below. He buttoned his jacket, tightened his woollen muffler and tucked it in, pulled his coat around him.

'That was lovely. Are you sure I can't give you something towards it, or at least pay for my ticket.'

'No. And that's the last word on it, or I might get cross.'

'Well then, thank you again.'

They strolled down the slope from the hotel.

'This is very symbolic for me,' Bob ventured.

'What is?'

'If Sangers is back in town it must be peacetime. It's like it was before. I remember how it felt back then to see the parade – the yellow cages rolling up the road with the snarling and growling inside – lions and tigers and whatnot. Camels and elephants plodding along, Red Indians on horseback, those beautiful painted caravans.'

'I remember us all running down the street when the shout went up,' said Mary. 'I only ever got to go once though. It was always so expensive.'

'I suppose they have a lot of mouths to feed,' said Elsie.

'It takes me right back to those happy days,' continued Bob. 'Did you know the horses were on war duty as well? It's not only the acrobats and clowns that are back after being demobbed but the animals too. Annie and Tiny, the two elephants, were working on a farm for the duration. We've all come through it and are coming together again like in the old days.'

'That's nice,' said Elsie. 'I like that.'

They joined the queue at the entrance to the great tent – children were running around, excited, and jostling each other.

'I feel too old to be here without children in tow,' said Elsie.

'You'll start to sound like your Smith if you're not careful. Let your hair down for once. Release that little girl inside you who wants to run around and see the animals in their cages.'

Behind them the traction engine was whirring away to make electricity for the lights, and men moved about carrying things into the tent: golden, painted mounting blocks, boxes of sawdust, bits of planking, buckets and chairs.

'Of course, this is all wrong,' said Bob, waving his hand towards the queue. 'The traditional way into a circus tent is under the flap, once it has already started and everybody is distracted. That's how we used to do it back in the day. There was none of this fancy electric lighting either, then.'

They were greeted at the entrance by red coated grooms proudly wearing on their sleeves their war service chevrons or gold braid stripes. 'The two and six seats are over there – that gentleman will show you.'

The band struck up some tunes and people settled onto the bench seats. Then the ringmaster cracked his whip and shouted out the familiar: 'Ladies and gentlemen. Boys and girls!' Then all of a sudden in rolled the clown: ridiculous yellow trousers striped in red, legs up in the air and bright ginger wig trailing on the sawdust, and he smashed straight into the ringmaster making him double over.

'Pimpo! You rascally…!'

Bob howled with laughter along with all the children. Elsie allowed herself a little smile.

Pimpo was chased. He somersaulted and tumbled, lost several waistcoats in his attempts to escape, kept losing his trousers – of which he seemed to be wearing many pairs – and pulling them up again. The ringmaster was made to look a pompous fool and everyone roared with approval.

Order was eventually restored and the ringmaster introduced "Mademoiselle Trevoni and the Sanger's School Horse Empress." The horses cantered and turned in formation, and the riders switched from one to another and stood up, balancing on their backs. The horses were beautiful – what a contrast from what they must have been like in France. The most beautiful of all was called Lily of the Valley, a pure white Arabian mare who danced in time to the music along with Mademoiselle Trevoni.

Then Pimpo showed up again and tried to copy the riders, getting it all wrong, and dicing with death between the horses' flying hooves, but doing it all so expertly – falling off, galloping alongside and getting back on, but facing the wrong way, even awkwardly bridging two horses at once.

He tried again to kill himself alongside his sidekick, Alberto, when the telegraph-wire walkers came on, falling and grabbing on to the wire at the last second. Elsie was too afraid for the clowns' safety to properly let herself collapse into laughter, but the more it went on the less real it seemed to become and she was dragged along by the general mood.

The sad looking elephants came on and were made to perform tricks. She thought of Lizzie pulling her loads of steel and machinery. That made her want to cry, not laugh. But at least Jack and Baby, the sea lions, seemed to enjoy themselves and were well rewarded with fish when they balanced and juggled balls and boxes on their noses.

A fearsome whoop announced the arrival of "Lone Face" and his savage troupe of Red Indians, thundering around the ring and jumping on and off. And of course Pimpo could not resist a turn.

After the African snake charmer there was another contretemps between the ringmaster and Pimpo, then a Grand Parade by the whole troupe before the band struck up God Save the King.

Elsie was exhausted – all her senses had been bombarded, and her cheeks ached from laughing.

'Did you enjoy it, Elsie?'

'Oh, rather. It really was something else. I haven't laughed like that in a long time. Thank you so much for inviting me.'

'I'm so pleased. Shall we go for a little drink?'

They headed to one of the more genteel pubs nearby to relive their favourite moments.

Smith watched the sun go down over the hill. It would soon be going-home time. The crowd would disperse, then he could go and collect his money and head home for a nice hot cup of tea and maybe soak his feet in a bowl of Epsom salts.

He heard a noise then suddenly it went dark, something had been thrown over his head.

'Oi! Geroffus!' he shouted. He reached inside his coat and pulled out the poker and swung around wildly. He made contact, heard groaning, then he got free.

'Bastard. I'll kill thi for that.'

He was face-to-face with a young lad – maybe only eighteen or nineteen: thickset, rough-looking. Behind him, up the slope were a number of other youths, perhaps a dozen all told. Where had they come from? Certainly not up the paths. Why hadn't he heard them?

'Lend us a hand, Fred. This one's a bit frisky. We got this, lads. The rest of you go up and get the money. We'll catch you up.'

Fred, a skinny, dark-haired youth with a stubbly beard stepped forward. The pair of them squared up to Smith, pulling lengths of wood, table legs or something, from their belts.

'Go on then, let's have it.'

Smith tensed, his poker raised ready to swing again. The thickset youth tried to swing at him. He jumped to the side and brought the poker down on the kid's shoulder. Seeing his mate go down, the other youth swung at Smith's head. He ducked but it caught him on the neck. He turned to face him, felt dizzy and nauseous. The youth swung again. Smith dodged, and smashed his poker into the youth's side, but as he did so he stumbled over something. He fell backwards and downwards. He heard a snap and felt pain in his leg. Something struck his back, then his leg, and then his head. He passed out.

They said good night at the tram stop on the Wicker, and headed to their homes. Elsie was so pleased for Mary: Bob was wonderful for her. She had always regarded him as steady, but now he was so much more than that. To the barest structure of character had been added complexity, refinement and richness. She could see there was a vulnerability to him that Mary had alluded to, but above all he was dependable. He had clearly never given up on finally capturing Mary – he adored her; that was obvious. She had been his talisman throughout the war – when he had agreed to call off their previous commitment when he enlisted, he had done it through love: because he wanted to set her free from possible pain. That was how Elsie reasoned events. How many men would do that? Most would selfishly cling to such a commitment as if it were all that could keep them afloat. Bob had let go and swum away for fear of dragging Mary down with him.

His eyes opened. Snowflakes fell onto his face – he could see them falling gently through the depths of the dark sky. He didn't know where he was. Then he remembered being attacked. He called out but his voice was swallowed in the darkness. He tried to move – a searing pain shot up his spine. He moved his arm and felt around: his left leg was at a very strange angle. Again he blacked out.

When she got home the house was empty. Smith, down the pub again. She made some tea and ate alone. As she had done many times, she left his plate covered up for when he got back – he could warm it up himself or eat it cold. She wouldn't wait up.

It was very cold. Where was he? He opened his eyes. It was night-time – stars in the sky. He couldn't move, but he turned his head. He could see the horizon. The hills over the town. In the sky was a bright quivering curtain of silvery light. Shimmering up from the curtain were beams like search lights becoming brighter then fading again; flickering up towards the dark clouds above the moors.

He was cold and thirsty.

Ellis had a fire going, had soup bubbling in a pot, put his arm around him. 'We'll be all right, mate. They'll never get us two.'

'I'll just put the kettle on and make you a nice cup of tea and a buttered pikelet.' She smiled at him. She was beautiful. And kind.

CHAPTER THIRTY-SEVEN

Elsie's brother Tom came into the living room and rubbed his hands together.

'Right then, girls, that's a van load. We'll have to come back for the rest, but one last trip should do it – don't tha reckon, Bob?'

'Yep. I've just checked. There's nothing upstairs now. So it's only that sideboard, the gramophone and an aspidistra in the front room and a few bits and bobs in here. '

'I'm really grateful to you both for all your work – would you like another cup of tea before you head over?'

'Another one? Blimey, sis. We've already had about fifteen this afternoon. No, we'll get off, shall we? We'll leave the kettle and have a sup when we get back from this run.'

'Yeah, we'll be back in about an hour,' said Bob. 'That'll give me time to run the van back round to my mate Pete's, after.'

'See you in a bit, then.'

The two men adjusted their caps purposefully and closed the door behind them, Bob blowing a kiss to Mary.

Mary finished wiping the teacups and put them on the side. 'I'll wait with you until they come back,' she said.

'Oh, there's no need. There's nothing to do here. Why don't you get off. I'm sure you've plenty to be getting on with.'

'Are you sure? I did say I'd pop and see the vicar about the hymns and readings sometime.'

'And did you decide about music?'

'Yes – something simple on the organ like you said. What was that one you were humming?'

'Stanford – one of his short preludes – the allegretto. It is just lovely. So right for you.'

'You've made me detest that Wagner thing as much as you now.'

'Well, good. At least I've had some positive influence over you.'

'And I can't exactly have anything German can I? Are you sure you don't want me to stop?'

'Of course. I'm a big girl. Thank you for all your help, too – it's been so much easier with two of us packing things away, and I'm so

251

glad you're going to make good use of all this stuff. It wouldn't have fetched much if I'd sold it.'

'It will set us up nicely for when we're married. And you mustn't feel obliged to us when you want any of it back – if you move to somewhere bigger.'

'Oh, there's no rush. My little room in Greenland will be perfectly fine until I find my feet, and there's not much I can fit in there.'

'And you are sure you don't want that gramophone?'

'No. It would only gather dust. You and Robert will get more pleasure out of it than me. I'll get my music at church, and I have promised myself to go to more concerts this summer.'

'Right. I'll get off then.'

'Ooh, before you go – just help me move the sideboard over there so that I can give the back of it a clean – it will be covered in cobwebs no doubt. I'm embarrassed by it – I don't know the last time it was moved... I'll get this end – that's it. Let's pop it in the middle of the room then the boys can shift it when they get back. That'll do. Oh dear, what did I tell you? Look at the state of it.'

'I'll give you a hand with it if you like?'

'Don't be daft. It'll only take a minute.'

'Well, we'll see you soon, Elsie. I'm looking forward to seeing your cosy little room when you've got it settled.'

'I'll have the kettle on ready. Bye, Mary.'

The house went quiet, and stillness and lifelessness descended on her, chilling her. The sound of every footstep she made held in the air, reminding her of how empty everything had become. She would do one last check. She climbed the stairs and stepped into the empty front bedroom.

She saw a woman weeping over something in a chamber pot. She saw Smith cowering on the floor after she had pushed him over; Lily's things scattered on the floor. She saw shards of glass on the counterpane and Lily fear-struck underneath, the curtains blowing in the breeze, and at the window she saw the shadow of a zeppelin across the night sky. She looked out into the street: damp and grey, the paving coated in a black film of mud and soot. A group of men and boys striding up the road with blue and white favours pinned on their lapels – on their way to the match. She had had to sell *her* boots.

She checked the small bedroom that had never been put into its intended use.

The front room downstairs was even colder than usual. There was only the aspidistra on the floor by the door and a rolled up rug. But Elsie saw the coffin on a trestle. Two whole nights had passed before they'd found him. Someone heading to work on the Monday morning, taking a short cut across the hill on the way to work. Accidental death they had said. He had deserved better.

They'd laid him out in the front room. His friend Morris had put the word round and on the day eight Sherwood Foresters in regimental uniform had carried him shoulder high up the road to Burngreave cemetery. The whole neighbourhood had turned out to line the route: young and old, including some very rough-looking characters standing at the kerb's edge, heads lowered as a war hero was taken to his final resting place. There was a bugler as they lowered him into the ground.

She squeezed out a damp cloth and cleaned the back of the sideboard, rinsed the cloth then hung it over the sink. She filled the kettle ready for when Bob and Tom returned. She stood in the middle of the room, her arms dropped to her sides. What now?

It was still some time before they'd be back. She started to wish she'd been selfish and got Mary to stay.

The skirting board where the sideboard had been was dirty. She would be ashamed for anyone to see that, so she got the cloth again and got onto her hands and knees. As she ran her cloth along she disturbed a dust ball lurking in the large gap between skirting board and floorboards. She noticed something else in the dust ball – a bit of bright, delicate metal chain. She put her little finger underneath to hook it out; she pulled at the chain and out came a necklace with stones coloured violet, green, and delicate pearly white. The necklace. From Henry. She teased it free from the dust ball as tears swam in her eyes.

She sat for a while, then held the necklace up and put it on before carrying on with her task. That done, she went to the gramophone put on a record, the one Henry had bought, wound it up and placed the needle on the edge of the disc. The machine crackled into life and she swayed to the melody. *When this nice little spot, we have come to at last, where the light is mysterious and dim.* She closed her eyes and raised the necklace and gently pressed the central pendant drop to her lips.

She still had a lot of living to do. She would write to the local schools inspector and enquire about being allocated a teaching post. There was always a need for good teachers – no more so than now.

She had so much to offer. To help young minds grow and learn. To help them make better choices. To learn from the mistakes made; to honour all the good people who had died trying.

A SUGGESTION

(to our artists)

Paint two vast heaps of mildewed human skulls
In pyramidal shape, with top depressed,
Two islands in a blood-red lake where hulls
Of stately ships rust-anchored rest;
Beyond in middle distance withered trees,
And blasted cloisters of some abbey proud
Through which trails, ghost-like, in the hidden breeze,
Black sulphurous smoke in semblance of a shroud.

Upon each pyramid a monarch stand,
Garbed in imperial robes of purple hue,
Each gripping firm the other by the hand
And whispering, Cousin, we have seen it through.
In distant background let fat vultures tear
Dead flesh from bones that seem from earth to spring,
And let your masterpiece this title bear
In letters deathly black – God save the King!

- Anon

Some words of Sheffield dialect

It is hard to capture the true sounds of dialect speech, and still be legible. Compromises have been made.

Gerroff! – get off!

Gi'– Give. So, "gi'o'er" = give over! i.e. stop!

Ha'porth – half penny's worth, useless person

Haife on it – half of it

Jammy – lucky

Jennel – a narrow passage/through route

Lummox – clumsy person

Mash (tea) – to brew

Misen thisen hissen – myself, thyself, himself

Nah then! – now then: a form of greeting

Nowt – nothing

Owt - anything

Pikelet – small oatcake, similar to a crumpet

Rec – recreation ground (often just an open grassy space).

Reight – right. A' reight – all right – used as a greeting

Scarper – run away

Scrape – margarine or dripping applied thinly

Sithee – see you/ goodbye

Snap – food taken for eating in the middle of a shift

Summat – something

Tha – thou (see also thi) this term are still used for the second person singular instead of 'you.' in Sheffield the 'th' sound is not as pronounced as in other parts of Yorkshire, being almost a 'd' sound. This has given Sheffielders the nickname Dee-dahs, in others parts of Yorkshire.

Thi – thee/thy

us – pronounced 'uzz' often used for 'me' or 'our.'

were – often used for was (it is actually a contraction of 'was' i.e. 'w,' but sounds just like 'were.' So, 'he were going to the shops,' is correct).

wi' – with

Acknowledgments

First of all my sincerest thanks to Joan Smith and family for their consent in my mining of *Grandad's Book*, the Great War memoir of Eric Needham of the Sherwood Foresters. Some of that mining approaches plagiarism, I freely admit, but I'd rather call it respect for a testimony I could not improve upon in a fictional telling. It is a remarkable piece of writing and all the more valuable for being a first-hand account. It is a historically important telling of life in the prisoner of war camps – in some ways the forerunners of the later concentration camps. Without it, my story would have been much weaker and I might have had to resort to sending Smith to the Somme, which has been done by better writers than me.

Thanks also, as ever, to Sheffield Libraries Local Studies Library where many a happy hour was spent going down all sorts of rabbit holes, up dead ends, and onto sidetracks. Also the library at the Imperial War Museum, which holds the papers of Captain Walter Wilkin. Our libraries are a fantastic resource and need to be treasured.

Thanks to my old friend David Hübner for his kind advice on the German language.

Also to Stephan Heinemann for putting me in touch with somewhere I could held hold of his book *Zwischen Demokratie und Diktatur*. Thanks Stephan for the correspondence and advice which prevented me from making a pretty serious historical error. And to Anke von Fintel at Landkreis Heidekreis for sorting the book out for me.

I am indebted to Michael Briggs (derbyshireterritorials.uk) for letting me have the photo of the unknown Sherwood Forester and woman used on the cover. I fell in love with it as soon as I saw it on the website ww1photos.org. It is uncanny how much they resembled the Smith and Elsie who lived in my mind for so long. If anyone knows who they are, please do get in touch.

Thank you Sarah Choonara for letting me put your words (more or less) into the mouth of Elsie on the feelings of joy at first discovering football. Again it is not something I could have improved on. (https://stringofpasses.wordpress.com/)

Dear Reader

If you thought this book was at least half decent, it would be really appreciated if you could do a quick review on Amazon, Goodreads or other online sites you use. Just a word or two would be great. 1889 Books is a small-scale undertaking so word of mouth is vital to letting readers know about it.

You can sign up for news and offers at www.1889books.co.uk, such as a free e-book of my first novel *The Evergreen in Red and White* set in Sheffield in 1897/98. If you liked *Built on Sand* I am sure you'd like this too.

The Winds Blew is a "sort of" sequel to *Built on Sand* – told largely from the points of view of three women with intertwined histories they are unaware of. There is Liselotte, a young woman growing up in 1930s Germany and facing the horrors of unfolding events; 500 miles away in Darnall, Josephine has her own struggles with death, poverty and identity. They come through the war and eventually meet many years later at the nursing home of the third character; but they never realise just how much they have in common!

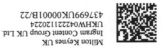

Milton Keynes UK
Ingram Content Group UK Ltd.
UKHW042211202224
437699UK00001B/22